BAD
SIGNS

BAD
SIGNS
R.J. ELLORY

THE OVERLOOK PRESS
NEW YORK, NY

First published in hardcover in the United States in 2016 by
The Overlook Press, Peter Mayer Publishers, Inc.

141 Wooster Street
New York, NY 10012
www.overlookpress.com

For bulk and special sales, please contact sales@overlookny.com,
or write us at the address above.

First published in Great Britain in 2011 by Orion, an Hachette UK company

Library of Congress Cataloging-in-Publication Data
Names: Ellory, Roger Jon, author.
Title: Bad signs / R. J. Ellory.
Description: First edition. I New York , NY : The Overlook Press, 2016. I
„2011
Identifiers: LCCN 2015044766 I ISBN 9781468311273 (hardcover)
Subjects: LCSH: Brothers--Fiction. I Hostages--Fiction. I GSAFD: Suspense
fiction.
Classification: LCC PR6105.L65 B33 2016 I DDC 823/.92--dc23
LC record available at http://lccn.loc.gov/2015044766

Manufactured in the United States of America
ISBN: 978-1-4683-1127-3

First Edition
1 3 5 7 9 10 8 6 4 2

ACKNOWLEDGMENTS

This is the ninth book I have released, and—as is always the case—there are too many people to mention. Those that I acknowledge are forever telling me they did nothing deserving of thanks, which—as we all know—is entirely untrue. So I express my heartfelt gratitude to my editor, Jon, also Jade Chandler, Susan Lamb, Juliet Ewers, Sophie Mitchell, Angela McMahon, Anthony Keates, Krystyna Kujawinska, Hannah Whitaker and all the Orion crew; to my agent Euan, to Charlie at AM Heath, Dominic and his team at WF Howes, to Amanda Ross and Gareth Jones at Cactus, to Judy Bobalik, to Jon and Ruth Jordan, to Ali Karim, Mike Stotter, to all those at Bouchercon, Thrillerfest and Harrogate. You know who you are, and you know what you did.

From the host of international publishers and festival organizers I have worked with, I must mention a few people specifically: Peter, Jack and Emer, Stephanie, and all the wonderful crew at Overlook; Francois, Leonore, Marie M., Arnaud, Xavier and Marie L. at Sonatine-Editions; Cécile, Sylvie and Carine at Livre de Poche, France; Sophie and Fabienne at SoFab; Fabrice Pointeau, Clément Baude, Christel Paris, Richard Contin, Catherine Dô-duc, Caroline Vallat, Marie-France Remond, Robert Boulerice, Linda Raymond and all the bookstore owners who made the French and Canadian tours so memorable. I must also thank Kevin and Brendan in Australia, Gemma in New Zealand, Anik Lapointe and Laura Santaflorentina in Barcelona, and Seba Pezzani in Piacenza for taking care of everything so incredibly well.

To my wife and son, my appreciation for everything, and to Guy and Angela for all their help and encouragement.

Most of all I thank you—dear reader—for your continued friendship and support.

This is for you.

Born under a bad sign,
I been down since I began to crawl.
If it wasn't for bad luck,
I wouldn't have no luck at all.

—"Born Under a Bad Sign"
Booker T. Jones/William Bell

CHAPTER ONE

By the time she reached her mid-twenties Carole Kempner had seen enough of men to be nothing other than disappointed. She bore two sons from two forlorn and wretched fathers, and it seemed that in all quarters and aspects those fathers were found sorely wanting. One was dumb and thoughtless, the other just downright crazy.

Elliott, the older of her two children, was born on January 2, 1946. Elliott's father, Kyle Danziger, was a transient oilfield worker, and he swept through Carole's life like a bad squall. Kyle was gone before Carole made her first trimester, perhaps because he could not envision himself burdened beneath the responsibility of fatherhood, perhaps for other reasons. Carole, believing that such a gesture might precipitate Kyle's eventual return, gave her son his father's name. And so he was Elliott Danziger, though from the first moments of speech he referred to himself as "Digger."

How Clarence, the second and younger of her sons, came to be was a thing all its own. His conception—merely eight months after Carole's delivery of Elliott—occurred in a moment of drunken awkwardness that was regretted immediately. That was indeed a low point, but things didn't improve much from then on. Suffice to say that the boys' childhood was grounded hard in violence and madness.

Just to begin with, Clarence's father—Jimmy Luckman—killed Carole stone-dead on a cool winter's morning while both Clarence and Elliott looked on.

Clarence was five by this time, Elliott a year and five months older. Jimmy was busy getting drunk. Carole, however, had set her mind to leaving once and for all. Perhaps she was simply exhausted with the disappointment. Or maybe she believed such

1

an action would serve the boys well in the longer run of things. Either which way, Jimmy Luckman didn't seem to agree with her plan.

So Jimmy—enraged at Carole's calumny and deceit, the way she seemed to have thought this thing through with no regard for *his* needs and wants—took a baseball bat and broke some crockery. He broke a window. He spiderwebbed the TV screen. Then he broke Carole's darn fool neck.

She went down like a stone. She was expressionless in the moment of impact, expressionless after the event. She could have been staring at a discount sign in a convenience store.

Jimmy Luckman appeared uncertain for some time. Later Clarence figured him to be calculating the odds. If Jimmy buried Carole, or perhaps chopped her up and drove out to Searchlight or Cottonwood Cove to hurl her piece by piece into a bottomless ravine, perhaps if he sent her headfirst down a dry well, or took her out northwest a hundred miles and left her in the desert for the coyotes . . . If he did this and told the world she'd finally left him for her mother's place in Anaheim and was likely never to return, then what were the odds? Would anyone ever discover the truth?

Eventually Jimmy Luckman told Clarence to sit quiet. *Wait here until she wakes up*, he said. *I'll be back soon, kiddo.*

Jimmy did not speak to Elliott. Elliott was neither his son nor his responsibility, and Elliott—slightly slower than Clarence, heavier, almost denser in some way—had always seemed to Jimmy as a distraction and a deadweight.

Jimmy—despite what he told Clarence—didn't come back soon.

He didn't come back at all.

Carole didn't wake up neither.

Three and a half hours later Jimmy Luckman, never a man to take after his name, was shot in the throat by an off-duty cop in a liquor store in North Las Vegas. He was trying to escape with nineteen dollars and sixty-two cents. Even today, allowing for inflation, it wasn't a great deal worth dying for.

Clarence waited patiently for the father that would never return. Elliott waited with him. They waited in the bedroom —one of four rooms in their first-floor apartment. The front door opened into the kitchen, the kitchen gave onto the sitting room, the bedroom with a narrow en-suite came last.

Frightened to leave their mother in case she woke, Clarence and Elliott took turns to venture only so far as the bathroom for water. They ate nothing however.

Their view to the street from the bedroom window was obscured by the walkway and heavy railings that circumvented the internal square of the apartment block. Above the railing and beneath the walkway above they could see a strip of sky. As it grew dark the stars appeared. Little Clarence talked to them. He asked them to relay a message to God. *Make her wake up*, he said.

Elliott merely watched his younger brother.

How Carole slept with her eyes wide-open Clarence did not understand. Whatever the reason, it did not matter. He just wanted her to wake up.

It was the most part of two days before anyone visited.

So it was that on the 5th of November Evelyn Westerbrook came by. She had always been Carole Kempner's closest friend. She came to tell Jimmy and Carole that Eisenhower had won the election and they should celebrate. She carried with her a copy of a newspaper, the headline of which read, "Ike to The White House!" Jimmy had left the front door unlocked. Evelyn let herself in. She called out after them. "Carole? Carole?" And then— "Jimmy? Jimmy . . . are you guys in?"

She came on through to the bedroom. She found both Elliott and Clarence asleep, Clarence's head against his mother's shoulder, Elliott resting against her tummy, his hand holding hers.

Evelyn woke the boys up. She called the police. What happened after that Clarence didn't really remember, except that he never saw his mother again.

It was a long time before he understood that she never did wake up.

Evelyn Westerbrook gave the police Jimmy Luckman's name. It wasn't long before they figured out who he was and where he'd died. Despite the fact that Carole had married neither Kyle Danziger nor Jimmy Luckman, the authorities afforded each boy their respective father's names. Elliott would forever be Digger Danziger, and Clarence would be a Luckman. Maybe that was the

3

start of his trouble, for Clarence Luckman was born under a bad star—that was the small and unavoidable truth—and people born under a bad star carry a bad sign their whole lives. Apparently this is so. And as far as people in general are concerned, there's bad ones and real bad ones. The second lot are pretty much broke beyond mending. Might as well shoot them where they stand. And shoot them the first time you see them. Anything else is just going to be a heavy sack of heartache for all concerned. Clarence was possibly in the first category, Elliott too, but those who would later most influence their lives were definitely in the second.

Clarence and Elliott, looking from the start like the longer they lived the worse it was going to get, were both shipped off to a boys' school outside of Barstow, California. It was a vast complex of buildings surrounded by a wall high enough to leave much of the day in shadow. The rooms smelled of dirty clothes and death, like a hospice for the destitute. In such a place life could be nothing but lonely and awkward. The kids ranged from seven to nineteen. The moment they hit their nineteenth they were released or moved on up to the big house. These were kids who had come up hard and bitter. Spent their childhood eating from hot dog stands and sleeping in bus depot restrooms if they were lucky. The attitude engendered by such experience was one of tight-wound nervousness. There was no way else to survive. Everything you didn't grab was grabbed by someone else. Sometimes people would kick and grab even when you'd got there first. Start out like that and it wasn't long before you figured all of life was colored that way. It was here that Elliott shined his light. The denseness, the slowness, became a methodical and pragmatic ability to deal with things that perhaps might have overshadowed Clarence. Elliott was the older boy, the big brother, and he wore his hat with pride and diligence. He was not afraid of people it seemed, neither kids nor grown-ups, and he was always there behind Clarence, always ready to step in and defend his younger brother if springs got wound too tight and fists were set to fly. He seemed to know when he was wanted, and when he was not. He had a temper for sure, much like his father, the transient oil worker, yet other times Clarence would watch Digger as Digger seemed to drift off in his mind to someplace where there was no one else but himself. He wondered if he was looking for long-lost

4

Kyle, just as Clarence often thought of his own father, the ironically named Jimmy Luckman, who—it seemed—had neither been really lucky, nor really a man.

"Digger?" Clarence would say. "Digger?" And it would require three or four urgent repetitions before Digger snapped out of it, smiled, and said, "What's up, little man?"

At Barstow they taught Elliott Danziger and Clarence Luckman to read and write. Clarence took to it quickly, Elliott a little more slowly. They were different boys in so many ways, though often mistaken one for the other. It was their eyes. They both had their mother's eyes. As they grew older they became less physically similar, but their eyes stayed the same. See Clarence, see Elliott, you saw Carole. How that physical attribute would contribute to an endless chain of troubles was both unknown and unpredictable. Safe it was to say that had they taken after their respective fathers—at least in looks—then life would have been a great deal simpler.

Life progressed in some vague fashion until Clarence was thirteen, and then he kicked one of the kitchen staff real hard in the pants. The man that Clarence kicked had been trying stuff that was about as wholesome as a roadkill sandwich. Elliott was there too, and he got down and gave that guy a wallop or two before the guards came to break it up. They took off, the pair of them, but the police caught up with Elliott and Clarence no more than three miles away. They beat them some, and then sent them to the juvenile hall in Hesperia. Here a different man tried the same sort of thing on Clarence, but had sense enough to tie the boy to a bed before he started. By the time Clarence got to tell Elliott what had happened, well, it was too late for Elliott to do anything about it.

And so it went on, Elliott Danziger and Clarence Luckman weathering their lot like stoics, and all the while they had in their minds the thought that there had to be something better than this someways up the road. Where that road started, and where it ended up, they didn't know. Such things were just details, and details came long after the main body of a plan. That's what Clarence set his mind to working on—a plan—and whether he was sluicing out piss buckets or peeling potatoes or spit-shining shoes that wouldn't stay clean for an hour, his mind was always working. Got close enough and you could hear the wheels turning, some kind of intricacy in there like a Frenchman's clock. The cogs turned, the ideas evolved, and maybe everything would have come right had he kept his ideas to himself.

But he didn't.

He shared them with Elliott. Older brother. Rock of ages. Elliott didn't have the vision or foresight of his younger brother. The boys were similar perhaps, but only in the thin thread that connected them through their mother. The rest was wildly different, and that difference would only become more evident as time moved on.

Elliott, now known as Digger to all and sundry, was a magnet for small and unnecessary troubles. Hesperia had served the local community with a juvenile facility for as many years as anyone could remember. Back before secession it had been a prison, before that something else. They had rooms that could sleep eight or ten, and Clarence and Digger were berthed side by side.

Within their first days at Hesperia Clarence noticed a shift in Digger. Slight, perhaps unnoticeable to anyone but Clarence, but there was a shift. He seemed bigger, a mite taller and wider, and he seemed to hold himself with a good deal more presence. This was more like a grown-up facility, and Clarence believed that Digger knew it would take more work to care for his younger brother.

"Your name is Clay," he told Clarence on the third or fourth morning after their arrival. "That's what you should call yourself. Clarence is all fucked up. Sounds like a homo name. Clay is much better."

Clarence was puzzled, but he nevertheless agreed. From that day forward he was Clay Luckman.

Digger was merely a year and five months older than Clay, but he started to look like a man when he hit twelve. He was willing to fight anyone, and did when it suited him. He lost more often than not, staggered away with his nose bloodied and his pride battered. But he never lost that pride, and he never lost his confidence and willingness to give it his best shot. His fists were all bone and no meat. His temper flared fast like a cheap firework, but he had the carry-through and balls to back it up. Nine times out of ten he went into battle for Clay, and Clay loved him for that. There was a loyalty there, a fraternity that meant the world to them both but for different reasons. Digger had charged himself with the responsibility for Clay's physical welfare, and Clay, well, he believed that at some point in the future Digger would be receptive to education, enlightenment, a wider mental and emotional perception of life. Digger was the fighter, Clay the negotiator. Digger was the pugilist, Clay the philosopher. Had both parts been worked into one boy, then that would have been some boy. But they were not. There were two of them, linked by blood, but separated by personality.

One time Clay asked Digger what he wanted.

"More to eat most of the time," Digger had replied.

"You know what I mean, Digger," Clay said. "From life. From the future."

That question had given Digger pause for thought. He did his little disappearing act, and he was gone someplace else for a good three or four minutes. "S'pose when it comes down to it," he eventually said, "I want the same things as everyone else. Enough smarts to keep out of trouble, enough money to get what I want, enough time to enjoy it."

Perhaps that was the deepest Digger would ever go. He had a view of life, a longer-term view, but present environment seemed so *present* that he rarely saw beyond the next meal.

Digger carried on fighting. He carried on losing. Clay wondered how much pride he did in fact possess, and how long it could be battered before it was entirely broken.

So as far as those that were charged with his welfare were concerned, Digger became both a trial and a tribulation. Rumor had it that Digger was going to be there through his eighteenth year, and then he'd be graduated to the big house. Rumor had it that had he not been a juvenile he'd have been there already. Rumor had a lot of things to say for itself, all except some way to determine the truth.

Digger seemed to find the notoriety and negative reputation somewhat of a charm and an allure.

"I'm a hot potato," Digger told Clay. "Far as the law is concerned, that's what I am."

Clay shook his head. He didn't understand.

7

"They got me for a salt and buttery," Digger explained, and then he bust a gut laughing.

Digger got like that. He blew hot and cold. A funny guy, very funny, and then all of a sudden serious. Clay sometimes wondered if he hadn't been hit in the head just a few too many times. It didn't make sense, but it seemed to Clay that everyone who'd given Digger a kicking had left a little of themselves imprinted on his personality. Or maybe it was that Digger, seeing someone stronger or faster or smarter, had snatched a little of their attitude away while they were pounding on him. Snatched that thing away and kept it for himself in the belief that it would make him stronger. All those bits of people were now there inside of him, packed up tight in his skin, and Clay didn't know from one mealtime to the next which one he was going to get next.

Clay loved Digger. He respected him. He cared for his well-being. He also stayed close because no one bothered him if Digger was around. Whenever he got mad with Digger, he had only to cast his mind back to the day of their mother's death, the way Digger carried water in his cupped hands all the way from the bathroom to where Clay was sitting. He did it many times. He'd figured that Clay was crying so much he'd just dry up and blow away if he didn't drink plenty of water. In Clay's mind there was nothing that he would not forgive Digger. He found himself rationalizing Digger's viewpoints, appreciating his left-of-center sensibilities, listening to his little dreams and aspirations. As time went on they just became closer. See one and you'd see the other. Some other kid said they were probably homos together, but Digger broke the kid's nose and he never said it again.

And the more they talked, the more it seemed that Digger's perspective and viewpoint widened. He listened to his younger brother. He started asking questions. He wanted to know *Why this* . . . and *Why that* . . . and Clay told him what he knew, or what he thought, or what he imagined was the truth. Digger taught Clay how to hit someone so they wouldn't get up so fast. He called it "lumberjack fighting," and Clay paid attention and toughened up somewhat. They were good for each other, and they started to connect not only as half brothers, but as real honest-to-God friends.

Perhaps Clay figured that was the point at which his fortunes altered. That now he'd outlived the irony of his name and gotten something good. Digger had a dark shadow, but he had a sense of humor and his mind was surprisingly fast. Clay knew he could always count on him in an awkward place. How awkward that place would be, and how it would happen, well, neither of them had the slightest idea.

"Nothin's really trouble till you're caught," was always a favorite line of Digger's.

One time—spring of 1961, Clay all of thirteen, Digger a couple of months more than fifteen—they were out on a field gang, all of them tied together with a length of chain, working like dogs, digging up rocks and stones out of sun-baked fields and loading them in the back of a pickup by the bucketload. The sun was high and brave. The wind out there didn't blow, it sucked. Sucked every ounce of moisture right out of you and replaced it with dead flies and dust. A hellacious thirst came upon Clay. Would've drunk a pint of warm piss had it been offered.

Duty guard was called Farragut. Sat on a horse and rode back and forth up the line making sure the boys worked hard and fast. Wore an expression like he'd had toothache his whole life. He was a compact knotted little man. If you hit him you would hurt for days. He would never go down without a bullet or two. Farragut was known as Shoeshine. Kicked boys in the ass of their pants all day and all night until his toecaps glossed up like river pebbles. He had true meanness deep inside of him, as tight and twisted as a box of snakes. He said little, but when he did the words sounded practiced.

"Toe the line and I'm behind you, boy. Cross it and I'll be the first agin you," he'd say, and "I told you with words to quieten down, boy. Next time I'm telling you with fists." Such tough poetry as this.

First time Clay met Shoeshine was his second day at Hesperia. "Seems to me you got only two expressions, boy," was his greeting. "Causing trouble an' asking for forgiveness. Well, you listen here now. I won't have the first and I won't give the second. That keeps it simple enough for both of us to understand."

Shoeshine had a cool box in the foot well of the service truck. Inside of the cool box were a half dozen or so chilled bottles of root beer. That day, April something-or-other of 1961, Digger took a liking to the idea of a root beer, a chilled root beer in a glass bottle with a crimped metal cap. Being Digger, he was suited to doing the job with his fists, not with his smarts, but this day was different; this day Digger had a mind to working some kind of angle on Clay.

"No way, Digger," Clay told him. "You get busted for some foolish stunt like that they're gonna beat you and throw you in the tool shed for the rest of the day."

"You think I can't take it?" Digger asked.

"Hell, Digger, sure you can take it. The point is not whether you can take it, it's whether it's worth it for some foolish dumbass bottle of root beer."

"But it sure would taste so good, right? You like root beer, right? Hell, everyone likes root beer. And it'd be so cold, and it'd taste so good, and it would be worth it, I reckon."

"Digger, you are sometimes so fuckin' stupid."

"Thirsty," Digger said. "Not stupid, just real thirsty."

It was a bad game from the start. Digger didn't say anything directly. Perhaps it was Clay's own fault by mentioning the fact that another transgression would see Digger into the tool shed with a few more bruises. Digger just kept on talking about the damned root beer. How cold, how tasty, how refreshing, how special on such a hot, hot day. Perhaps it had been his plan all along, but it seemed that Digger was trying to persuade and cajole Clay with his mind. Like he was set to hypnotize his younger brother. Later, after many other troubles, Clay Luckman would wonder if Digger had such a power, or if it was just his own mental process that was weak. Digger turned Clay's thoughts in such a way as to make him believe that stealing a bottle of root beer from Shoeshine was the only thing that could be done. Maybe it was Digger who did that, or maybe it was simply the memory of Digger walking back from that bathroom with his hands full of water.

"I know you don't agree," Digger said, "but maybe it's right to feel sore about people who have a lot of things. Like the more they have, the less there is for everyone else." He carried his broomstave across his shoulders like a yoke, his hands up and over left and right. He and Clay were walking to the edge of the road to get water. An old truck had been abandoned amidst the foot-flattened ridges of a fallow—four, five bullet holes in the radiator grille like the thing had quit one time too many. *To hell with you*, someone had thought, and took a rifle from the rear rack and shot the thing dead where it stood. *You don't work for me . . . hell, you don't work for no one.* Federal yellow flowers had grown up around the spare on the tailboard and made a crude wreath. Given enough time the seasons would take it all down to rust and dust. The other kids were coming down behind them. A five-minute break for hydrating, and then back to work. They gathered along a high dirt bank punctuated with rough handfuls of hardy sedge, dun and dry and dusty. This land hadn't seen rain for weeks, and the air itself made you cough. Fifty yards away was a deserted homestead; stone ruins like broken teeth, as if this were all that remained of some giant's fractured jawbone. Perhaps this was such a place where folks weren't s'posed to settle.

"Take this situation, for example," Digger said. "I'm one to latch on to an idea and let it take hold." He smiled. "Like this here root beer proposition. Seems to me that if you decide you want something, and then give up on the idea because it's too much trouble . . . well, you say this yourself. You gotta decide on a plan and then carry it through despite whatever obstacles come in the way, right?"

"Sure," Clay replied, the sense of resignation already evident in his voice. He knew where this was going, and he didn't like it. "I'm talking about what you want, Digger . . . what you want when we get out of here. I'm not talking about a bottle of root beer."

Clay looked sideways at Digger. He was waiting for a response, but Digger didn't say a word. He shielded his eyes against the sun. He looked out to where Shoeshine was watering his horse, and then back to the truck. The door was closed but unlocked.

Clay looked at Digger again and shook his head. Digger just returned an expression like he'd lost a piece of his mind and never cared to look for it.

"Some folks don't deserve to be wished well, wouldn't you say?" Digger asked.

"I think there's some good to be found in everyone."

"Sure, that's as may be, but with some folks you gotta dig real deep to find it."

"Yeah, I'd say so."

"Shoeshine for example—"

"It ain't gonna work, Digger. I ain't doin' this thing."

"Well, I see things different from you, Clay," Digger said. "I see a guy like Shoeshine, and he's got what he's got, and we ain't got nothin', but he's the bad guy here, he's the one who likes to kick kids and hurt them and whatever . . ."

"You are crazy," Clay said. "Always have been, always will be. Sometimes I don't know whether you're being serious or just winding me like a cheap watch."

"Whichever way you wanna take it," Digger said, and then he looked at Clay for a while longer, and then out to the truck, and then he smiled and said something about water being for horses and dogs and gardens.

Clay drank the water. Water was good enough for him. He didn't need a root beer, and he sure as hell didn't need the kind of trouble that would come from stealing one from off of Shoeshine.

"Seems to me that good things don't come find you. They stay where they are and you have to go looking. And hell, if they don't hide in the damnedest of places." Digger shook his head and looked out toward the horizon. "Bad things, however . . . well, let's just say that bad things is something else altogether. Bad things can find you anyplace, and sometimes it means a great deal to have someone there who can help you take care of them . . ."

"I don't want to go," Clay said. When he first thought of the words they sounded strong and definite. When they left his lips they didn't.

The tension between them was so solid you could have pushed it over.

Clay wanted to say *Fuck you, Digger*, but he stayed silent.

Looking at Digger then, he realized another facet of their difference. Digger was not stupid, never had been, but there was a shadow there, something that perhaps had come from his own father. Digger always appeared to be looking for the slant and pitch of the situation, how angles could be influenced to some small advantage. Digger was certainly no stranger to threat or violence, neither of them were, but maybe Digger was the sort of person to bring his own if none were present. It gave him the upper hand. Perhaps he believed he would make his mark more firmly on the world if he made others around him unsettled.

They went back to work for another two hours, scratching stones and rocks out of the dirt with their hands, an exercise that seemed to serve no purpose but to keep them occupied.

The feeling came upon Clay slowly. It was the kind of feeling that got right down into the basement of his gut and stayed there, slow-cooking like a pit barbecue. He believed that if he didn't do what Digger had asked of him then there would be discord between them. That was more trouble than he could weather. Clay knew that Digger would never threaten him, never hurt him. Nothing like that. It was not a concern for what Digger would do to him, but what could be taken away. Without Digger he would be adrift in this world. He would manage, of course, but the tension and agitation that would become part of his life without Digger there to defend and protect him would be a strain he could do without. He thought of the times Digger had pasted some kid who was grieving him. Without Digger as a shield perhaps that kid would come back for revenge. He had never really had to do such things alone. Yes, he began to think, perhaps all of the past avoidances would come back at him. Right when he least expected it. Saying nothing about the violence itself, the surprise would be enough to kill him.

Clay said nothing, but he watched the pattern that Shoeshine followed. The service truck sat at the side of the road, no more than twenty feet from the wheels to the edge of the hot top. The line of boys—more than eighty of them—stretched a good two hundred yards. Shoeshine paced his horse from one end of the chain to the other. He looked ahead of him, never back—not unless someone called for permission to take a piss. If that happened he would watch the boy until his business was done, and then he would resume the walk. Clay counted the time it took from one end of the line to the other. From the moment he turned he reckoned three minutes until Shoeshine was coming back the other way.

Next break time Digger said something to Clay. Said it low like a whisper, nothing direct. "Sometimes I feel like there's two sides to me. Sometimes I think the only reason I have a left hand is to stop my right hand from doing stuff it wants to." Digger tried to hide his smile, but it was there in his eyes. He was winding, winding, winding.

"You are so full of shit," Clay said. "You think you can make me do this—"

Digger laughed. "Hey, man, cool it. I'm just baiting you."

Clay opened his mouth, and then he hesitated. There was a change in his expression, a different light in his eyes. There was some shadow of grim determination that seemed to have taken hold. He looked across at Shoeshine, at the truck, back to Digger, and then he said, "I'll do it. Don't say any more. I'll get you your root beer."

Digger didn't say a thing. He didn't even smile. Expression on his face was suddenly serious and implacable, like he'd spent a lifetime walking against the wind.

Clay wondered then if Digger would try and stop him. Wondered if the whole thing had been nothing but a test. Now it was there, now Clay had agreed to do it, well, he had demonstrated courage sufficient for Digger to ease up. Digger would say the whole thing had been a prank, a stunt, and he had no more yen for a root beer than he did a snake sandwich.

But no, he didn't say a word.

There was a fraternal angle, a challenge, a thrown-gauntlet of sorts, and it had progressed too far to be reversed.

Clay made a small prayer. He thought of where his mother was, whether she could see him, and what she would say. He wondered if there was a heaven and a hell, and he wondered if the folks in heaven could see the folks in hell, and if he wound up down there with his father would he ever be able to speak to her again.

And then he realized how stupid he was being. It was a root beer. He was going to get his brother a root beer. Damn, the number of times Digger had bailed him out crap, this was the least he could do.

He waited until Shoeshine turned at the end of the row, and then he dropped his shovel and took a step.

The next boy in line stopped working.

Digger glared at him. The boy started up again. Seemed like the whole world went quiet. Seemed like the breeze stopped, the dust settled, the birds stayed right where they were in the branches of trees.

Clay's heart was in the middle of his chest, in his throat, in his mouth, and he could see everything twice. There were beads of sweat along his hairline. Seemed never to have bothered him before but they rolled down his brow and met his eyes and blurred his vision.

Three times he asked himself what the damn hell he was doing before he'd even made it two yards.

Shoeshine was still going the other way, his back to the line, his rifle across his knees, his attention all the way forward and nowhere behind.

Clay glanced back at Digger. Digger was leaning forward, his shovel in the ground, but he was not moving. His expression was unreadable. Clay wondered what would happen if he turned back. Would Digger forgive him? Would he just brush it off as a great joke that might have played out? Or would he make it a big deal? Would this put some irreconcilable rift between them that would never be healed?

Dead if he did, dead if he didn't.

Clay loved his brother, but hated himself. He feared Shoeshine, but more than that he feared the loneliness that he would have to endure without Digger by his side.

He looked back at the line of boys. He looked at the tool shed. He crouched lower to the ground and took another three steps. The truck was another fifteen yards. He wondered if he should just make a dash for it. There were boys farther down the line who would stop working as soon as they saw Clay run across the field. Shoeshine would hear him. He would stir the horse and chase him down within a heartbeat. He would knock him over with the butt of the rifle. Maybe the horse would trample him.

Clay swallowed. He gritted his teeth. He was going to do it. He *had* to do it. There was no other choice.

He pictured himself back in the ditch with Digger. He could feel the cool weight of the bottle in his hand. He could see the smile, the pride, the sheer unalloyed pride in his brother's eyes, and he knew that this was the way to make his mark with everyone else in the line. After this they would see him not as Digger's sidekick, the weaker brother, the one who was always being defended and protected, but they would see him as an individual in his own right.

This was his test, and destiny had brought him here.

He edged forward—another step, another two—his heart racing ahead of him, his pulse quickening in his neck, his temples, feeling the blood in every part of his body, his mouth dry, every hair on his head rigid with fear, but he took another step and he could see the truck getting closer.

Shoeshine was halfway down the line. He needed to gather pace if he was going to make it there and back. He took three more steps, three more again.

There seemed to be a united gasp all the way along the line. Eighty boys held their breath. Clay knew he was imagining it, but it was as real as anything he had ever experienced before.

Now was the moment. Now was his chance to make a dash across the last twenty-five feet and get that bottle out of the foot well.

Clay Luckman, believing he had broken the spell of bad fortune, held on to his belt and made that run for all he was worth.

Three yards, no more, no less, and his foot landed awkwardly on a protruding stone. Fist-sized, round every which you looked at it, the sole of his boot skidded off the surface and sent him sprawling.

Some kid laughed. Others laughed too. It was not so much the sense of ridicule that they found humorous, but the relief, that terrible instinctive reaction when you see some calamity befall another. A relief that it was not you.

Clay lay there for a second, dust in his eyes, despair in his heart, and then he tried to scoot around and head back for the ditch.

Shoeshine saw Clay Luckman before he'd made it five feet. He stirred that horse and chased him down just as Clay had envisioned. He did not use the butt of the rifle to knock him down, but rather booted the boy fair and square in the back of the head. Clay went down like gravity. His lights were out before he tasted dirt.

Shoeshine figured the boy had planned to take off in the truck. That's how he wrote it up. Clay didn't argue. Would have served no purpose. Shoeshine and Hesperia were going to believe what they wanted to believe regardless of what anyone said. Clay was up on an attempted escape charge. He went to the solitary block for a month. He stitched pants and shirts with rough thread, he washed piss buckets and shined boots and dug trenches and held his tongue. He didn't say a damned thing about Digger goading him up for the enterprise with the root beer, and he knew Digger would appreciate that.

When Clay came out it was May of 1961 and white folks were terrorizing colored folk for taking bus rides in Alabama.

Digger, having earned himself a reputation for trouble, seemed to now have passed a little of that reputation to his brother. They became even more inseparable, not because of any wish on Clay Luckman's part to be troublesome, but because they each possessed a need for reliance on the other. Possibly Clay might have survived far better without Digger. He would have taken the beatings that would have come without Digger to protect him, but he would have made it through. He might have figured out a way to exorcise Digger's influence and attention. As with all things there was a way to do it. As with most things he didn't know what it was.

Late at night, the sweltering darkness, the sound of dogs punctuating the throaty pitch of cicadas, Digger would whisper things.

"I seen enough bad in men to know that they could never really have been created in His image," he said. "Couldn't have been. And most folks think one way, say another, and then act in a fashion that contradicts both. Don't make sense to me."

Another time, saying, "There's a little bit more to being smart than just knowing how to get out of trouble. Real smarts is never getting into trouble in the first place. And unhappiness? Unhappiness is like a sediment. You don't know it's there until you empty everything else out. And when something good looks like it's gonna happen, well, you take it slow. Don't rush it. Don't drink that thing too quick or you'll get a mouthful of inevitable bitterness at the bottom."

And then he would reach over and prod Clay in the shoulder. "You listenin' to me? You listenin' to me there?"

17

Clay tried to hold on to his optimism, his wishes for the future, but too much of what Digger said made too much sense. He had seen his share of bad things. He had experienced his share of rough fortune and disappointment. If the first decade of his life had been a portent for the rest, well, there was a great deal more heartache and hopelessness on the way.

Clay didn't try to dissuade Digger from his monologues. He just lay there listening awhile, and then he slept the best he could.

Hesperia was a shadow of some other distant and better place. Children came and went. Sometimes faces would appear for weeks, days even, and then they'd be shipped off to some other facility on the West Coast. Seemed to Clay Luckman that he and Digger were part of the great unwashed and unwanted, a tribe of misfits. No one ever said the thing directly, but it was evident that such people as they were consigned to short lives filled with jail, with violence, with hardship and awkward death. Perhaps, early on, he decided it would be somehow different for them. They were not criminals like the other kids. They were boys with no parents that no one had wished to adopt and no one knew what else to do with. Clay, it seemed, was unaware of the bad star, thus ignorant of the bad sign that followed him, and though ignorance was never a worthy defense, it at least gave some small respite for the time it remained.

Digger had his darker moods, and during those times he would talk his bitter talk. He had a chip on his shoulder sufficient to break it, but most times it didn't show. Only thing that Digger ever said that Clay really took to heart was about being stupid. *Worst kind of stupid is the failure to learn from experience.* That was something Clay could understand. That was something that felt like a truth.

The quiet passage of weeks and months became the relentless passage of years. Both Clay Luckman and Digger Danziger became hardened in their own ways. Clay resolved in himself the desire to be free of Hesperia once he had gained nineteen years in June of 1966. Digger was still uncertain of his fate, whether he too would be released, or if they would send him up to the big house as they had threatened so often. Digger told Clay that he intended to escape before this happened. Escape or die trying. He was going out to Eldorado, Texas.

"You what?"

"Eldorado, Texas," Digger said.

"What the hell do you know about Texas . . . or anyplace, for that matter?"

Digger crouched to the ground and ferreted his hand beneath his mattress. He withdrew a folded piece of something-or-other, and when he spread it out on the bed Clay saw that it was some kind of magazine advertisement. "The Sierra Valley Estate," it shouted in big sunshine-yellow letters. Every house was picture-perfect, the adults were smiling, the kids were laughing, there were shiny silver barbecue sets on emerald-green lawns and sapphire-blue pools in every back yard. In that picture Digger saw everything he'd never had. Clay saw it too. It was enchanting beyond words. They saw what they wanted to believe, and each of them—in their own very different way—imagined this place, this "City of Gold," to be representative of everything they had been denied.

"Where d'you get that?" Clay asked.

"There was a magazine in the infirmary. I tore it out."

Clay reached out and touched the page. He could feel the warmth of the sun through the tips of his fingers.

Eldorado. Where kids have moms and dads. Where the grass is green and the sky is blue and you are never hungry and you can smile without someone wanting to wipe that smile right off of your face.

Eldorado, Texas.

Yes.

"We gotta got there," Digger said.

Clay looked at him. He couldn't have agreed more.

"That's what we gotta do, Clay . . . We gotta find someplace like Eldorado and make our fortunes and find some good things after all this crap we've been through."

"Eldorado," Clay whispered, and it sounded like just the sort of place where you had to leave all the bad stuff behind just to get there.

It was everything that they'd been denied, and how their intentions to remedy that denial became inextricably linked, and the consequences for both brothers could not have been foreseen. It was all related to a man that neither of them knew, nor had ever met. A man who came to Hesperia in a thunderstorm in the late fall of 1964.

DAY ONE

CHAPTER TWO

Earl Samuel Sheridan was a man who cared little for anyone but himself. His was a narrow and claustrophobic world, and beyond the borders of his own needs and wants there was little that engaged his attention. Earl had a quarter century of impatience embedded in his bones. Somewhere inside him was a nerve that was irritated by pretty much everyone. What they did, what they said, how they looked. Folks who knew him, even those who raised him up, understood it was only a waiting game before Earl Sheridan killed someone. Perhaps it was nothing more than an accumulation of minor incidents, but those who understood some aspect of human psychology knew that the power of small things should never be underestimated.

Earl Sheridan, all of twenty-five years old, was a handsome man. A little shy of six feet, broad-shouldered, fair-haired, he had the look of someone who spent most of his life in the sun and took to it well. He fell in with a girl who went by the name of Esther Mary Marshall. She could have just been plain old Esther, but no, she was Esther Mary, and that was the way she wished to be addressed. Her language was loose and slutty, and she wore makeup in church. Esther loved Earl. Her love was clear and uncomplicated. He lit a fire in her somewhere, and she knew she wanted him even though he was a violent man. The anger was in his bones and his blood, and she knew it was only a matter of time before he started sharing it with her. She was smart enough to leave him before it happened. One thing she wanted to say was that whatever he might have been guilty of, he never did inflict violence upon her. It was her departure that did it, almost as if her strength of character served to highlight Earl's own weaknesses. He could not keep a girl. She had left him. Deserted him.

Despite the fact that they had been together for less than six months, this betrayal lit a slow fuse in Earl Sheridan's mind.

The next girl he charmed wasn't so smart. Her name was Katherine Aronson. She possessed a quiet and unfailing optimism, and perhaps believed that with good sense and persistence she could get a light to shine in amongst Earl's darkest thoughts. She was heard to say one time that all it took to make a bad person good was for someone to expect it of them. That kindness and encouragement could be the best sort of discipline. She was never to prove her theory. Earl Sheridan felt no need for any higher emotion. Anger and bitterness had carried him thus far, perhaps would carry him all the way. He beat her senseless with his bare hands a month after she met him. She could have pressed charges, but she didn't. Earl Sheridan was a patient man, if nothing else. His patience was matched only by his anger. However many years he might have served for what he'd done, he would never have forgotten. Katherine knew he would have found her and killed her. Earl would have made it his reason for living. Additionally, Katherine believed that such things were a test of her faith. The brightest stars attracted the darkest shadows. She believed that Jesus had died on the cross for her sins, and that everyone had to make amends in their own individual ways. Sometimes those amends required the salvation of another's lost soul.

So they let Earl Sheridan out with a warning, and Katherine took him back. He said he was sorry, and he called her sweet baby, and she forgave him. Three weeks later he cornered her in the kitchen and put a boning knife through her heart. She was dead before she realized what had happened, dead before she hit the linoleum. Earl Sheridan did nothing by halves, especially relationships.

That action irritated the nerves of twelve jurors, a judge, and the state of California, and they decided to kill Earl right back. They had him up in Baker, had arranged a welcoming committee in San Bernardino State Penitentiary. Here he would reside while due process dragged its heels, and here he would remain until the necktie party. So that afternoon, November 20, 1964, they had Earl Sheridan meet with a doctor from Anaheim University Hospital. Earl was asked if he'd be willing to bequeath his eyes.

24

They were making great progress in the field of optical surgery. "Don't think that's such a good idea," Earl Sheridan told the Anaheim doctor. "Reckon most folks would best prefer blindness than to see the world through my eyes."

They handcuffed and shackled him. They put him in an armored vehicle with a black-and-white up front, a second one in the rear, and they began the one hundred-and-twenty-five-mile southward drive to San Bernardino at five o'clock in the afternoon. The storm came up unexpected and strong. It should have been a straight run along 15 all the way, nothing more than a dogleg turn where they connected with 138, but the rain came like a barrage of fists, and for a while they were down to ten miles an hour, little to see ahead of them but rain-hammered windshields.

Stopping in Barstow was out of the question. Barstow could provide them with little more than a sheriff's department holding tank. Victorville had a facility for orphaned girls and unwed mothers fallen on hard times. It was secure enough, but not to the standard required for a man on his way to hanging. Hesperia it would have to be, and by the time they reached it they had managed the ninety miles from Baker in three hours and twenty-five minutes. Sheridan had bitched all the way, and had it not been for the sound of rain on the roof of the car they might have listened to him. It was a little after eight thirty when the convoy pulled through the outer gates of Hesperia Juvenile Correction Facility, and they had all of eight warders awaiting that boy. Earl Sheridan had never seen such a welcome in his whole born life. He made some crack about how many half men it took to guard a whole man, at which point the convoy chief, a retired Death Valley Junction deputy sheriff named James Rawley grabbed the chain between Sheridan's cuffs and twisted it until Sheridan near pissed his pants with the pain. Each one looked at the other for a good thirty seconds, and then Rawley smiled all high, wide, and handsome with his broken, tobacco-stained teeth, and said, "Reckon about one ought to do it."

Had that challenge not taken place, had Sheridan not gone to his isolation cell with a sense of humiliation burning through his very being, then the events of that night, the subsequent events that would terrorize California, Arizona, and Texas, might have never happened. People were going to die, people who were utterly unaware of this inevitability, and even had they known —well, there was not a thing they could have done about it. That night had been scheduled to mark the departure of Earl Sheridan to his intended final residence, care of California State, but in reality it marked the beginning of the worst regional murder spree to date, a murder spree that would not be outdone until Evan Sallis went on a roll almost thirty years later.

Earl Sheridan went into isolation a sad and sorry mess. Soaked to the bones, his wrists bleeding, his shirt filthy, the cuffs of his pants looking like they'd been chewed to length. But he did have one thing that no one knew about. He had a metal comb. Had seen it on the floor of the car as Rawley twisted his hands down and threatened him with silence. In the moment that followed his release—hyperventilating crazily, his head down between his knees as if accepting defeat—he had reached right on down and picked it up. Jamming it into his shoe, moving it then beneath his foot, he had walked it all the way into his cell. They removed his cuffs when he was through the door, and they left him to his own devices.

"One night you're here," Rawley had told him through the grate in the door. "Tomorrow morning we drive you on down to San Bernardino and finish what we started."

Rawley walked away. Sheridan said nothing at all. It was only when Rawley reached the external door that he heard Sheridan singing. He knew what it was; that old Rabbit Brown song— *Sometimes I think you're just too sweet to die. And other times I think you ought to be buried alive.*

Things kicked off in earnest a little before ten that night. The storm hadn't let up, wouldn't until six the following morning, and by then much of the surrounding farmland would be a swamp of dirty oatmeal. Rawley's deputy, a skinny man named Chester Bartlett, brought Earl some dinner. Though nothing more than a mess of cornmeal, a couple of pieces of fatback, a fried egg, and a cup of coffee, Bartlett still needed the key to get through the door, and he still had to hold the tray while Earl got up off of the floor. Experienced Bartlett might have been at convoying chained prisoners from one part of the state to another, but when it came to attending a confined man there was a procedure and a protocol about which he was ignorant.

First Rawley heard of it was when Sheridan had already made it to the kitchens. It was here that he found Clay Luckman and Digger Danziger.

Chester Bartlett was bleeding out from a wide neck wound inflicted by a metal comb. He would die before they got to him. Earl Sheridan had used Chester's own keys to lock him in the isolation cell. Now he had Chester Bartlett's sidearm, a pocketful of shells to go with it, and he was about his business with vigor and excitement.

Digger had heard word of Sheridan. It had been news throughout the entire facility within thirty minutes of the man's arrival. There was something hypnotic and addictive about a hanging, more so about the man who was to be hanged. Faced with the condemned himself, Digger saw nothing but the opportunity to escape. He believed that if he allied himself to Earl Sheridan, if he showed him the way out of the facility, then both their purposes would be served. Earl had other intentions in mind. Earl saw two young hostages, a healthy collection of sharp knives, and a way to avoid the scaffold.

A rapid evaluation of the situation gave Earl Sheridan a clear comprehension of what he was dealing with. The older kid was up for the thrill, the younger one looked like he was going to piss his pants right where he stood. The older one would work with him, help him control and manage the younger, and the three of them would be out together. Somewhere along the line he could kill the younger one, perhaps kill them both, or if he was feeling humanitarian he could just ditch them on the road somewhere and go it alone. Go where, he did not know. For in amongst all the running and hiding, in amongst the rush and panic of this thing, he had forgotten to think about what would happen next.

By the time Earl Sheridan, Elliott Danziger, and Clarence Luckman made it to the main gate the entire facility was ablaze with searchlights. Dogs, men, guns; trucks revving in the back of the compound ready to chase this guy down to nothing if that's what was needed. Sheridan had Danziger and Luckman tied together with a whole mess of twine he'd found in the kitchen. It served the purpose, for he had those two kids on a leash just less than three or four feet long. Anyone with a twitch on their trigger finger could so easily have taken out one of the hostages instead of Sheridan himself. Sheridan demanded a pickup truck. He got one. He wanted three days' worth of food; he got that too. Facility governor Tom Young took his sweet time about organizing these things, charging every man present from the top down to work in the direction of double-crossing Sheridan, creating the appearance of cooperation, all the while looking for a way to bring his dreadful plan to a halt. The difficulty was the hostages. Young had his deputy on the phone to the local police, to the federal authorities. They had a convicted death row escapee, now responsible for another murder, and he had to be stopped. But in stopping him they could not endanger the lives of the two brothers. The simple fact that Tom Young didn't give a solitary damn about Clay Luckman or Digger Danziger was beside the point. The newspapers gave a damn. The taxpayers gave a damn. The public at large would be the ultimate judge and jury in such a scenario, and they always erred in the direction of the underdog. No, the boys needed to come out of this alive, and that—first and foremost—was in Young's mind as he tried to figure a way to outfox Sheridan.

When Sheridan demanded a shotgun to go along with Chester Bartlett's sidearm, well Tom Young told him to go fuck himself. It was then that he took one of the knives he'd taken from the kitchen and cut Clay Luckman's shoulder. It was a shallow wound, but it bled like a bitch, and Young didn't have much choice but to accede to the man's demands. Sheridan told them he was driving away. They were going to see which way he was going for only so long, and then he was gone for good. He said if they sent cars or trucks or helicopters or any of that shit after him then both the kids were dead. And he would shoot himself to boot. Save the State a few bucks but ruin the day for Young. Young—old enough and wise enough to recognize a crazy one when he saw him—held up his hands and said nothing. Kidnapping really did make it a federal mess, and as soon as Sheridan hightailed it out of the facility gates he planned to speak to the Federal Bureau of Investigation and tell them the mess was all theirs.

Sheridan and his charges went out of those gates a little before midnight. Facility governor Tom Young went back to organize the facility lockdown. Once the place was secure he called the FBI. He spoke with a man named Garth Nixon. Nixon said they'd take it from here. All he needed were details of the stolen truck and pictures of the two boys. They already had enough pictures of Earl Sheridan to make a snapshot album. Young wrote up a dispatch with the requested details, and sent one of his men out to the Anaheim Bureau Office. Nixon made it clear that Governor Young and anyone else involved in this fiasco was relieved of their responsibility for the matter. The bureau would attend to whatever internal investigative and resultant disciplinary action might be required for Rawley and his escort team. Earl Sheridan was a fugitive from the law, a condemned man on the run, and a kidnapper. Throw into the mix the charges for which he was going to hang and he was *numero uno* as far as the FBI were concerned. Had Nixon known then even some small aspect of Sheridan's nature, even the nature of sociopathological behavior in its crudest form, he would not have been so quick to criticize or censure his colleagues. He thought Rawley, Young, others of their ilk, little more than hicks and rednecks, no more capable of restraining and transporting a known felon across a hundred and twenty-five miles of countryside than he himself was capable of dancing an Irish jig. This was now Bureau business, and the Bureau would attend to it.

Forces were mobilized for the search. Pictures were distributed, radio bulletins were issued on the wires and relayed to all stations in the surrounding counties. It was the most excitement the FBI had seen in years, and they were going to take advantage of the publicity and media furor that they knew was coming their way. In such cases, Nixon knew that if you did not unofficially deputize the populace and get them alert and looking too, well, you were screwed.

Earl Sheridan was a matter of enormous concern, as were the kidnapped brothers, Clarence Luckman and Elliott Danziger. The state governor was apprised of the situation within a matter of hours. He made a personal telephone call to the widow of Chester Bartlett and ensured her that they were doing everything they could. He assured her that Earl Sheridan would be brought to justice.

Everything they could do was hampered by their lack of understanding of Earl Sheridan.

By six o'clock, morning of Saturday, November 21, Nixon had been deputized to Anaheim Field Agent Ronald Koenig, a fourteen-year veteran of the Bureau, a prior history in the Anaheim Sheriff's Department, before that a handful of years in the military, the last two in Berlin during the establishment of the East-West divide. He had been around the block and then some. He estimated that Sheridan would kill or release his hostages within twenty-four hours, that they would be found dead or alive within thirty-six, that Sheridan himself might manage another seventy-two or ninety-six hours, and then die in a hail of bullets in some small dust pocket of a town like Calexico or La Rumorosa. Of this he had no doubt. Sheridan would make for Mexico. He would be dreaming of sunshine, tequila, cool *cerveza*, and hot girls. A man like Sheridan was driven by his instinct and his dick.

Of this Ronald Koenig could not have been more wrong. Earl Sheridan was driven by his instinct and his hatred. He did not head south as was expected. He did not intend to ever get to Mexico. He went southeast toward the Arizona state line. He did not understand federal law sufficiently well to appreciate that he was now being looked for by the government entire. He believed that his salvation lay outside the state of California. Once he was over the border there was little anyone could do. He would steal some money, buy some clothes, color his hair, change his name. He would vanish. It was that simple.

How it then became something more than simple had a great deal to do with the quantity of hatred that Earl Sheridan felt for people whose names he didn't even know.

DAY TWO

CHAPTER THREE

The diner was just a little box of a place with a few seats in back for the coloreds. The menu was made up of wooden letters stuck to a board behind the till. A layer of dust and grease adorned those letters. It said that the menu had never changed, and never would. Fatback, meatloaf, ham and eggs, steak.

Sheridan had a fist of dollars from someplace or other. Clay did not know where he had come by them, but he also had a clean T-shirt, which he told Clay to put on. "Can't have you walking around with blood all over yourself," he'd told Clay. "Just attract flies and unwanted attention."

It was eight, a handful of minutes after, and they stood in the doorway of that diner as if they'd blown in on the back of some ill wind.

They'd slept in the truck—he and Digger tied together, and then the rope looped over the back of the tailboard and secured to the chassis. Earl—if he had slept, and he sure didn't look like he had—had been in the cab, the shotgun across his knee, Chester Bartlett's revolver in his lap.

Surprisingly—from the moment Clay had put his head down against the baseboard of the pickup to the moment he felt a rough hand hurrying him awake—he had slept. No dreams, no fear, nothing. He had slept like a newborn. Once he was awake he became acutely aware of how much his shoulder ached. The quantity of blood had belied the shallowness of the wound, but he was concerned it would become infected. There was little he could do at this juncture. The clean T-shirt concealed it but did not allay the discomfort he felt. Above and beneath whatever concern he may have had for his physical well-being, there was the blunt reality of Earl Sheridan.

"We're going to find breakfast," Earl had told them, and then he untied them, and even in that moment—even as he appeared to be friendly—there was something dark and unsettling about everything he did. Clay did not know how to describe the feeling. Like approaching a firework already lit that had not yet flared. You just didn't know. Was it a dud, or would it explode in your face?

Standing at the side of the highway, the three of them pissing into the wind, Earl had said, "Have to acknowledge you boys. Most kids would be crying like orphans in their first boys' home. A pair of wet and whimpering sacks of shit. Well, I'll tell you something right here and now. People feeling sorry for themselves just makes me mad as hell. Makes me feel like I *really* want to give them something to moan about, you know? So, it's good for you that you ain't bein' that way about this. You're takin' it like men, and I feel it's only right and proper that I acknowledge you for that." He shook his dick and put it back in his pants. "When we started out from that place I had a mind to kill the pair of you and leave you someplace, but I've changed my mind. Seems to me you never did me no wrong, and I don't have a right to hurt you for that. We've come from the same place, and more than likely we're gonna end up in the same place, right?"

Digger glanced at Clay.

Clay shook his head. *Say nothing*, that gesture said.

"Hey, I'm talking to you," Earl Sheridan barked. "You hear what I said?"

"Yes, sir," Digger replied.

Earl laughed. "Sir? Jeez, kid, you been in that place too long. You don't need to be callin' me no 'sir.' Lordy, lordy, you really are a pair of misfits and troublemakers. You been in that place all your life?"

"Ever since our mama died we've been one place or another," Digger said.

Clay said nothing. He wanted to maintain as much distance between himself and Earl Sheridan as he could.

"Your mama?" Sheridan asked.

"Yes, sir."

"You pair are brothers?"

"Yes, sir," Digger replied.

"Well, I'll be damned. I never would have guessed it." He

34

paused, frowned, squinted at one, then the other. "Well, now you come to mention it, I do see something there. Maybe in the eyes, huh?" He shrugged. "Well, okay then. Seems you pair have seen the sorry end of nothin' for quite some time, eh? Reckon a bit of a change is good for the calendar, whaddya say?"

"Sure thing," Digger said.

"Well, good enough," Earl said. "Reckon we should start with a good breakfast and then we'll figure out where the rest of our lives is gonna begin."

Clay listened to his brother talking with Sheridan, and though he wanted to tell Digger to shut the hell up, he could not. Ignoring the man would just make him mad, and there was no telling what *mad* would provoke him to do.

The town was called Twentynine Palms. It sat along 62 at the edge of Joshua Tree, a hundred or so miles from Hesperia.

Earl had already explained to them that he was doing what the authorities would least expect. "Tell you something now," he said. "Ninety-nine out of a hundred guys in my shoes would run right to Mexico. I know this part of the world. I've been causin' trouble here for as long as I can remember. Right now they'll have people in Palm Springs, maybe Moreno Valley and Escondido. Hell, maybe they'll even have people looking for us in San Diego 'cause they think we're gonna try and get in through Tijuana. There'll be roadblocks on all the highways . . . and shit, man, they'll be runnin' themselves ragged wonderin' where the fuck we disappeared to! Anyways, we ain't doin' nothin' of the sort. We're heading for Arizona, maybe even Texas. Texan girls are a sight to behold . . ." And then Earl turned and saw the waitress walking toward them with a smile on her face like Christmas.

She had on a peasant blouse with a pattern like a tablecloth. Red and white checks. The front tails were tied up in a fist-sized knot above her navel, and it pushed up her breasts like an invitation to all and sundry for something wicked and wonderful.

Earl Sheridan just stood there, dumb as a fence post.

"You boys wanna table or you gonna stand there till sundown?" she said.

Earl didn't speak.

35

"A table please," Clay replied, and the girl smiled and indicated the table right beside the window.

"You'll be wantin' breakfast, I presume?" she said.

"Three times," Clay said, and he elbowed Digger along the seat so he could sit down too.

Earl was still dumbstruck, like a mule hit by lightning.

The waitress leaned forward. Her cleavage was as deep as the San Fernando Valley. You could have pitched a silver dollar from the other side of the room and never missed that target. "My name's Bethany," she said. "I'll be your waitress today. Now d'you boys want coffee or milk or juice or what?"

"Co-coffee," Earl stuttered, and then he smiled like a fool and his cheeks colored up.

"Well, coffee it is," Bethany said, and then she turned around and walked away.

Earl watched her ass like it was the last train to freedom.

The food came. Digger ate with his arm down, his left hand guarding his plate, his right hand around the spoon in a fist.

Earl showed him how to hold it properly. "Like a pen," he said, "and you can put your left hand someplace else. No one around here is looking to steal your food."

There was fatback and grits, eggs, some waffles with syrup, even sausage-meat gravy and corn. The three of them ate enough for a Kiwanis Convention, and then they sat back and held their guts like Santa.

Bethany brought more coffee.

"You all here by your own sweet self?" Earl asked her.

Clay saw something flash in Earl's eyes. It was a dark thing, a bad thought. Clay could feel the tension in the man, tight like a spring.

"For a little while," she said. "My husband and I own this place together, but he's down the road apiece getting a spare tire for his truck. He'll be here in a while or so."

She went on in back of the diner. Earl waited no more than a minute, and then he told Clay and Digger to go get in the pickup out front.

"I'll be no more than a couple of minutes," he said, and he got up from his seat. "I have the keys to the pickup," he added. "Those guns in there ain't loaded right now, and won't be until I get back. You can make a run for it, but in the time it's gonna take me to finish up here you're gonna make it half a mile, and that's if you run like a pair of halfwit motherfuckers. My advice is just to hang tight until I'm done, and then we'll all leave together."

Neither Digger nor Clay argued. They sat in back of the pickup and waited. Clay wanted to say something, but there was nothing to say. He knew what was going on, he just didn't know how bad it was until Earl came running from the back of the diner with blood on the tails of his shirt. Clay knew then that he had hurt Bethany, maybe even killed her. Bethany was done for, and that was a cert. Earl tucked the tails in before he climbed up, but that didn't change the fact that Clay had seen them.

Earl fumbled with the keys. He dropped them, retrieved them, got them in the ignition and revved the car. The pickup kicked a whirlwind of dust behind them as they cut away from the front of the diner and regained the highway. Earl had a fistful of dollars, some fives, maybe a ten or so, and he stuffed it in the dashboard. There was blood on the money too.

"You kill her?" Digger asked.

Earl slammed his foot on the brakes. The pickup careered to a halt in the middle of the road. Before Digger had a chance to double-take he felt Earl's hand around his throat, felt the man's weight bearing down on him, looked right back into his eyes. Those eyes were black and depthless, as if all the darkness of the world resided there.

"One question is too many questions," Earl said, and his voice was low-slung and gravelly. "You understand me, little man?"

Digger said *Yes* with his eyes.

Clay started; could recall with such clarity when Digger used to call him that.

Little man.

"Good 'nough," Earl said.

He released Digger's throat, jammed the pickup into gear, and pulled away with a shudder.

Clay looked straight ahead, dared not to look anyplace else, but then he felt Digger's hand on his arm. The reassuring presence of his brother. *Hang in there*, he believed that gesture said. *I'm okay. We're gonna get through this. Somehow, someway we're gonna get through this. Might even make it to Texas. Might even see Eldorado after all.*

Clay wanted to cry, but he did not dare. He was scared beyond belief. Everything had happened so fast, and now here he was —trapped in a car with his brother and this maniac—and the maniac had just killed some poor unsuspecting waitress for the sake of a handful of dollars.

Out here it was different. Institutional rules did not apply in the wider world. For now Clay had no choice but to go along with this business, so he decided to keep his eyes and his words to himself. Earl Sheridan had killed Bethany the waitress. He'd killed her for money. For sex too, more than likely. The sex had lasted a minute, maybe two, the money couldn't have been more than fifteen or twenty dollars all told. This was the kind of man he was traveling with, and Clay wondered if he and Digger were even going to see the other side of tomorrow.

Still there was the reassuring grip of his brother's hand on his arm.

Clay kept his eyes forward. He didn't want to risk showing any signs of weakness.

They followed 62 and crossed into Arizona over the Colorado at Big River. By this time it was late morning and they had driven the hundred or so miles from Twentynine Palms without stopping. They connected with 72 at Parker and headed southeast. Earl wanted to get to the I-10 near Salome and then make a straight run into Phoenix.

"Couple of hours and we'll be in the biggest city you boys ever did see," he said. "Times like this a city's best. City has so many people you'll never find but one of them at a time. Make it to Phoenix and we're as good as gone forever." He laughed like a jackass, though Clay didn't tell him so.

Behind them a number of miles a hubbub of activity surrounded the small roadside diner at the edge of Twentynine Palms. Black-and-whites had come south from Ludlow, northeast from Yucca Valley. Twentynine Palms' sheriff, Vince Hackley, had been the first out there. Don Olson, owner of the Highway 62 Grill & Diner had called in an incident. Hackley knew Don, had eaten out at his place plenty, and when he got there he found the ordinarily level-headed and sober guy a mess of nerves and hysteria. In the kitchen he learned why.

Bethany Olson, for sure and certain one of the best-looking girls Twentynine Palms had ever known, was dead. Not only dead, she was gutted like a pig. From first inspection it seemed as if whoever had done this had set his mind to dividing her up three or four different ways. Her throat was cut—deep, like he had a mind to decapitate her. Perhaps growing frustrated at the difficulty of his task, he set about her torso and breasts, wide incisions that went a good two inches into the flesh. The upper thighs were also lacerated, her blouse shredded into a mess of wet, scarlet ribbons. Hackley went out front and called for reinforcements from the two closest towns, and he put a call into his dispatcher to get the county coroner from Desert Hot Springs. Next thing he did was go out and talk with Don Olson. The man was spotless. Not a speck of blood on anything but his shoes, and Hackley had some of that same blood on his own boots. Appearances indicated that Don Olson had done what he said: come home from the garage to find his wife exactly as Hackley had just seen her. Hackley didn't doubt for a moment that someone had raped her. If you had an urge to do that to some girl, well Bethany Olson was the girl you'd want to do it to.

The diner was cordoned off. The county coroner came down and started the unenviable task of controlling the crime scene and managing the body. Hackley and his two colleagues—Ed Chandler from Ludlow and Ethan Soper from Yucca Valley—began canvassing the area, looking for signs, clues, indications of who might have passed through here with murder in mind. Highway 62, all of a quarter mile away, had more than likely brought them in and taken them away. Hackley knew—more from intuition than experience—that the harder they looked the less they would see. There was nothing here, nothing to tell them who or why. Unless their man did some other thing, unless there was another incident that brought him to the attention of the police, then the likelihood of finding him was almost non-existent. That was the rub down here. Small-town murders came in two flavors. First was domestic, familial, neighborly. It was obvious who did it because there was no one else who could have.

Second came the unexpected. Never witnessed, always out of left field, as unexpected as weather. Three or four times in his quarter century he'd seen such things. Granted, none as violent and bloody as Bethany Olson, but he'd seen them. Robbery-homicides ordinarily, holdups and the like, one of them when he'd served in North Las Vegas back in the early fifties. Some schmuck had turned over a liquor store for little more than nineteen dollars, and Hackley's partner—off duty at the time—had shot the man in the throat. Hell of a thing to die for.

Big cities were different. Big cities there were always people who knew people, people who'd seen things, heard things, got word from so-and-so about such-and-such. Price you paid for the wealth of available information was the proportionately greater number of killings. You couldn't have one without the other. Seemed to be the nature of things.

So Vince Hackley was under no illusions. Don Olson didn't cut up his own wife, he was sure of that. This was not a domestic matter. This was something else entirely.

And whatever the hell it was, he hoped it had already left the state.

CHAPTER FOUR

That night, in the outskirts of Phoenix, Clay Luckman knew that if he and Digger didn't get away they were done for. That was as sure as sunrise.

Aside from a brief stopover for Earl to buy a shirt from a store and discard the bloody one, their journey had been uninterrupted. Earl then dropped them off a hundred yards from a turnoff on the highway. For some reason Earl had figured on Digger being more reliable than Clay, so he'd told Digger to hold on to Clay and stay right where they were for ten minutes or so.

"Down there is a motel. Whole bunch of cabins set in a half circle behind the main building. You wait here ten minutes and then come on down. I'm gonna get us a room, but if they see there's three of us they'll charge us three times. We'll all sleep there tonight, and then in the morning we'll head across Arizona into Texas or someplace." He took his jacket and wrapped it around the shotgun. The revolver went into the waistband of his pants, and he tugged his shirt out to cover it. He drove on down toward the motel. Clay could sense him looking back at them in the rearview.

"What the hell are we gonna do, Digger?" Clay asked.

"I don't know, Clay, I just don't know. I was scared he was going to kill us, but I don't think he will."

"He killed that waitress back there. You know that, right?"

"I don't know exactly what he did, Clay, and I don't want to know. You seen how he was when I asked him . . ."

"So what? You just gonna let him drag us all over the country-side until he gets tired of the company?"

"Hell, Clay, I ain't gonna *let* him do anything. This isn't my doing, you know? I didn't get us in this mess."

"And neither did I. All I'm saying is that we have to do something."

"And what would you suggest, you being the smart guy around here?"

"Digger . . . Christ, I don't mean it like that. I'm not blamin' you for what's happened. I'm just sayin' we have to do something fast before his patience runs out, or before he gets the idea we're slowin' him down."

"Well, I don't know, and right now the *only* thing we can do is go on down to that motel and see what happens."

Digger was right. But there was something else, something in Digger's tone that unnerved Clay. It was almost as if Digger was defending Earl Sheridan. Surely that couldn't be right? Surely Digger hadn't gotten the idea into his head that Earl was one of the good guys here?

"Digger . . . seriously . . . the guy's a crazy one. He done killed that girl back there. He was already on his way to hanging for something else, wasn't he?"

Not a word of response.

"Digger, I mean it. We gotta go someplace. We were gonna go to Eldorado. Let's take off for Eldorado together, eh? Let's us just do that and be done with him."

Digger was silent for a good three or four minutes longer, and then he got up and started down toward the motel. Clay watched him go. His heart was too heavy to bear. He felt the weight of conscience, the weight of responsibility, the weight of *fraternity*. If he left Digger alone with Earl, then Digger would be lost for good. Clay knew it, knew it with everything he possessed. He realized there was no choice now. He took a deep breath, he gritted his teeth and clenched his fists. He took a step, and yet again another, and he followed on after his brother because there was nothing else he could do.

In the cabin was nothing more than a flea-ridden bed, a ratty carpet, a tiny shower room with a sink and a toilet. It smelled like someone was buried underneath.

Earl talked incessantly. Clay tried hard not to listen to what he was saying, but Digger seemed to hang on his every word. Clay told himself that Digger was merely ingratiating himself into

Earl's favors in order to preserve both of them. If Earl liked Digger, then Digger was going to make it through the other side of this. And if Earl liked Digger enough, then Digger would at least have some leverage on defending his younger brother. That's what Clay told himself. What he believed was a mite different.

The poisonous words came, and Clay did his best not to let the bitterness infect his mind, but it was hard. In amidst all the lies was sufficient truth to start the fire, and that fire seemed to be lighting up a spark in Digger's eyes. Clay watched as Digger leaned in close, his shoulders down, his expression intent, as if here was all the wisdom of the world and he could not afford to miss a single word.

"Folks respect you because they're afraid," Earl told him. "Wife doesn't respect her husband because he buys flowers every once in a while. She respects him because she knows he'll let fly if she doesn't do what she's told. Reason wives never leave violent husbands? It ain't outta fear. I'll tell you that much. It's outta respect."

Digger's eyes were wide, his ears wider, and he seemed to just soak it all up like a sponge.

"Thing about being human is you know you're going to die. That awareness is there inside you. Doesn't matter what you do, how much money you have, how many people love you, at the end of it you're going to die. One thing we have in common. Levels the field for us all."

Earl smoked Lucky Strikes, chained them one after the other, used the last to light the next. The room was thick with acrid clouds, the window cranked barely a half-inch. It was warm, too warm to be sat inside, but lessons weren't over, and wouldn't be for a while.

"You hear these boys talk about killing someone. It's unreal. It's surreal. It's like I wasn't there. That's all so much BS. Of course you're there. More there than you've ever been. It's the realest thing you'll ever do, and that's a fact." Lighting another cigarette, and then, "Pain is the anvil upon which your personality is forged. Look at me. More pain in my life than a man can stand, but I got buckets of personality, and them buckets is spilling over. Hell, I got enough personality for three or four regular folk."

Digger seemed to take it all in, every word, every statement.

The most dangerous thing about Earl Sheridan was his confidence. Confidence was nothing more than certainty. Confidence was simply saying something you believed in. Trouble was that those with impressionable minds took certainty and self-belief as truth. Digger's mind had always been flexible. That was Digger's downfall. Those who lacked certainty took others' certainties as truths, however deceitful and shallow they were. The mind was like dough, and Earl Sheridan seemed set to leave his fingerprints all over it. Earl hated the world. That was obvious from the moment he opened his mouth. Clay had crossed paths with people like this before, at Barstow, at Hesperia as well. In such places he had acted as a buffer between Digger and such folks. Here it was different. Here there was no work party to distract Digger's attention. Here there was no rigorous schedule that would put them side by side in lockdown for eight or ten hours at a time, during which time Clay could disinfect Digger's thoughts and resultant erroneous conclusions.

It was in that motel room that Clay began to see a small ravine between himself and his brother, and with each word, with each passing minute, he saw that ravine widening to a gulf.

Earl Sheridan was a deranged and hate-filled man. If you looked too closely at that kind of hatred you'd go blind. Earl's reasoning seemed no more substantial than childish spite. He spoke of his father, introduced him into the conversation with the words, "Boy, if there was ever a book about being an asshole, that man wrote it." And Mr. Sheridan Senior occupied center stage for the next half hour. He did this, he did that, he did the other. He railed on Earl for speaking out of turn, for eating too much and eating too little, for walking too fast, too slow, for being stupid, smart-mouthed, simple, for sulking, for lying, for telling the truth. It was all a mess of contradictions, and if there was a grain of truth in what Earl was saying then it seemed no surprise that he came out the way he did.

After it got dark they went out to eat. Earl stopped at a liquor store on the way. He bought a six-pack and a bottle of rye. He offered a can of beer to Digger, snatched it back as Digger reached for it, and then for a moment or two he played that back-and-forth *You-can-have-it-no-you-can't* game until Digger was resigned in defeat. Only then did he give him the can. Earl seemed pleased with himself, pleased to bait a teenager and get the upper hand.

"Share it 'tween you," he said, "and drink it slow, 'cause you sure as shit ain't getting' no more." Then he went on to explain that come tomorrow there would have to be some changes in the way things were going as he had little enough money for himself, let alone anyone else.

"We'll get some money someplace," Digger said, holding the beer can like a prize, and the way he said it made it clear as daylight what he was thinking of.

"Maybe so," Earl replied as he pulled into the forecourt of a small restaurant with a red canopy and gold writing on the windows.

When Clay got out he looked down the street. It went as far as he could see and just kept on going. And it was not the only street in the place.

Once inside, Earl ordered up a feast of things. Some rib-eyes, potatoes, greens, gravy, some corn bread, and other stuff. He talked while he ate. The liquor had put him in good humor, and there he was, going off fast and funny in four directions like a talk show host.

Clay watched him. The man had about as much heart as a rattlesnake. He had a hundred different faces. He had layers and levels and facets. But Clay Luckman knew one thing—that however deep Earl Sheridan might go, whatever it was that lay at the heart of him was dead.

Looking sideways at Digger he realized that both of their thoughts were for Earl Sheridan in that moment. Clay thinking, *This man scares me more than death.* Digger—his head angled and alert like a hunting dog—thinking, *This man makes me laugh more than any man I've ever known.*

They were done eating by nine. Earl paid the check and left a two-dollar tip. He had drunk too much to drive, but Clay figured that if he was stopped he'd just shoot the cop anyway and what the hell. Either which way he wasn't going to let anyone stop him getting where he was going.

They made it back to the motel without incident. Earl gave them a blanket each, put them in the bathroom, and wedged a chair beneath the door handle.

"I hear a fucking sound out of you assholes tonight I'm gonna come in there and blow your fucking heads off, you understand me?"

There seemed to now be a light of admiration in Digger's eyes, and that light didn't seem to dim but a little. Perhaps he figured Earl was just being practical and businesslike. After all, he was a convict on the run. He was a man condemned to hang for the murder of Katherine Aronson. Now, if they caught him, they'd have to hang him for the waitress in that diner back in Twenty-nine Palms. Live like this and it behooved you to trust no one.

Clay thought about waiting until Digger fell asleep and then trying to go it alone. Maybe he could gag Digger with a towel, hold him down, force him to listen to some sense. He reckoned he might possess sufficient strength to do such a thing. And then Digger would have to make a choice. Come with him, take a risk and see if they could get away, or stay with Earl Sheridan. Given enough time, Clay knew he could set Digger's thoughts right again. He was just impressed with Earl, that was all. Earl was a tough guy. Earl was a man on the run. Earl had guns and liquor and money, and he could always get more of each. But if Clay could get through to Digger, appeal to him on every angle he could think of, then he might see the light of day and realize how he had been manipulated. Then there was the question of escape. Once out of the bathroom, Earl sleeping soundly, would they make it out and away before he awoke? Could they just smash through the bathroom door, both of them with all their strength, and rush at Earl where he slept? Two of them could maybe hold him down, use a towel or a pillow to suffocate him. Hit him hard and fast with the bedside lamp. Get one of them guns and just let him have it . . .

But Clay knew these were foolish and crazy ideas. First and foremost, he didn't have the nerve to kill someone. Knew Digger didn't possess that kind of nerve either. Didn't matter who they were. Second, Earl would hear their voices right away, and he'd come in there guns blazing. Clay didn't want to survive only for his own sake. He needed to rescue his brother from whatever delusions he now possessed, and because he felt it was his duty to stop this crazy man who had killed the waitress. He knew—in his heart of hearts—that he hadn't seen the last of Earl Sheridan's killing streak, and he knew that by the end of it one or all of them would be dead.

Clay Luckman lay there beside his brother. He started whispering something.

"Ssshhh," came the response from Digger—abrupt and direct. "You wanna get us killed, you damn fool?"

Clay wondered what would happen, and as he wondered he became more afraid than he could ever have imagined.

He believed then that he would die before a week was out, perhaps before the end of the next day. More chilling than that thought was the possibility that Digger's loyalties might be turned to such a degree that he would do nothing to protect him.

They were brothers, but they were different. Different fathers, different blood, different legacies. It was said that a child growing without a parent would always have aspects of their personality that they could not account for. There were things going on inside that were sourced someplace unknown, and Clay Luckman wondered about his own father, and he wondered about Digger's, too, and the more questions he asked of himself, the less answers he seemed to find.

He did not sleep. He listened to his brother as he snored. He shivered in the darkness and contemplated the end of his short and bitter life.

CHAPTER FIVE

When Bailey Redman was ten years old she realized her mother was a prostitute. She also realized that she'd been pretty dumb not to see this earlier. She'd told herself that her mother simply had a lot of friends, all of them men, all of them visiting at irregular times and just for a short while. Perhaps it was something she had learned at school, a conversation she'd overheard, a comment made by someone in the street, but her awareness shifted suddenly, almost imperceptibly, but sufficiently to understand that the things going on in the back bedroom of their small house in Florence, Arizona, were not games of pinochle and twenty-one. The games her mother played with her gentleman callers involved an absence of clothes and the exchange of money. It was in that moment that a great deal of other things became understandable, and a great deal more questions arose.

When Bailey Redman was twelve her mother told her the truth about her father. His name was Frank Jacobs, and when Elizabeth Redman had last seen him (which was in fact the night of Bailey's conception), he was an itinerant shoe salesman working out of Scottsdale. He was a good-looking man, unmarried, well mannered, and no, she did not have a picture of him, and no, she did not know whether or not he was still an itinerant shoe salesman working out of Scottsdale. Sorry, kid, those are the breaks.

On her thirteenth birthday Bailey Redman walked into town and visited the library. She found a telephone book for Scottsdale, wrote down the numbers for two *F. Jacobs*, one *Frank Jacobs*, and one *Franklin Jacobs*.

She called each of them in turn and asked them if they had ever slept with a prostitute called Elizabeth in a town called Florence back in January of 1949. Try to remember, she said. It would have been about the same time as President Truman was inaugurated.

Both *F. Jacobs* hung up the phone, as did *Frank Jacobs*. *Franklin Jacobs* paused however, and when he asked the caller's name, her age, and whether or not her mother knew what she was doing, Bailey knew that it was her father's voice she could hear at the other end of the line.

Bailey waited a week and then she took a bus all the way from Florence to Scottsdale, all of sixty-something miles, and with a shred of paper in her hand, the address of *Franklin Jacobs* neatly copied from the telephone book, she waited outside a narrow house with a stoop and a window basket.

When he came out of the house and walked down the street she knew. When he paused to open the door of his car, an Oldsmobile that had seen better days, she knew even better. She tucked the slip of paper in the pocket of her skirt and crossed the street.

When she stood ahead of him, just looking at him, neither smiling nor frowning nor anything else, he said, "You're the girl who called, aren't you?"

"I am," she said.

"What's your name?"

"Bailey Redman."

He did smile then, and he held out his hand. "I'm Frank Jacobs," he said politely.

"Pleased to meet you," Bailey replied.

"I think I better give you a ride home and talk to your mother."

And so it was, the evening of Wednesday, October 17, 1962, that the closest Bailey Redman would ever get to a family was reunited in the front yard of a small house in Florence, Arizona.

"How did you know it was me who got you pregnant?" was the question Frank Jacobs wanted to ask Elizabeth Redman. "I mean, considering your line of work an' all, I was just wondering how you knew to tell your daughter *my* name."

"It's something we just have," Elizabeth told him. "It's one of those things that women just *know*."

Frank Jacobs didn't question the issue. He had slept with Elizabeth Redman in January of 1949. The girl who had tracked him to Scottsdale looked so much like him it was unnerving. But she was beautiful, like her mother, and he did not resent the truth that had been presented to him.

He wanted to know if Elizabeth was secure, financially speaking, and if there was anything she needed.

"I didn't give you the problem, Frank," she said. "Not then, and not now."

"I understand that," he said, "and I appreciate it, but things have changed now." He looked at his daughter. "I'm a father now it seems, and a father has certain responsibilities."

"You're taking all of this very well," Elizabeth said. "I can't imagine there'd be many men who would take something like this in their stride."

Frank Jacobs, his hat removed, his top shirt button undone, seated there on the end of the couch in the small parlor, smiled ironically.

"I'm thirty-nine years old," he said. "I'm not married. I do not own a business. I am still working for the same people that I was thirteen years ago, still selling the same shoes for the same feet. All I know is types and colors of leather, cordovan wing tips, loafers, dress shoes, and sandals. I eat the same things from the same places. I go to see a movie once a month. I smoke the same brand of cigarettes as I did when I started back in 1940. Everything about me is predictable, routine, and regular. Now I am not so predictable. Now I have something that is neither routine nor regular, and I kind of like it." He looked at Bailey. "When Bailey called I knew she was my daughter. Don't ask me why. I just *knew*, same way that you knew that I was the one who got you pregnant. Now we're here, and we all have something to do with what has happened, and I'm asking whether you're okay, whether you need any help with anything, you know? I'm not a wealthy man, but I make a living, and I have no vices to speak of. I don't drink and I don't gamble, and as far as our rendezvous is concerned . . . well, I did that kind of thing maybe a dozen times in my life, and it's not something I've done now for the better part of ten years." Frank Jacobs hitched the knees of his pants and edged forward on the settee. "So that's where I am. Those are my cards on the table. I'm here if you need me, and if you don't then I'll go away again. I don't wish to bring you any trouble, and I don't think you want to deliver any up for me."

Elizabeth Redman smiled. "I recall you as a gentleman," she said, "and I'm never wrong about such things. I'm not going to ask you for money, but I get the idea that Bailey would like to get to know you, you being her father an' all, and if you have no disagreement with that then you can cover the cost of whatever she needs to come up on the bus and visit."

"That would be just fine," Jacobs said, and then he turned to his daughter. "Bailey?"

"Sure," she said. "Seems a hell of a shame we've missed thirteen years."

"These things happen," Jacobs said. "Everybody does what they do, rightly or wrongly, for good reason, and no one has the authority to judge another human being for their decisions."

"So it looks like you got yourself a father," Elizabeth said to Bailey, and Bailey smiled, and she tried not to cry, and when she leaned across to hug her father there was a moment of awkwardness between them that they both knew would pass with time.

Bailey fell into a routine. She visited with her father for a full weekend each month for nearly two years. By this time she was approaching fifteen. She was bright, she read voraciously, and had reconciled herself to the fact that she would never be normal. Her parents were a prostitute and a shoe salesman. She was an oddity, an idiosyncrasy, and there was something about this that she found immensely appealing. She loved storms. She loved angel food cake. She loved almost-ripe peaches, where the flesh was firm and bitter and the color had not yet come up fully. And though she was slightly afraid of cats, she could not help but love them too. Even if from a distance. She loved freckles on children, the smell of dark coffee. She loved corn and butter and the sensation of chocolate melting between her fingers, though she had experienced such a sensation only twice in her life and had yet to determine if it was the sensation itself, or the promise of chocolate itself as it was so rare. She loved old people with stories of youth, the sound of nibs on paper, the inky smell of new books, the rumble of three or four bass fiddles playing in unison. Most of all she loved being a girl, because a girl could love a boy, and boys were the best of all.

Frank Jacobs loved Bailey. He believed he'd never loved

someone so much in all his life. He didn't tell her for fear of embarrassing her, but he felt it in his heart and his eyes and his head and in the moments of solitude when she wasn't there and he wished she was.

And it would stay that way until Elizabeth Redman died.

Bailey understood the word that her mother used—*cancer*—but she didn't understand how or why she had it. Frank tried to explain it, but Frank was not the kind of man who was used to explaining much beyond grades of leather and discounts.

For a while the world appeared as if through aged, heat-blemished glass.

Elizabeth would find Bailey standing by the window, lantern-eyed and open-mouthed, as if to attract moths and then swallow them. She tried to console the girl, tried to make her see that things were never always simple.

"But why so complicated?" Bailey would ask her, and her mother would be unable to give an answer because she didn't know what the answer was.

A priest came by one time. It was a month or so after the news had come.

"If you are honest and forthright you will always meet challenges," he said. "The devil does not tempt the weak and the vain. They are already lost. The devil works hardest on those who are righteous."

"But my mother is a prostitute," Bailey told him.

"I know," said the priest, and he saw in her expression that this child was many years beyond her given age. Life had forced her to grow up fast. It had made her smart, but it also made her challenge him in a way that made him uncomfortable.

"Prostitutes aren't righteous, not in the eyes of the church and the Bible and whatever," Bailey said.

"Child, everyone is righteous in the eyes of God."

Bailey believed the priest to be uncertain and shallow. He looked like a man who doubted himself, doubted his faith, but kept on trying to convince himself and the rest of the world that he was right and God was just.

After a shock of such magnitude, some found solace in silence and solitude. Others craved noise and people, as if the insignificant collisions of smaller lives would be sufficient to distract them from their pain.

Bailey sought neither solitude nor noise. She sought understanding, but did not find it.

Once the priest had left, Bailey and Elizabeth lay side by side on the bed where Elizabeth had entertained so many gentlemen callers, and they said nothing.

Elizabeth Redman died on the morning of Sunday, November 15, 1964. Bailey was beside her when she passed away. The last thing that Elizabeth told her daughter was that she should listen to no one but herself, that her heart would always tell her the truth, and that if you started lying to yourself then you were screwed.

Bailey kissed her mother, and then pulled the sheet over her head. She walked out to the corner and called Frank.

"She's dead."

"I'm on my way," thinking that had it not been a Sunday he would have been on the road. Now he was responsible for his daughter. There was no one else. He was scared, excited, sad, a little confused. He drove twenty miles an hour over the speed limit and no one stopped him.

The funeral was held in Oro Valley, just north of Tucson on Sunday, November 22. The church was called the New Hope Missionary Baptist Church. Outside there was a sign that read *God's Math: One Cross Plus Three Nails Equals Four-given.*

Bailey didn't cry. She figured she'd done all the crying she was going to do earlier. Frank asked her if she wanted to say anything. What was she going to say? And who was she going to say it to? The only people in the church were herself, her father, the priest, and the undertaker who waited at the back for word that the coffin was ready to be interred.

Frank paid for everything. There was a little reception in a bar a block and a half away. They had sandwiches made up, some corn dogs and potato chips. Frank drank root beer because he had to drive. Bailey drank Coke.

"We have to go back to Scottsdale," Frank told her. "I don't know what to do about things . . ." He shook his head. "The house where you lived was rented. We just have to empty everything out and turn it back to the landlord."

"Leave it all there," Bailey said.

"What?"

"Leave everything there. I don't want any of it."

"But your clothes, your books, everything that belonged to your mother—"

"Leave it, Frank. Leave it all behind. I don't want to carry that stuff around with me forever."

"You're sure?"

Bailey didn't reply. She didn't need to. Frank knew enough of his own daughter to recognize what he was hearing. She was willful, no question. It was a good trait. The kind of trait that would help her survive alone.

They stayed the night in a cheap motel somewhere off of the interstate. Frank slept on the floor. He gave Bailey the bed, but she could not sleep. She went out in bare feet, in jeans and a T-shirt, and she stood at the back of the cabin and looked into the dark. Whoever told you that the night was silent wasn't paying attention. You heard more in half an hour of darkness that any span of daylight. The furrows of the darkening field like the nap of corduroy, the moon appearing as a hole in the black sky through which another universe could be seen. She could hear dogs howling in roundelays, echoing, reechoing, that final sound traveling out to wherever the land ended, and there to be swallowed by the sea.

The end of one thing, the beginning of something else. She didn't know what to expect, and thus expected nothing. She was unaware of Clay Luckman, of Earl Sheridan, of Digger Danziger. Had she known how their paths would cross she would not have believed such coincidence possible. She had once heard that old line "Coincidence is when God wishes to remain anonymous." Perhaps it was the same for the devil.

DAY THREE

CHAPTER SIX

The sun rose early. The light was as pale and clean as the face of a fresh-cut apple. Clay had fallen asleep listening to Earl curse. *Fuck. Shit. Cocksucker. Son of a bitch.* The man had spent his life taking wrong turns and had wound up in a cul-de-sac. The thing Clay saw, the thing he now understood, was that the darkness of man was not an illusion. Men and women—the bold and the brave, the anxious, the timid, the poor, the wealthy, the sincere and the shallow—all hoped that evil was an illusion, but it was not. Earl Sheridan stood as testament to that.

As Earl rose, as he oriented himself to where he was, as he removed the chair that he'd wedged beneath the bathroom door handle, Bailey Redman was elsewhere, even in that moment preparing herself for her mother's funeral. How her path would cross with that of Clay Luckman and Elliott Danziger was not yet known, and could not have been foreseen.

"Breakfast," Earl said. "And then you pair are gonna stay right beside me while I check out a few things in Phoenix."

Earl possessed the kind of calm stillness that people had just before they did something truly crazy. And, unbeknownst to him, his parents—his disciplinarian father, his puritanical mother—were now receiving a dozen telephone calls a day. Without variation they were all from strangers asking after their son. When had they last seen him? How did he seem? How was he as a child? Did they ever consider he would become a criminal and a murderer? A whirlwind of federal people had descended on Hesperia. The world wanted to know all about Earl Sheridan, about the boys he'd taken hostage, about Agents Garth Nixon and Ronald Koenig, about how a condemned man could escape the confines of the justice system with a bad attitude and a comb. They were looking for him south of Anaheim and Palm Springs.

They believed he was headed for Baja, California. The might of the federal government could be brought to bear, and was being mobilized even as Sheridan's parents fielded the incessant calls, but even the might of the government was nothing in the face of the entire continental United States. Sheridan was one man. Even with Luckman and Danziger in tow, this was only three. There were delays, misunderstandings, photographs that didn't replicate so well in the printing and reprinting. Earl Sheridan became unrecognizable as his image was dispatched time and time again to all the officers and individuals that possessed an interest in his identification and arrest. Most folks who had a mind to care just wanted him dead. It would save the state and the county the trouble of another trial for the killing of Chester Bartlett, the expense of feeding a maggot like Sheridan all the way through the arraignments, pretrial motions, the jury selection, the eventual incarceration on death row. Hell, it would even save the handful of bucks' worth of rope they'd use to hang him, perhaps the few cents of electricity that they might smash through his body like an errant hurricane if they had a mind to change the method of execution. Someone somewhere had to foot the bill for such things, and that someone could well do without the burden.

It was past nine by the time Sheridan and the two brothers left the motel and made their way into Phoenix itself. Clay Luckman had never seen such a place. Seemed more people were crammed into a block of the city than he'd seen in his whole life.

Clay walked breathless, amazed. Though Digger said nothing, a single look at his expression told Clay that he was experiencing the very same thing. It was a different world, could have been a different planet for the resemblance it bore to *anything* they had seen before. The clothes, the vehicles, the sheer quantity of everything that assaulted their senses. Sights, sounds, smells . . . hell, even the sky looked different to the one that would hang over them when they dug ditches and conspired to steal root beer.

Earl walked them to a diner. Had he not directed the way both Clay and Digger would have just stood wide-eyed and wondering in the street. He told them they looked like a couple of dumbass farmhands.

"Jesus Christ, anyone'd think you pair had never seen a real town in your lives . . ."

Earl was on the money, but neither boy replied.

Once in the diner, they sat in back in a booth, Earl closest to the window, watching the car, Chester Bartlett's sidearm tucked into the waistband of his pants.

A young man approached them, had on an apron, had a pencil and a pad of paper in his hand.

"Kinda steak you got?" Earl asked him.

"Only one kind."

"Kind is that?"

"Kind you eat."

Earl smiled. "That'll do, then. We'll have three of them. Eggs, potatoes too. Coffee for me. Ice water for the boys here."

Digger asked for coffee.

"Get what you're given and shut your fuckin' mouth," Earl said. "Be happy you're eating anything, boy."

Digger shut his mouth. He did not act offended. He acted respectful. Clay could see it in his eyes, in his demeanor, the awkward language of his body when Earl addressed him. The poisonous words appeared to be taking hold. Digger was now aspiring to be a contemporary of Earl's. A man had to have aspirations. Clay also knew that Digger could be mighty stubborn when the mood took him, no more so than when Clay lectured him on the rights and wrongs of things. There had been occasions when Digger had defied plain common sense, and for no other reason than to challenge Clay. Digger wanted to be right, and the greater part of being right was the refusal to admit when you were wrong.

They ate in near silence for a while, and then Earl punctuated that silence with more of his road-worn and ragged wisdom.

"Best food you'll ever eat is paid for with someone else's dollar," he said. Once more, he shared a few sentiments about his father. "Wasn't nothin' but a raggedy-ass son of a bitch. If half the ideas he'd had were only half useful he'd still only be a quarter of the man I am." Another pearl: "Don't get why folks read newspapers. All stuff that's already happened? Couldn't fathom it. Now a newspaper that told you what was *going* to happen? That would sure be a doozy." His words were clear and concise, but the mind behind them was not.

Later, a good deal later, Clay would think about those hours—the latter part of Saturday night and into Sunday, the things that happened that day and the following morning, and he would question why he didn't run. Perhaps he could have convinced Digger to go with him, perhaps not. Hindsight, ever the cruelest and most astute adviser, would tell him that the smartest damned thing he could have done was to have grabbed the gun from Earl, shot him dead center in the forehead, and then marched Digger out of the diner at gunpoint and turned themselves both over to whatever authority was the first to come along. If Clay had run alone, then there was always the good chance that Earl would have hunted him down and shot him. Digger could have done nothing to stop him. He didn't stand a chance. He knew that. But it was more than that. Earl Sheridan was car-crash-fascinating. Clay stayed—not because he feared for his own life, but because he feared for the lives of others, Digger's primarily, and if not his physical well-being, then surely his mental and spiritual salvation. Association with a man such as Earl Sheridan, especially by someone who seemed to possess such an impressionable mind as Digger Danziger, would require an exorcism. It would take a good while of talking and listening, of explaining, of patience and reorientation, to weed those evil thoughts out of Digger's head. And perhaps Clay thought he could do something to keep the body count down. Perhaps he believed that by hanging in there he could do something to ensure that there were no more Bethany Olsons.

Clay Luckman's responsibility was misplaced, his appreciation of the situation misconceived and ill advised, but he believed what he believed, and he believed he could do *something*.

Earl ate his breakfast. Digger watched in silence, almost as if he was waiting to hang on the very next word that Earl might utter. Clay felt sick to his stomach but forced down a number of mouthfuls. A time would come when he would need his strength.

They were out and on the road before ten.

It was past Phoenix, on the I-10 on the far-side of Casa Grande, that Earl saw the mercantile. That's what it was called—Pinal

County Mercantile. Perhaps it was the name that caught Earl's eye, pronounced it *penal*, and laughed some at the irony. It advertised *Feed-Seed-Tires-Tractor-Parts-Provisions-Boots-Dairy-Bakery-Etc.* It was a good-sized place, and Earl pulled over and tugged out the few dollars that he still possessed.

"We are low and then some," he said. "We're gonna go get ourselves a Coke and scope out this place."

The man behind the counter had a belly out ahead of him like a bay window. Maybe fifty, fifty-five, he was all smiles and welcomes. Earl got him talking, asked about the place, about Casa Grande.

"Sprang up in the late eighteen hundreds with the mining boom," the man told him. "And it's now the spring training camp for the San Francisco Giants."

"Is that so?"

"Sure is. Had the first exhibition game here in sixty-one. Willie Mays done hit a three-hundred-and-seventy-five foot home run."

"You don't say?"

"I do, sir, I do."

Digger went in back and put a couple of things in his pockets. Clay saw him; he scowled and shook his head. They had never been thieves. Had reason enough to steal things, but had never done so. Clay figured Digger was acting up simply to impress Earl.

Earl kept the man talking. He was the owner. His name was Lester Cabot. He'd owned the place near on twenty years, him and his wife. Had three sons, all of them lit out for bigger and better places, all of them still calling home for money. Earl was all ears and smiles.

"Surprised to find you trading on a Sunday."

"Well, son, we started opening on a Sunday as a result of a number of things. Lot of folks around here ain't much for churchgoing. Isn't the way it was ten and twenty years ago. And the bills keep coming, you know? And if I didn't provide what folks wanted they'd soon enough head someplace else. New stores opening up all over Casa Grande and a fancy-ass place in Florence, too. Gotta do what you must to keep the show on the road."

Earl asked about how busy Lester was. Lot of custom? Did he need a hand anytime?

"Well, son, it could be better, but it could be worse. We're doing okay here. Making enough money to keep the wheels on the wagon, so to speak."

And then Earl was buying another Coke, a couple of bags of corn chips, and he was telling Lester some joke about a woman with an ass as wide as a bumper. They laughed together—Lester and Earl—and Clay knew that Lester believed Earl a good feller, a sociable feller, the kind of man to pitch in and help out, a feller you could lend a couple of bucks to and never need to chase it up.

Once in the car Digger turned out his pockets, showed Earl what he'd scored. A couple of packets of chewing gum, some candy bars, a cheap pocket watch.

Earl slapped the back of Digger's head, told him he was a half-witted useless fucker.

"What if he'd seen you? What if you'd gotten caught, eh? Would've wrecked any chance of turning the place over. Jesus, kid, you got some balls, I'll give you that, but you ain't got no brains to speak of."

Digger looked sheepish.

"What candy bars you got there?"

Digger showed him.

Earl took one, tore the wrapper off with his teeth, and ate the chocolate.

"Dumbass motherfucker," he said as he pulled away from the edge of the road.

Clay looked sideways at Digger, watched him open up his own candy bar and start to eating. He didn't offer one to Clay. Clay was right there beside him, and yet it was as if Digger didn't see him. Clay was intensely aware of his brother however, and also aware of his own anger, his fear, his profound concern that with every passing hour he was losing Digger to the influence of Earl Sheridan. And what could he say? Nothing. And what could he do? Even less. Who was he—the younger brother, the weak one, the smart one with all the answers but no fists to back them up—against this mighty figure of a man, Earl Sheridan, killer, rapist and—if Digger had been asked—the all-American hero?

It was like watching someone float ever farther into the sea, and no matter how much you shouted for them to come on back, and no matter how far you stretched your hand out to pull them in, they were just fading away. Soon Digger would be nothing more than a ghost of something on the horizon, and then he would be gone forever.

"Tomorrow morning," Earl told them. "Sign on the door says they open up at six. We're going in there the moment the door opens, before they've had a chance to take any money to the bank. The whole weekend's takings. The busiest time I'll guarantee, and we're gonna help ourselves." Earl looked at Clay. "We are gonna sleep in the car, you pair tied together because I don't trust you worth shit. I'm gonna tie you the fuck up and then me and Digger here is gonna go in there and do the thing first thing in the morning."

That was all he said.

Digger didn't say a word.

Clay knew it was done then. He knew that Earl had chosen Digger, and he and Digger were going to do some terrible thing together, and tonight—perhaps, as Earl slept—would be Clay's last chance to rescue his own brother from whatever madness Earl was intent on selling.

Clay knew that if Lester Cabot opened his mouth in protest, if he tried to do *anything*, then Earl Sheridan was going to kill him. If he did that then he and Digger would be accomplices. Truth was that Clay figured Earl Sheridan was going to kill Lester Cabot regardless. Clay's emotions came all at once: a herd of wild things spooked into stampede. He could hear the Catholic Confiteor. Had heard it every Sunday at Barstow. "I have sinned through my own fault in my thoughts and in my words, in what I have done, and *in what I have failed to do*." And then the echo: "Through my fault, through my fault, through my own grievous fault."

Clay knew that his battle with Digger's conscience would more than likely be lost. Clay knew also that he would fail Lester come morning. He appreciated that if he tried anything then he would be dead in a ditch someplace and Lester would get smoked anyhow.

Earl gunned the engine, kicked a cloud of dust off the edge of the highway, and took off.

They passed a church. Outside it was a sign: *Jesus is the rock that doesn't roll.*

63

"That's funny," Earl said. "Smartass motherfuckers. Fuckin' church people. Me? I don't go to church. Only time you'll get me in there is on the shoulders of six strong men."

Digger laughed. He looked at Clay, expecting to see his younger brother laughing too. Clay didn't crack a smile. His mind was a million miles away. There was a resentful shadow in Digger's expression, and Clay saw it good.

"Gonna make our own rock 'n' roll," Earl said quietly. "Better to burn out than fade away."

Later, parked in some field beyond the outskirts of the town, Earl tied Clay and Digger together, and they slept all in a knot of arms and legs. Digger snored, Earl snored louder, and there was no chance of waking Digger without waking Earl. Clay knew then that his brother was more than likely lost, and again he questioned the woof and warp of all things. He wondered how their lives would have been had their mother survived. He wondered about a great many things, as was his nature, and—as always —there was scant understanding to be had of any of it.

In the cool half-light of a coming dawn, he shivered with the cold, he shivered with fear, and he knew he would likely never be so afraid as he was right then.

DAY FOUR

CHAPTER SEVEN

It had been a mess of things before the get-go. Even as the sun rose, even as Clay strained his way out of awkward and restless sleep, he had a feeling that it would all go bad. He knew it as he listened to Earl's bluff and bravado; he knew it as he watched Digger watching Earl, the light in his eyes, the small sense of awe that now seemed present in his expression.

Clay knew it most of all when Earl and Digger left him in the car, when Earl told him to stay put, to do nothing, not to even think of taking off.

Earl had leaned close, his face inches from Clay's, his breath rank and fetid like high-summer road kill.

"Digger here is my boy," he said. "Digger an' me don't have a great deal of use for you, but I ain't of a mind to kill you right yet." He was doing his utmost to sound threatening, and it was working. "We're gonna go in there, do what we have to do, and we're gonna come out real soon. Ain't gonna be more than three or four minutes all told. Like I said before, you can run only so far, and I'm gonna come after you and I'm going to cut you in a straight line from your throat to your dick, and then we're gonna throw your guts all around the place for the coyotes and the buzzards. That's if you run."

Behind Earl, Clay could see Digger looking at him. There was something in his eyes that he hadn't seen before. He looked awkward, sure, but he was still defensive, almost as if Clay was the only one that now stood between him and his destiny. Digger had made a decision somewhere, perhaps while he slept, there in the dark recesses of his subconscious, he had manufactured some convoluted rationale for what he now intended to do. Clay had never doubted his brother. Of course, there had been moments of anger and spite and hatred, but they had always been transient, based somewhere in petty jealousies or ill-founded assumptions. But now everything was different. Earl Sheridan appeared to have activated some sleeping gene, some dormant aspect of Digger's personality that Clay had never seen before. Until that point Clay had always been afraid *for* Digger, how the world saw him, how the world would treat him as he became an adult.

Looking into his eyes then—flinty and hard like gray, river-washed stones—Clay Luckman was afraid *of* him.

"So you make the decision, boy," Earl went on. "You hang in with us for a little while longer and we'll let you out someplace safe, or you can take a chance and run for it. Believe me when I tell you that I *will* come after you . . . I *will* hunt you down like a dog and kill you stone-dead in a dirt ditch if it's the last thing I do on this earth."

Clay believed him. Earl had a look on his face like he was about to do something he'd been wanting to do for the longest time. Only the night before he'd said something that gave Clay an appreciation of how left of center Earl Sheridan really was.

"God has a plan, sure," he'd said. "I'm just as much a part of that plan as everyone else. Someone crosses my path and I end up killing them, well, that must be part of the plan, see? It ain't complicated, it's just inevitable. Who's gonna be next, and why? Well, I have no better idea of that than they do. That's what makes the whole thing so fucking magical. He moves in mysterious ways, and it seems to me I must be one of them ways."

He'd said that, and it was those words that Clay Luckman could hear as he looked into Earl Sheridan's eyes and smelled his roadkill breath.

Maybe that now applied to Digger too. Maybe God did have a plan, and everything that had happened to date had merely been a precursor to the coincidence in time and space of Earl and Digger. No more Eldorado, at least not for Digger. The dream of what Eldorado might bring them, the life they would enjoy together, seemed a million, million miles away. Farther even than the dark star beneath which both of them had been born.

Clay Luckman looked at his half brother, and wondered what half they shared. Surely only their mother's half. This other half of Digger was now something Clay did not recognize. Did not *want* to recognize. He believed that the half of his brother that he loved, cared for, respected, and admired, had left. So scared had Clay been, so wound up in his own thoughts about what would happen to them, that he had failed to see that departure. But it *had* happened. No question about it.

"I ain't goin' nowhere," Clay said, and there must have been sufficient certainty and conviction in his voice because Earl leaned up and let him go. He sat there in the front of the pickup, right there ahead of the Pinal County Mercantile, and he knew that if Lester Cabot was in there then he wasn't going to be alive for long. Clay figured some people killed to rob whereas Earl Sheridan seemed the kind of man who would rob only to kill. Like he'd said before, *It's the realest thing you'll ever do, and that's a fact.*

Earl Sheridan and Elliott Danziger did not cover their faces when they went into the Pinal County Mercantile. There was no reason to. Whoever might have been in there, whoever might have seen them, wasn't going to be reporting any descriptions to any local or federal law enforcement officials. Only thing they were going to be reporting for was the afterlife.

Earl had a *thing* on. He was horny and aggravated, and he hadn't slept well, and he'd smoked too many cigarettes and there wasn't no breakfast, and he was in a mood. He had Chester Bartlett's sidearm, now fully loaded. He had the shotgun from Tom Young at Hesperia. He had the kitchen knife that he'd used to cut Clay Luckman's shoulder. He had Digger as his sidekick, a good enough kid, good enough to have around until he made a nuisance of himself, and then Earl would shoot him and push him down a dry well or some such. He could stay as long as he wasn't misbehaving. And he certainly had a good deal more balls than his candy-ass bullshit brother. On this job Digger would be able to keep an eye on the door while Earl terrorized the hell out of Lester and got all the money in the place. There had to be a good deal, a couple of hundred bucks, maybe more, and then there was always the possibility that Lester wasn't a bank-trusting man and he kept a safe in the basement or something. Earl felt good about the deal. He felt like his luck was going to turn. He'd managed to break out of custody. He was on the run. He'd had an appointment down in San Bernardino State Penitentiary for a necktie party, but he was going to miss that by a Texas mile. Things were on the up-and-up. Things were cooking up good on the front burner.

"You stay just inside the door," he told Digger. "You keep an eye on the highway, and keep an eye on the pickup. Make sure that little shit doesn't take off out of here, and if you see a car or a truck headed this way, don't matter who the hell it is, then you holler up a storm, you understand?"

"Sure thing," Digger said, and in his own voice he heard some desperate plea to be accepted. He wanted to be liked. He wanted to be accepted on the same terms. He was caught between one place and somewhere else, and he didn't know what he was doing. He was now in it up to his neck, and if he didn't start fighting he was going to get drowned. Earl scared him, of course, but Earl challenged him and excited him and tested his mettle. Earl was the real deal, an outlaw, a desperado, and there was something wild and exciting and addictive just in the air around him. Everything Earl said had a sort of skewed common sense to it. Digger was electrified. And Clay would come around. Clay would see the sense of it all when they had some money in their pockets and some halfway-decent chow in their bellies. Then they would part company with Earl Sheridan—these wild brothers of the road— and he and Clay would make their way on down to Eldorado and start life with a clean slate.

But there was one thing he had to know. One thing he had to ask Earl.

"Are you gonna kill that guy in there?"

"The guy in the store?" Earl asked.

"Sure, the guy in the store. You gonna shoot that man, Earl?"

"Gonna shoot you in the fucking head you don't shut your fool mouth," Earl said, and he cuffed Digger across the back of the neck.

Digger wanted to take this as nothing more than a bit of camaraderie horseplay. He grinned like a fool. He bit his lip and willed, willed, willed himself not to show a tear.

They went up the steps together and in through the door.

Outside, Clay Luckman peered up at the sky through the windshield. He wondered if he might see the dark star that was

70

following him. Dark stars—being dark—perhaps showed their faces in daylight. There was nothing but the bright sun, the clear blue sky, the fresh November air, the uncertainty of the future. Had he possessed someone or something to think of, he would have thought of them. There was nothing. There was no one. Whatever was out there had a natural kind of emptiness, an emptiness he had become accustomed to, and he wondered if the rest of his life was going to be this way. He remembered little of his mother, less of his father, nothing of his past before Barstow and Hesperia.

He looked right and saw Digger watching him from the store doorway. Digger had made a choice. He was with Earl now. Sure, Clay was his brother, but Earl was his buddy, his mentor, his leader. His *real* buddy. If Clay ran now then Digger would tell Earl, and Earl would chase him down and kill him. Hell, he might even kill Digger for the sheer rush of it. Be good and done with his hostages, for they were nothing but distractions and dead-weight. Clay didn't doubt this for a second.

Looking left, right, straight ahead, even over his shoulder, there was nothing but weather and distance every which way. There was no ravine, no gully, no wood, no forest, no outcrop of rocks, no river, no stream. There was no place to hide, no place to get lost. Out here he was a target, nothing more. He did not know how to hot-wire a car, and the keys were right inside the store with Earl. Hell, he didn't know how to do half the things that he needed to do. He felt ignorant, impotent. All the books he'd read in Barstow and Hesperia hadn't equipped him for this at all.

Clay didn't think Digger had it in him to kill anyone, least of all his own younger brother, but he sure as hell wouldn't stop Earl from carrying through with his threat. No, Clay decided, he was not going to run. He was going to wait it out, see what happened, see if this was happening because of Earl, or if it was his own dark star that had brought these things to pass.

Lester came through from in back and recognized Earl Sheridan.

"Howdy there," he said. "Thought you folks was all done and gone."

Then he saw the shotgun, the kitchen knife, the sidearm tucked into the waistband of Earl's pants, and he said, "You gonna shoot me, son?"

"May well do," Earl replied.

"Might I ask why?"

"Well, hell, I don't know. Maybe for no other reason than I figure to try everything at least once."

"You know what you get for murder down here?"

"What? Aside from the satisfaction, you mean?"

Lester shook his head. He closed his eyes for a moment as if in prayer, and then he said, "Well, it's a shame and a sin."

"Tell you what'd be a shame, old man," Earl said, "and that would be if you didn't empty up all your cash tills and whatever you have in back, and if you've gotten a safe someplace then it'd be good to go fetch whatever you have out of there as well."

Lester nodded. He was philosophically resigned to the situation. He knew there was no purpose for argument or contradiction. He could see in Earl Sheridan's eyes that this was a one-way deal.

"I got maybe a hundred, hundred and fifty bucks all told," Lester said. "I got but one cash till, nothing in back, no safe anywhere. Money goes right to the bank at the end of each day, 'cept weekends when we wait until close of business on a Monday . . ." Lester nodded understandingly. "But I guess you figured that one out, eh, son?"

"A hundred and fifty bucks? You gotta be shittin' me!"

"No, sir, I ain't. That's what we got. A hundred and fifty if you're lucky."

Earl lowered the knife. He stamped his foot just once like a spoiled brat kid having a tantrum. "And what the hell good is that gonna do me?" he asked. "Jesus Christ Almighty, fuck shit cocksucker! What the hell goddamned use is that to me?"

Lester shook his head. "I don't know, son. A hundred some-odd bucks more than you had when you came in here, I guess."

Earl looked pissed for a moment. His eyes flashed. Maybe he figured Lester was smart-mouthing him. He moved quickly, erratically, and before Lester could predict where Earl was going to go he was right there in front of him, right there ahead of the counter. Earl just dug that knife hard and sharp into Lester's shoulder.

Lester howled. Blood erupted. Some of it spattered the front of Earl's shirt.

"What the fu—" Earl started, and he backed up and looked at himself. He looked like he'd been the one that got stabbed.

Lester seemed unsteady on his feet. He held his right hand to his left shoulder. There was no shortage of blood seeping out between his fingers. He didn't say a word. He didn't hardly look at Earl in case his gaze aggravated him further.

"Fuck you!" Earl said.

"Son . . ." Lester said.

"Shut the fuck up!" Earl snapped. He put the shotgun down on a stack of seed bags and pulled Chester Bartlett's sidearm from his waistband. He took a couple of steps toward Lester and pointed that gun right between the man's eyes.

"Get the fucking money," Earl said.

Lester looked away. Earl glanced back at Digger. Digger's eyes were wide, his feet shifting backward and forward. He looked terrified and excited and overwhelmed and uncertain all at the same time. A wide patch of dark had spread across the lap of his pants.

"You keep your fucking eyes on the road!" Earl barked.

Digger blinked nervously, and then he looked back to the window.

"Now get me the fucking money!" Earl said to Lester, and Lester, bleeding profusely from his shoulder, backed up a step and turned toward the cash register.

He rung up, opened the drawer, lifted it with his good hand and took out a fan of tens and twenties. He took the ones from the drawer itself and put them on the counter.

"Put them in a bag," Earl said.

Lester did as he'd been asked.

Earl snatched the bag and stuffed it inside his shirt. He raised the revolver again and directed it at Lester's face.

"What else you got, old man?" Earl said.

"You got everything I got, son, and that's the truth."

Earl used his left and jabbed with the knife again. It caught the base of Lester's throat, and though the wound was neither life-threatening nor fatal, it produced another jet of blood, which scattered across Earl's shirt and hands.

"Jesus . . . what the fuck!" Earl screamed.

Lester seemed oblivious to the pain. Either that or the shock had rendered his system unfeeling. "It's gonna happen if you cut people like that," he said. His voice was measured and certain. Despite possessing no weapons, despite himself being the victim of this robbery, he was the one who appeared in control.

"Asshole!" Earl said. He turned and started toward the door, and it was only when he reached it that he paused and looked back.

He raised the revolver one more time, and this time he fired. Whether Lester was hit or not he did not know, for Lester just seemed to drop like a stone behind the counter.

Digger was on his toes. "Car coming!" he yelped.

"Fuck!" Earl said.

Digger hauled the door open and the two of them went down the steps and across the dusty driveway to the pickup.

Earl got in the driver's side and gunned the engine.

Lester appeared through the door with a double-barrel. The first shot punctured the fender a thousand times and burst the tire.

He didn't get a second shot.

Digger instinctively dropped beneath the firing line behind the door. Earl leaned over him, and with the shotgun he unloaded both barrels into Lester from a range of twelve feet.

Lester went backward, staggering, his arms flailing. He crashed through the doors of the store and didn't come to rest until he was out on his back on the floor within. Some of the shot went through the walls of the cool box at the top of the steps. Bottles of soda went off like firecrackers.

The car that Digger had seen was now no more than a hundred yards away.

Earl dropped the guns into the well. He put his foot on the accelerator, and with three tires and a flat he screeched out of the store driveway like a mad thing.

Dust and stones flew in a wide arc away from the edge of the highway, and when they hit the tarmac the sound of the collapsed tire rattled and rolled. Five hundred yards and the rim was already cutting through it. A mile and there was a cascade of sparks following them as they fled.

"Gotta get a new car," Earl said, and he didn't look back, didn't turn away from the road, his blood-spattered hands gripping the wheel as if his life depended on it, his teeth bared, his whole body tensed like a spring.

Digger looked back at Clay. Clay didn't meet his gaze. He tried to be invisible.

"Shoulda been there," Digger said, hurrying his words out excitedly. "Shoulda been there . . . he bled like a pig. Fat guy in there . . . he bled like a pig . . ." He laughed crazily, looked at Earl, looked back to the road. It was then that he became aware of the smell of himself, the urine that had soaked the front of his pants. He looked down, he looked at Clay, and there was something terrifying in Digger's eyes. Almost as if he was now frightened of himself, but had gone too far to come back.

Clay reached out his hand toward his brother.

Digger slapped it away. "Leave me alone," he said. "Leave me alone, Clay . . ."

The look that Clay gave him said it all. *You have a choice. It's not too late. We can get through this. We have been through everything before this and survived. Let me help. Don't do this, Digger . . . don't do this . . .*

But there was nothing.

Digger just glared at his younger brother, and there was something close to shame and hatred and . . . and *evil* in his eyes.

Something had surfaced within Elliott Danziger, and Clay did not recognize it at all.

The pickup was fighting to do thirty miles an hour. The sound was extraordinary. The sparks were flying out the back of the thing like a Fourth of July parade.

As far as Digger was concerned things couldn't have been more exciting.

As far as Clay was concerned they couldn't have been worse.

But then they had yet to reach Marana.

CHAPTER EIGHT

Soon enough they would start out toward Scottsdale, and Frank Jacobs would begin to understand the degree to which life would never be the same again. Wondering what was to become of him, what would become of her—his daughter, Bailey Redman; marveling at the circuitous paths of fate and fortune that brought things to the doorstep that had been left behind. If he'd known all that the future was yet to bring them . . . well, he would have been dismayed.

Earlier Bailey had said something. Her voice was quiet and gentle. She could have been speaking to anyone or no one, but he was there and thus he heard it.

"I hope sometimes that my life is a dream."

Frank looked at her, her skin as pale and smooth as cream. She was so pretty. Hard to believe he'd had anything to do with the making of her. Sort of girl some other guy would steal before she had a chance to love you. Heartache in a box, all parceled up neat for a birthday, delivered punctual by the federal mail.

"Yes," she echoed. "Sometimes I hope that my life is a dream . . . and someday I'll wake up and discover I'm an old lady, and that the life I've really had was extraordinary. A husband, a crowd of children, all of them loving me. A life of special memories . . ."

He didn't know what to say to that. Didn't know how to reply. So sad when a little girl wanted to wish her own life away, but Frank could appreciate the sentiment.

It was the old saw: Family and money—trouble when you got it, trouble when you ain't.

The motel room was quiet enough to hear his own blood. Then he got up and went out for food.

As he walked he thought of her. Bailey's mother. He remembered her, perhaps not as well as he would have wished, but he did remember her. Remembered the sound of her laugh. Remembered her smile.

What he felt then he could not understand. Some sense of relief? A burden of responsibility? No, not a burden, and not even responsibility. It was as if he had been all the while alone, and then he was not. How did it work? He had fathered a child, a girl, a beautiful girl, and he had never known. But was there something innate, something within him—almost preternatural—that *knew* there was some part of him alive in some other part of the world? And now, *only* now, as that part of himself was again reunited, did he feel whole once more? Was that the way it worked?

Bailey meant the world to him. She *was* the world, a huge part of everything, and he could not now conceive of any decision he might make without taking into consideration her thoughts and feelings.

She belonged to him. He belonged to her. They belonged *together*.

It scared him, but it made him happy. It caused him a fleeting sense of anxiety—Would they be all right? Would they make it?—but that anxiety was overwhelmed by a strange power of excitement. He imagined her at school. He imagined her at college. He imagined her married. Grandchildren?

And as he walked he found himself laughing, and there was a tear somewhere in his eye, and he let it go.

Things were so different now. Good different.

Frank Jacobs returned to the motel cabin with ham and cheese and milk and doughnuts and a sack of potato chips the size of a pillow.

He and his teenage daughter sat on their respective beds, and they ate for a time in silence.

After they'd eaten he smoked a cigarette. She asked for one, and though she was fifteen he couldn't say no.

"You smoked a long time?" he asked.

She shook her head.

"Longer you do it the harder it is to stop."

She shrugged. She smiled. She didn't care.

"So what are you going to do with me?" she said.

"You're going to have to come and live with me in Scottsdale."

Her eyes widened slightly, almost unnoticed, and then she looked toward the window. "Okay," she said, and in her tone was such matter-of-factness that Frank wondered if she'd ever been given the chance to make a decision all her own.

"I'll have to go on working, and you can finish school, and then you're going to have to work too," he explained.

She looked at him with patience and tolerance and a seeming lack of connection between his words and the reality they predicted.

"It will be fine," he said. "Everything's going to be just fine."

She didn't say a word in response.

"You have to try and believe that something good can happen any time at all, but you should never expect it too much. If you expect it, well, it won't come. Like snow at Christmas."

"I ain't never seen snow," Bailey replied.

"Maybe that's because you wanted it too much."

She seemed perplexed. A frown punctuated her brow like a comma. "So the way to get something is *not* to want it?"

"No, you gotta want it, but you only gotta want it but once or twice, not all the time, and then you hide that thought somewhere in the back of your mind and let it do the work without you."

Bailey Redman—quiet for a while, staring flat-eyed and curious through the motel cabin window—said, "I had a fish one time."

"A fish?"

"Sure. A gold-colored fish."

"Where d'you get a fish like that?"

"County fair or some such," she replied. She turned and looked at Frank with the same curious expression. She had the knack of making you feel like you should say something even when it was her turn to talk. "Loved that fish. Loved it a whole bunch. Fed it and fed it and fed it, wanted it to be big and strong and happy and everything." She shook her head resignedly. "Fed the thing to death."

She turned back toward the outside world, the world beyond the window, and Frank Jacobs sat in silence and wondered why she'd told the fish story. You could love something too much? You could kill something with love? He didn't know what it meant, and he made no comment, and he believed that the door he had opened by taking on this teenage girl was a door that would now never close.

In the same moment he could not have been more wrong, nor more right.

They left before eight. The reception guy eyed them suspiciously. Frank wanted to say, *She's my daughter, you fucking asshole*, but he did not. It was no one's business who she was, or why they were together. The world could take the time to find out, or they could stay ignorant.

They headed along the I-10, would take a route through Marana, Eloy, Casa Grande, on up past Chandler to Scottsdale. Somewhere over a hundred miles. An hour and a half, perhaps two if they stopped to take in the scenery.

Frank had a '57 Oldsmobile Super 88, a good, solid car that had nevertheless seen better days. Seventeen feet in length, four and a half thousand pounds in weight, and sometimes it ran like a coach pulling six horses. Hydramatic transmission, power steering and brakes, tinted glass, the Wonderbar radio, six-way power seats and whitewall tires—these were the things that the salesman had sold him, and never mentioned the sluggardly start, the fuel consumption, the top speed of one hundred and eight miles an hour that made the thing sound like it was wrenching its own guts out along the highway.

Bailey thought it was a *beaut*. She flicked on the radio, found some station out of Phoenix playing rockabilly and R&B. Frank didn't much listen to the radio, seemed to find nothing but gospel music and testimonial stations. Bailey leaned back in the passenger seat, put her heels on the dash. He wanted to tell her to get her feet down in the well where they belonged, but didn't think that reprimanding her for something unimportant was the best way to start this new thing they had.

Three miles away from the motel Frank commented on the heat. The vent on the driver's side was busted.

"We've lived in trailers," Bailey said. "You wanna know real heat you gotta live in a trailer with a metal roof. Days like that you gotta spend all your time just thinking about a cool breeze."

"What good would that do?"

"Think it strong enough and you can feel it."

Frank smiled. "That's crazy."

Bailey smiled back, and in that smile was something that said she knew things others didn't. "Rather be crazy and cool than sane and sweaty."

Frank laughed.

Bailey turned up the music.

Mist still hung on the open country, and somewhere—out there—was the sound of beasts, of creatures, of things with numerous legs laboring ceaselessly beneath a rug of leaves, the murmur of things unnamed and unseen in the long grass and furrows. Here was all of life, a life that had existed a good ways before people, and would exist a good ways after. They passed through towns that were not so much towns but a seeming random scattering of dwellings adjoined to the land. Unforgiving land. Land that would break a man's heart and hands in trying to farm it. Frank Jacobs had been traveling these roads for as long as he could remember. He knew them like the sound of his own voice. Whole generations were started and finished in these narrow places, places that were merely the widest parts in the road. The graves of all past generations were marked with nothing more than a shambles of hand-ferried rocks, in some special case a couple of two-bys banged together with cooper's nails. Either way such memorials were swallowed by time and weather within two or three turns of the calendar. Men and women born out of anonymity and gone back the same way. Children too, and sometimes in less years than it took to fallow a field after a good few years of crop.

It was a bleak and desolate place, at least it felt that way, but perhaps for no other reason than the way familiarity bred selective blindness to those things of interest or importance.

"You sell shoes, right?" Bailey asked.

He had told her before. Told her twice. Perhaps she was just figuring on a simple way to start a conversation.

"Yes, I sell shoes."

"For a long time?"

"Long as I can remember."

"You like it?"

"It's a job. It pays the way. Puts food on the table."

"What did you want to do?"

"Want to do?"

"When you were young?"

"I ain't so old now."

"When you were my age."

He thought for a moment, and said, "I wanted to play the piano. Wanted to play jazz piano in bars and clubs and maybe go to Hollywood and play piano in the movies."

"What happened?"

"Life happened."

"You could still learn."

"I'm all of forty-one years old, Bailey . . . I couldn't just up and start something like that at my age."

"I like the way you say that."

"What?"

"My name. Bailey."

"Reckon there's only one way to say it. Been sayin' it the same way since the day we met."

"I reckon you have," Bailey said, and eased back in her seat.

She wanted to stop in Marana.

"Thirsty," she said. "Is that okay?"

"Okay to be thirsty?"

"Okay to stop."

"Sure," he said. "We can stop."

He looked for someplace—a gas station, a convenience store, found one of each side by side and pulled over.

They sat for a minute. He lit two cigarettes and handed one to her.

"Your mother let you smoke?"

"Ain't never smoked before today."

"You do it pretty good for someone ain't never done it before."

"Well, I figure it can't be that hard, right? Everyone so busy tellin' everyone else that it's stupid to smoke cigarettes, well, I reckoned I'd better give it a go and find out for myself."

"And?"

"Could get to like it, I think."

She opened the door, stepped out onto the highway. She

walked ahead of the car and stood there in her three-quarter-length blue jeans, her flat-soled canvas shoes, her T-shirt, her fair hair tied back behind her head, and then she turned and smiled a smile of such warmth that Frank Jacobs felt the wind knocked out of his sails.

"Come on," she said. "I ain't got no money."

He got out and followed his daughter.

Inside it was all bright lights and shelving and things hanging on the walls and big-ass refrigerators in back stocked with juice and milk and butter and eggs and other provisions. They had homemade hand-crank ice cream in four flavors, and a sign that said you could mix them together if you wanted and make up your own tastes.

Bailey stood with her nose pressed against a cracker jar, as if the dry discs within were edible gold, as if you could eat just one and be blessed with good luck and eternal youth.

A man appeared through a curtained doorway. He had the kind of face for convenience store work—interested in everyone's business, ready to sell you whatever you looked at whether you needed it or not.

"Well, howdy there, good folks," he said.

"Howdy," Bailey said, and she crossed the floor to the counter and leaned against it.

"Just comin' through?" the man asked.

"Sure are," she replied.

"Well, I'm Harvey, and it'd be my pleasure to serve you with whatever you all need today."

Bailey held out her hand. "I'm Bailey," she said, "and that there is my dad, Frank."

They shook hands.

"Pleased to make your acquaintance," Harvey said. "So you folks got a ways to go?"

"To get where?"

"Wherever you're going."

"I couldn't say," Bailey replied. "I don't know where we're going. Maybe my dad's home, maybe not." She glanced sideways at Frank, who was still somewhere amidst the shelves. "I'm not the one who decides."

Harvey frowned. "Your dad's home isn't *your* home too?"

"Kind of," Bailey said. "I did live with my ma, but then my ma just died and I gotta go live with my pa, and this is pretty much the first day we've spent together where there hasn't been a bus ride at either end of it."

"Well, I hear some things here, Bailey, but that's just about as interesting as it comes."

"Yeah, I reckon so. Ain't nothin' so different as change, right?"

"Right." Harvey smiled. "So what can I get you?"

"You have chocolate cake?"

"I sure do. My wife made it herself. How many pieces you want?"

Bailey turned. "Dad? You want some chocolate cake?"

Frank walked up to the counter. "Chocolate cake? Well, sure, why the hell not?"

Bailey smiled at Harvey. "Four pieces, Harvey. One each for now, one each for when we get wherever we're going."

"Scottsdale," Frank said. "We're going home to Scottsdale."

"Figure you'll be wanting some buttermilk with that there cake," Harvey said. "Can get you a quart of buttermilk, fresh this morning, chilled as ice."

"Sure," Frank said. "And give me a carton of Luckies, a couple bags of potato chips, a half dozen of them cupcakes back there with the marzipan icing on, and a fifth of rye."

"Sure can," Harvey said, and then he looked out through the window as a car pulled up outside.

"Hell," he said. "See no one all day and then they all come at once."

Bailey walked to the window, and peering through the spaces between the signs and stickers and advertisements for Red Parrot Diesel and Burma-Shave she saw two men getting out of the car. One of them was older than the other, and the older one had blood all over the front of his shirt.

"Looks like trouble," she said, almost to herself, and couldn't have been more right.

CHAPTER NINE

Had Earl Sheridan arrived five, maybe ten minutes later, there would have been no Oldsmobile in the forecourt of the Marana Convenience Store & Gas Station. Frank Jacobs and Bailey Redman would have been long gone, would have heard nothing of Earl Sheridan, of Elliott Danziger or Clarence Luckman, except perhaps on the radio. But that was not to be.

Earl pulled over, saying, "The Oldsmobile. We're taking that motherfucker," and before the engine had stopped he was out of the pickup and running toward the store.

Digger went with him. Maybe Earl was going to shoot someone else, and he wouldn't want to miss that for the world. He was excited, all worked up inside like a bottle of soda that had been shaken and shaken and was ready to explode. Terrified too, his palms sweaty, his head feeling like there was some pressure inside it, like his brain was just too damned big for his skull. The rush was indescribable, and he loved it.

Clay watched them go, heart racing like a wayward locomotive, his mind overloaded, but somewhere beneath it the sense of resolution that now was the time. If he didn't go now, then he wouldn't be going. He knew Digger was lost. Digger would not be coming with him. If he was going to Eldorado, then he was going alone.

It was then that he saw the girl. His stomach was taut with fear. She was right at the back of the store, there on the right-hand side of the window. Instinctively Clay ducked down, and then he wondered who he was hiding from. He reached for the lever, opened the door, slipped out sideways, and dropped to the ground. He went to the left a few yards, cut back to the right, and hurried down the back of the store to an outhouse. It was then that the shouting started up.

"Give me the fucking keys!" Earl was shouting. He had the shotgun pointed directly at Frank Jacobs. There were just the two of them in the store. The guy in the suit and the guy behind the counter.

"I don't want any trouble, mister," Frank Jacobs said, and he went for the keys.

"Hold it right fucking there!" Earl screamed. "What the fuck you doing?"

"The keys," Frank said. "You want the keys, right?"

"Slowly, motherfucker, slowly does it."

Frank went slow. He took out the keys, held them out toward Earl.

Earl grabbed them, turned and tossed them to Digger.

"Go start the car," he said, and as soon as Digger had left Earl turned back to Frank and Harvey.

"Money," he said matter-of-factly. "You," he added, pointing the shotgun at Frank. "You give me whatever you've got, and you," he said, turning to Harvey, "can just empty the register and whatever else you got and hand it the fuck over."

Frank Jacobs gave Earl Sheridan twenty-four dollars. Earl looked at it like Frank had crapped in his hand.

Harvey emptied the till—notes, coins as well—and pushed the pile of money toward Earl. All told he gave up eighteen dollars and change.

"What the fuck is it with you people?" Earl said. "Do none of you people have any fucking money around here?"

Earl grabbed the dollars. The coins scattered across the floor. He turned just as Digger came back to the door.

"He's gone!" he said. "Clay has gone!"

"Fucker!" Earl replied, and then turned back toward Frank and Harvey with a wry smile on his face.

"Give my regards to whoever," he said, and emptied both shotgun barrels directly into Frank Jacobs's chest. Frank was sent careening back into the counter. Harvey was covered in his blood. Earl raised the revolver and pointed it at Harvey. He took a step forward. "You know what they say about a thirty-eight?"

Harvey shook his head, his eyes wide, his mouth open.

"That a thirty-eight is nothing more than an opinion with six reasons to back it up."

He fired it once, twice, three times. Harvey stood motionless for four, five seconds, the fists of scarlet growing across his chest and stomach, and then he folded to the ground as if the strings suspending him had been cut.

Earl turned to Digger. "Now where the fuck is that kid?"

Clay heard the sound of the car before he heard the voices of Earl and Digger as they came out of the store. He'd heard one shotgun blast, three other shots, and then the sound of another car.

The voices of Earl and Digger were drowned out as Earl started the Oldsmobile. Someone was coming. Some other car was headed this way. They weren't going to hang around looking for him. He crouched there in the outhouse, squatted down, arms around his knees, head bowed, and he prayed.

The Oldsmobile took off. The other car seemed to slow, and then it sped away too. Perhaps the second driver saw trouble and thought it better to get the hell out of there. That's what Clay would have done.

He reckoned he knew what had happened. Earl had killed the car owner, the store owner—he could pretty much bank on that. But the girl? Who the hell knew? Only one way to find out.

Clay got up slowly. He hesitated for a good two minutes before he opened the outhouse door and stepped into the sunlight. It had been dark in there and his eyes strained against the brightness.

The pickup—wounded, now lower on one corner—sat like a patient dog awaiting the return of its owner. The Oldsmobile was gone. The road to the store was deserted, as was the road away. Clay Luckman stood there for some time with his heart beating fast, his mouth dry, his eyes squinting against the sun, and he wondered if this was where it now got better, or where it now got worse.

He found her crouched on the floor in the middle of the store. She held the dead man's head, cradled it against her stomach. She looked up at Clay Luckman when he entered; her hands and her T-shirt were covered in blood. She said nothing with her mouth, but her eyes looked back at him with such a sense of pleading and desperation that Clay found it hard to be silent. But what was there to say?

And then she broke. It was as if she just snapped somewhere deep inside. The sound that came from her mouth was surreal, almost inhuman. That sound pierced whatever sense of strength and determination Clay had mustered, and he was rooted to the spot, beyond thought, beyond movement, and his heart broke like a clay pitcher.

Bailey Redman sounded like a girl dying, like every nerve and sinew and muscle and bone was being stretched and ground and pulverized by the weight of loss and grief.

Clay was stunned, in shock. He was breathless, immobile. He stood with his breath like a hot fist in his chest for minutes until she started hyperventilating, gasping, choking for breath herself, and then he took one step toward her. He went to his knees in slow-motion. She was looking at him, but Clay didn't even know if she could see him. He shuffled forward, trying his utmost to avoid the flow of blood that was making its way out across the foot-worn linoleum toward the door.

"W-We h-have to g-go," he stuttered. He thought of Digger. He thought of his brother, now lost to some other mad and insensate world of violence and unconditional hatred. His brother, who had been engaged in the human devastation that was now before him on the floor of the mercantile.

Clay tried to make his voice gentle.

There was no question in his mind about staying here. Two dead men, a young girl, a great deal of blood, and he was on the run from a juvenile facility. True, he had been taken hostage, but he had encountered authorities well enough to understand the railroad they'd put him on if he hung around. And there was also the possibility that Earl and Digger would come back. Earl was just about crazy enough to figure he needed beer and smokes, and he might just turn that Oldsmobile around and come hightailing it back here. Lord only knew when the next customer would come by, and even if they did they'd be unlikely to stop, more unlikely to lend a hand once they saw what had happened. Folks weren't naturally brave or calm in such circumstances, and Clay didn't plan on securing his future against the next stranger that just happened to drive through.

He steeled himself. He gritted his teeth and clenched his fists. He could handle this. He could deal with this. He could survive this ordeal as well as he had all previous ordeals.

"You—you need to get up," he told the girl. He sounded defiant and certain. He sounded like someone in charge. "You *have* to get up. You cannot stay here."

She looked back at him, said nothing, and shook her head.

"They might come back," Clay said, and as he voiced the words it became even more real as a possibility. Earl, wanting to ensure that there was no walking wounded; Digger wearing a hard-on for more blood and mayhem; the pair of them like a wide tornado in a narrow town.

Her eyes widened.

"Serious," he said. "I know who they are and they're fucking crazy."

The girl looked down at the dead man. She released his head and eased herself back on her knees.

"We need to get you cleaned up some," Clay said, and he reached out his hand toward her.

She took it. It surprised him that she did so. Perhaps in such a predicament it was better to trust someone than no one at all.

"Let's go in back," Clay said. "You have to get washed up, and I'll see if I can find something for you to wear."

He helped her up. They went out back together, found a small washroom with a sink and some towels. Clay hunted around, found little else but a man's undershirt. She took off her blood-soaked T-shirt, pulled the undershirt over her head. She tucked the hem into her jeans, rolled up the sleeves, but still there was room for a couple more brothers and sisters inside the thing.

"It'll have to do," Clay said. "Stay here for just a minute."

He went on back to the front door and scouted the road both ways. There was nothing and no one.

Clay checked the register, but all the money had been taken. He checked the jacket pockets of the dead man on the floor, but his wallet was also empty. He doubted Earl Sheridan would have left a dime behind. Clay found a canvas sack and started filling it with provisions. No cans, just bags of peanuts and chips, some cheese, some crackers and cartons of juice. He found a box of strike-anywhere matches, some smoked ham and beef jerky and a bag of pork rinds. Into the sack they went, always one eye on the front door, another on the exit into the back through which he'd taken the girl.

Everything was running on automatic. He knew he was in shock, but it was all on delay. He knew that later, sometime, he would see what was happening—*really* see it—and he would shake, he would vomit and curse and hurt inside. He knew that moment would come, but not now, not while true self-control was needed. Something took over. As if someone else was running his body. He did what he needed to do. He made decisions and carried them out.

This was a bad, bad thing. A truly terrible thing. What he was going to do he had no idea. He figured that Earl and Digger would take a new slant now. The authorities would maybe tie in the waitress from the diner, the old guy in Pinal County, and now this. They would find the pickup, connect it with Hesperia, and realize that they'd all been headed southeast toward Texas. Earl would realize this himself, and go someplace else. Not back north, for that's the way trouble would come looking for him. Maybe west? Three hundred some-odd miles and they'd reach the sea.

And what would be the smartest thing to do, him and the girl? Hell, it had to be to carry on the way they were going. And where would that take them? He had no idea, and he had no ability to resolve that question.

And it was then—as if fate conspired to best advise him—that Clay saw the paper there on the floor by the door.

He knew what it was before he reached it, and as he leaned down to pick it up the shock seemed to come over him like a quiet and gentle wave.

The effect it had was anything but gentle, and he dropped to his knees, the folded page in his hands, and he opened it carefully, tears running down his face, his breath catching and hitching in his chest. His hands shook, his vision blurred, but there was no mistaking the advertisement that had fallen from Digger's pocket. Eldorado, Texas. The Sierra Valley Estate.

Clay cried. For himself, his brother, his mother, even his crazy father. He cried for the future, and he cried because of the past. It lasted no more than three or four minutes, and then he managed to gather himself together. He took up the advertisement, folded it carefully and tucked it into his pocket. He collected up the bag, his provisions, his wits.

It was an omen, a portent. He would carry on to Eldorado. He had to. There had to be something out there worth all this pain.

And that's the way they'd stop looking. Maybe. Earl was not stupid. He'd put two and two together and understand that the authorities would have predicted his route, and now he'd go some other way entirely. That would be the smartest thing to do, no question about it.

Maybe Earl would double-blind everyone and carry on the same way, assuming that the police and the federal people would now be looking for him everywhere else but the way he'd first gone, but Clay believed that would have been too great a risk. No, Earl and Digger would be headed elsewhere, and that meant the safest thing to do would be to find the road to Texas.

Clay needed a map. He went back to the register, started hunting for anything that would help. There was a bundle of them, but they all seemed to be for other places—New Mexico, Louisiana and even Mississippi. He didn't find what he needed. He did find a small can full of coins, however, and tipped them out into his hand. Mostly quarters, some dimes, a few cents. Had to be all of seven or eight dollars in change. He stuffed the coins in his pocket.

It was then that he saw the gun. It was a small thing—a .32, maybe a .38 snub-nosed, but it sat like a sleeping thing just waiting to be woken. Next to it was a box of shells. He picked them up. Yes, a .32. Small, snug, little more than fist-sized, and the temptation to take it came too strong to resist. The shells went in one pocket, the revolver in the other, and he went in back to get the girl.

It took a while to drag her away from the dead guy in front.

She didn't say a word. She just stared, any emotion she might have been feeling absent from her face. Evidently her day was not working out as planned. Not for neither of them.

"We have to go," Clay urged, and he meant it, he *really* meant it, for now he believed that with his own dark star overhead, with whatever bad sign he carried showing no signs of abatement, then things could only deepen if he stayed. It was the devil and the deep blue sea—arrested and charged as accomplice to a double robbery-homicide . . . after all, hadn't he been in the pickup with Earl Sheridan and Elliott Danziger? Yes indeedy. Hadn't he come on in here with the intent to cause mayhem and murder? Yes, he sure as hell had. And what had happened for his accomplices and *compadres* to leave him behind? Hell knows, there was no predicting these people. They were crazy. All of them. They were neither loyal nor reliable nor predictable nor sane. They would not be there to say he had no part in it, and even if they had been that's not what they would say. Earl was definitely the kind of guy to take as many people down with him as possible.

And the other option? That he and the girl were still there when Earl and Digger came back. They'd been gone no more than twenty minutes. Earl could have stopped five minutes away and be right now considering the odds. Had he missed anything? Had the storeowner kept a safe? More realistically, did he need to come on back and kill Clay Luckman just to make sure that there was no evidence and eyewitness potential left behind? Clay could put Earl in the diner with Bethany Olson. Could put him in the Pinal County Mercantile. Clay could stick him with a double homicide right where they were now. And he was still hanging around and trying to convince this girl that they needed to leave? He *had* to get out of there.

Clay tried to recall faces—his mother's, his father's, anyone at all before Hesperia, before Barstow. It was as if those early years had been boxed away somewhere. Perhaps they would come back to him when he was old and dying and had no use for them.

Bailey was stunned, silent, overwhelmed, confused, lost. She was little more than a child, in one moment losing her mother to some terrible illness, in another her father to a moment of random, inexplicable violence.

"We need to go now," Clay said, and he started toward the highway.

She hesitated for a moment, perhaps to look back one more

time through the window and see her father dead on the floor, and then she followed on.

Within hours the Marana Convenience Store & Gas Station was swarming with officials from numerous departments. Marana extended along the I-10 from the line between Pima and Pinal counties all the way to the Tucson City line. They had a small departmental office, an annex to the Pima County Sheriff's Department. The department representative, Officer Nolan Sharpe, whose mental state by that time—ironically—was as blunt as a worn-out hammer, walked around and around the building with no certain direction or purpose. No one and everyone wanted the case. Once they identified the pickup it became federal, and they all breathed a sigh of relief.

Federal Agents Garth Nixon and Ronald Koenig were dispatched as the preassigned and active investigative officers, and they started to put two and two together. Lester Cabot at the Pinal County Mercantile, now Harvey Warren and some unknown guy at the store. The pickup made it Earl Sheridan for sure. Earl and his two hostages, and that's if the hostages were still alive. They had not headed for Mexico, but southeast for Texas. Why Texas? Who the hell knew? Maybe Earl had a sweetheart down there. Bethany Olson still didn't figure in the math. They had yet to make the connection because she'd been all the way back on 62 outside of Twentynine Palms, California, and appeared to have no link to what was happening in Arizona. Back in Twentynine Palms itself Sheriff Vince Hackley, Ludlow's Ed Chandler, and Yucca Valley's Ethan Soper were still scratching their heads and trying to make sense of something that made no sense at all.

Earl Sheridan and Elliott Danziger were heading west along the I-8 in Frank Jacobs's Oldsmobile, whereas Clay Luckman and Bailey Redman were ten or twelve miles away en route to Tucson.

Bailey didn't say a word. Twice they stopped, and she drank juice and ate a handful of pork rinds, but still she did not speak. Clay wondered if she was just dumb, or maybe mute or deaf, or if the witnessing of these events had sent something awry in her mind. Wires got loosed somewhere along the way and never reconnected. Hell, you had to credit her with the ability to still walk a straight line after what had happened. Who the guy in the store was he did not know, but he guessed it might have been her pa.

Every time she heard a car, which was rare, she stopped dead in her tracks. Standing on one foot at the edge of the highway, her thumb outstretched, she remained expressionless as the meanest drivers in the world flew by in a hail of pebbles and a cloud of dust. Give such drivers an empty bus and they'd leave the twelve disciples standing at the edge of the highway.

And then she kept on walking, right there beside him, silent as ever, never looking at him, not even in his vague direction, just straight ahead. The sun came up high and his shadow stretched long, and she walked inside it as if the coolness suited her. She matched him step for step, and even though he was almost a man, and she was nothing but a slip of a girl, she made it a point of pride to never slow him down. If nothing else, he would always be able to say she kept up.

He talked to her on the way. He talked to her just so he could hear something other than dust and wind. He told her the names of plants that he saw, and though he knew that he was wrong with some of them she did not correct him. Perhaps because she did not know herself, perhaps because she did not care. Checker-bloom, buttonbush, partridgeberry, sumac, cattails, arrowheads, nightshade, jimson, bullbriers, balsams. He made some up for fun. Just to see if she would react. "That one there is called rat-pellet. They call it that because you can use the seeds to poison rats. But humans can eat them no problem. If you eat them they taste like cotton candy. Slightly burned maybe, but cotton candy all the same."

Nothing from her. Nothing at all.

He realized after a while that he was actually talking to himself. He was trying to hang it all together for his own sake. He'd seen what he'd seen for sure, and there would never be a living day when he wouldn't remember what he had seen. But more than that, cutting right through to the heart and quick of everything, was the fact that Digger had gone. His brother. His defender, his protector, his mentor in so many ways. Gone. Disappeared into the wilderness like some kind of mad animal. And all because of Earl Sheridan. Or perhaps not. Perhaps it was just that bad luck was following them everywhere, and separating them was as good a way as any to weaken their collective defense. Perhaps everything until now had been merely an indication of the true horrors to come.

At one point the girl stopped to inspect a tree bole, a hole burrowed into it as if a nest for something long gone. And then they walked on, veering away from the highway a little into the adjacent fields, their footsteps flattening the ridges of newly turned fallows.

Clay Luckman had been alone like this before. At Barstow, at Hesperia, surrounded by people but nevertheless alone. It was times like this when everything in the world felt alive. Not only the grass and the trees, but the rocks and the dirt and the stones, and the air itself felt suffused with some age-old energy that carried all the history of the earth in its fickle shifts of direction. The earth remembered everyone who had walked upon it—their names, their faces, their footfalls—and if you listened carefully you could hear the wind speak of these things with a voice as old as God. Clay knew such ideas were fanciful, but he wished to believe them. Imbuing life with some element of magic gave him hope. Hope that there was a reason for all things. Hope that the future was even now learning from the mistakes of the past.

They went on walking, Bailey—whose name he did not know— right there beside him, and yet nothing for company save his own dark and fearful thoughts.

CHAPTER TEN

"We should go back and get him," Digger said. "He's my brother . . ."

"Only reason to go back would be to kill him," Earl replied. "Hell, I should have killed him yesterday. We ain't goin' back now, that's for sure. We're gonna find ourselves the first place on the road that's got a bank and we're gonna get ourselves some running-away money, and then we're going to Mexico."

"But—"

Earl rounded on Digger suddenly. His face was enraged, his eyes wide with hate. "He was nothin' but a punk-ass kid, you see? He ain't nothin' to you. You got a new brother now. You got me. Way this is goin', we'll be home free and rich before the week is out. We gotta get ourselves on a road to Mexico. Get to Mexico and we're gonna be just fine."

"Ain't never been to Mexico," Digger said, not knowing what else he could say in that moment.

"Well, you're goin' now, son, you're goin' now."

Wellton was where they would end up somewhere after noon that Monday. One hundred and ninety miles from Marana give or take, but they had Frank Jacobs's Oldsmobile, and the Oldsmobile lived up to her name—old, but mobile—and she puttered along like a heavy thing and didn't give them the urgency they were after.

"That man sure had a surprise on his face when you shot him," Digger said. Had Clay been there he would have heard two things in Digger's tone. The first was fear, a sense of awestruck horror regarding where he was, the situation he had gotten himself into. But above that, drowning out the lesser emotion, was a need to be acknowledged, a need to be accepted by Earl on Earl's terms, the need to be seen as a contemporary, an equal. Perhaps some deep-seated insecurity, perhaps the simple fact that he had never before belonged to anyone or anything, but Digger *wanted* to be recognized, he wanted to be heard, he wanted to be *wanted*.

"Hell, everyone has a surprise on their face when you kill 'em. They never expect it. Even when you stick a gun right up their nose."

"How does it feel? To kill someone?"

Earl smiled. "Damned if I know. Just a matter of business as far as I'm concerned. Something that needs to be done, and you do it the best you can."

"Wonder what it feels like to die."

"Only the dead know that," Earl replied. "Sad, huh? Don't matter what they say before they're dead. Don't matter what they feel. Fear, terror, how they plead with you, whatever they confess to, whatever promises they make, well, it don't matter worth a bucket of shit 'cause they's still alive, see? I think I am still trying to find out the answer to that question, and until I find it I'm going to keep on looking. It's like searching in a dark room for a shadow that wants to stay hidden."

"How many people you killed?"

"Not enough."

"How do you decide?"

"Hell, there ain't no decision in it. Like I said, you do what you gotta do. I mean, it's like this, see? Some guys spend their lives lucky, always reaching the home plate before the ball. Some people have lives like that. Even their shit smells good, you know? People like us . . ." Earl turned and looked at Digger, and in his expression, in the flash of his eyes, there was something. Camaraderie. Fellow-feeling. Something fraternal. Digger saw it, and it filled his heart with pride. In that moment he believed that Earl Sheridan *was* indeed talking to him as the equal he so desired to be.

"Some people are like that, right? Well, that ain't me and you, my crazy little friend. We were fucked from day one. We were fucked before we even got out of bed. Tell you this now . . . only time I ever went to a party was by mistake. Story of my life. Walked in unexpected and they all looked at me. Maybe I convinced myself wrong. Maybe I told myself they'd all expected someone else to mail an invite. But no, it wasn't that way. It was that most of them hadn't even thought to ask me, and those that did? Well, those folks didn't want me there anyway. People only think of me when I'm right there in front of them. Rest of the time I'm invisible. Know what I mean?"

"For sure I do," Digger replied, and believed that he did know. He knew precisely what Earl was talking about, and the more he heard this kind of thing the more he managed to convince himself that there was something common between them. Earl, if not a contemporary, if not a kindred spirit, was at least someone who could appreciate the kind of crap he'd been living with all his life. He was an ally, that much if nothing else.

"People like us ain't given shit, so we gotta take it. You have to keep your own self-respect. That's the important thing. You can't let yourself slide. You gotta stay sharp, on the money, right? Only time you're in trouble is when you can no longer smell your own stink. Keep your wits about you. Get what you can, but don't be foolish. Like back there at the store. They'll figure out who it was from the car. And if they catch that little cocksucker he'll squall like a girl anyhows. Thing is, by the time they get it all figured out, we'll be on the beach in Ensenada drinking *cervezas* and getting the old trailer hitch polished good by a senorita or two."

"You got it all sorted out," Digger said.

"Hell no, we ain't never got it sorted out really. We just do the best we can. I'm still too easygoing." Earl grinned. "Like you boys. I shoulda killed you stone-dead an hour after Hesperia, but I'm too soft. Guy I knew back in the joint, believe me, this boy could smile as sweet as Jesus, stick a knife right through your heart, use your own damned shirttails to wipe it off, and then sit down for dinner. And he'd use the same knife to cut his steak, and hell, if he wouldn't still be smiling. That's the kind of guy you wanna work with. That's the kind of businesslike attitude you gotta cultivate."

Digger smiled. Earl smiled too.

"Hell, everyone's crazy." Earl winked. "Shit, even Moses was a basket case."

It took a moment, but Digger got it. They laughed like a pair of dumb hyenas. Digger could see the man behind the image then. He was no longer scared of him. At least not so much as before. In a way he felt proud. Proud that a man such as Earl Sheridan would want to keep someone like him around. He thought about the dead people back in Marana, and he had to admit that he felt very little at all for them. Then he thought about Clay, and he realized that they were different, and perhaps it was because they had different fathers. Whatever the reason, well, it didn't matter. He couldn't stay hitched to his little brother for the whole of his damned life. Was only right that they should go their separate ways at some point. And if not now, then when?

So it was that they fell in together, and if Earl Sheridan's heart was nothing but a dark and twisted muscle, then Digger's was a heart of shadows and possibilities. If Katherine Aronson had been right, if all it took to make a bad person good was for someone to expect it of them, then Elliott Danziger was screwed from the get-go. Earl Sheridan was bad from the inside out and back again, and he attributed those same qualities to everyone he met. Earl Sheridan expected the worst of people, and here—in his new-found acolyte—he had decided to expect the very worst of all.

Earl truly believed that nothing he ever did came out of blind anger. Sure, he had plenty of things to be angry about. Too many to list. But he never permitted that force to go tornadoing around the place arbitrarily. A power like that needed to be controlled and channeled. A man had to have self-discipline. A man was measured by his actions, and thus his actions should be measured.

This was what he believed, and he was going to believe it for just a few hours more.

They arrived at Wellton, Yuma County, a handful of minutes after noon.

Earl was hungry. Digger just wanted to hold Chester Bartlett's sidearm and point it at someone. He wanted to know what it felt like, even if the thing wasn't loaded. The anticipation of such a thing was far more meaningful and important than lunch.

"We're eating before anything else," Earl said. "It'll give us a little time to settle after the journey. We can get a measure for the place."

Driving down the main road it seemed perfect. Not too big, not too small. The bank—Yuma County Trust & Savings—was pretty much as Earl had imagined it would be. That was what he was interested in. The bank. The money inside. How far they would make it was dependent upon how much they could get. There'd be two or three tellers, a loans manager, an assistant manager, a general manager—all of them deskbound, pen-pushing cowards without an ounce of guts between them. Closest they'd ever get to challenging anything was shooing strays out of the yard. A bank like that would handle traffic for all the farmers and breeders and cattlemen in the county. Monday afternoon, start of the new week, an entire five days' stock of cash delivered in only hours before. Sweet as candy and twice as rich.

A block and a half down and over to the other side of the main drag they found a diner. Half a dozen regulars, people familiar enough with whatever was going on in Wellton to glance in their direction but give them no real pause for thought. Earl Sheridan didn't know, but Wellton was the last real town on I-8 before the county line at Yuma, and then you either went right to California or left to Baja. Wellton was on the Gila River. They got boatmen and ferry travelers, people from San Diego en route to Phoenix, and for what it was worth a couple of unremarkable strangers were nothing to get excited about.

Earl took a stool at the counter, asked for a menu.

"Menu's on the wall," the waitress told him. She was fifty, maybe fifty-five, too much makeup, her hair lacquered into a monstrous beehive. She was trying to look ten years younger and just made the whole deal worse as a result.

"We'll have the meatloaf," Earl said. "Coffee for me, RC for him."

Earl tapped a smoke out of the pack and lit it. They didn't speak before they ate. Earl wanted to think. Digger didn't want to interrupt the thinking. The meatloaf was garbage—dry and tasteless, but Earl hosed ketchup all over it and wolfed it down. Digger sucked down the ice-cold cola like it was his last drink before the desert.

Quarter to one and they were back in the car. Earl smoked a couple more cigarettes. He had the barrel of the shotgun down in the well, the butt alongside his thigh. He held the revolver, checked the chamber several times. One had gone on Lester, three on Harvey. There were only two bullets left. He had eight shotgun shells, and that was that.

"You fired one of these before?" he asked Digger.

"One time," Digger said.

"Well, it ain't rocket science. Usually just pointing the damned thing is enough to get people cooperating." He handed him the gun. "I'm giving you this 'cause I trust you enough, but I don't have a conscience, son, I really don't. I may even shoot you yet, but right now it's gonna take more than one of us to rob that place and I have a mind to get it done."

Digger held the gun like he would a woman's breast—gentle, like he loved it. "You can trust me," he said. "And you don't need to shoot me, but if you do then I'm gonna be happy that you was the one that did it."

Earl smiled, and there was an odd twist in his expression. "Shit, son, I believe you is as crazy as me."

Just as Garth Nixon and Ronald Koenig reported back to the Anaheim Field Office that they had the Hesperia pickup outside a gas station in Marana, Earl Sheridan and Elliott Danziger got out of Frank Jacobs's Oldsmobile and started back down toward the Yuma County Trust & Savings to commit perhaps the most ill-advised and badly planned bank robbery in Arizona's history. Earl figured himself for John Dillinger, was thinking of beers and blow jobs in Mexico. Digger could feel the weight of Chester Bartlett's revolver in his pants pocket, and for some reason it made him feel like a real man. Clay? Hell, Clay had no idea what he was missing out on. This was gonna be a gas.

CHAPTER ELEVEN

First and foremost, there was a security guard. His name was Alvin Froom. Alvin was all of five seven, little more than one fifty. He wasn't a big man—never had been, never would be, but he had a mean temper, perhaps fueled by resentment about his size and stature. The .44 he carried was too big for him, but it gave him a sense of well-being. He'd shot little more than trees in the woods and busted Frigidaires in the dump site, but he hit more than he missed despite the kick of the thing.

Alvin had a wife. Her name was Rosetta, perhaps after the stone. She was most of two forty, and then some. Why Alvin chose such a big girl was a puzzle to many. Maybe little guys were afraid they'd be carried away by a strong wind so they got someone real heavy to hold on to. The relationship was good. They were friends before marriage, had stayed friends afterward. Alvin figured there were some men who went home only to fight with their wives. As far as he was concerned, there were enough battles beyond the door, and the last thing he needed was to find them once inside.

Monday morning Alvin was on the ball. He'd had a good night's sleep, a good breakfast, and after work he and Rosetta were heading out to a new picture theater in Yuma to see a movie. The manager, Audie Clements, was in his office. Loans manager, Lance Gorman, was dealing with the younger of the Leggett sons from the T-Bone Ranch, a fifteen-hundred-acre place that sat in the vee between 95 and the Gila River, and the tellers—June Fauser, Laurette Tannahill and Jean Rissick—were tending to one another's business in between the odd customer. Monday morning was generally slow, and this one looked no different.

It stayed no different until a problem came through the door in the shape of two men—the taller, older one carrying a double-barrel, the younger with a .38.

The taller one didn't say a word. He had the gun up ahead of him and in Alvin's face before Alvin had a chance to blink. He told the younger one to take Alvin's gun, and the younger one did so.

"My name is Mr. Heartache," the taller one said, "and this here is Mr. Trouble."

The younger one grinned like a fool. He had an unremarkable face, but there was something about his eyes that seemed strange. That's what they would recall when asked. Amidst the shock, the disbelief, the few that could remember anything about appearances simply commented on the younger one's eyes.

"I'll say this just once and once only," Mr. Heartache went on. "You may think you have seen us before, but believe me when I tell you that you have not. Fail to cooperate, fail to do exactly and precisely what we tell you to do, and whatever heartache and trouble you might have experienced before will be nothing compared to today. Do we all understand one another?"

June Fauser, the oldest and longest-serving of Yuma County's bank officials, had hit the silent alarm the moment Mr. Heartache opened his mouth. Wellton sheriff, Jim Wheland, was mobilizing himself and three deputies. They had dry-run such scenarios a number of times, and there had been an incident in the spring of '61 resulting in the successful arrest of an armed bank robber. Wheland was sober, straightlaced, levelheaded, and businesslike. He was also ex-military, had served in Korea in the mid-fifties, and there was very little about smalltime hoodlums that concerned him. This was the class of individual into which he placed the likes of Sheridan and Danziger. He had no idea that he was about to face a death row escapee with homicidal intent.

Quarter past one and Earl Sheridan had Alvin Froom, Audie Clements, Lance Gorman, June Fauser, Laurette Tannahill, and Danny Leggett up against the right-hand wall with their hands on their heads. Jean Rissick—because she was not much older than twenty-three or -four and pretty as a picture—was employed to bag up whatever cash was at the tellers' stations. Beyond that Earl wanted to know about the safe.

"The s-safe is pretty m-much empty," Audie Clements told him nervously. He figured the straight truth was the only thing that would give him odds on surviving this nightmare. "We—we empty out on a Friday night, and then we don't get a delivery in before about three or four on a Monday afternoon. Everyone around here knows that—"

Sheridan stuck the shotgun in Clements's face and told him that he was not from *around here.*

"I d-don't know what to say, mister. You got the right day, but you're about three hours early."

It was then that Sheridan heard cars out front. He sent Digger to the door.

"Cops," Digger said. "Three cars."

"Mo. Ther. Fuck. Er." Sheridan emphasized each syllable violently. He turned to Audie Clements. He put the shotgun in his face once again. "You got an alarm here?"

"An alarm?" Clements shook his head. "No, not unless you try the safe."

"Liar. Fucking liar," Sheridan said. He swung the butt of the gun sideways. Sharp, a real kick to it, and the solid stock impacted against the side of Clements's face with a ferocious sound. He went down silently, bleeding from the corner of his mouth before he even hit the ground.

"Who set off the alarm?" Sheridan said.

June Fauser looked resolute—terrified, but determined not to show it. Laurette Tannahill and Jean Rissick were holding each other. Jean was crying. Until that point she'd imagined Earl Sheridan as quite handsome. Both of them, in fact, though the younger one was still very young to be involved in something such as this. Until now, well, this had been a story to tell the girls. Now the scenario had taken on a completely different pitch and tone. Now it looked like someone was maybe going to die.

"Who?" Earl repeated, and his voice came like a gunshot. He lowered the shotgun toward Clements's spread-eagled body and rested the barrels against his temple. "Who? Tell me now or his head is mystery meat from here to the sidewalk."

June Fauser stepped forward. She opened her mouth to speak.

The only thing that issued from her lips was a stunned *Uuuuggghhh.* Both barrels, released simultaneously, provided sufficient force to fold her in the middle like a rag doll. She slumped backward against the heavy wooden barrier with a sickening crunch. Lifeless, she simply slid to the floor and lay there.

Jean and Laurette started screaming. Earl snatched the revolver from Digger and fired a single shot into the ceiling.

"Silence!" he hollered.

Digger looked as scared as Danny Leggett. The guy in the convenience store was one thing, but this was turning out to be something else entirely. Had he had any piss in his bladder it would have been all across his pants once again. Now he knew that he was in this for keeps. There was no way back. It was just forward from now on. Roll with it, or die.

Earl handed Chester Bartlett's gun back to Digger, reloaded the shotgun, and centered the room. He leveled the weapon at waist-height. Jean, Laurette, Danny Leggett, Alvin Froom, and Lance Gorman gave him their undivided attention. Audie Clements would be alive for another eight minutes and then a blood vessel would burst in his brain and kill him. June Fauser, fifty-one years old—mother twice, grandmother four times over, married for thirty-two years, resident of Wellton for thirty-seven—was already long gone. She'd been dead before she hit the counter.

"Now, where is the rest of the fucking money?" Earl said calmly. He knew if he killed enough people he'd get out of there. That was the basic difficulty with most robberies. People lost their nerve. They were afraid to shed a little blood. The ones that got away were the ones who didn't back down when it came to the shoot-outs. And hell, he was already on his way to the hangman. If they got him alive then it wouldn't make a gnat's asshole worth of difference.

"Wh-what Mr. Clements said w-was right," Lance Gorman ventured. Not a brave man by nature, he nevertheless understood that with the incapacitation of the manager, the absence through sickness of the assistant manager, it was his job as loans manager to step up to the plate. It was sometimes necessary to take your place and say what was needed.

What he said, however, was not what Earl needed to hear, so Earl unloaded the shotgun one more time. This time he went for the head, and took most of the left side clean away with a single barrel.

Now it was bedlam. Alvin Froom fainted, as did Jean Rissick.

Laurette Tannahill, spattered from thigh to throat in brain matter and blood, screamed like a fire siren. Digger, thinking that perhaps he needed to show his colors and make his mark, walked toward her and aimed the gun at her face. She didn't quiet down as he'd imagined she would. She just screamed more. Blood was now pouring from a nasty gash above her left ear. Danny Leggett just stood there like a tailor's dummy in a store window. His eyes were wide, his mouth open, the front of his pants all dark and wet where he'd pissed himself.

Earl put a shell in the empty barrel. He grabbed the back of Laurette's dress and hustled her toward the door.

"Get the fucking money," he told Digger.

Digger grabbed the canvas cash bag that Jean Rissick had filled from the tellers' stations. Later, when he counted it, there would be seven hundred and forty-three dollars. More money than he'd ever seen in his life. In that moment all he was aware of was Danny Leggett still standing there.

"What about him?" he asked Earl.

Earl seemed to notice him for the first time. He smiled. "You wanna kill him?"

Digger felt the bottom drop out of his stomach. He looked at the gun in his hand, at the man ahead of him. Then he looked back at Earl.

"Oh, for Christ's sake," Earl said. He gave the shotgun to Digger, snatched Chester Bartlett's handgun, didn't hesitate for a second. Danny Leggett didn't have time to even raise his hand or his voice in protest. Earl aimed the gun at the young man's forehead and pulled the trigger. He didn't fall. Not immediately. There he stood, a neat punctuation mark centering his forehead, a fist-sized mess at the back, and he just stood there—those same staring eyes, that same open mouth.

Earl laughed, and then he took one step back and let fly with an almighty kick to the man's knees. He fell like a tree then. A single drop, no flailing arms, no roll. Boom, down, like a stone.

Earl, still hanging on to the collar of Laurette's dress, looked at Digger disapprovingly and said, "Am I going to have to take care of everything myself?"

He gave Digger the revolver, took back the shotgun, didn't wait for a response.

Digger stood there, blood spatter on his hands and face, across the front of his shirt, his eyes wide, his mouth open, a vague sense of disconnection and disorientation permeating everything he thought and felt. Before it had been different—in Pinal, at Marana. Both times he'd been looking the other way when Earl had done his killing. It hadn't connected. Not like this. This was up close. Right up close in front of him. The man was alive. The man was dead. That was all it took. And it could have been him. He— Elliott Danziger—could have done it. Then he would have known if killing someone was the *realest* thing in the world.

Earl was out the front door onto the steps, Laurette as a shield, the shotgun pointing out beneath her armpit, his voice clearly audible to Sheriff Jim Wheland and his three deputies.

"Hey there, motherfuckers! Back up and get the fuck outta my line of sight. We're taking a car and this girl and you ain't gonna get anyplace near us for ten fucking miles!"

Jim Wheland came up from behind the open car door and stood looking at Earl Sheridan. It was Jim Wheland who saw the younger one come out behind Sheridan. Now he had two to contend with, and that doubled the odds on this going all to hell and back again.

"Well, son, I don't know that I can let you do that," he said, and his voice was measured and calm and matter-of-fact. The one with the hostage looked crazy, like there was some mad light burning right through him. The younger one just looked terrified.

"Hell, Sheriff, you got some stainless-steel cojones there, ain'tcha? And what the hell makes you think you have a choice in the matter?"

Wheland smiled.

"Fuck you!" Earl said. "I don't wanna fuckin' listen to you anyway."

Wheland took a shotgun load to the shoulder. He would survive, but at the time he believed he wouldn't. The force of the thing threw him back against the rear fender of the car and down to the ground. He was out like a light, and would stay in the dark until it was all over.

It was in that moment that Digger knew he wasn't going to make it out of there alive. He dropped to the ground and started shuffling sideways. He used the fact that all eyes were on either

106

Earl Sheridan or Jim Wheland to get alongside the sheriff's car and flatten himself against it. He had the money bag in his left hand, the empty revolver in the right. It was then that he saw Wheland's .38. Wheland must have been holding it when he was hit. It was no more than three or four feet from where Digger crouched, and using the bag as a sufficient weight to drag the thing back to him he was soon armed once more.

Earl got Laurette out ahead of him. He had one barrel empty, one loaded, and he guided her to the door of the sheriff's car. Digger got in back, had Wheland's gun in his hand, kept his eyes on the three deputies, all of them staring back at Earl Sheridan with deer-in-headlights eyes.

"Digger!"

"Back of the car, Earl," Digger replied.

Earl lost connection for a moment. He turned for a split second to push Laurette Tannahill into the rear of Wheland's car, and it was in that split second that he was alone, unshielded, defenseless. The deputy that shot Earl Sheridan was Alvin Froom's brother-in-law. A head taller, ten pounds heavier, a good deal more handsome, Lewis Petri would now carry the legend for the rest of his days. The man that shot Earl Sheridan. Like his own Liberty Valance thing going on. Alvin would always be the one who fainted in the bank, no more capable of securing a paper bag than a financial institution. The love of a good, heavy wife couldn't hold him from the shame he felt. He would later drink himself into forgetfulness and his wife would divorce him for a skinnier guy called Stanley Osler.

Earl span sideways and careened off the wing of the car. It was a neck wound, deep enough to bleed him out if he was left unattended.

Digger knew it was now or never. He vaulted the back of the driver's seat, and had gunned the car into life before Earl had a chance to move. Laurette Tannahill, merely a couple of years older than Jean Rissick and almost as pretty, was in the backseat. It was her presence alone that prevented a barrage of gunfire from the deputies. Already there was trouble enough. They didn't need a dead girl, this time courtesy of the Wellton Sheriff's Department.

Digger floored the sheriff's car. He went in the direction the car had been pointing—back toward Casa Grande along the Tucson-bound I-8.

Behind him two deputies stood over Earl Sheridan while the third went into the bank to survey the carnage. Four dead, two unconscious, the sheriff hit, Earl Sheridan too. The second robber on the run with a hostage. And it was only Monday afternoon.

Outside, Lewis Petri and the second deputy, Reggie Sawyer, kneeled beside Earl Sheridan. The wound in his throat was a good one. Blood wasn't leaking, it was pumping. Not a great deal at a time, but there was little doubt that this was the end of the road.

"Who was your accomplice?" Petri asked. "Who took the girl?"

Earl smiled. "F-fuck y-you," he gasped. The pain hit him in that moment, and then there was something else. That mad light in his eyes, something malign and wicked, and he tried to smile with his facial muscles closing down and it came out like a sneer.

"I'll t-tell y-you," he stuttered. "F-fuckin' ass-assh-holes . . ." He tried to turn his head but he couldn't. "Uuugghhh," he exhaled, a sound not unlike that uttered by June Fauser as she was launched across the bank toward the counters.

"Fu-fuckin' co-cock-cock-su-suckers," he said, and then he grabbed the collar of Lewis Petri's shirt and pulled him closer. "Yo-you wa-wanna know hi-his n-name?"

"Just tell us who took the girl," Lewis said.

"Too-took the g-girl, sure. Bu-but we did th-that guy back in P-Pinal County, and th-those guys i-in Marana . . . and my friend . . . my friend, he di-did th-that swee-sweetass b-bitch in Twe-Twentynine Palms. He fu-fucked her g-good and th-then he killed her . . . and he killed the other kid as well, the Da-Danziger kid . . ."

"His name?" Petri said. "What is his name?"

"His name is Cla-Clarence," Earl said. "Clarence Lu-Luckman took your fu-fucking girl . . ."

Of all things to say, this was his last. Earl Sheridan died less than a minute later. It was 1:43 p.m., afternoon of Monday, November 23, and he went with a smile on his blood-spattered face, sick bastard that he was.

CHAPTER TWELVE

Two in the afternoon, walking for the best part of five hours, resting every once in a while in silence. They'd covered twelve miles, and not once had a driver stopped for them. Clay thought people from Arizona must either be the least kind or the most suspicious people in the world.

Still the girl had not spoken.

She did look at him, and in her expression was malice and bitterness and fear and sex. Perhaps the sex only to deny it if he asked.

He didn't know what to think of her, and then after three or four miles she just stopped dead in her tracks, sat down at the edge of the road, and bawled like a baby. She did not make that sound, that wailing and heartbreaking sound that she had made back at the store. Clay didn't know if he could have handled that again. This time she seemed to fold into a tight ball, her knees up to her chest, her arms around them, her face hidden as she sobbed her little heart out for a good fifteen minutes. And then, almost as unexpectedly as it had started, she got up, wiped her face, and carried on walking. He reckoned the guy back in the store *must* have been her father. She was all tore up in rags and tatters. She was a mess. Whoever the hell she was, she wasn't talking. Most people had a whole suitcase of problems, and they would just share them out like candies. This one was different. This one had her own thoughts, and after four or five hours of nothing Clay figured it was best to leave her alone with them. She would talk in her own time, or she would not.

Clay himself, well, he was hot and irritated. He could feel things moving inside his shirt collar. He would have given his eye-teeth and most everything else for a lemonade stand. He had the coins from the store at Marana, and he would have bought a whole pitcher and shared it with the girl. But there was nothing. Other folks' houses—some of them along the roadside and some of them set back; people working in the fields here and there; a crowd of women coming out of the trees, and then cutting back in like they'd forgotten something. Things went on the way they did, and he and the girl were just invisible people walking through the midst of it. Where he was going, why he was going there, hell, he didn't know, but he was going anyway.

Clay thought about his brother. He thought about Earl Sheridan. He guessed they'd be doing something dark and dangerous someplace. Earl would kill some more people, rob some more money, and he'd wind up dead or disappeared. He hoped that would happen, he really did. He figured that that'd be as good a humanitarian act as could be perpetrated by one human being for another. Earl seemed hell-bent on turning Digger into an awkward mess of horrors, and the sooner Earl was put out of everyone's misery the better. Maybe then there would be a chance for Digger. He would get himself straight, get it all figured out right again. Clay doubted it, but there was no harm in hoping.

Another mile elapsed and Clay started talking. He just opened his mouth and started talking, just assumed that the girl was listening and let it go.

"That thing back there. That was a hell of a thing. You know who those people were? The older one was Earl Sheridan. He was supposed to be hanged somewhere down south but he sprang me and the other one from a juvenile place at Hesperia and took us along as hostages. He stole a car, and he robbed money, and he didn't only kill those folks back at Marana, he killed some others too. A waitress in a diner in Twentynine Palms. I didn't see him kill her, but I know he did. I think he raped her too. Anyway, I've never seen such trouble in all my life and he did that all in just the few days since he took us along with him. And the other one. That was Elliott Danziger. And he's my half brother. Same mother, different father, and only a year and a half between us. Everyone calls him Digger. He was a good brother, a real good brother, but I think he had a weakness in his mind and now he's under the influence of that other crazy son of a bitch. He sort of latched on to Sheridan, and Sheridan is one of them people that

110

always needs to have someone looking up to them or they don't feel like no one. I think if he doesn't get away from Sheridan then he's gonna wind up just like him, 'cause I reckon there's some people that are just born bad, you know? I don't know what you think about that, but that's what I reckon. There's some people that are just born bad, and it don't matter what you say or do they're always gonna be bad. Earl Sheridan is like that. And then there are some people who just fall under the influence of the bad ones and becomes bad themselves. On their own, well, they seem to be fine, but hitch them up with a bad one and they all go to hell together. Digger is like the second type of person. Me, on the other hand, I was born under a dark star. You know what that is? Well, I'll tell you. A dark star is like a conjunction of the planets. You know what conjunction means? It means a combination of events or circumstances. Well, when I was born I believe there was a conjunction of the planets. One planet was one place and one planet was someplace else, and then there were a whole bunch yet someplace else again. And they have a magnetic force. That's what they do, the planets. They have a magnetic force or something and they control the tides and whatever. Anyways, they was out there in whatever positions, and I was born just at the wrong moment, and that's why my name is Luckman, 'cause I ain't never gonna get none . . ."

Clay paused, watching the girl. She just went on walking, but there was something about the way she was walking that was different. Perhaps it was his imagination, but she seemed a little less tense, her shoulders a little less rigid. Maybe the sound of his voice soothed her. Maybe she thought he was as crazy as Earl and Digger, and now—by saying what he was saying—he was demonstrating that he wasn't completely off his head. He figured there was nothing to lose by carrying on.

"Anyways, I've spent many a night looking up into the sky and searching for my dark star. I know it's out there. I even gave it a name. You wanna know what I called it? Well, I'll tell you. It's called Hesperion. I called it that after the juvie place I was sent to. I went to one place called Barstow, and it was real bad there, and then they sent me to this new place at Hesperia, and I figured that it had to be better than Barstow and it wasn't. It was then that I knew there was a dark star. It was then that I knew there was never going to be anything good for me. So I called it Hesperion, and it kinda sounds like Latin or Greek or some other old language. Anyway, make sense or not, that's what I called it. And it follows me. It watches over me. It makes sure that I don't ever really get a good deal on nothin'. That's its job. Make sure Clarence Luckman is never a lucky man."

He fell quiet again. He had never voiced these thoughts. He wondered whether he would make things worse now that he had spoken them out loud. Would the bad luck intensify, or would it diminish? Was it strengthened or weakened by sharing?

He stayed quiet for a while. He asked the girl if she was hungry. She reached out her hand for the canvas bag, took out a moon pie and some pork rinds.

"Don't matter a damn who you are, you can't live on moon pies and pork rinds," Clay said. "You should eat some cheese or something. Some ham, you know? You should have some protein in you."

The girl stopped, her mouth crammed with pie, her fist filled with rinds, and she looked at him like a disapproving schoolteacher.

Clay smiled. "Hell, you sure are as pretty as I don't know what, but you have a sour face on you sometimes. But considerin' what's happened I can't fault you for that. You go on and eat whatever you wanna eat. Sure as hell ain't none of my business."

The girl turned and resumed walking. Clay followed on behind her, a pace and a half behind.

If it was going to be like this all the way to Tucson, then so be it.

CHAPTER THIRTEEN

By three o'clock Garth Nixon and Ronald Koenig understood what had happened. The report from Deputy Sheriff Lewis Petri at Wellton had been precise and specific. Earl Sheridan was dead. Clarence Luckman, one of the hostages from Hesperia, had escaped. This Luckman kid had apparently killed Elliott Danziger, his own half brother, was responsible for the death of a waitress in Twentynine Palms, had colluded and collaborated with Sheridan in the deaths of Lester Cabot at the Pinal County Mercantile, and then Harvey Warren and an unidentified male at the Marana Convenience Store & Gas Station. They had also wounded Sheriff Jim Wheland, and killed Audie Clements, June Fauser, Lance Gorman, and Daniel Leggett at the Yuma County Trust and Savings Bank in Wellton itself. Worse still, this Clarence Luckman had driven away from the bank in the sheriff's car, taking with him a young woman called Laurette Tannahill. Based on Clarence Luckman's performance thus far, it seemed unlikely that she would be alive for long.

Koenig and Nixon now had a real honest-to-God trans-state, interstate, multiple homicide killing spree on their hands.

All they knew was that Clarence Luckman and Laurette Tannahill had driven away along the I-8. If he kept to that road he would pass through Gila Bend, Casa Grande, and then have the choice to go back toward Phoenix, or head toward Tucson. If he had any smarts at all he would have ditched the sheriff's car immediately, and already be driving another stolen vehicle. They were uncertain as to whether he was armed, but presumed he was. Sheriff Wheland's sidearm had yet to be located. And if Luckman wasn't armed, well, he soon would be. A fugitive of this type would not go far without securing further weapons.

Contact was made with the Hesperia Juvenile Correction

Facility. Governor Tom Young was asked to send over all documentation, photographs, fingerprints, and related information to the FBI Field Office at San Bernardino. They would courier the files to the field office at Anaheim. Anaheim would ensure that the information was forwarded not only to Koenig and Nixon, but also to whatever official bodies were brought in to collaborate on this case. Right now they had a manhunt on their hands. Clarence Luckman was a wanted killer, a fugitive, a runaway, and—as of this moment—it looked like he was going to be one hell of a lot more trouble than Earl Sheridan had ever been. A shoot-to-kill policy would be implemented almost immediately, the wires would burn red hot with dispatches and county-wide alerts, and if this Luckman character was not secured within twenty-four hours then the news would have to go public. Radio warnings, announcements on the television, whatever it took to secure Luckman would be activated. This was the biggest thing either Nixon or Koenig had seen in their respective histories, and—beyond such cases possessing the potential to make or break careers—there were lives at stake. Enough people had died. There would be no more.

Elliott Danziger ditched the sheriff's black-and-white eight miles away from Marana. He was not that far from Oro Valley, co-incidentally, though Oro Valley was on the I-19 and he was on the Tucson road. Laurette Tannahill had done little more than sob quietly, seated there beside him in her blood-spattered cotton print dress and matching sweater. She was all of twenty-five years old, brunette, delicately featured, and Digger knew that at some point he was going to have to do something with her. First and foremost, there was business to attend to, and that meant a new car, a change of clothes, perhaps the acquisition of some more weapons. He had enough money to be getting on with, all of seven hundred and forty-three dollars, but that was beside the point if he didn't get control of his own emotions. He gripped the wheel to stop her seeing how much his hands were shaking. He said nothing so as to avoid showing the fear in his voice. Now he was in deep. Too deep. He would swim or drown, that was the truth, and the only way to swim was forward. He could not go back. He was an accomplice to however many counts of murder.

He was a bank robber. He was like John Dillinger, worse than John Dillinger. And he had his own hostage now. Strange how the tables turned. The hostage had become the kidnapper. White had become black. Day had become night. He was damned if he was going to give himself up. This was not his fault. He had been an unwitting accomplice, but they wouldn't listen to him. He could pretty much guarantee that they would shoot him down in the street like a dog. All they would care about was the money and the girl. Not him. They wouldn't even give him a fair trial. Earl had been right about that for sure. There were some people who weren't even given a fair shake of the dice. Not ever. Maybe now it was time to turn things around for himself, and if he had to do it with a gun, then so be it. Why should everything go right for other people? Why should he be left behind?

Everything that had happened . . . hell, everything that had happened had come at him like a whirlwind. He was choked up in his chest. He knew he was supposed to be feeling something, but he didn't know what it was. Guilt? Shame? A sense of responsibility for the position he was in? He had a stolen car and a hostage and a gun. Earl was back there outside the bank. Earl was no longer directing the play. Earl couldn't show him what to do next. He had to make his own decisions. It was a simple choice: Turn round and give himself up, or carry on. It gave him pause, but not for long. His mind had been infected with a virus, and it was too easy to succumb to that virus.

The house that caught Digger's eye was set back from the edge of the highway a good two hundred yards. He could see the pickup from the get-go, and it was a good one. Looked pretty new, all clean and white and ready for the road. Digger took the left turn down a wheel-rutted path that ran directly to the property, and he shared a few words with his passenger.

"Now, don't you worry your pretty little head, sweetheart. We're just gonna get ourselves another vehicle, and then we'll be on our way. I'm gonna go on in there and have a few words with the owner here and we're going to come to an arrangement. I'm gonna take the car keys with me, and you can run all you like, but I'm gonna be out again in just a moment and I'll see you wherever you are. Cooperate and I'll let you out a few miles down the road. Run away and I will kill you stone-dead. We understand each other?"

He knew he could no more kill her than he could have killed Clay, but he had to sound mean, he had to sound like he meant business, and the only way he could do that was to imagine what Earl would have said. That was what he would have to do. He would have to *be* Earl, even though such a thing was a crazy idea. It was like a game, a game of pretend and making stuff up. He would be Earl Sheridan, if only for a little while, if only until he figured out who the hell he really was and how he was going to survive this mess.

Laurette managed an awkward hitching acknowledgment, and Digger pulled to a stop ahead of the house. Before he got out he hunted around in the dash and the foot wells. He found a cloth, maybe for cleaning the windows or some such, and he tied it around the lower half of his face. He carried his gun down by his side and Laurette believed he wasn't going to be making a deal with anyone. What she didn't know was that Digger's heart was racing fit to burst. He didn't know what he was doing. He was both scared and excited. He had never been on his own. Not like this. Not where he was the one in charge, the only one who needed to be consulted. It felt good. It also felt bad. Whatever might have been going on in his mind, he knew that doing nothing was no answer.

"Hello there!" he called out as he entered through the screen door and stepped into the hallway.

"Hello!" he called again.

The sound of footsteps across the upper landing.

Digger backed up a step toward the front door, Wheland's revolver down by his side. He waited for the sound of footsteps on the stairwell, and then he called out again.

"Sorry to be intruding like this, but I have some car trouble out here and I wondered if I could make a telephone call or somethin'?"

"Who is that down there?" a voice called. The voice of a man.

"My name is Charlie, sir. Charlie Wintergreen. I ain't no one in particular. I'm not from these parts . . . just me and my good wife passin' through here and got ourselves an ornery vehicle." Digger was nervous, on fire, and he could hear the sense of uncertainty in his own voice. He stood still, knew that if he moved the man might see that his hands were actually shaking.

The man was smiling. The smile disappeared when he saw Digger standing there, gun in his hand, a kerchief tied across his face. He was dark-haired, broad in the shoulder, a kindly face. He'd anticipated no trouble. Trouble didn't really happen in these parts, at least nothing to speak of.

"I ain't after no trouble, son," he said. "What do you need? Money? A car? You don't need that gun there. My name's Gil Webster—"

Digger raised the gun. Something came over him. It was like the shadow of a tree as you walked through sunshine. He felt momentarily cooler. He felt taller, wider, stronger, faster. He didn't know what it was, but it was good. It was the gun that did it, no doubt about it. The gun gave him power, gave him self-control, gave him Earl's spirit.

Digger tightened his finger on the trigger. He still didn't know if he'd be capable of pulling it, of actually killing someone, but the feeling of that thing in his hand was mighty reassuring. "And my name is whatever the fuck you want it to be," he said.

Gil Webster lowered his head ever so slowly. He took on a crestfallen expression, something of disbelief in his eyes. He shook his head slowly. "I ain't got much of anythin' that'd be of use to you here, son," he said.

"Like you said, you got some money and you got a car, that's enough for sure."

"The car you can have, and I got maybe ten or fifteen dollars in the house—"

"You alone here?"

"Yes, I am."

"Who else lives here?"

Gil Webster hesitated. He had a wife. Her name was Marilyn. She was up north in Lake Havasu City visiting with her mother. They'd been married so long he couldn't think a thought without her. He'd already decided not to tell Charlie Wintergreen anything. If this went the way he hoped it wouldn't, then this crazy son of a bitch might just be crazy enough to drive up there and kill her too. They say it took a full turn of the calendar to reconcile yourself to the loss of a loved one. You had to weather each anniversary once—one birthday, one Christmas, just one of every special occasion. If you made it that far then the odds were you'd make it all the way. Gil didn't reckon Marilyn would do it. She wouldn't take her own life. She wasn't that kind of person. She'd just lay down and go to sleep and never wake up like them native Indian fellers could do. And then he stopped and wondered why he was thinking these thoughts. He was scared, that was all. This kid didn't want anything but whatever money he had and the keys to the car. The car could go. It was insured. Such things were never worth fighting for.

"I can get all the money I have in the house," Gil said, "and you can have the keys to the car."

"Good 'nough," Digger said. "Well, let's get busy, eh?"

Digger followed Gil Webster through the house. He emptied his pocketbook, a coffeepot on a shelf in the kitchen with a handful of dollar bills in it. He even checked the bureau drawers and found another five bucks. All told there was twenty-three dollars, and he handed it over to Digger with the keys to the pickup.

"You got a root cellar?" Digger asked.

"Sure have."

"Show me."

Gil Webster crossed the room and stepped into the kitchen. In back there was a door that led down to the cellar. The key was in the lock.

"Down you go," Digger said. "I'm gonna lock you down there and you're gonna keep your fucking mouth shut for at least an hour, and then you can do whatever the hell you like. I'm gonna be up here for a while, and if I hear you making any fucking noise I'm gonna come down there and shoot you in the head. You understand me?"

Gil nodded. Looked like he was going to come through this. He kept thinking of Marilyn. He kept thinking of the moment the police caught up with this son of a bitch and threw him in lockup. Probably give him a good hiding for his trouble.

He walked to the cellar door and opened it. He took a couple of risers down and then looked back at the young man.

It was in the moment—the moment he looked back and saw Charlie Wintergreen looking down at him—that he knew there was some other agenda. There was a flash in the boy's eyes, something dark. Hard to describe—a dark light?—but that was the only way he could describe it. There was a dark light in the boy's eyes, and that light said there was something wicked in his thoughts.

Gil Webster stood there for a moment, and he felt something indescribable. It was mental, emotional, physiological, even spiritual. It was beyond anything. He had looked death in the face and survived it.

"Go," Digger said, and Gil Webster went on down the stairwell. He heard the door lock behind him, and he resigned himself to sitting quietly for an hour. Maybe he'd make it two or three just to be sure.

As Digger closed the door he stopped. Something arrived in his thoughts. Something real. So terribly, terribly real. He knew then, as well as he knew his own name, that Earl was dead. That neck wound, the amount of blood that he'd lost, the poor son of a bitch wouldn't have survived. Not out there, not in the middle of damned nowhere. Digger closed his eyes for a second, and he felt something, and it was like a religious thing, an overwhelming thing. Like them preacher fellers who talked about being filled to bursting by the love of Jesus and all that shit. Well, this was like that, but better. This was like being overcome by the spirit of Earl Sheridan, and Digger knew that everything he did from this point forward would not only be for himself, but for Earl as well.

A moment later, his gun and the kerchief in one pocket, the money and the car keys in the other, he was out front again. He got into the sheriff's black-and-white and pulled it around behind the house. There was a shed there, big enough to park the car inside, and the doors were unlocked. It didn't take more than a minute to get the vehicle hidden inside, and then he took the girl by the hand and walked her back to the house.

She didn't know about Gil Webster. Perhaps best. She might have gone all hysterical, screaming for him to come on out and save her. Digger took her upstairs, showed her into Gil and Marilyn's bedroom, and stood there for a moment looking at her.

"I reckon I'm going to do some stuff to you now," he said. His voice was calm and measured. "I ain't done this before so I don't know how it goes, but I got a pretty good idea. You can either cooperate or you can resist. If you cooperate then everything's gonna be fine. I'm gonna leave you here and be on my way. If you resist then I'm gonna do what I want to you anyways and then shoot you in the head."

He paused, looked at her closely. "You hear me?"

Laurette Tannahill didn't say a word. She looked back at him, fierce defiance in her eyes. She'd known this was coming. She'd tried to prepare herself for it. She'd kidded herself into thinking that this was something she could do. Truth was, if this went the way she thought it was going to go then she might never be able to deal with it. She'd heard one time of a girl in Payson who was raped by some feller, and the girl was so traumatized she ended up taking a whole handful of pills. She didn't die, but something snapped in her mind and she was never the same again, and now she lived in a place for crazy folk somewhere near that meteor crater south of Flagstaff.

"You done this before?" Digger asked her.

She nodded.

"Well, good 'nough. Then it ain't gonna be a new experience for both of us. Now git your clothes off before I tear 'em off you."

Laurette stood there for a moment. There was no choice. If she did this she might make it through. She might not, but she had to increase the odds as best she could. If she didn't do it then she was history. She knew that for sure. She could have run, but how far would she have got? Nowhere at all. This place was a desert. There was nowhere to hide, no one to go to. Hell, she'd just sat there in the car terrified and frozen and disbelieving of everything that had happened. This morning she'd woken up and it had been a normal day. If someone had told her . . .

"Get a move on!" Digger said.

She took off her sweater. She kicked off her shoes, and when she looked down at them she saw that they were spattered with blood, as were her stockings, as was the lower hem of her dress. She wondered whose blood it was.

Bile rose in her throat.

She reached under her skirt and unclipped her stockings. She rolled them down and took them off. Now she had on nothing but her dress and her bra beneath. This was it. This was where it got nasty.

She reached behind her back and tried to get the zip. She struggled.

"Here, let me do that," Digger said.

The moment his hand touched her she shuddered. That was the thing that did it. That was the thing that kicked everything into focus and made her realize where she was, who she was with, what had happened, what was *about* to happen . . .

She let out a cry. She started to sob. Her breath came up short and she coughed.

Digger yanked down the zip, and then he grabbed the shoulder straps and pulled them down. The dress fell in a single drop and bunched around her feet.

Instinctively Laurette covered herself with her hands.

Digger reached up and grabbed the front of her bra. He tugged it roughly and it hurt her.

"Off," he said.

Laurette hesitated. Digger raised his hand to slap her, and realized he could not. He felt stupid then. He felt ugly and stupid and ignorant. This was not him. This was not the way he thought about women. This was Earl Sheridan.

Laurette flinched as he raised his hand, but she didn't make a sound. Tears filled her eyes and the color rose in her cheeks. Her breathing was swift and shallow, and for a moment Digger hated what he had done to her, hated what he had made her feel. He felt sorry for her, and then he felt angry at himself for being so weak.

Laurette looked back at the bed. She noticed the beautiful cushions there. Looked like every one of them had been hand-stitched. She'd had sex twice before, once with Lenny Bisbee, another time with Charlie Gibson. They were still dating, she and Charlie, and she figured it might go all the way to them getting engaged. Maybe not. Maybe he was the kind of guy who . . .

She felt his hand on her shoulder, and though Digger's thought was to comfort her, perhaps to even tell her he was sorry, to explain that he had in fact hurt no one, Laurette took that gesture as one of threat. He was going to push her back toward the mattress, and he was going to put his hand between her legs, and then he was going to undo the button on his waistband . . .

She twisted suddenly, pushed him away, took a step toward him.

"God damn you!" he said. "I was only—"

"God damn you back!" she shouted.

Digger stood there for a moment. He felt nothing. He had been trying to get aroused. The girl was there, most of her clothes on the floor, and he knew what to do, but damn it if he couldn't get a hard-on. "Son of a bitch!" he said. "Goddamn son of a bitch!" It wasn't him, it was the girl. That was the problem. The girl was the fucking problem. He looked at her, the white skin, her fat ass, the way she glared back at him. He looked at the stupid pillows, the names embroidered on them—*Marilyn and Gil*, another one—*Five Years of Happiness Together*, and the whole thing just made him mad.

Frustrated, angry, upset with himself, the girl, the situation, he reached back and took Wheland's gun from his back pocket.

It was then that she slapped him. He hadn't expected that. She just let fly and slapped him, and he felt that sudden rush of blood to his face. He stood there with the gun in his hand and he didn't know what to do.

For a second he hesitated, and then he said, "Get back on the bed! Get back on the fucking bed!"

"Or what?" she said, and in her tone was such defiance that Digger was taken aback.

"Or what?" he echoed. "Or I'll fucking shoot you—"

"Do it," she said. "Do it! Just fucking shoot me, why don't you? Shoot me right now, because you ain't doing this to me."

Digger was stunned into silence. He took a step back. The gun felt too heavy in his hand.

The girl shifted forward. Pretty much naked though she was, she seemed suddenly terrifying. She took another step toward him and he backed away farther.

Digger raised the gun again. "Sit d-down," he said, and he felt his voice crack.

"You sit down," she said. "You can say what the hell you like. You are not going to rape me. You can kill me, but you are *not* going to rape me."

Digger felt sick. He felt like a scolded child. He had been trying to apologize, and now he was the bad guy. Wasn't this just another example of what Earl had been telling him? Some people had all the cards stacked against them, and there was nothing that could be done about it.

"You couldn't even do it if you tried," she said, and she realized then that he really was backing away, that she had him on the defensive, that he was no more capable of shooting her than he was of raping her.

"Son of a bitch," she said. "You pathetic son of a bitch—" She raised her hand then, as if to slap him once more.

Incensed, angry, more ashamed than anything else, Digger hit her. He just let fly wildly and the gun connected with the side of her head and she went over like a tenpin.

She fell onto the bed, blood already visible on her cheek and jaw line, and Digger stood there for a second with nothing in his mind but rage and terror.

He looked down at her, and it seemed in that moment that everything—every shame, every rebuttal, every denial, every ignominy that had befallen him—was now personified and represented by this girl. There were tears in his eyes.

You pathetic son of a bitch.

He hit her again. Hit her hard in the side of the head. And then again.

It was then that he felt it. Felt the blood rushing to his groin, felt his dick coming to life, and he started to feel nauseous, strangely disgusted with himself, and then it passed almost as soon as it had arrived. In its place was a sense of panic and disorientation. He wiped the side of the gun off on the bedsheet, and he leaned close to the girl and he could hear her breathing, shallow and rapid, but still breathing. He didn't know what to feel. Relief that she was still alive? That he hadn't killed her? Anger toward her for making him feel ashamed? For making him feel so *pathetic*?

Digger started backward toward the door, and then he turned suddenly.

The room ahead of him was blurred through his tears. His nose was running and he felt like a little boy, a scared little boy, and he hated himself and he hated her and he hated the world.

He had to get out of there. Had to get out of there and as far away as possible. He looked down at the gun in his hand, the

123

blood on the chamber, and he felt the tension in his groin and the weakness in his knees, and he wondered for a second if it was like this for everybody.

He almost lost his balance as he flew down the stairs and out to Gil Webster's pickup. He jammed the vehicle in gear and screeched away, his heart racing, his mind overwhelmed with a thousand different thoughts.

Do what Earl would do, he kept thinking. *Just do what Earl Sheridan would do.*

But he didn't know what Earl Sheridan would do, and Earl was dead for sure, and the fact that there was no one to tell him what to do was the scariest thing of all.

CHAPTER FOURTEEN

As Digger Danziger fled the Webster house, Clay Luckman and Bailey Redman caught a ride in the direction of Tucson. The pickup slowed to the side of the road and waited for them. The driver was a rough-looking feller, his eyes the sharp blue that came from walking into the sun most days of your life. In back of the pickup was a mess of cornstalks and old tin cans.

"You can get in there. Can take you most of the way to Tucson, but then I'm turning off, okay?"

"Any distance you can take us would be . . ." Clay started, but the driver had already revved the engine into life and his words were drowned out.

Their let-off was all of three miles from the city limits, and there they waved goodbye to the pickup and stood side by side at the edge of the highway—silent, breathless—as if watching for someone they knew would never come.

It was late afternoon. Clay was exhausted. He knew the girl was too, but she would never show it, certainly wouldn't say it.

He also knew that there would be only so much time before pictures and radio dispatches would be alerting the world to who he was, the fact that he had gone on the run from Hesperia.

"I think we need to find somewhere to rest up," he said. He looked out to his right and left, seemed to be considering direction from intuition alone.

As an aside, almost to himself, he said, "Would make sense if I knew your name. That is one word you could say without upsetting too many folk."

He looked at her. She looked back. She tried to smile but it didn't come out so good.

"No?" he asked. "Okay. I was figurin' you was maybe gonna be a nun or some such. Like you'd taken a vow of silence."

Clay decided left and started walking. He hoped to find a barn, a shack, a shed—something long enough to lay down in with a roof over their heads.

The girl followed him—dutiful, implacable, silent.

A thousand yards from the road they came upon a place. The roof was sagging, but the walls were solid. A deserted storage barn, an intended home, he had no idea what purpose the building had served, but for tonight it would suffice. In back was a rain barrel with clean-looking water to the brim.

"This we can drink if we boil it first," he told the girl. "It ain't gonna be a comfortable night, but it'll be better than sleeping out under the stars." He looked to the sky. "And I have a feeling rain is coming."

Inside was a stone floor, a broken chair, a table with three legs. Spiderwebs crisscrossed the corners and angles, and dust as thick as cloth was laid out on every surface. A collection of metal cooking pots were scattered around. Old cutlery, rusted and useless, a newspaper dating back four years, its pages nothing more than sepia-colored memories of things long-forgotten. Clay moved things about. He used the remnants of an old blanket to brush dirt and mouse droppings away from the side of the room, and then he told the girl to wash one of the metal pans.

"Scoop water out of the barrel in back. Don't put the pan in the water itself. It's clean enough and I don't want it all dirty."

She took the pan without a word, went out there and started.

Clay broke up the chair, kicked the remaining three legs off the table, stacked them in the fireplace beneath the chimney. He hoped the chimney wasn't blocked with old nests and crap. Soon enough they'd find out. The newspaper, a few handfuls of kindling from outside the door, and he had the fire going. The chimney was okay. The room could cope with the smoke.

The girl returned with the pan.

"We're going out," he said as he took it from her.

He led the way and she followed. They spent a while gathering up broken cornstalks, those with heads still attached, and when they had an armful or two they went back inside. The heads went into the pan, the stalks into the fire, and soon they had the thing half-filled. Clay added water, set the pan near the edge of the fire and let the thing heat up. It boiled it up into a sticky mess and they wolfed it down while it was still too hot to taste. Clay shared out the last few items that he had taken from the convenience store. That was it. Now it was all down to what money they had, what money they could get. He counted out the coins. Seven dollars and forty-two cents. He took out the gun, the box of shells, and before he had a chance to stop her the girl had taken the gun and was holding it by the grip between her fingers so it pointed down to the floor.

Her eyes were questioning.

"Just in case," Clay said. "In case those people come back."

She returned the gun to him. She lay down on her side, her face turned away, and he heard her sigh.

Clay lay down too. The floor was cold and hard and unforgiving. Beside him was the kicked-out window, and through it he could see the sky darkening quickly, the nascent stars, the promise of thunderheads. He watched the wind move the clouds. He felt the hot fist of poor nourishment cramping his guts. *Pay for this come morning*, he thought, *squatting in a bush someplace with my ass like a fresh bullet wound.*

The rain came then—fast, relentless, hammering at the ground as if to make a point, as if to prolong some eternal argument between the dirt and the sky. Water channeled and roiled around the edges of the old house, and in it was carried all manner of things.

He closed his eyes for a moment, and then he felt her close up against him. Her body was cold and thin and awkward. She approached him for warmth, for the certainty that they would sleep better if they shared what heat they could muster between them.

In those last moments of wakefulness Clay Luckman wondered what had happened to him. He questioned the present, the past, and he realized that life had a way of preparing you for nothing at all. Tomorrow they would reach Tucson, and what was waiting for them there? Nothing. Absolutely nothing. The authorities would be looking for him, and for her too he imagined. It would help greatly if he knew something—anything—about her. And if the police or the federal people got hold of Earl and Digger, God only knew what lies and calumny they would spew. Earl would more than likely tell the world that all the killing had been Clay's doing, and then it would be Clay's word against that of a convicted felon. Hell of a chance for fair judgment if that happened. Even as he lay there he imagined police cars crisscrossing the countryside, wireless announcements, his picture in the newspapers and on the TV. Fate and fortune had brought him here, and fate and fortune—he felt sure—had something else in store for him tomorrow.

It was barely evening, and yet Clay Luckman and Bailey Redman fell asleep to the sound of the rain and each other's breathing, and it seemed after a while that one was indiscernible from the other.

CHAPTER FIFTEEN

Tucson, "The Old Pueblo," overwhelmed Elliott Danziger completely. Thirty-second largest city in the continental United States, bordered to the north by the Santa Catalina and Tortolita mountains, to the south by the Santa Ritas, the Rincons to the east, and the Tucson Mountains to the west. The city was breathtaking to him. Never had he seen such a place.

Near the old city center, right there at the corner of Stone Avenue and Broadway Boulevard, he pulled Gil Webster's white pickup over to the edge of the street and sat there for a good while. He was angry. He was still scared. He was upset about what had happened with the girl back there at the house, but his shame and guilt had evolved into something closer to resentment. He *resented* her. That was how he felt. He even half-hoped she'd die. Or maybe have brain damage and spend the rest of her life having to be spoon-fed by cruel nurses. He knew also that now he was in trouble *for* himself and *by* himself. There was no Earl to cover for him. There was no Earl to blame it on. He had locked a man in his cellar, beaten a girl unconscious, and stolen a pickup. He also had a gun that belonged to the police and the proceeds of a major bank robbery.

He was also hungry, and he needed to eat. He had no shortage of money, but there was something so strange and new and paralyzingly huge about the place that he felt afraid to leave the vehicle. It took him a good fifteen minutes to feel centered and focused and oriented. He didn't like to carry so much money on him, but he had no choice. He was not going to leave seven hundred bucks in an unattended car. He needed a change of clothes as well. The things he was wearing were grubby, sweat-stained, and there was blood in the treads of his shoes. He couldn't look at it. The girl had made him feel ashamed, made him feel like a child. He wondered when she would come around, or when someone would find her, and if they would find the man in the basement too, and if . . .

It was all so many *ifs*, and regardless of everything blood was blood, and it wasn't so smart to go walking around with evidence of your deeds on your footwear. He divided the money into four roughly equal parts, put two bundles of notes into his inner jacket pockets, the other two in the front pockets of his jeans. The gun was too difficult to conceal on his person, so it went under the driver's seat. There were only four bullets. He thought of how to get more, and then was scared at the thought. Why would he need more? Because he was on the run, because he had hurt the girl . . . maybe even killed her? And then he thought of Earl, and what Earl had said, and he felt a sense of resolve amidst his nervous thoughts. He had to be a man. He had to make a decision and carry it through. He had to keep on going. He paused, and then he went for the advertisement in his back pocket. It was not there. Hell, it was not there! He checked the other pockets, knowing full well before he checked that it had gone.

Damn! Hell and damnation! That was important. That had been his goal.

And then he paused and thought for a moment. Maybe it was an omen, a portent. Maybe the fact that he had lost it was fate playing a hand. Clay talked about fate. Clay believed in fate. Maybe Clay was right. Perhaps the fact that he no longer possessed the picture meant that he had moved beyond seeing it on the page, and now he had to see it for real. That would make sense. Out of the imagination and into reality.

Yes. Of course. Eldorado. That's where he was going. That's where he'd been going for the past five years.

Digger locked up the pickup and took a walk, paying attention to landmarks as he went so as to find his way back when the time came. More people than he had ever seen crowded the streets. Music could be heard from bar doorways. Women sat talking in laundromats. Restaurants with lighted windows showed people laughing, eating, drinking, doing what regular people did on a Monday evening in Tucson. He felt self-conscious and out of place. He felt like a bohunk hick farmhand come to the big city.

Well, howdy, y'all! He felt naive and unschooled in the nature of many things, and he started to resent the people who looked at him as he passed by.

Ten minutes and he found a small place on Sutherland Street. There were people his own age inside an adjacent record store. They were dressed up in skinny-legged pants and flat shoes in pastel colors. Some of the boys had on sweaters and ties. The girls had mountains of hair perched on their heads. They wore cosmetics, had long dark lashes, scarlet red lips, and necklaces and bangles and little purses that seemed too small to carry a pack of smokes. They danced in the store. They were provocative and coy. They looked like they were teasing the boys, and they knew what they were doing. Digger despised them immediately. They reminded him of the girl from the bank. She had slapped him. Jesus Christ almighty, she had slapped him! He calmed himself. He told himself that he had been in control. He told himself that she was stupid and fat and ugly anyway, that when he did it for the first time he was going to do it with someone pretty and smart and respectful.

In the diner he ordered meat and potatoes and beans. He ordered a glass of malted milk as well, and he took a couple of bread rolls from a basket next to the till to eat while he waited. He was one of three customers, the other two minding their own business—one at the counter, an old man with nothing more than a cup of coffee ahead of him, and then a younger woman at a table three down and one to the right. Digger smiled at her when he caught her eye. She smiled back, but there was a tension in that smile. She was in her twenties, late-twenties he guessed, and she had a flat and unremarkable face. He wanted to tell her that he was no threat, that she was not his type, but he knew well enough that spontaneous conversation with strangers was as welcome as hives.

He ate slowly. He did not circle his plate with his arm. There was no one here going to hurry him, no one going to steal his food. He started to relax. He was in the big city. He was in Tucson. Earl was more than likely dead. Clay was Christ-only-knew where, shit-fool-coward, useless half brother that he was. They would find Gil Webster in his basement and the girl upstairs in the bedroom. They would find the sheriff's car in the barn out behind the property. They would realize that he had taken Gil Webster's white pickup, and they would be looking for that. Best collect the gun and get another ride. Anything would do. Something inconspicuous, something that wouldn't be missed for a while. He would give them the jump, take the lead, be running so far ahead of them that they'd never have a chance to catch him. And where would he go? That would be their question. Eldorado, that's where. Somewhere they didn't know about, and somewhere they would never think to look.

For now the details didn't matter. Tonight he needed to find some new clothes, some new boots, somewhere to sleep, and then in the morning he would get another car and make a decision. What would happen he didn't know, but the faster he moved the more likely he was to dictate the outcome. That much he knew. Of that much he convinced himself.

He finished up his dinner, paid the check, left no tip. He looked once more at the unremarkable woman in back of the diner. Her eyes were empty and registered nothing.

Out on the street he headed back in the direction he'd come, stopping at an open-fronted market where jeans and tees and checked shirts were on sale. He bought what he needed, carried them away in a large paper bag. Boots too he found at another store, bought a pair of rugged, thick-soled lace-ups that would survive three Russian winters and a walk through the Ozarks. In the pickup he changed, put his old shoes and clothes in the paper bag and twisted the top tight. The gun went in his jeans waistband, the tails of the shirt to cover it, and then he wiped down the internal surfaces of the car, levered the door with his cuffs over his hands, and then locked up from without. He dropped the keys down a storm drain ten yards down Stone Avenue and didn't look back.

Three blocks away he saw a young dark-haired woman carrying a bag of groceries out of a store. She was cute-looking, had that whole ponytail-hair-tied-up-behind thing going on. She wore short tight pants that reached her knees, flat shoes, a T-shirt that emphasized the curve of her waist and the substance of her breasts.

She looked good enough to eat.

Digger waited for her to make fifteen yards, and then he started to follow.

CHAPTER SIXTEEN

Federal Bureau of Investigation Agents Ronald Koenig and Garth Nixon had confirmed the identification of Frank Jacobs by eight that evening. Yes, they had a pocketbook, a couple of things on his person that carried his name and address, but nothing substantive like a driver's license or official ID card. So many times an ID had been assumed, and so many times that ID had been proven wrong. Substantiating his name had meant sending people to his home in Scottsdale, a good hundred miles or so north. What he was doing in Marana they did not know, and from what the Scottsdale field agents could tell them there was nothing unusual about Frank Jacobs's home aside from the staggering prevalence of shoes. Jacobs's Oldsmobile had been employed by the fugitives in Marana, and thence to Wellton for the abortive and murderous bank robbery. With the death of Earl Sheridan in Wellton, the remaining fugitive—this Clarence Luckman—had taken Jim Wheland's car and made his escape.

A report had come in from a hysterical Marilyn Webster about the discovery of her husband, locked in his own basement by a gun-wielding teenager, a second unknown woman in the bedroom, badly hurt, still alive but fading fast. But that report had gone to the police at Gila Bend. It would not be until the following morning that Wheland's car would be found out behind the house and the sheriff's department would contact the federal authorities. Webster was unable to identify the young man who had locked him in the basement. He'd had a kerchief tied around his face. Laurette Tannahill would not be telling anybody anything at all for quite some time it seemed, and thus the authorities were blindsided.

At that moment Koenig and Nixon had eight killings to deal with, all the way from Bethany Olson in Twentynine Palms to

Danny Leggett from the bank at Wellton. Seemed that the death of Earl Sheridan had not marked the end of the trouble. Laurette Tannahill, if she didn't pull through, would make it nine. Even at eight it still ranked as the most significant killing spree in Arizona's history for over forty-five years, and despite the fact that Earl Sheridan had been killed at Wellton, it looked like trouble was still making its way westward. The earlier record holder had been one Window Rock resident called Bernard Fenney. Fenney exemplified all of the craziness it was possible for a man to maintain. One Saturday afternoon he took it upon himself to march into the Hubbell Trading Post and let rip with a couple of shotguns. The shells he used were of his own invention, stuffed with lead shot, fish hooks, bits of glass, saltpeter and ball bearings. Once he'd laid down half a dozen people in the post, he went walkabout. The authorities finally trapped him in a cabin up near Keams Canyon, and they just wound up hurling some dynamite in there to finish the thing. Fenney had killed fourteen, wounded as many again, and by the time the dynamite did its work there was too little of him left to get an explanation.

But that was history. That was now folklore and ghost stories for kids who didn't eat their greens. *Eat your collards or Fenney will come find you.* This was now, right here and now, and eight was enough of an issue to have raised the antennae up in Phoenix. Both Koenig and Nixon were good men, men of stature and reputation, but even heroes have lice and neither of them wanted this to be the swan song of their respective careers. Clarence Luckman might have been lucky this far, but if it had anything at all to do with them then his luck had just about exhausted itself. Koenig and Nixon filed reports and made phone calls. They alerted their superiors all the way to San Francisco and Los Angeles. They were told that more men would be assigned and dispatched, those to assist in the location of Clarence Luckman, others to search for the body of the unfortunate half brother, Elliott Danziger. Radio announcements alerting citizens to keep a lookout for Clarence Luckman had already started through three counties, and more would follow. Luckman's picture was duplicated time and again, and copies of that picture were driven in every direction on the compass. He swiftly became the most wanted individual for the last twenty-five years of FBI operations. And Clay Luckman—hunkering down in a collapsed barn somewhere in the middle of nowhere—did not have the faintest idea of what was about to befall him.

CHAPTER SEVENTEEN

She was twenty-three, and she lived alone. Her name was Deidre, but everyone called her Dee. Dee Parselle. Her mother worried far too much about her, but her father was a leather-worker in Apache Junction and he believed that a girl of twenty-three should be independent and focused. He had given her the money to find an apartment, and she'd found one—right there above the hardware store on Peridot Street. Four rooms—a sitting room, a kitchen, a bathroom, a bedroom. She'd been there for seven months, she had friends who visited, and there was a guy she'd met through her work as an orthodontist's receptionist, a guy with an impacted bicuspid called Ben. She thought he might be *the one*. Ben, however, didn't feel the same way about Dee. He wanted to fool around as all boys did, but did he want something beyond that? She hoped so. She really did. Ben—unbeknownst to Dee—had already figured he might move on anyway. After all, they had been going out for three weeks and she still hadn't let him past second base.

Monday evening she'd gone to get groceries. Her apartment was above the store and accessed by a wooden stairwell and walkway. It gave her privacy and altitude, and when the summer came she would put a chair out there and smoke cigarettes and listen to the record player from her sitting room, and she would have potted plants and maybe she would paint the railings, and things were going to be good.

Monday evening she let herself in through the screen, the front door, and she kicked it shut behind her and went on down the hallway to the kitchen on the right to set her bag down. She didn't go back to close the door for a good two minutes, and when she got there a young man was standing on the walkway looking at her through the screen and she jumped, startled, and wondered if she hadn't dropped something. He was little more than a silhouette against the light behind him, and she could not see his face.

"Miss?" he said.

She took a step closer. "Yes? What can I do for you?" She wanted to sound unconcerned, but there was a querulous edge to her voice.

"I just wondered if I could get a drink of water," he said, and there was something innocent in the question, and yet at the same time Dee was thrown into a confusion of feelings as he raised his left hand and placed it against the screen.

"Please," she said. "Wait there . . ."

But he came on through, and it was only then that she saw he had a gun in his hand and a kerchief tied around the lower half of his face, and at first there was a tightening in the base of her gut, and then her knees started to weaken, and she had to place her hand against the wall to stop herself from fainting.

"Wha-what do you w-want?" she stammered, and now she did sound afraid, even to herself, and she had never been a tough girl, never been a fighter, never been one to take the offensive, and even though running at him with her fists and nails and screaming at the top of her voice, catching him off guard and unawares, pushing him back into the screen—which would certainly have given way with his weight—and seeing him fall out onto the walkway, perhaps even stagger back and lose his balance against the banister and go appetite-over-tin-cup backward to the yard below . . . even though this would have been the smartest thing to do there was no way in the world that Dee could have done something like that . . .

She was completely unable to do a thing except allow a brief whimper to escape her lips as he advanced on her.

He was gentle at first, taking her by the arm and guiding her through into the sitting room.

There was something deeply disturbing in his eyes. They were blue, a good strong blue, and not a shade of gray in them, but the blue was cold and unfeeling, and she knew from the moment he asked her the second question that she was done for.

"You here alone?"

She nodded. She started to cry.

"Stop crying!" he said, and though his voice wasn't loud it was nevertheless hard and direct and uncompromising.

She stopped crying.

He pushed her away from him to the middle of the rug. She stood there, her arms in front of her, her hands out toward him as if pleading. She didn't speak, *couldn't* speak, and she felt like she was going to pass out right there and then.

"What's your name?" he said.

She shook her head.

"You don't have a name? Everyone has a name, sweetheart. Now, what is your name?"

"Dee," she said, and the sound was involuntary, as if there was now no longer any connection between physiology and thought. She didn't think to tell him her name, she just told him. He asked and she gave.

"Dee," he repeated. "Dee. Dee. Dee."

"Ple-please d-don't hu-hurt me . . ." she gasped, and her eyes were so filled with tears she could see him as little more than a blur.

"Now, Dee . . . sweetheart . . . what makes you think I want to hurt you? Do I look like the sort of person who goes around hurting people?"

She didn't know what to say. *Yes, mister, you look like that kind of person . . . exactly that kind of person. No, mister, you . . . you what?*

She said nothing.

"I asked for a drink of water, that was all. If I'd wanted to hurt you I would have hurt you. But if I wanted a drink of water . . ." He left the statement incomplete. There was something happening. Something unexpected. He felt . . . felt what? Sorry for her? It upset him that she was so afraid?

Digger smiled to himself. Jesus, what on earth would Earl say? *You fucking pussy! Christ Almighty, are you a man or a fucking mouse? Give it to her, Digger! Just fucking give it to her! Fuck her and shoot her and be done with it!*

But no. There was something about this girl. She was pretty and fragile, and there was something almost *trusting* in the way she looked at him. Almost as if she believed what he was telling her.

"Sit down," he said.

She did so. Didn't hesitate, didn't question the instruction.

She sat on a plain wooden chair that was there beside the kitchen door.

Digger stepped back. He lowered the gun fractionally. "You scared of me?" he asked.

She nodded. "Ye-yes . . ."

"Well, okay, I understand that. That makes sense to me. If I was home and someone came to the door with his face all covered up and a gun in his hand . . . well, I reckon I'd be scared some too, right?" Digger smiled beneath the kerchief. "Well, for sure it would have to depend on how big the guy was and whether or not I figured I could take him, but if he was a good deal bigger than me and he had a gun, or maybe two guns, then sure I'd be a little nervous, just like you."

He looked at Dee as if waiting for acknowledgment. She gave none.

"But that's not the deal here, sweetheart. I just need a place to lie low for a while, and I see you in the street and you look like the kind of girl who'd take pity on someone less fortunate, and there we are. We can make the best of it, or we can make the worst of it."

"Ar-are y-you in tr-trouble?" she asked.

Digger laughed coarsely. "Hell, sugar, ain't we all . . . from the moment we're born to the moment we die? Ain't nothing but trouble from one to the end with a few distractions along the way."

"I mean . . . I mean real trouble . . . like, with the police or something?"

"No, what do you take me for, a criminal? I ain't no criminal. I'm just down on my luck and things haven't gone so good, but there's always a light somewhere, right? You just need to make your mark someplace, and then people start respectin' you again and it all straightens out."

"You're gonna hide here or so-something?" she asked.

"Hide? Who said anything about hiding?"

"Someone must be af-after y-you . . . if you're carrying a gun an' all . . ."

Digger looked at the gun in his hand. He raised his eyebrows, almost as if he were surprised to see it there. "Well . . ." he started, and then he shook his head. "Well, that's a long story . . . ain't important."

"You can st-stay here for a while if you like," Dee said. She tried to smile. She shook her head. "I ain't so afraid . . . I mean . . . I mean, you don't look so terrible to me, mister."

Digger frowned.

Dee raised her hand and withdrew it. She raised it again, slowly.

Digger lifted the gun. "What the—"

"It's okay," she said. "I ain't gonna do nothin' . . ."

He watched her, the way her hand reached out toward him, and then the tips of her fingers were against his face, and for a moment he was intrigued, curious as to what she was doing, and then she tugged down the kerchief slowly, and she smiled when she saw his face.

"You're a handsome man," she said. "You ha-have beautiful eyes as well . . ."

Digger felt himself color up. He didn't know what the damn hell was going on here, but all of a sudden the last thing in the world he wanted to do was hurt her.

He could hear Earl's voice—*Go on, give it to her! Fuck her and shoot her! Fuck her and shoot her, you pussy!*—but the sound of that voice was fading.

For a moment he closed his eyes, and he felt the sensation of her fingertips on his cheek, and then he knew what she was doing.

He jerked back, raised the gun, but she was not trying anything. She was just looking at him—slightly surprised at his reaction — but still smiling gently.

"What are you doing?" he said.

She frowned, a fleeting shift in her expression, and she shook her head. "Nothing," she said. "Just looking at you . . ."

The fear seemed to have vanished from her voice.

What was she saying? That she wanted him here? That she thought he was good-looking, a nice guy?

Suddenly Digger had a vision of Eldorado. He remembered Clay, how they peered at that magazine advertisement and imagined the life they could have in such a place.

He felt a rush of emotion in his chest.

Digger and Dee in Eldorado.

Elliott . . . he would be Elliott in Eldorado. Dee and Elliott. Elliott and Dee.

Something hurt in his throat. He closed his eyes. He felt a tear somewhere, almost as if he were going to cry.

"It's okay," she said. "What can I do? I'm just a girl. I'm here on my own. You're bigger and stronger and faster than me. I'm going to run? How far would I get? And even if I did get there, what would I tell anyone? This nice boy came to my house and we sat and talked for a while, and he seemed like such a nice boy . . ."

And the way she said that—*nice boy*—didn't seem anything but a compliment. He was a *nice boy*. To Dee, he was just a *nice boy*. Someone his mother would be proud of.

"You look tired and hungry," she said. "I make great sandwiches. I can make you a turkey and white cheddar with some mayonnaise or something. Maybe you want a pickle and some chips, huh? You look real hungry . . ."

Digger smiled. "Yeah," he said. "I kinda am . . ."

"So go wash up. You go shut the front door, and you go wash up and I'll make us a sandwich, and we could have a root beer too. I got some root beer in the icebox, and we could just talk for a while. You can tell me about yourself and how you wound up in Tucson." She started to get up from the chair. "We could pretend, you know?"

Digger raised an eyebrow.

She smiled. "We could pretend we were . . . you know? Like we were on a date or somethin' . . ."

Digger didn't know what to say, didn't know what to think.

"Go on," she said. "Close the front door and you go on back and wash up before we eat . . ."

Digger got up from the chair. He stood there for a moment.

She took a step forward. He didn't back up. His arm hung by his side, his hand loose on the grip of the gun.

She tentatively raised her hand and touched his face once more. "I don't even know your name," she said.

"Ell . . . Elliott," he replied.

"Well, go on, Elliott . . . go on back and wash up."

Elliott hesitated, and then he tucked the gun in his jeans pocket, walked to the front door, and pushed it closed, and then he followed her direction as she pointed in back of the apartment to the bathroom.

Once there he stepped back and looked into the living room. He could hear her in the kitchen. She was making sandwiches.

Elliott Danziger stood for just a moment in the bathroom. He could see his own face looking back at him, the kerchief still around his neck like some kind of cowboy. He untied it, stuffed it in his pocket. He took out the gun and held it in his hand. It was cold and heavy. He felt ashamed. He felt disgusted with himself for treating such a poor, defenseless girl so badly. That was just damned awful of him. Such a nice girl like that. Such a . . .

He shook his head.

Jesus goddammit, why'd he have to be such an asshole all the time? Clay wouldn't have spoken to her like that. Clay wouldn't have thought such things about her . . . that he was going to fuck her and shoot, or maybe stab her and whatever. What the hell was wrong with him?

He had to tell her sorry.

He put the gun in the waistband of his jeans and walked back to the living room.

She was silent. No sound from the kitchen.

Elliott frowned.

And then there was something. A sound like . . . like someone dialing a phone?

Elliott started toward the kitchen, and that's when he saw it. Saw it because he damned well nearly tripped over it.

The cable across the carpet.

He sped up. *No!* he thought. *She didn't . . . no way, she didn't!*

She just dropped the phone when she saw him appear in the doorway.

Her own sudden intake of breath was the loudest thing she had ever heard.

Digger reached to his left and ripped the cable from the wall. With his right hand he was already holding the gun.

Rage filled him to bursting. He boiled over inside. He felt more anger than he had ever experienced, so much so that he believed his body might just explode.

"I was just—just going to tell my mom I'd—I'd be—be l-late for d-dinner . . ." but she was already crying, and the terror was in

142

her eyes, and the lies were on her lips, and Digger could see them, could smell the betrayal and deceit in the air around her, and he hated her then, hated her more than was possible . . .

Oh, how Earl would have raged now, how Earl would have torn her limb from limb!

She stood there, her eyes closed, her whole body shaking.

He raised the gun. He cleared his throat, and then touched the barrel of the gun to her forehead and looked right at her with his fiercely blue eyes.

"Open your eyes," he said, and his voice was strong and commanding.

She did as she was told.

"Ple-please . . . I didn't mean to . . ."

He slapped her with his left hand. The shock of impact jarred throughout her entire body.

He raised his hand again. She shook her head. She pressed her hands together as if in prayer.

"N-no, don't h-hit me again," she said.

He didn't move. He just looked at her.

She started to cry then.

"Shut the fuck up, you sniveling fucking bitch . . . Jesus, you're all the fucking same, aren't you? Walking around out there, all dressed up pretty, and then when it comes down to it you don't want to know. I was nice to you. I was real nice to you. 'Go wash up. I'll make a sandwich . . .' "

She felt her knees give, and she dropped suddenly, and she hit the floor. She thought one of her teeth was loose. She thought about Ben's impacted bicuspid, that she would get a twenty-five percent discount on her own orthodontic work because she was an employee . . .

And then he was kneeling beside her, and he had his hand on the back of her neck, and he was squeezing real hard. For a moment she wondered whether he was going to choke her to death, but then he released his grip and walked away. She wondered if he was leaving. She rolled onto her side and tucked her knees up into her chest, and she wrapped her arms around her knees and hugged them tight, and then she realized that he hadn't gone to the front door, he'd gone to the kitchen, and when he appeared in the doorway he had a knife in his hand.

"Oh God," she said, and she started crying again, and he took two steps toward her and he knelt beside her, and he just dug that knife into her shoulder.

He closed his eyes as he did it. And when he opened them and saw the blood he seemed to gag.

He took a deep breath, and he dug the knife in her again.

Digger's mind turned over and his heart was filled with something he couldn't describe, and it took all his concentration to hold on to the thing and not drop it right there on the floor.

He felt really sick and really afraid. And then he felt stupid and hateful and incensed with her betrayal. He had been betrayed. Betrayed by this girl, and the one from the bank, and betrayed by Earl, and before that by Clay, and before that by his mother and his dumbass father . . .

Betrayed by the whole fucking world it seemed, and the betrayals just kept on coming like a wave.

Dee opened her mouth to scream, but he put his left hand over her mouth and she felt like she was going to suffocate because he blocked her nostrils as well, and then he dug that knife in a third time. She had betrayed him . . . was going to call people . . . which people? The police? She had planned all along to call the police, and now she was going to betray him some more by screaming at the top of her voice and bringing other people here, and then he would be in for it. Then he would really be in trouble. She was not going to do that. He couldn't let her. It was her or him—that was the truth—and the choice was not difficult.

He stabbed her in the breast and he felt her surge upward against his hold, and he knew if he took his hand away from her mouth she would just start hollering like a fire siren, and Digger —filled with the certainty that this time he would not be outdone and outsmarted by a fucking girl—set the knife aside and used his other hand to choke her as well. She fought back, and she was no weakling, but he got his entire weight on top of her, and within a minute she was limp and lifeless and silent. She was not dead, merely unconscious. He had no intention of killing her. He just needed her to shut the hell up.

He stood up slowly, and he looked down at the girl. He was motionless for quite some time and he thought about what he had done.

A minute ago he had hated her. A minute ago he'd wanted to hurt her and punish her and make her feel like nothing. A minute ago she'd represented everything that was despicable about other people. Everyone that had made him feel useless and ashamed for being who he was.

But now, seeing her there on the floor, he felt something else. He wanted to wake her up, to tell her he was sorry, that he didn't mean it.

Digger knelt down beside her. He listened to her breathing.

He wanted to cry but he didn't dare. He was scared Earl Sheridan might be around someplace, like his spirit might still be in the room, and he would think of him as nothing but a frightened little boy. Which was how he felt.

"I'm sorry," he whispered. "I'm really sorry."

And in hearing his own voice he realized how pathetic he sounded. He wanted to kick her. He wanted to stab her some more. He picked up the knife, but then merely wiped his finger-prints from it with the hem of his T-shirt, and dropped it again. He cursed himself for not buying two pairs of jeans.

Closing his eyes, he took a deep breath and then slowly released it.

It was done now. There was no going back. He'd made his decision.

He got up. He used the kerchief to wipe his prints from every-thing he'd touched in the apartment.

He paused at the door, looked back at her, shook his head.

If ever he'd needed confirmation that people were all the same, well, this had been it.

He left the apartment quickly, walked down to the street and was away and gone within a minute.

Dee Parselle was alive—barely—but she was alive. She'd man-aged to hold on to her life, but—in all truth—she'd managed to hold on to little else.

145

DAY FIVE

CHAPTER EIGHTEEN

Rich sunlight shone through the punched-out window of the door. The girl was still sleeping. She had pulled away during the night and curled into a fetal position, her knees drawn toward her chest, her face down amidst her hair. Her breathing was slow and deep.

Clay sat up. He looked around and oriented himself. When she woke they would walk into Tucson and get some breakfast, and then ... well, then he didn't know. She needed to talk. She needed to tell him her name, where she was from, where she needed to be returned to. There would be family awaiting her somewhere, and Clay imagined they would be worried. They had come this way simply because Clay had believed that Sheridan and Digger would go the other. Whether he was right or not now didn't matter. They were a handful of miles from Tucson and they needed food. He also wanted to smoke cigarettes. That much he knew. He had smoked little before, had liked it, and now for some reason craved the sensation. He would buy cigarettes in Tucson as well, and damn the cost.

When the girl woke he told her they were going to walk into the city. She looked at him with the same flat absence of expression.

"I don't know if you just can't talk," he said, "but I think it's gonna get to a stage where I find your silence too uncomfortable to bear. I helped you away from that place 'cause I believed you might have wound up dead if you'd stayed there. And the man that was dead ... hell, I don't know who he was to you—"

"He was my father."

Clay was silenced. He stood and looked at her with his mouth half-open for a good while, and then he closed it without saying a thing. He didn't know whether it was the shock of hearing her voice, or the significance of what she'd said.

"His name was Frank Jacobs and he was my father," she went on. Her voice was soft, a rounded tone, and something of the deeper South in it. "And I thank you for getting me away from there, but I left him behind and I don't know that I'll ever be able to forgive myself for that."

Clay smiled as best he could. "He'll have forgiven you," he said. "Worst thing that could have happened for him was to have you killed as well."

She nodded. "I reckoned the same thing."

Clay cleared his throat. He held out his hand. "My name is Clay Luckman."

She took his hand. "Bailey Redman."

Clay frowned.

"My mom and dad weren't married."

"I see," he said, "and where is she now?"

"We were just on the way back from Oro Valley. She died and we went down there to bury her."

"Hell, you ain't doing so well for good luck now, are you?"

"S'pose not."

"So you're on your own now?"

She shook her head. "I got you."

"Yes, sure, but I mean no family. No aunts and uncles, grandparents maybe?"

"Nope," she said. "No one."

"Shee-it," Clay exclaimed.

"And you?"

"Me?"

"Sure. Where's your folks?"

"Hell, I lost them a good long time ago."

"So it looks like we're in the same trouble, then."

"Seems that way."

"And those people . . . the ones that killed my dad. One of them was your brother?"

Clay nodded. "My half brother. Crazy half, it seems. The older guy was an escaped convict. He was on his way to get hanged someplace south I think and he broke out and took us with him as hostages."

"So you're on the run too?"

"Sure am. Sure they've got me all fixed up for a couple of murder charges already. Mostly they'll be looking for Earl Sheridan. That was the older one's name. They'll just be looking for him to finish what they started."

"And your brother . . . your *half brother*?"

Clay shook his head resignedly. "I think he made his choice. I think he's gone the way of the devil. What little time I had I tried to talk some sense into him, but he had his mind set on not listening."

"Why were they gonna hang the other guy?"

"I think he killed someone already. Capital offense an' all that."

Bailey tilted her head to one side. "That's something that never made sense to me," she said.

"What?"

"The death penalty. I mean, how does killing someone prove that killing people is wrong?"

"You got me there," Clay said.

"So what do we do now?"

"Well, that's what I've been thinking about. I got a handful of dollars, get us food and whatever for two days, maybe less, and then we gotta get smart."

"Where were you headed?"

"Originally I wasn't headed anyplace. This was just the direction I went in 'cause I figured the other pair would head west. Now I'm thinking we should head for somewhere called Eldorado in Texas."

"What the hell is in Eldorado?"

Clay smiled. He pulled out the advertisement and showed her. "Pretty houses with green lawns and swimming pools."

"And what the hell are we gonna do there?"

"I don't know," Clay replied. "I just feel that my brother ain't gonna go there. That's the way we were all going, and now that all this has happened I reckon they'll double back and go some other place entirely. And if my brother don't go there then Earl Sheridan ain't gonna go there neither, and the farther away from him I am the better I'll feel."

She shook her head. "I don't under—"

151

"It was somewhere we were going to go together, somewhere we always talked about. He'll figure that if the cops get me I'll tell them about how we were always going to go to Eldorado. He'll be smart enough to stay well away from it, I'm sure."

"And that's it? That's your plan?"

"Yeah, that's my plan."

"So really . . . well, really you don't have a plan?"

Clay smiled wryly. "Sister, I ain't never had a plan in my life. This is about the closest I've ever got to having to make a decision. You spend your life in places like I have . . . you get up when you're told, you eat when you're told, you work when you're told, you sleep when you're told. There ain't a single decision to make. This is a whole new world of mystery and madness for me."

"Maybe we don't have to make a decision."

"Eh?"

"Maybe we just keep on going and see what happens."

"That ain't a plan."

"Seems to me there ain't a great deal of point plannin' anythin' in this life. I planned to spend the next few years with my mom and then maybe go traveling around, maybe get a job or something, and all the while I was gonna keep on visitin' my dad in Scottsdale and get to know him properly. Now they're both dead and the only person in the world I know is you."

"I'm sorry about your mom and dad."

"What're you sorry for? You didn't have nothin' to do with it."

"You know what I mean . . . I'm sorry that something so bad as that had to happen to you."

"Yeah," Bailey said. "Me too."

"So we're gonna walk into Tucson and get some breakfast, okay?"

"Okay," she said.

Clay paused. "How old are you?" he asked.

"Fifteen years old," she said. "Sixteen in October next year."

"Right," he said.

"And how old are you?"

"I'm seventeen," he replied. "Be eighteen come next June."

"I ain't gonna have sex with you," she said.

Clay turned suddenly, his eyes wide. "What? What the hell d'you say something like that for?"

"My mom told me that men think about sex like three hundred times a day."

"Well, I don't know where the hell she got that kind of information from."

"She was a prostitute."

"She was what?"

"She was a prostitute. You think that's bad?"

Clay shook his head. He was all sixes and sevens. "I don't think nothin' about it. Don't make a blind bit of difference what she was." He hesitated. "I mean . . . er, I didn't mean that disrespectfully or nothin'. Hell, you know what I meant . . ."

She was laughing. "It's okay. I was just teasin' you."

"Well, don't. Jesus, girl, enough of that sort of talk. The idea of having sex with you didn't even cross my mind—"

"Why? You don't think I'm pretty?"

Clay took a step back. He was finding it difficult to speak.

"You wind up real fast, Clay Luckman," she said.

"Enough," he said, and wondered if there wasn't something wrong with her, something in her mind. Maybe something was broken. Maybe the sudden and unexpected deaths of both of her parents had snapped her somewhere inside and she was now all over the place and then some. Clay wondered what something like that would do to someone.

"Let's go," she said. She turned and started walking toward the doorway.

Clay followed her. He would have to watch her carefully. What he'd gotten himself into he didn't know. Out of a pan and into a fire was the phrase that came to mind.

CHAPTER NINETEEN

Back at Gila Bend the sheriff's department duly informed the federal authorities about the discovery of Wheland's car behind Gil Webster's house. By ten that morning both Nixon and Koenig had arrived at the Webster house. Laurette Tannahill was already in the hospital. She had slipped into a coma almost immediately as a result of the head trauma. Her vitals were weak, and there was no hope of her identifying anyone. Gil Webster could help them little. He gave an estimate of height and hair color, of course, but the young man's face was covered with a rag and he could not make a positive identification. They showed him a photograph of Clarence Luckman, to which he responded, "Yes, sure, it could have been him. Looks about the right age . . . similar sort of shaped face . . ."

Both Nixon and Koenig were veterans of the business. They had seen their fair share of attacks and killings. Stabbings, shootings, hangings, decapitations, drownings; they had experienced the stench of a body left to rot for days and days, had felt the instinctive gag reaction when faced with dismembered body parts, had seen the very best of people subjected to terrible things by the very worst of people, and they remained open-minded and sober. The upper bedroom of Gil Webster's house, however, seemed to possess an all-pervading melancholy the like of which neither had experienced before. It was the pattern of blood on the mattress perhaps, the shape of Laurette Tannahill's face still evident there upon it. It had ceased to be impersonal when Nixon had spoken to Laurette Tannahill's mother only the evening before.

"We are doing everything we can Mrs. Tannahill. *Everything*."

It was as good as a promise. And now that promise would be broken. They had done what they could, but not *everything*. If they had done everything then surely Laurette would be home by now?

Garth Nixon stood there for a long time. He thought of his wife, his son, his nephews, his nieces. He thought of Ronald Koenig's wife and children, people he had never met, would probably never meet, but people of whose existence he was aware. Laurette Tannahill and her parents were much the same as them. Their daughter had made it through childhood— through coughs and colds, through measles and chicken pox, through bumps and scrapes and falls and teenage crushes and first loves and school prom, and here she was—all of twenty-five years old, working in the bank—and someone had waltzed right in and snatched her away. That didn't happen to twenty-five-year-old women. It just couldn't. And then to bring her to some stranger's house, to lock him in the basement, to take her upstairs and beat her senseless? It just didn't bear considering. But it had been considered by this Clarence Luckman—not only considered, but done—and now the girl was in a coma, and they had to tell Mr. and Mrs. Tannahill that things hadn't turned out the way any of them had intended.

Luckman was working alone, it seemed, and from the absence of Gil Webster's white pickup Koenig and Nixon at least had a vehicle model and registration plate for which they could put out an alert. That alert went to Phoenix, Scottsdale, Mesa, Chandler, Glendale, Buckeye, Casa Grande, Wellton, Yuma, all the way southeast to Oracle, Oro Valley, Tucson, and Tombstone. Right now they knew nothing of his intentions. He could have headed in any direction, so all directions needed to be covered. Reproductions of the most recent pictures of Clarence Luckman, courtesy of Tom Young's staff at Hesperia, were also circulated to eleven local sheriff's departments and the federal offices in the region. Both Nixon and Koenig concurred that a dissemination of flyers or posters beyond the immediately relevant counties was not best advised at this stage. Alert a fugitive to the breadth of the search and he could go to ground. That's what they were concerned he would do. People had a way of just vanishing. Luckman had been Sheridan's accomplice, and now he had attacked and harmed in his own right. As far as this one was concerned people were expendable. No, they would continue to contain it within official parameters for a little while longer. All relevant county and federal officials would be informed, those pictures would be in the hands of all pertinent departments and units, and they would find him. Come what may, they would find him. The only questions were how rapidly, and how many lives would he take before they secured his arrest or confirmed his death.

It was as they left the Webster house that Koenig said something to Nixon that put it all in perspective.

"You want to find a boy like this, you have to think like him."

That was the kicker, the real wrench in the gut.

Clarence Luckman was a boy, not even a man, and he had done this thing.

It chilled Garth Nixon to the bone, and he was not a man to be easily unsettled.

CHAPTER TWENTY

The details of the white pickup arrived at the Tucson Sheriff's Department just before eleven that Tuesday morning. Had the call-out on the Parselle girl come a fraction later duty detective John Cassidy would have been in his office to see the report. Perhaps he would have given it some mind, perhaps not. It would only be later that the details of that vehicle and the scene he was to find in Deidre Parselle's apartment would become connected.

Cassidy was all of thirty-four, still ardent and purposeful enough to believe that right was right, wrong was wrong, and there was an identifiable division between the two. He had come into the sheriff's department in June of 1950, just three months after his twentieth birthday. He worked hard, asked questions, studied, paid attention, was sufficiently humble to believe he knew nothing until he knew something, and had been promoted to detective in August of 1962. By that time he had been married to Alice Frankenshaw for four years and three months. They had always said that when he was promoted to detective they would think about starting a family. They did more than think about it, they worked hard at it, and for the first eighteen months it seemed that a family was not something they were destined to possess.

In the spring of 1964 John drove Alice to a specialist clinic in Phoenix and she was examined and inspected and questioned and probed. They came back and told the Cassidys that there was no identifiable pathological reason that Alice could not bear children. Which begged the question, was there something wrong with John? They kept on trying, and in August of 1964, just at the point where they figured it was time for John to also be examined and inspected and questioned and probed, she caught. Neither of them could have been happier.

157

The Cassidys lived in a house on Brawley Street, a house that was bought and paid for in full. After the death of John's mother three years before he'd sold the house his parents had lived in for the best part of a quarter century. It was the house where he'd spent his teenage years, and though there was a sense of nostalgia and affinity, there was a stronger sense that it was *their* home, not his. He felt nothing when the family property was bought, nothing but the promise of a new future. He bought the Brawley house for cash, had a little left over to redecorate and modernize the kitchen, and though it was small it would serve him and Alice just fine until they decided to have a second baby. John's father, Eugene, a brusque and businesslike man even when he was in the best of moods, had passed away from cancer of the liver all of eight years earlier. He had worked for the Midwest Railroad Company for the eleven years since his release from the U.S. army at the end of the war. He had seen action in France and Belgium. That was all he ever said. He had *seen action*. The expression he wore when he said it made it clear that it was not something he wished to discuss. He had lost a brother out there, a younger brother, and there seemed a sense of hardheaded intolerance toward any non-Americans since that point. His opinion about his only son's chosen vocation was never voiced. When John graduated the police academy Eugene was there to see him. Afterward, at the small soiree his mother had arranged for close family and friends, Eugene had taken his son aside and looked at him for what seemed like an interminable time. Gripping his shoulders firmly, looking directly into his eyes as if to gauge the very heart and soul of him, he had merely smiled and nodded his head. That was the best acknowledgment his father had ever given him. It was all John could have hoped for and more. *You did okay by me*, that moment said. *You are my son, and I am proud to call you so.*

When Eugene contracted cancer and was diagnosed, he said little if anything. He resigned himself to death as a man resigns himself to going to bed. It was what it was, and it was nothing more complicated. When John's mother cried, she cried alone. She did not share her grief with her husband, and it stayed that way until the moment he closed his eyes for the very last time. He accepted no remedy save doses of morphine to ease the pain toward the end, and he expressed no wish for treatment. He was not a religious man, but he seemed to believe in the fatalistic nature of things. This was *supposed* to be, this was the way that had been chosen for him, and who was he to question some higher dictate? He passed away in the early morning of Monday, August 13, 1956.

The funeral was on the following Friday, the 17th, and Alice went with John as a courtesy. At that time they'd had known each other for little more than six months, and would not be married for the better part of another two years. They sat separately, John with the family, Alice with the family's friends, but at the wake that followed he stayed by her side and talked to almost no one but her. Perhaps he had already decided that the closeness he felt for her then would be the closeness that defined the remainder of their lives together. He knew there was no question of anyone else. He knew he would marry her. He knew she felt the same way. And once they were married, their relationship continued as if nothing had changed but the element of cohabitation. They fit. It was that simple. And they seemed to fit in all ways possible. Where he was tidy, she was clean. Where he was pragmatic, she was imaginative. Where he was relentlessly hard-working, she taught him to relax, something that he seemed incapable of doing, even at the most appropriate of times.

As John Cassidy drove out to Dee Parselle's apartment that late Tuesday morning he was aware of the fact that Alice had passed her first trimester, that all was going well, that there were no adverse indications, and that—if everything continued as predicted—he would be a father in April of the following year.

The scene he found in Deidre Parselle's apartment blanched his mind of his parents, of Alice, of the baby, of trimesters and birth classes and choosing colors for a nursery. The scene he found cleared his nostrils, raised the hairs on the back of his neck, broke a sweat beneath his hairline, and caused him to hesitate for a good forty-five seconds before he dared step into the room.

From eyewitness reports Deidre Parselle had somehow managed to crawl out of her front room and onto the walkway above the rear yard. It was here that she had collapsed, and it was here that she'd been found. An ambulance had been called, the police too, and while Deidre was rushed to the hospital an initial examination of the scene was undertaken to try and determine what nightmare had unfolded there.

It was this same scene that confronted Cassidy as he hesitated in the doorway of the apartment. The girl had been stabbed three or four times from initial reports, but it could have been more. She would make it, but she was traumatized, sedated, in and out of surgery, and saying nothing of her attacker. She seemed so far beyond rational communication that any clear description was impossible.

The quantity of blood on the carpet surprised Cassidy. There was also a kitchen knife—heavy, bloodstained and damning. Cassidy got as close to it as he could, used his ballpoint pen to turn it slightly, to tilt it gently against the light. The blade was thick with clots, but there seemed to be no evidence of any clear print. He also noted that the telephone cable had been pulled from the wall, and the telephone itself was on the kitchen floor. The assailant had presumably done this upon entering the apartment as a precautionary measure. He kneeled back on his haunches and stayed immobile for a while. Uniforms were in the doorway, one of them on the walkway outside the front door to ensure that unauthorized persons did not enter and compromise the integrity of the crime scene, and Cassidy took the time to just look, to perceive, to absorb and try to understand what was there in front of him. Psychology fascinated him. Psychology had been afforded no significant place in criminal detection, but the rationale and mentality and perspective of the perpetrator seemed to him all-important. Perhaps one day they would start to consider such things, but at the moment he was limited to what he could see with his eyes, what he could touch with his hands, the answers he received with his ears. Beyond that it was all suspicion, supposition, and superstition. Oddly enough, it was only Alice who listened to him with interest when he spoke of such things. Alice—all of five two, a hundred and ten pounds, petite and demure and delicate, and yet possessive of a stronger mind and stronger stomach than most of the veteran police officers he knew—believed her husband when he expressed his opinions, that someday soon the method of investigation would shift in a completely different direction, that they would start to spend money at federal level to investigate the motives and

160

methods and viewpoints of hardened criminals. There was a reason for the crimes. There was *always* a reason. If they could understand and appreciate where that reasoning came from, well, then there might be a way to predict and prevent such things happening.

But for now it was simply the facts: the probative physical evidence, the fingerprints, the eyewitness statements, the girl in the hospital.

Cassidy shared a few words with the uniforms who had responded to the call-out.

The call had come in at 10:31, a call from the girl's landlady. Rent collection day was always the last Friday of the month, in this case the 27th, but the landlady—Rena Fitzgerald—was planning a few days away with her sister in Prescott, and had called Deidre on the previous Saturday afternoon and arranged to collect the rent that morning. Hence she had come over, and thus she had found the girl on the walkway. Why had the arrangement been made for a Tuesday morning? Wouldn't Deidre have been at work? A call to the orthodontist's office verified that Deidre had taken a day off. Did this have anything to do with the time of her attack? Had her assailant been aware of her taking a day off, and had planned the attack in such a way as she would not be missed until the Wednesday morning when she failed to show for work? No one could verify that save the assailant himself, and if that was the case then he must have known her. The first line of investigation would be to question the landlady, determine whether she had touched or moved anything in the apartment. Subsequently he would question Deidre's colleagues, anyone who might have known her professionally, anyone who might have had access to employee information at her place of work. Next would be her friends, and beyond that he would pursue any line of inquiry regarding social gatherings, recent events she had attended, any clubs, groups, hobby circles or church congregations she belonged to. This was an attempted murder, no question. If the girl died, well, it would be his third homicide investigation. The first had been the strangling of a wife by a jealous husband, only for the husband to find out that the wife had never been unfaithful. The second was a heartbreaker. A young girl, all of eight years old, caught between an abusive father and an alcoholic mother. The mother wanted to leave, the father wanted to prevent her. The mother wanted to take the girl. The father wished to deny her. To solve the problem he killed the child. Shot her dead while she slept. Then he took an overdose of sleeping tablets and drank a fifth of whiskey. He neither took enough pills nor drank enough liquor, and he woke up a day and a half later in a police cell. That had been a year before, and he was up in the penitentiary at Flagstaff awaiting the result of his second appeal against the death penalty. His appeal wouldn't wash. He would go to the chair. It was just a question of how long he could get the state to prevaricate.

In Cassidy's view, the attack upon Deidre Parselle was the most important case of his career to date. His rationale was simple. The first two murders had been murders, of course, but they had been emotional killings, crimes of passion. Jealousy, envy, revenge, whatever the feeling behind the action had been, they had not been planned and premeditated for pleasure. The attack on the Parselle girl, the fact that she had been stabbed, left for dead in her own apartment, indicated something else entirely. This *had* been for some other reason. There were no signs of rape or sexual molestation, so what possible motive could someone have had? Pleasure perhaps? At least whatever degree of sick pleasure such an attack would engender in the perpetrator. And then there was the stabbing itself. The perpetrator had not cut her throat. He had not stabbed her once through the heart. He had stabbed her in the breasts and the shoulder. Symbolic of womanhood, motherhood, the womb and the breasts. The growth and care of children. Had he stabbed her with the intent to deny her children? Was this a psychological attack as well as physical? There had been rage, but a controlled and channeled rage. There had been anger, but the anger appeared focused and concise. There was a method to his madness, a motivation to it, a reasoning behind why he had done this thing. That, and that alone—once identified—could narrow the number of persons they would be looking for. Cassidy believed this, believed it with conviction, and he made notes while he was there in the apartment so he would not forget his train of thought while present at the scene. The fundamental truth was the Deidre Parselle attack excited him—cerebrally, almost physiologically. There was a rush of excitement in his lower gut, the sense that here he had found something to challenge his preconceptions about the nature of the criminal mind. He would speak of it later with Alice, and though he could never divulge the specific details of the crime scene, though he could never share the results of his interviews and inquiries, he could give her the general gist of the thing, the way it felt, the way it appeared to be going, and she would play devil's advocate and challenge his assumptions every step of the way. Intuitively, he felt this case was important, and he believed that something important would come of it.

The Pima County medical examiner arrived shortly before noon. With him came a freelance photographer who was employed on contract to the police department for such work. Fifty-three years old, hardened and cynical and world-weary, he nevertheless visibly paled as Cassidy explained what had happened.

"Just when you think you've seen the very worst, someone comes along and tries a little harder," he said. His flashgun popped and the scene was caught in a flash of brilliant luminosity. Almost monochrome in its starkness, Cassidy was momentarily startled by the unnaturalness of the scenario. He knew that once the carpet was replaced, once the blood spatter was cleaned up and the walls repainted, it would be no one but Deidre who would remember what had really happened here. And, in time, even those memories would fade. Perhaps.

Cassidy stood on the walkway for a moment, and then he made his way down to the car. He suspected that the knife would give no prints, that it had been wiped clean, and if it did they would be partial and smudged and inconclusive. This was the way of such things. This was where such investigations began—with too little information, too few facts, and in truth it was where most of such investigations also ended.

John Cassidy did not hold out a great deal of hope for the identification and arrest of Deidre Parselle's attacker, but he was going to do his utmost. Not just for her, but for all of the victims who wound up with no one to give a damn.

CHAPTER TWENTY-ONE

Elliott Danziger stood before the mirror in the clothing store and looked at himself. Tan-colored chinos, a blue button-down shirt, a leather jacket, brown boots. He looked like a ranch hand with money, a famous rodeo star home for the weekend. The store clerk told him he looked a little like James Dean. Elliott figured the guy for a homo maybe, and he didn't respond.

He paid the money and left the store, found a diner on Bayard Street and sat in a booth by the window and looked at girls while he ate his lunch. After leaving the woman's apartment the night before, he'd found a rough boarding house at the edge of the suburb. He went in, paid for one night, shut himself in the room, and washed the blood off his jeans. Then he sat on the edge of the bed and cried. He didn't know why he was crying. He did not feel sorry for what he had done. He did not feel guilty. In considering it, he perhaps felt a degree of shame. He wondered what he would say to her if he ever met her again. Would he tell her *Sorry*? He didn't think so. He didn't know what he would say. He thought about what he had done and then he tried to focus on the girl, but his mind drifted toward the knife and the stabbing and the blood, and it was in those moments that he felt most aroused and excited. Afterward he wondered if such thoughts made him a crazy person. He didn't think so.

His jeans were still damp when he put them on in the morning, but it didn't matter. He walked around for a while, had some breakfast, bought himself the new duds, and threw the old clothes away. He still had upwards of six hundred and fifty dollars in cash. Now he needed a car. Buying one was out of the question. A few bucks for some new clothes was acceptable, but a car? Secondly, he had no driver's license, and it didn't matter how much money he had, without a license he wasn't getting a legit car, simple as that.

There was no hurry. He could enjoy a little of Tucson. The girls sure were pretty enough to start a prison riot, and the thing that had happened the night before had given him a taste for a little excitement.

He stayed there in the diner for a while, seated in the booth, the pressure of Sheriff Wheland's gun in the back of his waistband and beneath his jacket, the feeling of money in his pockets, and a dull ache in his groin every time he saw a pretty one go by the window. Some of them glanced his way, and every once in a while he'd get a smile in return.

After a while he went to the restroom. He sat in a stall for a while, just sat there on the seat, and he thought about stuff. Then he went out, and even though he had not taken a piss or anything, he still washed his hands. Cleanliness was next to godliness an' all that jazz.

He looked at his reflection in the mirror above the sink.

He tried to smile, but for some reason he could not. Smiling just seemed to hurt the muscles in his face.

In the mirror he saw the man he would become. He did not see the boy he was.

In his eyes he saw depth and character. He saw self-possession and the grim determination to survive that had carried him thus far, a determination he believed would carry him all the way. Where it would take him, well, it didn't matter. He did not have to choose now. He did not have to ever choose. He was alone, and yet never lonely. He could have company whenever he wished. He could have any company he chose.

Elliott knew he was special. He'd known this from the first day he'd ever conceived a self-aware thought. He knew he was important, that there was a reason for his existence. These things, these recent diversions, were not his purpose. They were merely things with which to occupy himself while he waited for the clarity that he knew would come. Where it would come from, perhaps more important, *who* it would come from, he did not know. It would not be God. God was a weak man's answer to a weak man's problems. No, the clarity would not come from God. There had been a point where he believed the clarity would come from the spirit of Earl Sheridan, but so far Earl had kept himself to himself.

Everything that had happened thus far had been a trial. He had been found wanting, but he had persisted, and through persistence he had found his inner strength, and now he was not afraid to hit back, to take what he wanted any which way he wanted it. That was what life was all about. If you didn't take it, well, someone else would. Earl had known that. Hell, he'd known that himself even before he met Earl. It had just taken some real-life situations to bring that awareness into reality.

Digger looked at his own reflection and he tried to remember something his ma might have told him about his father. Anything at all. Good, bad, important, irrelevant—anything at all. There was very little *to* remember, and he struggled for a while. He believed that once he located one thing then others would follow.

He remembered a dog. The sound of a dog barking. He remembered the smell of dirty bodies. He remembered the smell of sweat and liquor and the taste of something salty in his mouth. He remembered being hungry. Oh, how he remembered that! He remembered holding a bird in his hands, and holding it so tight it stopped moving and how he put it in a box and hid the box somewhere. He couldn't remember where he hid the box, or what the box looked like. He could not now even remember the feel of the bird as it had tried to escape from his hands.

He remembered the sound of his mother's voice. He remembered her going away one time. He remembered how she looked when she returned. He remembered the last time he saw her alive, and then the time he thought she was alive and she was not. He remembered when Evelyn came, and how he knew—even at that age—that something had happened that was *a bad thing*. The first of many *bad things*. He remembered the policeman. He remembered the man who came in the car with a stretcher, and the way they carried her out of the house and how her arm suddenly appeared from the edge of the stretcher, her hand hanging down, and how they didn't see that her hand was banging against everything as they made their way out of the house with her. He remembered someone laughing, and someone smoking a cigarette, and someone asking if he was hungry. He remembered crying.

And then there was nothing for a long time.

After that he remembered the first home, and then the second, and how scared he felt for so long, and how the only person in the world he knew was Clarence.

He remembered corridors and dormitories and other boys and people who shouted, and always the heavy footfall of unnamed people who meant him harm.

And then the talking. Endless talking. People with flat, gray eyes talking forever and ever and ever about things that meant nothing. "Why this, Elliott? Why that, Elliott? Why the other, Elliott? Elliott. Elliott. Elliott. Why are you so violent? Why are you so bad? "

"Because I want to be," he said. "Because I fucking want to be, okay? I don't need any other kinda reason. I fucking well want to. Now fuck off and leave me alone."

But such an answer didn't seem answer enough. And so on and on they went with the questions.

A Mormon came. He was a tall man with white hair and he wore glasses. He said that if Elliott didn't *curb his ways* and *come to the Lord* then he would wind up in hell.

I think I'm there already, Elliott said.

The Mormon smiled and shook his head. "You have no idea, child. You have not the slightest idea of what awaits you if you don't turn your face to the Lord and pray for his forgiveness, and ask for him to come into your heart and bless you with the peace that is His love."

"Is that so?" Elliott asked.

"It is," the man said. And then he went on to say that there were sins that could be atoned for by an offering on an altar . . . and then there were sins that the blood of a lamb, or of a calf, or of a turtle dove, could not remit. And he said that sins such as those must be atoned for by the blood of a man. If Elliott went on doing these terrible things, and thinking these terrible thoughts, then it would be his blood that would be taken. He would find himself carrying a sentence of death over his head, not only in this life, but in the life ever after.

"Go fuck yourself with your life ever after," Elliott said, and the

167

man fell quiet and then he seemed to cry, and then he left the room and Elliott never saw him again.

And after that they stopped asking questions, as if they'd decided that Elliott Danziger was too powerful to break. Whatever mold might have been used, whatever material he might have been cast from, they possessed nothing with the strength to break it. That was the simple and incontrovertible truth. Elliott Danziger was tougher than all of them combined, and—if he had needed it, which he didn't—there was all the proof you would ever need that he had been made for better things.

For a while there was nothing of significance. He hurt a boy one time. He was a bigger boy and he tried to fuck Elliott in the ass. Elliott said he would rather suck his dick. The boy said okay, and when the boy put his thing in Elliott's mouth Elliott bit it so hard it almost came off. For that they put him in a room by himself and left him there for six weeks. He never told Clarence why he was in solitary. He never said a word about that. They put his food through a slot low down in the door. He didn't see sunshine or breathe fresh air the whole time. When he came out he had to see a man called Lansford. He remembered Lansford's name because Lansford made him repeat it several times, and he made him say "Yes, Mr. Lansford, sir" every time Lansford told him something.

"You are a bad person. Through and through to the very core of you, you are a bad person."

"Yes, Mr. Lansford, sir."

"I do not see that you will ever be free from some sort of institution, Danziger. I think you will see walls and bars for the rest of your life and when your life is over, probably because we will execute you, then you will go to hell and burn forever for your sins."

"Yes, Mr. Lansford, sir."

"I know that you think I am a fool. I know that you think you're better than all of us. I know that you believe yourself smarter and more capable, and you think you have all the answers to everything that needs an answer . . . but let me tell you, and this I want you to hear good and proper. You are an evil child. You are an evil, evil, wicked, destructive child. Your mind is poisoned and perverse. You are sick and cruel and desperately insane, and there is no cure for the likes of you. You are mentally disturbed and there is some sick disease in your brain, and there is nothing that can mend how broken you are."

"Yes, Mr. Lansford, sir."

"See, even now you are smiling at me. Even now you think this is a joke. You take that dirty little smile off your face."

"Yes, Mr. Lansford, sir."

"I said take that dirty little smile off your face, Danziger! Get rid of that smile right now!"

"Yes, Mr. Lansford, sir," he said, but apparently that wasn't good enough because Lansford started beating him then, and Elliott took the beating and he never said a word, and he never averted his gaze from Mr. Lansford, and he never stopped smiling.

And when Lansford was done—sweating, breathless, still angry but too exhausted to hit Elliott any more—he stood over Elliott and said, "So boy, what do you have to say to me now?"

And Elliott, still smiling his dirty little smile, said, "Go fuck yourself, Mr. Lansford, sir."

Lansford kicked him then and broke one of his ribs, but it was worth it.

After Lansford they left him to himself. He stayed out of the way, kept his head down, didn't get involved in conversations or arguments or fights. He just stayed with Clarence. He needed to look after Clarence. He needed to make sure that no one did anything to hurt Clarence. He didn't make friends. He didn't make enemies. Sometimes he had people he took a shine to, people he figured thought the same way he did. Most often they didn't. He tried to tell them a few truths, a few of the real facts about life, but most often they were too dumb to listen and appreciate the value of what he was telling them.

And then he met Earl Sheridan, and Earl understood. Earl knew exactly the kind of thing that Digger was talking about.

And as soon as he met Earl, well, Clay showed his true colors. He turned like the worm that he was. He became just the same as everyone else. Cocksucker. Motherfucker. Son of a bitch.

But Earl knew the deal, the real deal, the whole deal. Such a guy! A real man. A hero. And those assholes in Wellton had to gun him down! Motherfuckers! What he was doing now had to be some sort of retribution for that. What he was doing now sort of helped to rectify the balance. He was doing these things for himself, but he was also doing them for Earl. Earl Sheridan. Even his name sounded like something for a king!

And these motherfuckers, liars and betrayers and sons of bitches . . . with their stupid fucking smiles and trying to make him think that everything was fine, everything was all right, everything was going to be okay if he just trusted them . . .

Pleading and crying and sobbing like a fucking baby, goddammit he was mad!

Elliott stepped back from the mirror. He realized there were tears in his eyes.

He raised his hand—suddenly, almost surprising himself—and he slapped himself hard across the face. As hard as he could. For a second he felt nothing, and then the pain came, and his cheek reddened violently, and he could see the impression of his own fingers.

He stood there for some seconds, eyes closed, holding his breath, and just waited until the sensation subsided. Then, glancing once more at his own reflection, Elliott left the restroom.

As John Cassidy drove away from the yard beneath Deidre Parselle's window, Elliott put two quarters on the table and left the Bayard Street diner. He headed back the way he'd come, back toward the girl's apartment, but before he reached the corner he turned left down Holbrook and went looking for a car.

CHAPTER TWENTY-TWO

As overwhelmed by Tucson as Digger might have been, Clay was more so. It was the number of people that shocked him. Bailey had seen Scottsdale and Mesa, even Phoenix. She had taken the bus back and forth many times and spoken to strangers on numerous occasions. Compared to Clay Luckman, Bailey Redman was worldly and experienced. Turning the first corner as they came out of the suburbs they were besieged by a crowd of church folk. They were handing out leaflets and religious tracts and pennants and button badges saying *Jesus Is Love* and *I Am the Way, the Truth, and the Life*, and their mouths were full of words and smiles, yet their eyes were flat and dull and doubtful. Bailey grabbed Clay's arm and pulled him off the sidewalk. She hurried him across the road out of the melee, and he let her pull him because he felt awkward and naive and uncertain about where he was going.

Around the corner, on a stoop ahead of a tall house, a man waved both hands like a guilty politician, and he shouted something about the mayor and the republicans and a need for change at all levels of government. Watching him was a whole mess of dirty kids, tougher-looking than most adults. Clay paused. Bailey pulled him again and they were hurrying away.

"Where does this road go?" he asked.

"Goes to wherever it gets and every place on the way," she said, and she laughed at him and he felt like a little kid.

Where the road went was the center of Tucson, and here they slowed down and she gave him a little time to absorb what he was seeing. Storefronts and street signs and advertising hoardings and newspaper vendors and lemonade stands and cars going this way and that at a hundred miles an hour. He felt as if the wind had been knocked out of him. He felt as if Shoeshine had given him a good kick in the seat of his pants and he'd landed in the future.

Jesus Christ, he kept thinking. *Jesus Christ. Jesus Christ Almighty.*

"Come on," Bailey said, and she took his hand once more and they were walking again. Left, right, left, right, he couldn't see where she was taking him, and he soon forgot what was left behind them. There was too much to see, too much to hear, far too much to take in.

Unaware that Earl Sheridan was already dead, Clay Luckman would have been even more surprised to know that Digger was right there in Tucson as well, just about finishing up his lunch in a diner on Bayard Street, not five blocks from where he stood. Digger's intent now was to cross out of Arizona and get into New Mexico. Once out of the state he could make his way to Texas more easily. He knew they would find the sheriff's car behind the house near Gila Bend, that now he would be a fugitive just like Earl Sheridan. What he didn't know was that the federal authorities actually believed him dead, that they were even now looking for someone called Clarence Luckman. That would have humored Digger. That would have put a smile on his face as wide as the Mississippi.

It would be an hour before Gil Webster's white pickup was discovered abandoned in a street in Tucson, another two hours before Garth Nixon and Ronald Koenig were informed of the discovery. They wouldn't arrive in the city until late that afternoon, and by then the Tucson Police Department had been apprised of the identity of Clarence Luckman, that he was armed and dangerous, that he was sociopathic and potentially homicidal and more than likely planning to attack again. These were all parts of a jigsaw, and the pieces had yet to align. They would, but they needed time. Late that evening, when the pieces were drawing close, John Cassidy would resolve in his own mind that there was no connection between Deidre Parselle's booking a day off work and her subsequent stabbing. He had questioned her work colleagues, the few friends she had in the city, and they'd all expressed the same reaction. A wide-eyed and disbelieving shock. Her parents were inconsolable, and this was something Cassidy could appreciate. The shock attendant to such an event was easily understood. Save the police themselves, the county coroner, the

172

medical examiner, there were few people who ever experienced such brutality. Homicides, even attempted homicides, were rare enough in Tucson City. Cassidy hoped that such crimes would remain a rare and unusual phenomena, but he believed that they would not. Ever attempting to maintain an optimistic slant on things, he could not help but be aware of the fact that the social order was slipping. By inches, yes, but it was slipping. Coincident with the assassination of Kennedy the year before, there seemed to be a brashness and superficiality appearing in society. Television was consuming people's lives. The quality of things seemed to be deteriorating. People had less time for others. Perhaps it was his imagination, perhaps not. If the brutal assault that had been perpetrated against Deidre Parselle was anything to go by, well, he could see the direction in which things were headed. It was not good, not good at all. Made him wonder whether the world he was bringing a child into was really a world he would wish on anyone.

So it was that FBI Agents Garth Nixon and Ronald Koenig, also Elliott Danziger, Tucson PD detective John Cassidy, the parents and friends of Deidre Parselle, Gil and Marilyn Webster, the widow of Harvey Warren from the Marana Convenience Store & Gas Station, the staff of the Yuma County Trust & Savings Bank in Wellton, Laurette Tannahill amongst them, even those who discovered the body of Bethany Olson in the diner outside of Twentynine Palms, were all drawn into the drama as if attached by the fine threads of some unseen web. Had Earl Sheridan not plunged a boning knife through the heart of Katherine Aronson, had she in fact pressed charges against him for the earlier assault and beating he had given her, things might have turned out different. But they had not.

Clay Luckman and Bailey Redman arrived in Tucson in the early afternoon of Tuesday, November 24, 1964, and they found pictures of John F. Kennedy still hanging in stores and diners, a black ribbon tied across them. Only two days had elapsed since the first anniversary of his murder, and there had been memorials and words in church, and the mayor had made a statement to the press about his immeasurable sadness, a sadness he now carried with him each and every day of his public and personal life.

Bailey Redman, both perplexed and amused by Clay Luckman's seeming naïveté of the world at large, merely steered him into a diner and sat him in a corner booth, saying, "Now we're going to have lunch," aware then that she was feeling that sadness herself, but not for Kennedy. The sadness she felt was for her father, before that her mother, and it seemed that she was so tangled up with emotions she didn't know what to feel or how to express it. She had cried at the side of the road. She remembered that. She had tried to sob her broken heart out, but her heart was still broken. Perhaps it would come back again—a wave of overwhelming grief, and she would begin to reconcile herself to what had happened. Somehow she doubted it. Somehow she figured that these events would take a lifetime to recover from, and even then the recovery would be incomplete.

Bailey ordered for them both. Hash browns, sausage, gravy, malted milk. Before the food came Clay got up, said he was going out for cigarettes. He returned with a pack of Lucky Strikes, one of them lit already and in the corner of his mouth.

The food came and they ate in silence. When he paid the check he was reminded of how much money they didn't have. There was very little like the weight of empty pockets.

He held out the few dollar bills and the collection of change. "This is something we have to do something about," he said.

"We do," she replied, and yet neither of them offered an idea of what that something might have been.

They left the diner just as Elliott Danziger decided on a dark gray Ford Galaxie parked behind a house on Montrose. The keys would be in the house or in the car. Either which way he was getting them, and then it was goodbye, Arizona. He instinctively touched the butt of the revolver through his jacket and made his way to the rear yard gate.

CHAPTER TWENTY-THREE

As bad luck would have it, the owner of the Ford Galaxie on Montrose Street lived alone. His name was Walter Milford, and he too had been born under a dark star. He was fifty-eight years of age, had served his country in Salerno, running into battle with his comrades as part of Operation Avalanche, and then amidst the ranks of allies as they fought for Monte Cassino. Invalided at the end of the war as a result of deteriorative blindness and a serious leg wound, Walter Milford walked with some difficulty even now, the better part of twenty years later. He often woke with an ache the size of Tennessee, used a heavy cane when he walked, and the discomfort he suffered set his tone at resentful and varied little across the dial. His eyesight, having grown ever worse year by year, was now at the stage where he saw shapes and shadows, little more, and the car that he'd once driven was little more than an ornament. It was maintained solely for the periodic visits that Walter's son made—Thanksgiving, Christmas, sometimes Easter—and he would drive Walter out to a restaurant and Walter would listen patiently as his son detailed the trials and tribulations of his advertising firm. Walter's pension provided him with a quality of life that left a great deal to be desired.

The young man that knocked on the back door of the house that Tuesday afternoon merely gave him further cause for bitterness.

"I was wonderin', sir, if you had a jug of water. My car seems to be overheated—"

"The hell you think this is, a goddamned garage?" Walter replied.

Digger smiled apologetically. "Don't see as there's any excuse to be discourteous, mister," he replied.

"Don't give a damn what you do or do not think," Walter said, "and I'd be more than pleased if you'd get off my goddamned property right now." He got up out of his chair, used the cane to lever himself to a standing position, and he stood there glaring at the teenager.

Digger withdrew the gun from the waistband of his pants. There was no reaction on Walter's face. Digger was surprised. He did not appreciate the fact that the lack of reaction was occasioned by Walter's inability to see the weapon.

"Got a gun here, you old fucker," Digger said.

"Why, you little asshole—"

"Fuck you, old man."

"You two-bit no-good son of a bitch. What the hell do you want? You've come here to rob me? Is that it?" Walter took a single step forward.

Digger came through the screen, through the open inner door, and he stood there in the hallway. They were now little more than twelve feet apart. Digger had the gun down by his side. He possessed the advantage. The old man was scared shitless. He could tell by the flicker in his eyes.

The feel of the gun in his hand gave Digger such calmness. He felt high. He felt elated. He felt as if his whole being had been touched by the hand of God.

"To rob you?" Digger said. "Don't see as how you got anything worth robbin'."

"So what you here for? You've come to kill me?"

"Maybe."

Walter sneered contemptuously. "You don't scare me, you little punk. You think I'm frightened by a sawed-off little punk like you—"

Digger smiled inside. He raised the gun and aimed it squarely at Walter's chest. "I think you're gonna pee your pants, old man," he said. There was a derisive and condescending tone in his voice. He wanted the old man to say he was scared. He wanted the old man to admit that he was terrified.

And whatever Walter Milford might have felt, he was damned if he was going to show some darn fool teenager with a pistol he was frightened. He'd faced Nazis in Germany, fascists in Italy. He'd been in bar brawls with American sailors. He'd chased down a purse snatcher one time in San Diego and given him the kicking of his life. He wasn't going to be threatened by this . . .

"Where are the keys to the car?" Digger asked. He held the gun steady. Strange, but it didn't seem to weigh anything at all.

"You go burn in hell," Walter said. A red rag to a bull.

Digger smiled. He took two steps forward. If he fired now the force of the bullet would knock Walter Milford clean on his ass.

"Give. Me. The. Keys. To. The. Car."

Walter smiled back. "Go. Burn. In. Hell."

Digger came at him, but Walter was quick. With his heavy cane he swung upward and caught Digger's forearm from the underside. The gun went flying across the room, hitting the mirror above the mantel and cracking it from corner to corner.

The pain was considerable, but Digger was so enraged he simply lashed out sideways with his clenched fist. That fist caught the right side of Walter's face, broke a couple of teeth, and Walter staggered but did not fall. Digger went for the gun, retrieved it, aimed it once more. Walter raised the cane again, and this time he brought it down on Digger's left shoulder. It was more the weight of the cane than the force with which it was delivered, but the shock and impact was sufficient to catch Digger off guard and bring him to his knees. Digger lost his grip on the gun a second time and it clattered away and hit the baseboard. It was then that the dark star over Walter Milford came into its own. Raising the cane high above his head, a moment away from bringing the full force of it down on Digger's head, Walter was stopped dead by an excruciating pain in his chest. His heart cramped viciously, and he let out a howl of anguish. His grip on the cane was relinquished involuntarily, and he dropped it. Digger was up on his feet, running across the room to get the gun. He thought to shoot the old man as he knelt there on the ground, both hands on his chest, his face a mask of agony as he gasped for air. He hesitated for a moment, and then made a move for the kitchen.

Walter Milford lashed out with his left arm and caught Digger sideways. Digger fell awkwardly, jarred his elbow against the arm of a wooden chair. He howled in pain, and even as he struggled to get to his feet Walter was lashing out again.

"Jesus fucking Christ, old man!" he shouted. "Give it a fucking rest!"

Digger swung his arm out and his fist connected with Walter's shoulder, but Walter didn't go down. He was right there on his feet, cane in his hand.

Digger held the gun steady, aimed right at Walter's head. "You back off, old man, or I'm gonna shoot you right where you stand."

"Ha!" Walter snorted, and he pulled his arm back as if to bring that cane down on Digger's head with every ounce of strength remaining.

Digger was fast. He was younger and stronger and his blood was up. He just lunged forward and punched Walter Milford in the chest. Walter's breath was knocked right out of him. He dropped the cane and fell backward. The side of his head caught the edge of a low table. He was unconscious before he hit the ground.

Digger caught his breath. He stood there, gun in his hand. There was a bright and shining light in his eyes, and his heart was racing, and his stomach was churning, and he felt the singular and unmistakable pressure of the moment in every ounce of his being.

He didn't take a moment to consider the fact that he'd nearly had his ass kicked by a blind man.

"Fuck you," he said, and he felt brave and bold and powerful.

He stood there until his heart slowed down, until the pulse in his temples and his neck returned to normal.

But he hadn't gotten his ass kicked. He'd beaten the old bastard into submission, and now he could just shoot him in the head for his trouble. He had the power of life and death. He had total power over the old man. He could kill him, or let him live.

Digger took a step back and looked at the gun in his hand.

There was nothing like it in the world. There *could* never be anything like this in the world. This was God's work. This was the devil's work. This was not religion, it was better than that. This was an epiphany, an exorcism, a channeling of such force that his mind and body could barely contain it. Whatever it was that he experienced in such moments was the most important thing in the world. The most important thing a human being could *ever* experience. Earl had been right all along.

And now the old man was unconscious, and there was no hurry. He could get himself together. He could wash up, find some new clothes, look for any money the old guy might have.

A handful of minutes later Digger was upstairs in the bathroom stripped to the waist. His blue shirt was on the floor, his face and neck and hands and arms were scrubbed clean. He had wiped down his leather jacket, found a clean shirt amongst the old man's things, and he was ready to go.

Downstairs once more, Digger checked to see if the old man was still breathing, and left him lying right there on the floor while he searched for the keys to the Galaxie. He found them in a dish on the countertop in the kitchen. He went through cupboards and drawers, located Walter's "emergency fund"—a bundle of ones and fives and tens tied together with a piece of string, tucked right there in the back of the cutlery drawer. He counted out thirty-seven dollars, stuffed the notes in his jeans pocket and went back to the front.

Before he left Digger looked around the lower floor of the house until he found the basement door. A light cord inside the doorway illuminated a flight of stairs. He descended slowly, felt the chill of the darkness and damp, established that there was little down there but old clay jugs, water pitchers, a trunk full of military clothing with a box of medals on top, work boots with the laces tied together, a couple of old canvas sacks that smelled of mold, a broken ladder, an empty tea crate. Back upstairs he got a good grip on the cuffs of Walter's pants, and he dragged him to the basement door. He got his arms under Walter's shoulders and made his way down one riser at a time. The old man wasn't so heavy, and he laid him down on the basement floor. He was still unconscious, still breathing, but he sure as hell was going to wake up with a sore head. He looked down at Walter Milford on the floor below. He felt nothing at all.

"Scared now, little man?" he said. His voice was measured and peaceful. "Are you? Just a little bit? Just a little unnerved by today's experience?"

He enjoyed the silence that came in return.

Then he took the gun from the waistband of his jeans, and—holding it steady—he aimed it at Walter's head. "Bang," he said, and smiled.

He put the gun back in his chinos.

He closed and locked the door soundlessly, and made his way out to the car.

CHAPTER TWENTY-FOUR

John Cassidy, en route from one appointment to another, stopped off at home at approximately quarter past four that afternoon. He had spent the afternoon speaking to Deidre Parselle's parents, her work colleagues, her friends, with an air of sadness about him that reminded him more of the loss of his mother than his father. Alice called it his *shadow*. She said she could sense it when it was there. She said that it was as obvious as daylight and sunshine, and yet only she could perceive it. The *shadow* was what made him question all things. The *shadow* was the thing that made him a cop, made him a detective, made him seemingly more interested in the dead than the living. Aside from her, of course. Her and the baby.

She saw the shadow around him as he came across the backyard and in through the kitchen door.

"What happened?" was her first question, and before he had a chance to respond she added, "Who died?"

John smiled. He held out his hands and she stepped toward him. He held her for a few moments, or rather *she* held him, because she knew at times like this she was an anchor for him, a reminder that there was light and life in between the darkness and dying.

"A young woman was attacked," he said. He did not say her name. Protocol prevented divulgence of specifics. He could tell her that someone died, but not their identity.

"Murdered?" Alice asked.

"No, not murdered, but she was attacked very brutally." John sat down at the kitchen table. "You have some coffee on the go?"

She shook her head. "You know I don't drink it anymore. I'll make some—"

"It's okay," he replied. "I have to go soon anyway."

"I'll make some," she repeated. "You'll stay long enough to have a cup of coffee."

She busied herself in silence. She asked no more questions. He would speak when he was ready.

"It was a sex attack, I think," was his opener. "He didn't rape her, but he stabbed her in the breasts . . ."

Alice didn't turn. Cassidy *felt* her close her eyes for a moment and withdraw inside.

"In her home or elsewhere?"

"In her home."

"So there's a reasonable chance he knew her."

John shook his head. "I don't think so. I think if he knew her he would have made sure she was dead. I've heard of enough killings of enough spurned lovers to know that often there's just a single wound. The throat is cut. A knife through the heart. A single gunshot to the head. Almost as if they want to make it as swift and definite as possible."

"Was the house broken into?"

"It was an apartment, up a stairwell and along a sort of balcony. It was above a hardware store." He paused. "And no, I don't think he broke in. There was a bag of groceries on the kitchen counter. I think he followed her home."

Alice Cassidy stopped what she was doing. "Peridot Street?"

John looked at her. His expression confirmed the question.

"Was it the orthodontist's receptionist? That girl?"

John didn't say a word.

"Christ Almighty, John, I've spoken to her." Alice crossed from the stove to the table and sat down facing him. "I was making inquiries about getting a new orthodontist. You know, after you had that trouble with the abscess and everything, and I went there. I had to wait a while to see him, and I just got talking to her. Pretty girl, early twenties, dark hair, and she said she lived above the hardware store on Peridot Street."

Again John didn't speak, which were all the words Alice needed.

She shook her head slowly, resignedly. "Lord Almighty," she said as she rose from the chair. "What on earth is this world coming to?"

A half hour later John Cassidy left with those words echoing in his head. *What on earth is this world coming to?*

He did not need to tell Alice to say nothing about the girl who lived above the hardware store on Peridot Street. She took what he did very seriously, and a breach of confidentiality between them would have been a mortal sin in her eyes. She watched him go, and she didn't want him to, but he'd told her he had to interview more of the girl's friends. The longer he left it, the less would be remembered. He said he would try and be back by seven. She knew well enough that she couldn't expect him until she saw him.

Instinctively she checked the front door and the back. She knew it was foolish, that whoever had done this thing was more than likely three hundred miles away by now, but she felt that crawling sense of unease that always arrived with bad news. She did not understand how fine the thread was that attached her to these things, but she appreciated that the thread was there. The same thread that now drew Ronald Koenig and Garth Nixon in from Gila Bend to look at Gil Webster's abandoned pickup, the same thread that was now stretched over two hundred miles southeast as Elliott Danziger started to feel hungry on the I-10 between Lordsburg and Deming. He had left Arizona behind, was now a good sixty miles into New Mexico, and he had decided to stop at the next diner he saw, wherever that might be along this road.

Clay Luckman and Bailey Redman, however, were ready to be involved in an altogether different kind of trouble, and that trouble had started when Bailey saw an advertisement for an open-air drive-in theater showing a horror picture that very evening.

She'd looked at that poster for a little while, and then—with a mischievous smile playing around her lips—she had said, "I have an idea."

CHAPTER TWENTY-FIVE

There was enough blue left in the sky to make a sailor's suit. It was close to six, the sun was down all but remnants, and they lay in the long grass on a bluff that overlooked the drive-in. The screen was the end wall of a vast warehouse facility. Brick-built, it had to be sixty feet high and forty feet across. The wall had been painted white, a black border had been applied to all four edges, and from a distance it looked like the frame for a missing photograph. The drive-in was nothing more than a fenced area, an entrance to the right, an exit to the left, and enough open expanse to cater to a good three or four hundred cars. The really important thing was the diner.

Established in 1936, owned by the same family for twenty-eight years, the Lunch Box was now a thriving little business lorded over by Jack Levine and his sister, Martha. Jack was close on sixty now, his sister five years younger. Jack had never married, considered women more ornament than use, save when he got the urge, and then he found a good deal of use for a couple of forty-something widows he knew, one in Sells, one in Benson. Martha, however, had been married four times, carried eleven children, nine of which survived childhood and went on to cause their own brands of trouble in other folks' lives. Her last husband, Hobey Gerrard, had died just two years before. Some kind of embolism. He'd left her sufficiently provided for with a comfortable house in the Tucson suburbs, and she helped out her brother because he needed the help, not because he paid her. Without her the Lunch Box would have gone to ground years before, though Jack Levine would never have countenanced such a thought. Its success was all his own. The arrangement worked just fine, rather like a Greek marriage. He was the head, she was the neck. She turned the head any which way she chose, and he remained ignorant of the fact.

The drive-in was a co-managed enterprise. The brains was the warehouse owner, Barnard Melville, a wool dealer whose family hailed from Tuba City and Cameron back before God was born. The warehouse did its warehousing, but Barnard was as close to an entrepreneur as the Melville family had ever produced, and he had once seen a drive-in theater in Payson, and there they had shown a film against the wall of a factory building and it had lit a spark in his brain. Jack Levine and he had shared the cost of the wall painting, the projector, the lease of the films themselves, and the Lunch Box stayed open until every last car had driven away. Burgers, fries, hot dogs, fried chicken, malted milk, soda, cookies, muffins, coffee, and candy. Two hundred or more cars, four hundred or more occupants, a dollar fifty a head on average, and Jack Levine and Martha Gerrard ran the whole operation fortnightly, paying the going rate to the girls who waitressed, and those girls got to keep the change that was ordinarily left on the side trays that clipped to the doors and upon which the food was set while the passengers made out.

It was that knowledge that had inspired the idea for Bailey Redman. Distracted teenagers, the noise of the movie, the darkness, the side trays, the change left there for the waitresses. Two hundred cars, even at ten or twenty cents per car, added up to a good deal of money.

The movies that Jack Levine and Barnard Melville rented and showed were old-time B-stock, never less than five or six years out of circulation, but the clientele—on the whole—didn't care a great deal. That evening was Edward L. Cahn's 1955 monster masterpiece *The Creature with the Atom Brain*. Mad ex-Nazi scientist uses radio-controlled atomic-powered zombies to help an exiled American gangster wreak vengeance on his enemies and return to power. Standard fare for such an evening. Ironically, Cahn—director of such masterworks as *The Four Skulls of Jonathan Drake* and *The Curse of the Faceless Man*, had also directed a film called *Riot in Juvenile Prison* back in 1959. Such an irony would have pleased Elliott Danziger, and—had he been alive—perhaps Earl Sheridan too.

The schedule included a newsreel, a short, and then the main feature at seven forty-five. Running an average of eighty or ninety minutes, the show was done somewhere after nine. Bailey had a

185

plan. They would creep down there around eight fifteen. From where they lay in the long grass looking down into the drive-in they could see the clock next to the water tower in the yard of the fire station. Cars were already beginning to make their way into the enclosure. People were walking across to the Lunch Box to book early orders that would be delivered once the picture show had begun.

Clay didn't know what to think of such a thing. It was stealing. He smoked a cigarette. Bailey smoked one too. When they were done smoking he thought about it again, and it was still stealing.

"I don't know," he said, and he let the statement hang there for a while. After the while had elapsed and she had not responded, he repeated that he didn't know, and then he said, "Whichever way you look at it, it ain't our money. Either it belongs to the people in the car, or it belongs to the waitresses."

Again Bailey Redman didn't reply.

Clay, lying on his back, rolled over and propped himself up on his elbows. He made a cup with his hands and rested his chin in it. "Stealing is a sin."

"Starving is worse," she replied.

"Sure, I get that, but you don't always have to come by money by doing something wrong."

"I agree," she said. "You got to work."

"Right."

"Work is done by adults. I'm fifteen, you're seventeen, neither of us is any use for anything right now, and even if we were we'd have to work a week or two before anyone'd even give us a dime. Hell, I don't even see how we could get a job unless we lied about our ages, and lying's a sin too."

"So it's a matter of which sin is worse."

"Life is always a matter of which sin is worse."

"That's a slanted viewpoint for someone as young as you."

"It's a slanted life."

"So what you're saying is we don't have a choice?"

Bailey rolled over on her stomach too. She leaned up on her elbows the same as Clay. She kicked up her feet at the back and scissored her lower legs back and forth. "Sure we have a choice. Go down there and get some of that money or stay right here and die of starvation in the grass."

Clay smiled.

"What are you smiling for?"

"Listening to you."

"What's so funny?"

"How simple and dramatic you make it sound. We don't have a choice but to steal money. It's simply a question of which sin is worse. If we don't commit one sin or other then we'll starve to death in the long grass."

Bailey Redman didn't reply. She was manipulating him. He knew that. He could see through her like glass.

"Okay," he said, "but not all of it."

"We won't have time to take all of it."

"So we just crawl around on the ground, reach up, take the change off the trays that are hooked to the sides of the cars, and then we run away."

"That's about the size of it, yes."

"And if someone sees us?"

"You run like a madman."

"And if one of us gets caught?"

"Then whoever it is will get the chair," she said, and rolled onto her back once more.

"You're such a wiseass."

"Well, you know what John Wayne once said?"

"What was that?"

"He said life is tough, but it's tougher if you're stupid."

CHAPTER TWENTY-SIX

There was something about the guy at the counter. Sure, he was seated with his back to Digger, but it was the *way* he was seated with his back to Digger that was disrespectful. His hunched shoulders, the manner in which he grunted at the waitress, the sound he made when he drank his coffee. All these things.

It was a small enough place, maybe a little bigger than the Olsons' place back in Twentynine Palms, but it couldn't have catered to more than thirty or forty people at full stretch. The chicken-fried steak they served Digger was the best steak he'd ever eaten, no doubt about it. He was all set to tell the waitress as much, maybe even leave her a tip, but then he got this disrespectful shit off the guy at the counter and everything else in his mind went to hell. The guy was in his early forties, jeans, a denim jacket, a red-and-black-checked shirt, a kerchief tied around his neck and knotted in back. He had a hat on the stool beside his own, a beat-to-shit fedora or some such, and the way he took a stool just for his fucking hat made Digger angry.

Digger had a mind to say something, had a mind to go ask for the stool beside him just to see if he'd move the damned hat, but he steeled himself.

There were two types of trouble. There was the kind of trouble you got out of when it came a-calling, and there was trouble you got into 'cause you created it yourself. The first was inevitable, whereas the second was just foolish. Digger was not of a mind to go making a nuisance of himself. He had to be mindful of drawing attention to himself.

But then, as simply nothing more than a provocation, he saw the guy just shift up on one butt cheek and break wind right there where other folks were eating.

A disgusted shudder went through Digger, and he knew there was no way he could let this kind of disrespect lie.

Digger got up slowly. He took his check and his cash to the counter, stood behind the stool where the man's hat was seated, and he nodded to the waitress.

"You got your check there, honey?" she asked.

"Think I'll have just one more cup of coffee," Digger said. "If that's no trouble, miss."

"Why, hell no, sweetheart. You just set yourself down wherever an' I'll bring on over a pot. Just made fresh." She smiled at Digger, such a warm smile, such a friendly smile, and Digger knew that Earl would have liked her real good too.

Digger stood there. He waited for the man to move his hat. The man went on pretending that he hadn't seen Digger. That was just the first provocation. It was intentional. Digger knew it. Any doubt he might have had was swiftly dispelled when Digger tapped the man on the shoulder and said, "Excuse me, sir . . . I wonder if you'd mind movin' your hat there so's I could take a seat here . . ."

The man didn't move. That was just the second dismissal.

"Sir . . ." Digger started.

The man turned. He turned slowly, as if he was merely trying to locate a fly, a buzzing fly, a dirty buzzing little fly that was now starting to annoy him.

He looked at Digger.

He was an ugly man. He had pockmarked skin and heavy-set brows, and he looked like he was the kind of guy who'd kick a dog just for the hell of it.

"Go sit someplace else, kid," he said.

Kid.

Kid?

"Ain't no shortage of seats in this place . . . you just run along and find someplace else to sit . . ."

Run along?

Digger gritted his teeth. He felt a strange sensation of distance between himself and the man, as if suddenly there was a gulf between them, as if there might be echoes if he spoke again.

His blood was boiling. He glanced at the fork, right there on the counter. He saw the man's hand, the way he'd placed it beside that fork as he'd turned. Like an invitation. With one swift motion Digger could have taken that fork and driven it through the man's hand and stuck that damned stupid hand right there to the counter.

That's what Earl would have done.

But then Digger stopped.

No, Earl wouldn't have done that.

There were two types of trouble. The second type was just plain foolish.

The waitress appeared. Digger smiled at her. She was a nice lady. She had a fresh pot of coffee and a clean cup, and she just went on and poured him some coffee and passed it over, and Digger took it and gave her the money. He gave her an extra quarter for being so pleasant.

"Why, thank you, sweetheart," she said. "You have a safe trip now, wherever you're headin' off to."

"Thank you, ma'am," Digger said, and he turned and walked back to the table.

He drank his coffee. He watched the man. He nursed his rage.

However this guy had planned to end his day was not the way it was going to end.

Digger was the soul of patience.

It was all of twenty minutes, and then the guy got up, donned his hat, straightened his kerchief, tossed a couple of quarters on the counter, and left the diner. Digger counted to ten and followed on after him.

Had he left it any longer he wouldn't have seen the dark blue '58 Chevy pull out of the lot and turn onto the I-10. He was heading east, same direction as Digger, out toward Las Cruces, perhaps El Paso. The truth was something Digger would never know for sure, and didn't care to know. The driver of the Chevy, one Marlon Juneau, was a Canadian out of Wynyard near Quill Lakes in Saskatchewan. He was down to see his sister, Helen, and the Chevy he drove was a rental he'd picked up in Albuquerque when he'd come off the train. He'd intended to follow the Rio Grande right down 25, and go straight on through to Las Cruces. Here he would have cut back northeast to her place in Alamogordo. Some-where around Hatch he'd screwed up, gone southwest on 26 for some damn fool reason, and hit the I-10. He'd seen the diner and pulled over to eat. He wasn't a driver, hadn't driven this far in ten years, and it didn't suit him. The constant jiggering and juddering fouled up his guts something awful, and he'd wished more times than Christmas that he hadn't had to come. But he did. No question. His sister's useless piece-of-shit husband, a man by the name of Tate Bradford, had walloped her again. Not the first time by any means, but this time he'd walloped her good. Broken her cheekbone, concussed her, and she'd had the police over to help her evict him. He'd gone, bitter as poison, but was likely to return. She had called Marlon late Sunday afternoon, and Marlon had made arrangements to get there as fast as possible. Took a train from Regina to Rapid City, South Dakota, a second from Rapid City to Denver, a third from Denver to Albuquerque. Over twenty-four hours, sleeping as best he could, but all knees and elbows, impossible to get comfortable, hungry and awkward and ever more riled at the prospect of facing off with Tate Bradford over his damaged-goods sister. It was a ball of bullshit, but then what could he do? Family was family, and family was blood and you were bound to it.

The run to Alamogordo was all of a hundred and fifty miles, and he figured he would make it by ten. He wasn't going to get there any quicker, and if Tate was on his way back to break his sister's spine with a shovel there wasn't anything he could have done about it. Marlon Juneau wasn't a fatalist, but a realist. He was getting there as quick as physics and geography would allow, and if geography put Tate and Helen in the same place before he got there then he'd be too late. It was that simple.

It wasn't until he was a good thirty miles from the diner that he even noticed the Galaxie behind him. He noticed it but paid it no mind. A Ford Galaxie was a Ford Galaxie, and there was nothing unusual about it. When the Galaxie overtook him he didn't even look to see the driver. He watched it disappear up ahead in the twilight and flicked on the radio. He didn't give that vehicle a second thought until he caught the flash of something in his headlight a hundred yards up head. The Galaxie was pulled over at the side of the road, the hood was up, the driver—a young man by all appearances—was waving his arms over his head and flagging him down. Detours and distractions was all he needed now, yet, despite appearances, Marlon was one of the world's Samaritans, this evidenced by the fact that he'd dropped his life to come to his sister's aid so many hundreds of miles away, and he felt the least he could do was give the young man a ride to the next garage where he could get the help he needed. The highway was all but empty, and if the number of cars he'd seen thus far were anything to go by then this boy would be stranded a good while yet if he didn't lend a hand.

Marlon pulled over, climbed out, and even as he walked toward the Galaxie he was saying that he really couldn't hang around. Twelve feet from Digger and there was a flicker of recognition in his eyes. The kid from the diner. What the hell was this about?

"I'm on up to Alamogordo," Marlon said. "Got some family trouble up there and I need to arrive in a hurry. I can give you a ride to—"

And his voice fell quiet when he saw the handgun that appeared from behind the young man's back and was then aimed right at his face.

"Oh shit," Marlon Juneau said in a flat, matter-of-fact voice.

"Oh shit is right," Digger replied. He came out from behind the open door and took a step toward Marlon.

CHAPTER TWENTY-SEVEN

Seven forty-eight p.m., evening of Tuesday, November 24. Clay Luckman and Bailey Redman lay in the long grass on the sly bluff overlooking the makeshift drive-in movie theater. Every once in a while Clay thought he could smell the hot dogs and fried chicken being cooked up in the diner below, and it made him awful hungry. Digger Danziger stood at the side of the I-10 a handful of miles outside of Las Cruces, and he wondered if he should kill the disrespectful asshole right there and then or goad him somewhat. He was leaning toward the latter. And then there was Tate Bradford, half a skinful of something cheap inside of him, and he had decided to drive down from Tularosa to Alamogordo and resolve this bullshit with Helen once and for all. It was a decisive thought, a thought fueled by bitterness, empowered by the belief that he had lived a life filled with hard-done-bys and disadvantages, and he was too good a person to let it go on any longer. He had hit her, for sure, but she had deserved it, and the bitch had called the cops. Un-fucking-believable. You didn't call the cops on family. You didn't call the cops for personal shit. Totally, totally un-fucking-believable.

John Cassidy was coming home, however. He pulled up outside the house and hesitated for a moment before he got out of the car. The interviews he had conducted that evening had pretty much confirmed for him that he was dealing with someone outside of Deidre Parselle's circle of family, friends, colleagues, and associates. Everything thus far indicated that her attack had been perpetrated by a random acquaintance. What had been done, more the manner in which it had been done, had led him to the conclusion that he was dealing with a sociopath.

John came up through the backyard as usual, entered through the kitchen, and was overwhelmed with the smell of pot roast. He called Alice's name, heard her as she made her way down the stairs and along the hallway. He kissed her, held her hands for a moment, and then took a seat at the table.

"Have a glass of beer or something," she said. "Dinner'll be another fifteen minutes or so."

"I'm okay," he said.

"Bad?"

He shook his head. "No, not any worse than it was before. I spoke to a couple more people. She was a good girl. Never in any trouble—"

"Until now," Alice commented.

"Right," he replied. "Until now."

She paused there before the sink. "Seems it's always the ones who are never in any trouble that wind up in the worst trouble of all."

John didn't hear her comment, didn't ask her to repeat it. His mind was on the last comment the last interviewee had uttered as he'd left their house. *Damned shame*, they'd said. *That girl never had a bad word for anyone. Sweet as pie. Just as sweet as pie.*

That's what her killer thought, John Cassidy had wanted to say, but he didn't. He'd held his dark tongue and his dark thoughts, and he'd smiled and thanked them for their time, and left their house without sharing his shadows.

"Think he's gone by now," John said. "I think he blew in and blew out like a tornado."

"You reckon he attacked anyone else?"

"While he was here? We haven't heard of anything, but you never know."

"What does Sheriff Powers have to say about it?"

"I haven't spoken to him. Just with Mike Rousseau."

"You'd have thought that something as important as this would have warranted attention from the sheriff, not just the deputy."

"It doesn't work that way anymore, sweetheart. Bob Powers is a politician. He's running a reelection campaign. All the duty rosters, assignments, supervision, case reviews . . . everything gets handled by Mike Rousseau now. It's better that way. I've always worked better with Mike."

"How is he?"

"He's good. The twins are moving schools. They had some difficulty. He said that Caroline was going to call you about some clothes she wanted to bring over for the baby."

"I saw her today," Alice said. "She's planning on bringing them at the weekend."

There was quiet for a time. Just the sound of the oven, the sound of plates, of cutlery, of the refrigerator door opening and closing. Sometimes he wanted music in the house. He liked some of that new jazz that came out of Phoenix. Not now. Now he wanted quiet. His mind was a storm of things. Thoughts, sounds, colors, images, the pattern of blood in the nap of the carpet . . . He closed his eyes for a moment. He inhaled deeply, exhaled slowly, felt a shiver along his spine as he considered the kind of human being you would have to be to do something such as that to a girl like Deidre Parselle.

Mike Rousseau, deputy sheriff for only three years and already frayed at the edges, told him that it was more than likely a vagrant, an opportunist thief who had seen the girl entering her apartment and come in for money. Finding little—simply because girls like Deidre Parselle weren't the kind of people who hid hundreds of dollars in their homes—he decided he was going to take something else from her.

"Animalistic, that's what it is. Some kind of animalistic thing comes in on them, and they just go wild."

Who *they* were Rousseau didn't go on to clarify. It was assumptive. Everything was assumptive until it was not.

Cassidy didn't buy *opportunistic* or *animalistic* or anything else. He believed he knew the motivation behind the attack: *necessity*. He believed the perpetrator *needed* to do that to Deidre. He was of the viewpoint that there was a dissociative mental condition, a condition where the rational parts of the mind disconnected from the irrational, and a new perspective came into play. It was not insanity in the clinically validated way. The people he was considering were more than capable of carrying on their lives like anyone else, but only so far. At some point something gave way, and then an impulse or an urge came into force, and it was an impulse and an urge that could neither be denied, rationalized, anticipated, inhibited, or prevented. It had to be satiated. That was all. The impulse had to be carried forward into action, and

195

only then would it be satisfied. Then it would sleep—for a while—and the individual would spend some time trying to convince themselves that they had not been present for the enactment of the impulse, and perhaps they would feel a sense of guilt, but the dissociative state helped them overcome that guilt. It was not *them*. It was another part of themselves that they could neither predict nor control. How else could someone do this kind of thing, and then go smoke a cigarette and buy a soda? How else could—

"John?"

He looked up. Alice stood there with a plate of food.

"Elbows?"

He moved his elbows and she set the plate down ahead of him.

"Stop thinking," she said. "Start eating."

John and Alice Cassidy were in the sitting room when the visitors came. The knock at the door was brusque and certain. John got up, frowning. It was past eight thirty.

He flicked on the outside light. Through the frosted glass half-moon in the upper part of the front door he saw two broken-up silhouettes. Two heads with hats. He hesitated, glanced back at Alice, who stood in the sitting room doorway, and then he opened the door.

"Detective John Cassidy?"

"Yes."

"Good evening, sir. Sorry to bother you at home. My name is Garth Nixon, and this here is Ronald Koenig. We're from the Federal Bureau of Investigation, and we'd like to come in and speak with you."

IDs were presented, and John Cassidy stood there for a moment, and was certain of nothing but the fact that their appearance was due to the attack on Deidre Parselle.

Koenig was evidently the more senior of the pair. Cassidy put him in his early fifties, and he had that authoritative, almost military bearing that made you feel he should be respected. The younger one, still a good ten or twelve years older than Cassidy himself, was also businesslike, matter-of-fact, straight to the point.

Cassidy took them in the sitting room, asked if they wanted

coffee, water, anything? They declined politely, and they waited silently until it was obvious that Alice needed to leave the room before they would speak further.

Koenig did all the talking, seated there with his hat on his knee, his voice calm, his attention focused.

"A convicted murderer by the name of Earl Sheridan was being transported from Baker, upstate California, to San Bernardino, for his execution. En route the convoy was slowed by a storm, and they decided to hold Sheridan in a juvenile facility in Hesperia overnight. Sheridan killed a guard and took two of the inmates of the facility as hostages. He escaped from Hesperia and headed southeast into Arizona. On the way a waitress in Twenty-nine Palms by the name of Bethany Olson was killed, also a man called Lester Cabot in Casa Grande, two more men in a convenience store in Marana, and then—while attempting to rob a bank in Wellton in Yuma County—four more people were killed and the sheriff was wounded. Sheridan himself was killed as he tried to escape from the bank, but one of the hostages, a seventeen-year-old by the name of Clarence Luckman, took one of the bank employees hostage, a young woman by the name of Laurette Tannahill, and got away in the sheriff's car. In the few moments before Sheridan died he said that Luckman had been the one to rape and kill the Olson girl, and that Luckman had been an accomplice to the murders in Marana and Casa Grande. He also said that he and Luckman had killed the other hostage from Hesperia, a teenager called Elliott Danziger. We have now learned that Luckman and Danziger were in fact half brothers, same mother but different fathers. Danziger was the older by a year and a half. Luckman went on the run, and on the I-10 near a town called Gila Bend he stopped at the house of a man called Gil Webster. Here he locked Webster in the basement, and then he took the girl from Wellton into an upstairs room and beat her senseless." Koenig paused. "He attacked her very brutally, Detective Cassidy, very brutally indeed." Glancing at his watch, he sighed and shook his head. "We learned just an hour or so ago that she didn't make it. She died in the hospital."

"So Luckman is now on the run, unaware that he's wanted for her murder as well?"

"Whether he believed he had killed the girl or not, we don't know, but irrespective of whether he killed the Olson girl, or was accomplice to the other murders, he is now wanted for homicide in his own right. And after he assaulted this girl he took Webster's pickup, which we have now traced to Tucson. We arrived just a little while ago. We spoke with your deputy sheriff, Mike Rousseau, and we are of the opinion that Luckman has been in Tucson for some time—"

"And he is the one who attacked Deidre Parselle?"

Koenig was silent for just a heartbeat, and then he nodded his head. "We believe that this is the case. Rousseau told us of this incident. The manner of assault, the brutality inflicted . . . these things have led us to believe that we are dealing with the same perpetrator."

"And you have this Gil Webster's pickup here in Tucson?"

"Yes, we do. It has been impounded by your sheriff's department."

"So now he's either on foot, hiding, or he's secured another vehicle," Cassidy said.

Both Koenig and Nixon said *Yes* in unison.

"And my assault case has now become a federal homicide case and I am excused from the investigation?"

Koenig smiled understandingly. "Not quite," he said. "We believe that Luckman will head out of Arizona as fast as he can. Considering the route that he has taken thus far, we believe he's going to continue into New Mexico, perhaps even Texas. We have instigated the highest alert possible, all county police and local units are being apprised of the situation. Until now we have limited our dissemination of this information to the federal offices in each area and the relevant police and sheriffs' departments, but soon we will widen the zone of activity. Radio announcements will be made, Luckman's picture will be distributed to gas station owners, convenience store owners, banks, motels, and suchlike. This will soon be the biggest single manhunt that the state has seen. Myself and Agent Nixon here have to follow him, of course, which means that we cannot stay behind in each town or city to investigate an incident. We have to leave that for the local authorities. The reason for speaking with you is to introduce ourselves, to present you with the facts you need to know, to answer your questions, and to gain your cooperation."

"In what way?" Cassidy asked.

"That any and all facts you might uncover in your investigation of the Parselle girl's attack be passed directly to our Anaheim office, and they will ensure that the information reaches us wherever we might be."

"Yes, of course," Cassidy said. "I can do that."

"Excellent," Koenig replied. "And now, are there are any questions you have for us?"

"You have given pictures of this—is it Clarence Luckman?—to Deputy Sheriff Rousseau?"

"We have, yes. He has assured us that copies will be made and distributed to all of his mobile units and beat officers."

"And the pickup that was taken from Gila Bend is impounded here and will stay here?"

"It will stay here, yes, but we have specialists coming down from one of our field offices in Mesa and they are going to take the thing apart to look for any further clues that may assist us. It is unlikely that there will be anything, but we have to be as thorough as possible. In such cases the slightest thing can be very helpful."

Cassidy said nothing for a few moments, and then he rose from where he was sitting and walked to the fireplace. He rested his hand on the mantel and looked back at the two agents.

"Can I ask why Clarence Luckman and his half brother were in the juvenile facility?"

"They were there as orphans," Koenig replied. "Danziger's father, as far as we can understand, left before the child was even born. Luckman's father murdered the boys' mother when Luckman was five, and then the father, James Luckman, was shot and killed while trying to rob a liquor store."

Cassidy frowned. "The facility at Hesperia was a state orphanage?"

"No, it was a juvenile criminal facility."

"But neither boy was there for having committed any criminal act?"

"Well, originally Luckman was at a juvenile facility at Barstow, but he assaulted a member of their staff and he was sent to

Hesperia. There was a question as to whether the assault was purely self-defense, but he was sent anyway. The brother went with him." Koenig smiled wryly. "Seems Clarence Luckman was just very unlucky from the get-go, which is ironic, considering his name."

"And he and this Earl Sheridan killed Elliott Danziger?"

"This is what Sheridan reported to the police at Wellton before he died. Danziger was the older of the two brothers, and was a source of trouble at Hesperia. He was guilty of numerous infractions of facility regulations, incidents of violence and mayhem, and there was a strong possibility he would have been transferred to the state penitentiary when he reached nineteen years of age."

"At San Bernardino?"

"I believe so."

"Which is where this Earl Sheridan was going to be executed."

"Right."

"And Sheridan and Luckman killed Elliott Danziger?"

"Yes, it seems they did."

"Why?" Cassidy asked.

Nixon looked at Koenig. Koenig looked at Nixon. They both turned back to Cassidy.

"We have a theory," Koenig said.

"Which is?"

"Sexual."

Cassidy frowned.

"Earl Sheridan had a long history of homosexuality. He was involved in sexual encounters with numerous men at the prison in Baker. We believe that he was sexually involved with Luckman, and that Danziger might have been openly critical of this involvement. We believe, in all likelihood, that Sheridan killed Danziger as a response to some comment or reaction to what he was seeing between the two others."

"But his own brother?"

"Half brother," Koenig said. "And if the incidents that have transpired concerning the girl at Wellton and the Parselle girl here are anything to go by, I don't think we are dealing with anything even remotely approaching a sane and rational human being. We are dealing with a psychotic, and there is nothing predictable about the behavior of such individuals."

"Two's company, three's a crowd," Cassidy said.

"Precisely," Koenig replied. "We don't think that Luckman killed Danziger . . . well, we didn't at first think that Luckman killed Danziger, but then when the girl from the bank was attacked, and now this one in Tucson . . ." Koenig left the statement hanging.

"Situational dynamics," Cassidy suggested. "Until he meets Sheridan there is nothing to provoke the homicidal or sociopathic tendency, but when he finds someone of like mind it lights the fuse, so to speak."

"You sound like you have some experience with this sort of thing," Nixon said.

Cassidy smiled. "An interest, that's all."

"What you're saying is a very strong possibility," Koenig said.

"And this girl in—where was it? Twentynine something-or-other?"

"Twentynine Palms. A woman called Bethany Olson. She was raped and murdered."

"So Sheridan didn't limit himself to sexual encounters with men."

"Sexual preference might be men," Koenig said. "His appetite for sexual sadism could be reserved exclusively for women."

"But the ones who were killed at the bank. Men as well as women, right?"

"Yes."

"Well," Cassidy said, "I don't envy you your task. Your case is federal, and it's a homicide now. I have just the one stabbing to contend with."

"We *hope* you have just the one, Detective Cassidy. There is the possibility that you may yet find another victim here in Tucson. And there's always the possibility that the Parselle girl wasn't attacked by Luckman. Doubtful. We know he was here. The pickup gives us that much for certain. The likelihood that we have two sociopathic maniacs on the loose in the same city is slim, wouldn't you say?"

"I would, yes," Cassidy said.

"So that's where we stand," Koenig said. "We have our vehicle specialist on the way from Mesa, but I don't think he will tell us anything further. We hope that there are no more victims in

Tucson, and we have our work cut out trying to predict where Clarence Luckman will go from here."

"You have left contact details for your Anaheim office with Deputy Sheriff Rousseau?" Cassidy asked.

"We have."

Both Koenig and Nixon rose to their feet.

"All of this has to be kept under wraps for as long as possible, Detective Cassidy," Koenig said. "I believe you understand enough of what has happened here to appreciate the necessity for the utmost confidentiality."

"Of course, yes, it goes without saying."

"I can also tell you that we are approaching this with a view to immediate resolution. If this Clarence Luckman is seen, then we have orders to address the matter with the most extreme prejudice."

"You have a shoot-to-kill policy in force?"

Koenig smiled knowingly, but said nothing in response.

"I understand," Cassidy said.

They shook hands, all three of them, and Cassidy showed them down the hallway to the front door.

Alice appeared from the kitchen and joined him as he stood watching the federal agents drive away.

"Bad news?" she asked for the second time that evening.

"Yes," he replied, and yet couldn't shake the question that had come to mind the moment he'd been told of Clarence Luckman. Why would an apparently honest teenager, having spent twelve years of his life in state facilities, having never really gotten into any kind of trouble, suddenly become a brutal sexual sadist? Not only that, but an individual capable of killing his own half brother. Because he met someone of like mind? Because he had been withheld from enacting his impulses and satiating his appetites while incarcerated? Perhaps, perhaps not. It was hard to conceive of the idea that a seventeen-year-old would be capable of doing the kind of thing that had been done to Deidre Parselle, and before that the girl taken hostage from the bank. Again, it was further evidence that cultural structures and social restraints were coming apart at the seams, and out through the gaps the very worst kind of people were escaping. Were things getting worse, or was he just becoming more cynical and intolerant?

John Cassidy closed the door on the darkness without, and followed his wife back to the kitchen. Omitting names and specific locations, he relayed to her precisely what he'd been told by Nixon and Koenig. She sat there silently, listening intently, and when he was done she didn't say a word for quite some time.

CHAPTER TWENTY-EIGHT

They lay on their backs for a while in the dusty darkness. Side by side, pressed against each other, and Clay Luckman could feel the warmth of her body against his, the touch of her hand against his leg, and he was aware of little else but her—this Bailey Redman—and he felt the need to hold her, to close his arms around her, to draw her even tighter toward him, but he didn't dare move.

He tried to think of her as his kid sister, but he could not. There was barely anything between them in years, and though he wanted to feel fraternal and protective, he nevertheless felt a great deal more. He felt things for which he did not know the name, and those things made him feel alive.

The light from the movie screen cast shadows that fell behind the cars. It was within these shadows that they then crouched and hunkered and waited. A little after 8:35 they moved. She went first. She smiled at him, and in the darkness he saw the white of her teeth and the whites of her eyes, and he couldn't help but smile back. She crawled from the back fender to the side of the door, and with her slim hand she reached up and felt along the tray with her fingertips. She found something, came crawling back, held out her hand, and showed him as if to prove she had been telling the truth. A dime and three cents. Clay nodded. He reached out and touched her shoulder, pulled her close, whispered in her ear. *That way.* He pointed to the right. *I'll go that way, you go the other way, meet you over there.* And again he pointed, far out across the field to the right-hand side. *Behind the diner.* She nodded, smiled again, and off she went. He watched her, the way she flattened herself to the ground and inched forward on her elbows and knees. Like a soldier going under the wire. He watched her until she disappeared into the shadows and then he

204

made his own way from the back of the first car and started along the rows.

Every once in a while the screen lit up with some brightly illuminated scene. The movie was loud enough to obscure any noise that he and Bailey might have made, and the vast majority of the occupants were far too involved in what they were doing to be distracted by the slightest noises from outside, but still there was something fearful about what they were doing. They were stealing. There was no other way to describe or define it. It was theft, larceny, an offense punishable by a trip back to Hesperia—perhaps somewhere else, somewhere worse. And for her? The orphan. Christ only knew what would become of her. But he could not let her starve. They had to have money, and they were too young to work, and what choice did they have? Devil and the deep blue sea. Stealing money from teenagers. Is this what his life would now be like?

Clay crawled on, reaching up his hand to touch-search the small shelves with his fingertips, finding coins here and there, stuffing them in his pants pocket without looking to see what he'd found. It seemed to go on forever. Car after car after car. The ground was hard and dusty, his hands dry with the dirt, his knees and elbows chafed and sore as he went on to the next one, and the next one, and the next one.

Somewhere along the line he knocked over a cup of soda. It dropped suddenly, half-full, and spattered across his legs. He rolled sideways, and pressed himself into the pitch darkness beneath the car. His heart thudding, his palms sweating, the stickiness of the soda on his ankles, soaking through his pants, the smell of it, the feeling of the car above him moving, shifting, and his certainty that whoever was inside had heard the cup go over, was even now opening the door, stepping out, was ready to crouch down and look beneath the vehicle. And then there would be a cry, a shout, and headlights would go on, and kids all over would straighten their clothes and look up, and then their lights would go on too, and whoever was running the show would switch off the movie, and for a moment there would be silence, and then Clay Luckman and Bailey Redman would be dragged out from wherever they were hiding and turned over to the authorities . . .

Something like that. And maybe he'd get a kicking. Not her, not the girl, but him. Some thug with a buzz cut would give him a pounding for stealing the change. Prove himself a man. Show his girl that he was bigger and stronger than this rat-faced, dirty, skinny teenager who had sunk so low as to steal burger change from a drive-in.

Even though his heart thudded, even though no door opened, no feet appeared, no lights were switched on, Clay Luckman felt a heaviness in his chest that he had never felt before. He waited a minute more, and then he edged to the side of the chassis and looked out from beneath the car. He could see the night sky. Clear of cloud, the deepest blue, each star and asteroid and meteorite and planet bright and white and beautiful. But somewhere amongst them was his dark star, the one that was following him, the one that had been there the night of his mother's death, the one that had watched him as he lay with her in the apartment bedroom waiting for the father that never returned. Where was his dark star?

He moved off again, edging on his back from one car to another, rolling over as he moved between the rows of vehicles, gathering speed as he went, until finally—nearing the end of the last row—he had gained confidence. Thirty, forty, fifty cars he had passed, and not once had he been seen. The coins jangled in his pockets. He could feel the weight of them. He felt stupid and shallow and light-headed and brave and intoxicated with nervousness, all of these things simultaneously, and he was only ten yards from the front of the diner when he saw Bailey burst out from the shadows beneath the movie screen and run like a scared jackrabbit across the last expanse of scrubbed earth. She disappeared behind the diner. She had gone unseen. She was safe.

The last two cars there was nothing but a single coin between them. From the size of it he reckoned it was a quarter. He dropped it in his pocket, crouched and waited as a sequence of images on the screen suddenly illuminated the darkness, and then the sequence was over and Clay hurried to the side of the field and pressed himself against the chain-link fence. He hunkered there for a just a moment, and then he ran to the end of the fence, head down, shoulders hunched, knees bent. He came to the far end and slipped down the side of the diner.

And then the door opened. He hadn't seen it. A couple of steps, a railing, a rear door to the diner, and he was there—standing upright, as clear as day as the light streamed out of the building and a man stood there with a cigarette in one hand, a lighter in the other. For a second neither moved nor spoke. Clay saw every line on his face. He saw the sweat on his brow, his stubble, the open-necked shirt, the hairs on his chest that poked through the aperture, the grease stains on his apron, the way the cord was looped around the back and tied in front . . .

"Who the—" he started, and then he frowned, and then he figured the kid for a stowaway, a kid too young to drive a car, too young to get a girl, a kid who wanted to watch the movie for free.

Clay Luckman—frozen for a second—decided to move, and when he did he went like a rocket.

He took off, rounded the corner of the diner, shouted for Bailey, and she was right there beside him.

The sound of the man followed them as they flew away from the back of the building and across the short expanse of ground to the street.

"Hey! Hey, you kids! What the hell d'ya think you're doing? Get the hell outta here!"

He walked a few steps, but he was too heavy and too old to run. His name was George Buchanan, and he was the diner's short-order cook, and he worked full-time in another diner that sat on the I-19 between the outskirts of Tucson and the town of Green Valley, and he did the drive-in movie shift for a few extra bucks, cash in hand. He saw those two kids fly away from there, and he didn't know whether the second one was a girl or another teen-age boy. Younger for sure, because whoever it was was smaller and faster.

He walked back to the rear door of the diner and lit his cigarette. He inhaled deeply, exhaled again and watched the smoke break up and disappear into nothing. Hell, he thought, and smiled nostalgically. That age he would have done the same damned thing himself.

CHAPTER TWENTY-NINE

Men were different. Digger was aware of that, had been since he'd tried to have sex with that girl from the bank. The guy in the bank, the one with the wiseass face, the one Earl shot in the head . . . well, seeing that had been terrifying, but it had been a rush as well. A real kick of a thing. The girl in the apartment, the one he stabbed, well, that was a different playground altogether. With the girls there was the sex thing. With the guys there was now just the impulse to hurt them, to show them that he—Digger Danziger—was in charge, that he was the one with the power and the say-so. With the pickup guy that he locked in the basement and the old man he'd restrained himself. He could have killed them, but he didn't. Had he been scared? Had he known that once he crossed that line it was all downhill from there? He didn't know. But now it didn't matter.

This guy, the one from the diner, with his jeans and his denim jacket, the red-and-black-checked shirt, the damn fool kerchief tied around his neck and knotted in back, and the hat he wore, the one he'd parked on the stool back in the diner, and his eyes all wide and surprised like he didn't know this was coming, like he thought he could get away with disrespecting Digger 'cause he figured Digger wasn't going to be man enough to do anything about it . . . this guy was an asshole of the first order.

"Now, look here, son . . . I am real sorry about what happened back there at the diner—"

"Shut your fucking mouth," Digger said, and he said it with an edge, and there was that Elvis lip thing going, and he half-closed his eyes and squinted at the man, and the man fell silent. He really did *feel* Earl around him. Inside him even. Like someone possessed.

"Son . . . I didn't mean any disrespect—"

"Yes, you fucking well did."

"I'm sorry . . . lookee here, I really am sorry . . . I got a lot on my mind right now—"

"I said for you to shut the fuck up," Digger said.

"Son . . ."

Digger closed his eyes for just a second, and then he took a step forward and leveled the gun at Marlon's face.

"Don't. Call. Me. Son," he stated emphatically.

Marlon closed his eyes too, but he kept them closed.

Do it.

Just fucking do it.

Digger took a deep breath. He could hear Earl's voice goading him. Earl was smiling. He could hear it in the tone of every word. Oh, son of a bitch, he could feel the rush! Earl would have gotten such a kick out of this.

"What's your name?" Digger asked.

"Marlon," the man said. "Marlon Juneau."

Digger heard the quake and quiver in his voice. He was trying to be a tough guy, but he was already coming apart.

"Marlon Juneau," Digger repeated. He took another step forward. There was now no more than ten feet of dirt separating them. Digger held his gun steady. He thought of Earl, what a great guy he was, and how the cops outside that bank had shot him down like a defenseless animal. Bastards.

"Marlon fucking Juneau. Like Marlon Brando, right?"

Marlon nodded. His throat was dry and his hands sweated, and his eyes felt like powdered glass had been sprinkled in them, and the pressure in his bladder was sufficient to inflate a car tire.

"How old are you, Marlon?"

"For-forty-two."

"And where are you from?"

"C-Canada."

"'S a big fuckin' place. Anywheres particular in Canada?"

"Wynyard near Quill Lakes in Saskatchewan."

"Is that so? Near Quill Lakes in Saskatchewan."

"Yes—yes," Marlon replied, and he knew—as he'd known within the first minute—that whatever was going to happen now wasn't going to be good. This wasn't a straightforward robbery. This wasn't a roadside rollover for the car and the cash.

This was a performance. This was some crazy motherfucking kid with a gun and a dark light in his eyes. Oh, how he wished he'd moved his hat. Oh, how he wished he'd just been pleasant. But he'd had things on his mind, and he wasn't thinking straight, and usually he was so polite . . .

Marlon looked up at Digger. "Look, if it's money you need . . ."

Digger smiled. "You have no fucking idea how much money I got. You ain't never seen that much money, you dumb motherfucker."

Marlon opened his mouth to say something else.

"Anyways, I thought I told you to shut the fuck up."

Marlon closed his mouth.

Digger weighed the odds. He had four bullets left, was aware that they weren't going to last forever. If he ran at the man—suddenly, forcefully—he could knock him down, beat him in the head with the butt of the revolver, maybe knock him out. But the man wasn't some skinny-ass son of a bitch. He had some girth and substance to him. Whatever happened, Digger knew one thing. The time had come. The time had really come. Two girls, two men, all of them had lived. He'd let them live. They had disrespected him, but he'd let them live. That was true mercy. That was true strength. But now . . . now it was time to show Earl that Digger was a man. Elliott Danziger was a *real man*. He wasn't no scared little boy. If he had the power of life and death, well, every once in a while someone had to die, otherwise it wasn't real power, was it?

"Get on your knees," Digger said. "Down on your knees and put your hands on your head."

Marlon hesitated for a moment. He was wondering if the kid had the nerve to shoot him, if the gun was even loaded, if the speed he could muster from a standing start would carry him across ten feet of dirt before the kid had time to react. That was what it came down to. Could he get to the kid before the kid pulled the trigger? Intentionally, involuntarily, it didn't matter—could he reach the kid before the gun went off?

He looked at the kid's eyes. Damn it, he couldn't have been more than seventeen or eighteen, and here he was pulling strangers over at the side of the highway and threatening them with a handgun. What the hell was happening to the world? What was happening to the America he knew? He'd sure as hell have some story to tell his sister when he got to Alamogordo.

When the kid took one more step forward and stared him down with a look of such unadulterated viciousness, he knew that there would be no involuntary reflex pulling that trigger. This was a wild one, a crazy one. If he pulled the trigger he was going to do it because that's precisely what he wanted to do, and for no other reason. Maybe if he complied . . .

Marlon Juneau stepped back, and then went down on his knees, raising his hands as he did so and placing them on his head.

Digger smiled. He went left, walked around Marlon and reached the car. Keeping his eyes on the kneeling man he looked in through the open door, saw nothing but a flask, a paper bag with spots of grease showing through, a pair of sunglasses, an enamel mug.

He switched the gun to his left and reached for the glove compartment.

"Holy Mary Mother of God," he said. He reached in and took out the .45.

Marlon closed his eyes and said his first prayer for three decades. He didn't know the words to anything formal. As an adult he'd never stepped foot in a church. He just said whatever he could think of in the heat of the moment. *Oh God, please don't let me die. Not here. Not now. I've been as good a man as I knew how to be. I've got a sister who's in trouble . . . well, you know that, Lord, and I wanna do everything I can to help her, otherwise—*

"Son of a bitch," Digger said. He had the revolver tucked in his pants waistband. The .45 was heavier, and there was a solid feeling to it, and he pushed the button beside the trigger and the clip slid out and it was full of bullets.

"Does this work?" he asked Marlon. He walked around until he was looking down at him. He held out the .45 so Marlon could see it.

"Far as I know," Marlon said.

Digger frowned. "Far as you know? What the hell does that mean?"

"Never had reason to use it," Marlon said.

"It's all loaded up and everything," Digger said. "Looks fine to me. Don't see any reason it shouldn't work. Do you?"

Marlon shook his head. He didn't want to know, didn't want to find out. Last thing in the world he wanted was proof that the .45 was fully functional. He'd had it for two years, bought it off a man in a saloon in Fort Qu'Appelle for twenty dollars and a bottle of Slackjaw. The guy was ex-army, had brought it back from the war, had half a dozen of the things and was damned near giving them away. Marlon had never owned a handgun. A rifle sure, but not a handgun. Had done a little hunting, had a shotgun, a Remington, but not a pistol. Bringing it had seemed like a good idea. Keep it nearby just in case. Just in case of what? In case he and Tate Bradford had an old-style showdown in Helen's backyard? Now how foolish did he feel? Hauling that damn gun along was the stupidest thing he'd ever done.

The kid was standing over him. He had the .45 in one hand, the revolver in the other. He had a smile on his face like a drunken clown.

Marlon was scared, more than he'd ever been, and his bladder went. He felt the warmth escaping down his inner thighs and he felt like a child woken from a nightmare, afraid of the dark, struggling to understand what he'd seen, whether it was real or imagination, whether there really was something in the wardrobe, something hungry, something homicidal . . .

Digger saw the man's pants as the dark shadow spread across the front.

In that moment he saw himself, remembered how he too had pissed himself like a little kid. Oh, how he hated the fact that Earl had seen that. And Clay? Clay, wherever the hell he was, he would remember that too, how Digger had pissed himself out of sheer terror. God, that was just so shameful!

Well, not now. Now he wasn't scared. Now he was here and he had his guns and he was in charge.

Digger raised the guns simultaneously. He pressed the revolver against Marlon's left temple, the .45 against the right.

"Motherfucker," he said, and it wasn't a derogatory term directed at Marlon, but simply an exclamation of how damned good he felt.

"One . . . two . . . three . . . four . . . five . . . six . . ." he counted, and then he stopped. "Son of a bitch!" he said, and then he stepped back and did this little dance. Like an Irish jig, like some-one was playing a fiddle or something, and he just couldn't help himself from having a little dance to celebrate the moment. He stopped dancing, came back to face Marlon, and he put the guns right where they'd been.

"Where was I?" he asked, and then he nodded. "Sure . . . six . . . seven . . . eight . . . nine . . ." He paused again. "You ready for some fireworks, Marlon Juneau from . . . where was it you was from?"

Marlon didn't speak. He couldn't. He had his eyes shut tight. He had a lump in his throat like a fist.

Digger frowned. He lowered the guns. He tucked the revolver in his waistband, made a fist and then tapped the top of Marlon's head like he was knocking on a door.

"Marlon!" he shouted. "Hey, Marlon! You home?"

Digger took the revolver in his hand again.

Marlon opened one eye. He looked up at the crazy kid.

"Sas-Saskatchewan," he whispered.

"Saskatchewan! Too right, motherfucker!"

Digger put the revolver against the left side of Marlon's head, the .45 against the right. He hesitated for just a second. "Ten," he said, and then he pulled both triggers simultaneously.

It was as if someone had released a grenade inside a water-melon. The body that knelt there continued kneeling right there. The top of his head just disappeared in a cloud of something, and there he was—Marlon Juneau from Wynyard near Quill Lakes, his shoulders, his neck, and then pretty much everything gone from the nose upward.

Even his sister wouldn't have recognized him, but that didn't matter anyway.

Digger was stunned. Then he started laughing, and then he did his dance again, waving the guns in the air like a drunken cowboy on Independence Day.

He stopped suddenly, took a step toward Marlon, and looked again at the mess that had been the man's head.

"Shee-it," he said, and with his knee he pushed the man over. "Shee-it and Shinola with sugar on top."

And then he started puking. It was a reflex. It was the thrill, the excitement, the horror, the disgust, the sheer amazement at what

213

he himself had just done. He dropped both the guns, put his hands on his knees, leaned forward, and puked violently, and he just kept on going until there seemed to be nothing left inside.

When he eventually raised his head he couldn't believe how good he felt.

In that moment it felt like eighteen years of disrespect and shame had just vanished with the breeze. Digger believed he'd become a man. He had been tried, and this time he had come through. He had not been found wanting. Nothing like it in the world.

He could feel everything and nothing. He believed he was someone and then no one in the same instant. It was as if a wind had blown into one ear and out the other, and in passing through it had taken everything bad with it. He felt clear and simple and as straight as a Texas highway. He could see the past, the present, and the future all in one go, and he could see himself rushing on into that future like a freight train. Wasn't nothing gonna stop him now. There wasn't no one gonna make a fool of him again.

Digger walked around the body for a good while longer. He kept getting up close and looking at the mess he'd made. He wanted to feel nothing. He just wanted to reach a point where he could look and look and look and feel nothing—no nausea, no fear, no regret, nothing. He wanted to feel like this kind of thing was the most natural thing in the world. He could sense Marlon's blood on his face, could taste it on his lips, feel it drying on his eyelids and on his hands. Even his clothes were beginning to stiffen. There were bits of bone on his boots, and he had no doubt that just a short while earlier those bones had been right there inside Marlon Juneau's discourteous and disrespectful head. Well, he wasn't gonna be discourteous and disrespectful again anytime soon.

Digger felt centered. He felt calm. He believed he had made it through the other side of something real important.

And then it was a matter of practicality and reason. He needed to get cleaned up. He needed to get rid of the clothes, get rid of the body, get himself straightened up and flying right.

In the trunk of Marlon's car Digger found a suitcase. In it were pants, shirts, socks. They were clean, pretty much the right size, and would serve the purpose. There was also a can of gasoline and some rags.

Digger stripped down to his shorts. He used the rags and a little gasoline to wipe the blood from his hands and face. It evaporated quickly, but the smell gave him a high that he liked. He threw his own blood-spattered clothes into the back of the car, and then dragged Marlon's body back into the driver's seat. Then he dressed in the clothes from the suitcase, used the rags to wipe off his boots, and he was set. He surveyed the scene once more. He could see Marlon sitting there in the driver's seat, half his head gone, the rest of it sprayed across the ground where Marlon had been kneeling.

Digger couldn't help but grin.

He grinned like a fool; like some inbred, mouth-breathing wild man out of the backwoods of beyond.

And then he leaned his head back and howled like a coyote into the evening sky.

Twenty-five minutes later Tate Bradford would arrive at his estranged wife's house in Alamogordo. An argument would ensue, all the while Helen praying that the headlights of Marlon's car would be suddenly visible through the front windows, but they would never come. Just as Marlon's last thought had been for Helen, so Helen's last thought would be for Marlon. At 9:43 that evening—Tuesday, November 24—Tate Bradford grabbed his wife by the throat and banged her head against the corner of the mantel above the fireplace. She went down immediately, was dead before she hit the ground, and then he stood there for a long time before calling the police. The Alamogordo Sheriff's Department was out there by ten thirty, and Tate Bradford confessed to killing his wife in a rage. Even as they took his confession Digger Danziger was driving away from the burning wreckage of Marlon Juneau's car. He'd doused the thing in gasoline, and set it alight. By the time it was reported Digger was an hour away, outside of Las Cruces and heading along the I-10 toward Anthony and El Paso. He was hungry, could've eaten a dead skunk given enough ketchup, but he didn't plan to stop until his heart slowed down and was beating right again. Marlon Juneau had been the best thing ever. The way his head exploded.

The way it felt when the guns went off together. The sound and the fury. Where had he heard that expression?

That's what it was for him: the sound and the fury.

The control. The power. The life and death thing all going on. He had to do it. He couldn't help himself. He'd wanted to do something like that ever since that old guy had whacked him with the cane. Now who was the chief, eh? Now who was the big boss of the hot sauce?

Earl Sheridan had been right all along, God bless him. It was the *realest* thing he'd ever done, the *realest* thing he'd ever experienced.

The road came up at him ceaselessly, and then span out behind him like a black ribbon, and the headlights picked out the white lines as he followed them toward the next rush. He had never been happier in his life.

CHAPTER THIRTY

They ran until they gasped for air. They ran until their legs were rubber and their hearts were pounding, and they laughed like foolish hyenas, and at one point Clay stumbled and whacked his knee on thick root and the pain was sudden and sharp and it made him laugh even harder despite the fact that it now hurt when he ran. They didn't stop running until the light of the movie screen was a dim and distant ghost some five hundred yards away. And then they stopped because no one was chasing them, and because they believed that if they took another single step they would die.

They collapsed on the ground—some barren field with stones and dry roots and the rigid imprints of heavy boots—and they lay there heaving air in and out of their lungs, and every once in a while turning sideways to tuck knees into chests and laugh some more.

"God Al-almighty," Clay said, and that started Bailey laughing some more, and the sound of her laughter made him feel some-how better, as if this ridiculous escapade had helped to jar loose the memories of the last few days. Tragedy was overcome by living life. Best way to deal with loss was to gain as much as possible every place else.

Minutes later they were quiet, just the sound of breathing, the night sky growing brighter as their eyes became accustomed to the shadows, and then the question of what they would do now arrived in Clay Luckman's mind.

"How much?" he asked her, and she turned out her pockets and he did the same, and they set the coins down in the dirt and started counting.

"Fourteen dollars and twenty-eight cents," he said. "Not much, is it?"

"I ain't never seen that much before . . . not that was mine."

"Gonna feed us for a few days, maybe a week if we skip a couple of meals."

"Better than no dollars at all," she replied. She sat back on her haunches, wrapped her arms around her knees, and then she looked up at the sky and sighed.

"What are we doing?" she said.

"Runnin' away," Clay replied.

"From your brother and the other one?"

He shook his head. "Not anymore. I think they're long gone. I think we've lost them for good."

"So where are we going?"

The silence between them was thick like oatmeal.

"Where?" she repeated after a while, and Clay sat in the dirt with fourteen dollars and change and wondered what he could say that would make either of them feel better.

"Tell you the truth, Bailey," he said, "I don't know what we're doing. They get ahold on me I'm goin' back to Hesperia, and this time they'll find a reason to keep me until I'm an old man. And you? You're still a kid as far as the state is concerned, so Lord only knows what they'd do with you."

"We could hide out from everyone until we're eighteen years old and then we could do what the damn hell we wanted."

"Sure we could, but we ain't gonna live on what we steal from drive-in movie theaters."

This time it was Bailey who stayed silent. She lay on her back, stretched out her legs, and put her arms up straight behind her head.

"I'm hungry," she said.

"Best go get something to eat, then," Clay replied.

"And tired."

"We'll eat, then we'll sleep."

"Where we gonna sleep?"

"Hell, I don't know, Bailey. Your guess is as good as mine. Figure we'll find some old house or somethin' like we done before."

"We should get some blankets or something. Maybe like a coat or whatever. Something that's gonna keep us warm. Ain't the time of year to be sleepin' rough outside with no blankets or nothin'."

Clay lay down beside her. He folded his arms across his chest and looked at the stars. She was right. Soon it would be cold enough to see your own breath. And then what? The pair of them dead-frozen, hypothermic and stiff and useless for anything. Another couple of nameless graves in the potter's field.

"This is bullshit," she said.

"Sure is."

"Ripest kind of bullshit I ever heard of."

"Couldn't agree more."

"So where d'you think we should go?" She rolled over on her side, crooked her arm and rested her chin in her hand. From where Clay was looking, the moonlight, the shadows, Bailey Redman looked like the kind of girl who would grow up ever so pretty. She was going to break some hearts he figured, more than likely his own just to get the pattern started.

"You remember I told you about that place called Eldorado?" he said.

"Yeah sure, what about it?"

"It's in Texas. Schleicher County in Texas. I really think that's where we should go."

"Because of that dumb advertisement you showed me?"

"The advertisement, yes, but I also think anyplace called Eldorado is gonna be lucky, you know? It's the same as that South American city that was made of gold."

Bailey looked at Clay askance, like there was something loose and rattling behind his forehead.

"You got a better suggestion?" he asked.

Bailey Redman thought for a while, and then shook her head. "Don't s'pose I do."

"Better to have somewhere to head for. If you ain't headin' somewhere then you're either wanderin' or lost."

"And you know how to get there?"

"Texas is east, that's all I know," he replied. "We just keep going east until we see signs or we find a map or somethin'."

She didn't say anything. Clay Luckman took a deep breath. He figured there was rain on the way. He got up and brushed down his clothes. "Don't know how far Texas is, but it ain't around the corner. Seems we got a way to go."

"Everybody's got a way to go," Bailey said.

"You gonna be this philosophical all the way there?"

She nodded, hid a smile.

Clay buried his hands in his pockets. "Let's walk back into Tucson and get hot dogs and root beer."

Bailey sat up, came to her feet, stood looking back toward the drive-in theater.

"Someone see you back there?"

"Yeah, the cook I think. He came out back when I was running past."

"They'll call the cops for sure."

"Maybe, maybe not. Maybe the waitresses'll just think that they didn't get no tips. Maybe the people in the cars will think that the change they left was already taken by the waitresses. The cook'll just think I was sneakin' out after seein' the movie for free. He ain't gonna report that to no one. Bet that happens all the time."

"Yeah."

Clay started walking, Bailey following on behind. Now that they'd slowed down, now that they weren't running like banshees, he realized how cold it was. Bailey had been right. They'd need coats or blankets or something if they were going to sleep rough. And Texas? This Eldorado place? A crazy idea, but then any idea right now was as crazy as any other. He sure as hell wasn't planning on going back to Hesperia, and he didn't want Bailey Redman in some juvenile place either. That was no way to start your life. He'd done it, and look how things had turned out for him.

They didn't speak. They walked side by side. The lights of Tucson grew brighter. Clay Luckman wondered if things were going to work out, if they were going to get better, or if the dark star he'd been born under was just going to follow him all the way to the end.

CHAPTER THIRTY-ONE

Sleep did not come easily. A little before ten thirty John Cassidy rose from his bed and made his way quietly from the room. Down in the kitchen he poured a glass of cold milk and sat at the table. All he could think about was Elliott Danziger, the boy that Clarence Luckman and Earl Sheridan had killed. Maybe the federal agents were right in their suppositions, maybe Sheridan and Luckman were homosexual lovers and the second hostage had been killed. There was little that surprised Cassidy anymore. But was that all they knew? What had Sheridan actually said in his dying moments? Had he told them how Danziger had been killed? Had he told them where Danziger's body was? Had they found it, and if not, were they looking for it?

These questions turned around in his mind, and they continued to turn without resolution until he heard Alice coming down the stairs.

"I hadn't meant to wake you," he said.

"I woke anyway," she said. She placed her hands on her stomach. "Seems I can't go two hours without needing to pee these days."

She stepped up behind him, placed her hands on his shoulders. "You're troubled about this case?"

"I am," he replied. "Not just the Parselle girl, but the other things. I am finding it very hard to understand how someone could change so rapidly. A teenager, an orphan, never been in any real trouble, and all of a sudden he's a homicidal maniac . . . so much so that he colludes in the murder of his own half brother."

"Well, like you've been saying for I don't know how long, there's a great deal that the police and the federal authorities don't understand about the criminal mind."

"I know that, Alice, but this . . ." He shook his head. "There's just something about this that doesn't make sense."

She came around the table and sat facing him. "What?" she said. "What is it that doesn't make sense?"

"That, for starters. The fact that this kid, all of seventeen years old, could suddenly be in cahoots with someone like this escaped convict, killing people, robbing banks, Lord knows what. And then the convict, this terrible mentor that he's suddenly adopted, is killed, and the kid goes off on his own spree." Cassidy inhaled deeply. "I don't know. I just don't know."

"Well, there isn't a great deal you can do about it right now, and the other thing you have to take into consideration is that it isn't your case, and in all likelihood it isn't ever going to be."

"I want to call the people who were at the bank," he said. "The ones who were there when the convict was shot. He must have said something more when he died. He must have said something more about the other boy that they killed."

"And if he did?"

"Then maybe I can suggest—"

"Suggest what, John?" Alice interjected. "Suggest nothing is what. This is a federal case. Those two men who came this evening, they didn't come to invite your cooperation in anything more than the attack on the Parselle girl. They want you to investigate what happened, and if you find out anything that could be helpful to them then they want you to report it. That's all they want, John."

He was nodding before she was done. "You're right," he said.

She reached out and closed her hand over his. "I know how mad you get about these things," she said. "I know how much you want to help, but when you're sheriff—"

"Mike Rousseau won't be sheriff for another ten years yet, and then he's going to serve for—what?—twenty years? By the time I get there I'll be retiring."

"We don't have to stay here, John. We can move wherever you want to."

"What about federal?" he asked, and it came right out of the blue.

"Federal?"

"Sure. They don't work the same way. You're not restricted to

222

one town, one city. Like those fellers today. They came from Anaheim in California, and now they're all the way down here in Tucson. They get to investigate exactly the kinds of cases that I need to be investigating, Alice. They get to work with people who understand the kinds of things I'm talking about. There's things that these people have in common. These murderers and rapists and whatever. There's things that they have that are common denominators. I'm *sure* of this. If I could only get some more firsthand experience then I could show people exactly what I've been talking about these past few years."

"And you think they'd listen?"

"Federal investigators, sure. They aren't small-minded like Bob Powers and Mike Rousseau. I mean, they're good people an' all, but—"

"I know what you mean, John."

"Too narrow a view, right? Too narrow to start thinking about anything beyond the immediate case, the immediate evidence. And sometimes they look so closely at these things they miss the entire picture—"

"Enough," Alice said. "You need to sleep. This thing has gotten you all riled up. You need to get some rest. You can call whomever in the morning and start asking about a federal application, or you can go find out whatever else you can about what happened to Deidre Parselle."

John Cassidy looked at his pregnant wife. He wondered what he'd done to deserve her. If he wanted to join the federal authorities she would back him all the way. If he traveled for his work she would make sandwiches and a flask. If he was gone for days at a time she would ask for nothing more than a call to let her know he was okay. If he asked her the question—*What did I do to deserve you?*—she would smile and tell him that she often asked herself the same thing.

"Some people just work better together," she'd once said. "Some people just belong. Always have done, always will. It isn't complicated."

He didn't fall asleep immediately. She did, however. She was sleeping for two. He lay next to her, the warmth of her body, the smell of her, the sense of inseparability he always felt at such moments, and he recalled her words and wondered if she was right. *It isn't complicated.* Always thinking, always wrestling with things, finding himself agitated and dissatisfied whatever he was doing. This was his flaw. Wherever he was, he always believed that what he was looking for was someplace else. Only at times such as this, just the two of them, did he feel some sense of stability. She was his anchor. That's why they worked.

This case? The indescribably brutal attack on the Parselle girl, and all that was now attached to it . . . was this the watershed, the point about which everything would revolve? Why this one? Why did this feel so important? Why had this raised the question of what he was doing with his career, of whether he should now leave the sheriff's department and apply to the Federal Bureau? Because he could do more good there? Because the theories he had went unheard in Tucson? Even the most irrational mind had a rationale. Even the most deranged and insane killer had a modus operandi and a purpose behind what he was doing. Were there influential factors? Were there common denominators in education, family background, social interaction, income bracket, locale? Did these situations present some sort of *dynamic* that produced an Earl Sheridan, a Clarence Luckman? And if so, then what could be done to predict, inhibit, or prevent such outcomes? What could be done to help identify potential victims, for surely—if there were patterns in the makeup of killers—then there could also be aspects of certain individuals' personalities and characters that made them victims? Or was he delusory? Was he imagining an ideal that could never be?

He drifted away finally, the last image he remembered was that of the photograph Deidre's parents had shown him of how she'd looked as a child. It was almost as if he could hear her asking the question . . .

Why? Why me? Why did this have to happen to me?

It was a question he did not understand, a question for which he had no answer. But he was *sure* he was going to find out.

CHAPTER THIRTY-TWO

Digger made it to El Paso just as Luna County Sheriff's Department officers were cordoning off the burned-out '58 Chevy outside of Deming. The registration number went into the system before midnight. It wouldn't be until ten on Wednesday morning that they would identify the rental company that owned the car, not 'til eleven that they had official word back from Albuquerque regarding the possible identity of the man inside the car. One Marlon Juneau, driver's license giving a Saskatchewan address, and what the hell he was doing way south in New Mexico, beyond that what had transpired that put him in a rented Chevy and burned to hell, was a different matter altogether. Sheriff of Luna County, Hoyt Candell, weathered and cynical and seen-everything-twice, was himself a little surprised. He'd seen a burned body before a couple of times, but bodies burned in house fires and suchlike. This boy was different. This boy looked like he had no head before he was set alight.

Digger had left Marlon Juneau behind, though he would think of him often. However, what was done was done. El Paso was his destination now, and whatever he might find there for amusement. It was a straight run he guessed, and he thought less of where he was going and more of what he was going to find on the way. He did not think about being stopped or caught or arrested or anything else. He just thought how killing Marlon Juneau from Saskatchewan had made him feel. Like a god. That was how it was. Like a fucking god.

Digger kept on driving until he found a motel, a run-down crescent of cabins with a flickering neon light somewhere in the suburbs, and then he walked out to find a late-night diner serving hamburgers and fries and tepid root beer that tasted like antiseptic mouthwash. He would be asleep by midnight, laid on his back, fully clothed, exhausted from the excitement of it all.

Clay Luckman, soon to be a wanted fugitive in two states, and Bailey Redman, the girl who did not exist, ate three or four twenty-five-cent hotdogs apiece and then walked back the way they'd come. Without coats, without blankets, they hunkered down beneath a fall of straw in a barn near a farmhouse. A heap of windfall branches were stacked against the near wall, and they imbued the air with a woody rot that seemed potent, like something fermenting, something strong. Bailey slept almost immediately, but Clay lay awake—much the same as John Cassidy—and wondered about the nature of things. He felt as if he'd been born with nothing and had pretty much all of it left. The Patron Saint of Losers. He listened to the girl breathing, and he wondered what would become of them. They'd started out running away from Earl Sheridan and Digger, and now they were headed for someplace called Eldorado, and for no other reason than some dumb ad in a magazine. It was a foolish, crazy-headed thing to be doing, but what other choices were there? If he turned himself in to the authorities he would go right back to where he started. And the girl? An orphan now, fifteen years old—what would she have to look forward to? A ward of the state, three years of neglect and abuse and bad food? This was the way it had been for him, and he wouldn't wish it on anyone else. Save Digger perhaps. Yes, he would wish such a thing on Digger.

He wondered where they were now. Had they caught Sheridan? Was he dead? Or had they driven him right on down to wherever and finished the job they'd started? And Digger? Had he been caught too? Had the authorities tracked them both down and shot them dead? Or was Digger still on the loose, doing whatever he wanted and not giving a damn about anyone else? Clay tried to think about what had happened to his brother. He could not understand it. He tried to think of him dead on the highway, finally trapped by some police roadblock and riddled with bullets. He felt almost nothing.

He thought about the people that would be looking for him. He—Clay Luckman—was an escaped convict too, of course. Is that how it would end for him? Brought down by a single shot from a marksman's rifle even as he was trying to explain what had happened?

Clay looked up. There were gaps between the boards in the roof of the barn. He could see darkness there, and through the darkness the stars. Maybe he was right. Without a destination they were simply wandering or lost. Eldorado, the Golden One, the city of promise and fortune and good luck for all who reached it.

He smiled to himself. *Dreamers*, he thought. *Pair of foolish dreamers*. And he knew—somehow he just knew—that it had to get better from here.

DAY SIX

CHAPTER THIRTY-THREE

"**Y**ou're the deputy sheriff there in Wellton?" John Cassidy asked.

"Well, I am, yes," Lewis Petri said, "but not the same way you'd consider a deputy. There's three of us, and we share the job so to speak. Two days a week, each of us covering the missing day on a rotational basis. It's just the way it is down here, you know?"

"But you were there at the bank when Sheridan was killed?"

"Well, yes, but all three of us were there."

"I thought—"

"Situation like that we all get a call-out."

"I understand that you were with Sheridan when he died?"

"Yes, I was, sir."

"I wanted to know precisely what he said, the exact words."

"Well, the exact words he said were the exact words I put in my report, Detective Cassidy. He said that this Clarence Luckman took the Tannahill girl. Then he went on and said that they killed the guy in Pinal County and the guys in Marana. He also said that Luckman raped and killed the girl in Twentynine Palms, this Bethany Olson, and that they had both killed the other hostage, Elliott Danziger."

"You're sure that's what he said. That *they* killed the man in Pinal County and the other two in Marana, but *he*—meaning Clarence Luckman—raped and killed Bethany Olson and was also accomplice in the murder of Elliott Danziger?"

"Well, sir, you have to understand that it was a pretty tough situation we had up here, and things were going off left, right, and center, you know? We were all pretty much stressed to our limits with what was happening—"

"The best you can remember, this was what Earl Sheridan said before he died?"

"Yes, sir, as best as I remember."

"And he didn't say anything about where the other hostage had been killed, how he had been killed, where they'd put the body?"

"No, sir, not a word beyond what I already told you. He wasn't alive more than a few seconds, and that was all he said."

"Right, Deputy, that's been very helpful," Cassidy replied, fully aware of the fact that it had not been helpful at all. Individual and specific recollection of precisely what someone else had said during a moment of tremendous stress and pressure could not be considered reliable. Not at all. Sheridan could well have said the exact opposite, that *he* had raped and killed Bethany Olson, that *he* had murdered the men in Casa Grande and Marana, that . . . well, that anything at all had happened. Deputy Lewis Petri had heard what he *believed* Sheridan had said, and not a word of it could be sworn for sure.

Cassidy ended the call. He went through to see Rousseau, explained that the federal people had been at his house the night before.

"They were here too," Rousseau said. "Me and Bob, we both spoke with them, told them about the Parselle girl before they came out to you. This is some deal, ain't it?"

"They want me to get as much information on the assault on the Parselle girl and pass it on to the federal office so it can be relayed through to Anaheim."

"They told me as much. So what's your plan?"

"Go back there. Look at the scene again, see if there's anything else that has been missed. Apparently there's a vehicle team coming down from Mesa to go through the car with a fine-tooth comb."

"Truth of the matter is he's long gone," Rousseau said. "Sick son of a bitch is more 'an likely over the border into Sonora or someplace. If it was me I sure as hell wouldn't hang around to enjoy the scenery."

"Sure you're right," Cassidy replied, "but I got to check everything and then check it again. Sure wouldn't appreciate them coming back and telling us we'd missed something."

"Hell, John, I wouldn't worry too much about it. Like they said, it's a federal case now. People like us can't be expected to do that kinda work for the money we get paid."

Rousseau smiled. Cassidy smiled back. Cassidy didn't feel that way at all, but there was not a great deal of point in saying so. Bob Powers had the same attitude, and that's why the sheriff's mantle would go to Mike Rousseau, and ten years from now Cassidy would be hearing the same speeches and wondering why he hadn't gotten out when he could.

"I'll be onto it, then," Cassidy said. "You radio me if something else comes up I need to attend to."

"For sure I will," Rousseau said.

Cassidy left, a healthy degree of uncertainty in his mind as he walked to his car out behind the building. He had viewed the Parselle crime scene every which way he could think of. He had questioned friends, colleagues, family members. He really didn't see there was anything else that could help him or the federal people. They were right—it was Luckman, a crazy boy with a head full of fury set to make his mark on the landscape any which way he could. And he was headed east by all accounts, perhaps to New Mexico, on to Texas, even south into Mexico to see if he couldn't evade the law that way. If there was a worse mess than this someplace, well, Cassidy was sure as hell glad it wasn't his.

He started the engine and drove back out to Peridot Street. The door was still taped, the balcony and stairwell still marked as a crime scene. He sat in his car and just looked at it. This was where she lived. This was where Clarence Luckman had followed her to, and this was where her life had suddenly changed direction. And to do that to a girl? To invade her home, to stab her and choke her? What kind of a thing would drive somebody to such actions? What possible rationale could someone possess for such brutality? It was definitely not something that could be understood within any acceptable context. But then, wasn't it the case that all people believed they were rational? What they were doing in their minds and what they were doing with their hands were never the same thing. Clarence Luckman was terrorizing and hurting a young woman with her whole life ahead of her. That was in reality. In his mind he was . . . well, he was what? Avenging a betrayal? Punishing a rejection, a crime, a mortal sin? What was he doing as he kneeled beside her and plunged that blade into her breast? Did he talk to her as he did it? Did he explain to her what he was going to do, and why? And why now? Why—all of a sudden—has this thing been unleashed inside of him? What was it that had lain dormant all these years, only to find release in such circumstances? Impulsive. Intoxicating. Something possessive of such power that it overrode all censorship, ethics, morals, social restraints, any slightest sense of what would be considered right in the eyes of the majority.

And did he feel guilty? Was Clarence Luckman even now weeping quietly somewhere, aware of what he'd done, regretful, filled with self-loathing, reassuring himself that he wasn't completely responsible, that he had been *taken over*, convinced that next time—*if* there was a next time—he could manage it, control it, subjugate it? Or had he now a taste for the thing? Was he now planning or committing or walking away from another heinous crime?

It was a remarkable case to be involved in, even on the fringes, but he was involved, some part of it did belong to him, and he felt the need to be as engaged and contributory as he could be.

John Cassidy closed his eyes. He breathed deeply for a little while, and then he exited the car and crossed the street to the stairwell. What better place to contemplate his next step than the crime scene itself? He made his way up slowly, looking at each riser, trying to see everything it was possible to see, and with each step he felt more and more certain that Clarence Luckman's killing spree would be a defining path for them both.

CHAPTER THIRTY-FOUR

Having left Detective John Cassidy's house the night before, federal agents Ronald Koenig and Garth Nixon telephoned the field office in Anaheim to ensure that every county sheriff's department between Tucson, Arizona, and San Antonio, Texas, had been kept up to speed on the case. Photographs of Clarence Luckman had been distributed widely, and more were being printed. As Koenig told Cassidy, soon every gas station and highway-side diner would know what Luckman looked like. His name would be on the wireless, his face would be on the TV. The I-10 went on through Houston, Baton Rouge, Pensacola, Tallahassee, and finally wound up in Jacksonville, Florida, where it stopped merely because the earth did. For now Koenig believed that San Antonio was far enough, and thus the sheriff's offices for the counties of Pima, Cochise, Luna, Doña Ana, El Paso, Lincoln, Otero, Pecos, Sutton, Kerr, Bexar, and everywhere in between received a teletype cable from the federal authorities. Clarence Luckman was armed, dangerous, unpredictable, and on the way. A roadblock schedule was drawn up. At first they would cover the interstate and the secondary highways, and then—within a further twenty-four hours—they would have the men and resources to extend roadblocks to the primary routes between the towns. This served not only to cover the possibility that they would in fact stop Clarence Luckman in a stolen car, but also to show his picture to travelers who may have seen him.

One of those counties was Hoyt Candell's, and a little after one that Wednesday afternoon he took it upon himself to call the federal office in Las Cruces and inform them of the burned-out car and the semi-decapitated man that had been found outside Deming the night before. Las Cruces got very interested very quickly, and as Koenig and Nixon were still in Tucson they went out there themselves to take a look-see. Koenig and Nixon took what details they could from Candell. Marlon Juneau's name, the details of the rental firm, his home address, his place of work, and when they got there they were already working on the basis that this incident might be the work of Clarence Luckman. Why? Simply because it was downright odd. It was Luckman's anticipated route, the I-10 itself, and he had last been in Tucson and Luna County was about two hundred miles east. For something that made no sense at all, it seemed to make a great deal of sense.

The scene itself was a debacle. The remains of the blackened, burned-out car sat at the side of the highway like a stationary nightmare. A couple of pickups were parked on the other side, and the occupants were out on the highway, walking up and down, looking at the vehicle, the dead man inside, like there was something important to be learned from this scene.

First task Koenig undertook was to ask them to leave.

"There ain't nothing to see here," he told one man.

"Sure as hell there is, mister," was the reply he got. "There's some dead feller with half his head missing sitting in a burned-out car."

The onlookers didn't give a damn who the suits were—federal or otherwise—but when Koenig told Candell that they *had* to go, Candell took it upon himself to reason with them. They did go— eventually—and Koenig and Nixon surveyed the wreck, the dead man inside, and wondered what the hell would happen next. There was no way to confirm that this was Luckman's work, but it had to be factored into the equation simply because of the sheer incongruity of it.

"Last murder around here?" Nixon asked Candell.

"Two years, a little more perhaps. Woman stabbed her husband in the throat with a kitchen knife when she found him out for cheating on her. Didn't mean to kill him, just to teach him a lesson, but she hit his juggler and that was the end of that."

Koenig looked at Nixon. Nixon looked back. An unspoken appreciation that the more they thought of this the more it could be Luckman.

They informed Hoyt Candell that it was his task to maintain the confidentiality of the environ, to ensure that the inquisitive county residents and passersby didn't violate the integrity of the crime scene. People would be down from Mesa—vehicle investigation specialists—and they would examine the car closely, and then tow the car away.

"And the dead feller?" Candell asked.

"He goes with the coroner once the car has been examined," Koenig replied.

"You know what killed him, 'cause seems to me that he had half his head missing before he went in there, wouldn't you say?"

"Appears that way. Perhaps a shotgun. Several handgun rounds—"

"Have to be an awful big handgun, or right up close and personal to take the top of his face away like that."

"Yes, it would."

Candell frowned. "Kind of sick son of a bitch does something like that to someone? And what the hell for?"

Koenig shook his head. He smiled faintly, which was the first sign of personality or humor he had demonstrated since he'd arrived at the side of the I-10. "Sheriff, your guess is as good as mine. This man we're after, Clarence Luckman . . . well, let's just say he's done some pretty terrible things."

"Looks like he's of a mind to do a whole bunch more," Candell said.

"Yes, it does, doesn't it?" Koenig replied, and was amazed to find that such an admission based on someone else's statement created quite an effect on him. Had he been any less professional and businesslike in his attitude he might have stopped to consider all the lives he was now responsible for, the people who would step across Clarence Luckman's path and find that that single step had marked the end of their life. The number of lives he could now save was entirely dependent on how quickly he found the boy. The boy? Yes, he was still a boy. Seventeen years old and capable of atrocities such as this. Atrocities such as this *maybe*, for there was no way to confirm that this had in fact been Luckman's work. But Koenig was professional and businesslike in his attitude, and he had worked hard and long to ensure that emotion, sympathy, intuition, and especially assumption played no part in his considerations of a case. But in this instance intuition and assumption had crept in; there was something about the burned and dead body in the car that rang a bell. It made him *feel* something.

And as far as this Clarence Luckman was concerned, well, there was little to expect but his timely end. They would find him. It was inevitable. How quickly was the question, but it was *when*, not *if*. And when they saw him they *would* kill him. This was the way it was going to be. Word had gone out. Shoot to kill. No questions, no hesitations. Shoot *to kill*.

Koenig and Nixon were at the scene less than an hour. They shared a few words and decided to head on for Las Cruces. There was a small field office there, and from that point they could coordinate their next steps with the agents in Anaheim and Tucson. If Marlon Juneau had been the victim of Clarence Luckman's unpredictable temper, then Clarence was still heading east along the highway and he would have made it to Las Cruces. If this was Clarence's handiwork, then it did indeed look like he was heading for Texas.

CHAPTER THIRTY-FIVE

They found a map without difficulty. A small gas station some-where between the outskirts of Tucson and the turnoff for Highway 83. The man inside was helpful enough, let them look at the thing without making them pay for it.

"Here," Clay said, and he put his finger right on Eldorado. "This is not a coincidence."

Bailey could see what he meant. They were on the I-10, and the I-10 went all the way from Tucson through New Mexico and into Texas, and right there—right in front of their very eyes, about thirty or forty miles the other side of Fort Stockton—the I-10 turned off to Highway 190, and where did Highway 190 take them? Hell, if it didn't take them right into Eldorado.

"You can't tell me that this doesn't mean something," he said. "The exact highway we're on takes us right to Eldorado. You gotta see that that means something. We just have to stay on this road and we'll be there, though I sure as hell ain't intending on walking the whole way. That must be—what?—six or seven hundred miles."

"We'll get a ride," she said. "Bet there's trucks that come all the way out of Tucson and on down to El Paso every day. That must be near as damn it half the way in one go."

Clay folded up the map, put it back in the wire rack. He bought a couple of moon pies and a bottle of Coke. They had eaten eggs in a diner en route, but already Clay was hungry again. With each dime he spent he realized that they were running on prayers and little else.

They started walking again—that vague middle ground between someplace and someplace else. This was a flat and unrelenting land. The trees were squat and awkward. Anything taller than a shoulder was invariably man-made. There were rusted gas pumps, once bold turquoise and visible for a hundred yards in any direction, now simply part of the landscape, behind them the station, now fallen into disrepair, the wood stolen for fires, for house repairs, for flatbeds. An outhouse, a shed for tools and what-nots, a water tower, a weathervane, a corroded sign that read *Don't Take a Curve at Sixty-Per. We Hate to Lose a Customer—Burma-Shave.* Folks ill equipped and unsuited for such terrain had arrived with ideas. The heat, the dust, the sandy-throated dryness, had beaten those ideas into submission. Whatever determination and dollars might have been invested here had been left behind.

Clay would have called it godforsaken, but he didn't believe God had anything to do with such a place.

It was late morning, and somewhere back at the outskirts of Tucson Jack Levine and his sister Martha, the owners of the drive-in movie theater, were sharing words with Barnard Melville. They had already spoken with George Buchanan regarding the absence of tips for the drive-in waitresses the previous night. George had told them of the boy he'd seen, couldn't have been more than seventeen or eighteen. George had figured him for nothing more than a free seat for the movie, but now it seemed that two and two made four. Maybe the boy had been stealing tips from the window shelves. Jack wanted to call the police. Barnard said it wasn't worth it. The police had one hell of a lot better things to do than chase some kid around Tucson for the sake of a few bucks. There were five waitresses. They had come up short for the night's work. Barnard, big-hearted feller that he was, dug a five-buck bill out of his pocketbook and gave it to George.

"Give 'em a dollar extra each from me," he said. "And keep a weather-eye open for this kind of thing. Next time they can go without."

That was the end of it.

Had they called the police, had a black-and-white come over, the officers might have shown George Buchanan the picture that had come through from the federal office just a little while earlier. Yes, George would have said, that looks like him. But I can't be sure. Not a hundred percent. It was dark. He surprised me. I only saw him for a split second and then he was gone.

Had that information reached Koenig and Nixon it would

240

have merely confirmed something that Koenig was now beginning to suspect. Why, with the proceeds of the Wellton bank robbery, would Clarence Luckman have wasted his time stealing pocket change from a drive-in movie theater? Simple. Because he was crazy. Because he was irrational, impulsive, spontaneous, opportunistic, and most of all he was unpredictable. Koenig, faced with George Buchanan, would have told George that last night had possibly been the luckiest night of his life. "That kid," he would have said, "would have killed you right where you stood and never thought another thing about it." And it was that sentence, the use of the word *kid* that said it all. What they had here was a teenager—arrogant, knew everything there was to know, bucking authority, packed full of hormones and energy, and to boot he was as crazy as a shithouse cockroach. The worst kind of nightmare. He caught people unawares and off guard, like Bethany Olson, like Laurette Tannahill and Deidre Parselle. Teenagers don't do this kind of thing. Teenagers are a little rowdy sometimes, sure, but they aren't dangerous. Clarence Luckman was out to prove them different, and he was doing a damned fine job of it.

So Jack and Martha, George Buchanan, and Barnard Melville went back to their business and didn't consider it again, wouldn't even think of it until Clarence Luckman's picture started appearing in the papers. But that wasn't going to happen for a while. That wasn't going to happen until Elliott Danziger really started swinging for the fences.

Clay and Bailey kept on walking. Churches every five hundred yards—Evangelical Covenant, First Baptist, Community Congregational, Church of the Nazarene. And they all had signs— clever words and turns of phrase that seemed incongruous in this setting. *Fire protection policy available—talk to Jesus inside. Forbidden fruits make many jams. Seven days without prayer makes one weak. Let Jesus into your heart. If you don't like it, the devil'll take you back.* They sure liked their religion down here, Clay thought, and wondered why it was always the poorest that seemed to possess the greatest faith. Maybe if you had enough money behind you you didn't need God taking up space.

They walked a good three or four miles before lunchtime, and then they sat at the side of the highway and imagined how good it would have been to drink another Coke.

Bailey made mention of plants and creatures. Guessed what they were. Blacksnakes. Leopard frogs. Fireflies. Goatsuckers. Other things that Clay had never seen the like of before.

Out of the blue she said something else. "If love is so great, how come it breaks so many hearts?"

Clay was lost for words, mumbled, "I don't know, Bailey." He didn't know if she was speaking of her mother, her father, or someone else.

"I miss my dad," she went on. "I miss my mom, but I knew she was sick, and I knew she was going to die, but my dad . . ."

Clay tried not to look at her, but he couldn't help it.

"And your brother . . . do you miss him?"

Clay nodded. "Sure I do. Miss who I thought he was, not who I think he's become."

"Why do all the bad things happen to just a few people? And why is it never just one bad thing, but one thing after another, and then another thing after that?"

Clay sighed. "Think you're gonna have to ask that question of someone a lot smarter than me, Bailey."

He looked at her and she was smiling. "What?" he asked.

"I like the way you say that."

"What? What did I say?"

"My name. It sounds good when you say it."

"Bailey."

"Right," she said. "Bailey."

He felt his cheeks color up. He dared not look any way but straight ahead.

"You think we're going to die, Clay?"

"Die? Die of what?"

She shrugged her narrow shoulders. "I don't know," she replied. "Bad luck maybe?"

Clay couldn't think of anything to say, and so he said nothing.

There was silence for a good minute, and then she said it once again. "I miss my dad. I really, really do."

A little later they got a ride.

"Can take you as far as the turn-off at Deming," the driver told them. He had four teeth—two up, two down. The hand he extended to help Bailey on up into the cab of his truck was short the little finger. Maybe he had a habit for losing bits of himself as he traveled. "Have to go on up to Hatch," he said, "or I'd take you farther."

Clay got on up beside Bailey, and they took off.

"You pair headin' home?" he asked.

"Yes, sir," Bailey said. "Me an' my brother. We've been down in Tucson visiting, and now we're heading on back to Las Cruces."

"Hell of a way to be goin' by yourselves. You ain't got no kin to drive you?"

"No, sir," she went on. "We're visitin' our gramma, and our pa is away working at the moment."

"What's he do then, your pa?"

"He sells shoes. Drives around the country selling shoes."

"Hard job."

"No harder than drivin' a truck I shouldn't reckon."

The man smiled. His teeth showed like broken picket posts. "Well, I guess you're right there, missy," he replied. "Name's Milt. Milt Longfellow. And you might be?"

"I'm Caroline, and this here is my brother, Jack," she said.

"Pleased to make your acquaintance," Milt said, and there was little else he had to say for himself until they came up on Deming.

A cordon had been erected with sawhorses and ropes around a burned-out car at the side of the highway. Police were evident, a couple of black-and-whites and a vehicle that looked like a hearse.

" 'S up here?" Milt inquired, and they slowed somewhat as the scene unfolded around them.

A cop stood by the side of the road and waved them on, and as the truck went by Clay looked directly at him, eye to eye, and for a second he imagined that there was the faintest flicker of recognition. It was nothing, merely imagination, and then they were on past the wrecked car and whatever had happened back there, and the road was once again ahead of them—empty and flat like a gray ribbon laid smooth on the landscape.

It stayed that way—quiet, peaceful almost, and then the signpost for Hatch to the left was coming up and the truck was slowing down.

"Gotta part ways here," Milt said. "Pleased to have your company. You take care of yourselves an' each other now."

"Will do, mister," Bailey said.

Waving, standing there side by side as the truck pulled away left to Hatch, Clay asked her why she'd lied about their names.

"I didn't lie," she said. "I just told a different kind of truth."

He frowned.

"There's people that need to know things, and there's people that don't. We ever get ourselves in some kinda trouble . . . well, the less people who know where we're going the better."

He couldn't disagree with her, and so he didn't. They started walking, now sixty miles or so from Las Cruces, and he started to wonder whether the trouble she'd spoken of was some kind of omen. She'd had no scarcity of bad luck, that was for sure. Maybe she too had been born under a dark star. Perhaps they were both carrying bad signs, had been drawn in together because of it, and the two of them were destined for heartache whichever way they went.

CHAPTER THIRTY-SIX

If Elliott Danziger gave any later consideration to his actions, those considerations would have centered around pride and a sense of accomplishment. There was a case he'd heard about way back, in Kansas as far as he could recall, where two guys had done a whole family—mom, pop, son, and daughter. It had taken two of them, and they'd done it under cover of darkness. Well, everything Digger had done he'd done alone, and he'd done it in daylight.

He slept well in the motel cabin. The bed was sufficiently firm, the pillow adequately soft, and he left the window open an inch to get some fresh air into the room. There was little he hated more than a room with no windows. He woke to the sound of the traffic on the highway a quarter mile away. He lay there for a while, aware that it was past nine o'clock, a strange smile on his face when he considered how much money he had, how much freedom, how much anonymity. No one knew where the hell he was, and it felt good. Had he known that his actions were being ascribed to his half brother he would have felt a mixture of emotions—a sense of satisfaction and wonderment that things were working out so well for him, against that an awkward feeling akin to jealousy. No, not jealousy, more a kind of injustice. Someone else was getting the credit for his work. However, he was not aware of this fortuitous misrepresentation of the truth, and thus felt little but the sensation that came with a brand-new day. A brand-new day in a brand-new life. There was no breakfast, but—more important—there was no one telling him what to eat and when to eat it. There were no locked doors aside from those he locked himself. There were no raised voices, no challenges, no provocations, no insults, no threats of violence . . . save those, of course, that he chose to administer himself. He was afraid, but only a little, and that fear was easily remedied. He only had to think of Earl and he felt strong, almost bulletproof. This was the way things were supposed to be. This was the way they were always meant to have been. He'd just had to be patient. God bless Earl Sheridan for breaking him out. God bless Earl Sheridan for showing him the way, the truth, and the light. In fact, fuck God. What the hell had God ever done for him? Nothing, that's what. It was him and the memory of Earl Sheridan, and that's all he'd ever need.

Digger left the motel and drove in a straight line. It was a good half hour before he realized that he'd missed the I-10 connection somewhere a couple of miles back. Vexed, he did a U-turn, and it was en route the way he'd come that he saw a diner set back from the road a way. He was hungry, famished actually, and he pulled up ahead of the place in Walt Milford's Galaxie and wasted no time getting inside.

Maurice Eckhart hailed from Gunnison, Colorado. Fifty-one years old, carrying a dozen or so pounds too much for his height, yet healthy and hardworking, a churchgoer, a good man. His wife, Margot, should have been a showgirl. At twenty-one she was five eight with a thirty-six-inch bust, a twenty-five-inch waist, and thirty-four-inch hips. The whole package was balanced gracefully on thirty-nine-inch legs. She'd studied ballet since she was five, supported and encouraged by both her parents, but when it came to career choices it was her father, Hendrik Kristalovich—a lapsed Presbyterian, a one-time Calvinist—who drew a line in the sand. Margot possessed neither the nerve nor the determination to cross that line, and out of spite she married Maurice Eckhart, a man nine years her senior, a man she met while waiting for an interview for a secretarial position in an elementary school in Plainview. Maurice happened to be there for a similar reason. He worked for a firm that manufactured and sold school supplies— textbooks, journals, pencils and the like. They had captured a good percentage of the market in Colorado and were looking to branch out into Texas, New Mexico, Kansas, and Utah. The deputy principal, supposed to be seeing them one after the other, was running a good hour late, and Maurice and Margot got to talking. Maurice was not successful in securing an account for his provisions, but he did secure a date with Margot. He would have been a good catch for any normal girl, but Margot was no normal girl. Her looks apart, she was smart. Not just book smart, but wise beyond her years. She had read voraciously as a child, and perhaps it was this extracurricular education that had given her the sympathy and compassion that others found so magnetic. Perhaps it was a quality with which she had arrived, and it was her mission to share it with the world. Her mother, a timid little woman of no great consequence, insufficiently strong to carry another child once Margot had been born, merely provided a somewhat weak shoulder for Margot to cry on. Margot's mother, Joan, would never have taken her daughter's side in a familial conflict. That was not what a good wife did. A good wife bent to her husband's will, and—once bent—she stayed out of shape.

In later years, their two children entering their teens, Margot Eckhart would have time to reflect on her life choices. They had been wrong for the most part, but she was a woman of character and substance. She did not make a bed and then presume not to lie in it. Maurice was honest, faithful, loyal, decent, a good provider, and then there were the children. At twenty-three she had Dennis, at twenty-five she had Linda. They had her looks and Maurice's steadfast character. They were the best of both of them combined. They were children of whom any parent would have been proud, and that was something that was never regretted, never up for trade, never something to wish back so one could start over. Now Margot was forty-two, still great-looking, still balancing everything gracefully on her thirty-nine-inch legs, and possessive of the philosophically resigned attitude that life was lived forward. It could have been better. It could have been worse. Maybe some things turned out the way they did because that's the way they were supposed to.

Late morning on Wednesday, November 25, the Eckhart family was heading out of Lubbock, Texas, Margot's hometown. Maurice, always in charge when it came to maps and directions and routes, had insisted they avoid the northbound Interstate 27 this time. I-27 had been a nightmare a couple of times before, and he didn't want to repeat it. I-27 would take them only so far as Amarillo, and then it would be a mess of state highways before they could join the I-25 at Springer or Raton. *No*, he'd said, and said it with some degree of definitiveness. *It may seem like a longer way around, but I plan on driving the two-hundred-and-fifty-odd miles to El Paso, and there we can go north into Colorado, all the way to Pueblo, where we can simply join the 50 west to home. Once we reach Pueblo it's no more than a hundred miles and we're there. Whatever time we might lose driving to El Paso we'll gain by taking the interstate all the way north. Trust me, it'll be quicker in the long run, and besides, the kids'll get to see some of Texas and New Mexico.*

Maurice had logic on his side. They had travelled on the smaller state highways and it had taken them all of four days. He couldn't bear the idea of another four days home, and he figured the 25-route would shave a day off the return. This mammoth one-and-a-half-thousand-mile journey was another matter entirely. This mammoth one-and-a-half-thousand-mile journey had been to bury Margot's father.

To make sure the bastard's fully and completely dead, was Maurice's sentiment, and he said it once and once only. Maurice Eckhart and Hendrik Kristalovich had never seen eye to eye. Margot was too good for any man. That was Hendrik's resolve. Margot appreciated her husband's resentment. Nigh on twenty years married, a good home, two wonderful grandchildren, stability, respectability, everything that a father could wish for his daughter, and the best Maurice got of it was a brisk and business-like handshake on the rare occasions he and Hendrik crossed paths, a comment about how it was too long between visits and the children were growing so fast. Joan Kristalovich had been dead a good five years. *Dead from emotional boredom*, Maurice said, and Margot smiled and said nothing despite the fact that she knew Maurice was more than likely right. If a life has no purpose then it finds a way to stop living. The cancer that took her mother was diagnosed and done within a month. She had it, and then she was dead. Margot went down to Lubbock to be with her, and the speed with which she deteriorated made it impossible for her to leave. After the funeral Margot stayed behind with her father for another week. A week was sufficient to establish some sort of routine for him, for he was a man who had never attended to any domestic matters. A week was also brief enough for her to maintain her tongue and her temper.

Margot had to be honest, though it pained her to admit it.

When she heard of her father's death—sudden, unexpected, a fatal stroke while waiting to cash a check at the Lubbock Savings & Loan—she experienced a combination of sadness and relief. The journeys they made back home—once by train, once by air (which made Linda awful sick and they vowed never to do it again), most times by road—were exhaustingly long. Christmas and the tail end of summer. December and August. Twice a year they went, often for a week, but the two or three days' traveling at each end made it the better part of a fortnight. Now they wouldn't have to do it again. They were all going, and going for the last time. Linda was seventeen, Dennis was nineteen, and they were plenty old enough to take a responsible part in what needed to be done. The house would need emptying, cleaning, perhaps a lick of paint here and there, and then they would get it on the market and sold as soon as possible. Hendrik Kristalovich's personal business affairs could be managed by Maurice and the Lubbock family lawyer. The Eckharts hoped to be there no more than a week, but Maurice had been given compassionate leave from the same school supplies firm he had once sold for, the firm he now co-managed, and they had some leeway. It was November, a better time than the high summer, and it was far enough away from Christmas not to spoil it. So they would spend Thanksgiving in Texas; there could be worse things.

That prescient and unknowing thought, nonchalantly considered as Maurice decided to pull over for a brief stop at a diner before they reached El Paso, could not have been more right. They were many worse things, and the Eckharts were soon to meet one of the very worst of them.

Maurice had been driving for a little more than three and a half hours. Linda and Dennis had been asking for bottles of Coke and bathrooms for an hour, Margot wanted to freshen her makeup and stretch her legs. State highways notwithstanding, they had made good time—Lubbock to the outskirts of El Paso before lunch.

"Quarter of an hour," Maurice said as he drew to a stop outside the diner.

"Half," Margot said. "Half an hour."

Maurice conceded by raising no objection.

The kids took off with a dollar apiece, Margot walked around the car a couple of times and then asked Maurice if he wanted to go inside for a cup of coffee.

"We should probably get a bite to eat as well," she said. "Once we're on the other side of El Paso we'll be on the interstate and you won't want to stop."

Maurice nodded in agreement. "Yes, okay," he said. "Makes sense. Go shout to the kids. Tell them we're having an early lunch."

Maurice headed on into the diner. Alone he did not draw Elliott Danziger's attention, but when the wife followed on, the two kids in tow, Elliott looked up and watched them as they made their way to a table in the corner. The daughter looked a little like the girl back in Tucson, the one with the shopping bags, the one he stabbed with the kitchen knife. She had her hair tied up, two tails like horses, a bright yellow band around each. He thought how good it would be to hold on to those tails while he fucked her in the ass. The mom was sweet-looking as well. She had legs—long, long legs—and she had on those skin-tight pants that women wore, the ones that came down just below the knee. And then there was the dad and the son.

Something happened in Elliott's mind. He ceased to see four, and he saw one: a family.

What it was that happened he did not know, could not comprehend, but he knew he felt different. There was sadness, something nostalgic, some strange emptiness that ran right through the middle of his heart and out the other side. Aside from that there was resentment, spite, anger, hostility, a dry mouth, sweaty palms, and the hairs on the back of his neck stood to attention like convicts at muster.

A family.

He thought of Clay, hateful little bastard son of a bitch that he was, and for some reason he wished he were there, eating with him, smiling perhaps, the two of them making some wiseass joke about something or other the way they once did.

Son of a bitch traitor bastard Clay.

A family.

Mom, dad, son, and daughter.

Mom laughed about something as she stood at the counter, and she reached out and touched her husband's arm. There was affection in that gesture. Digger wanted to stand beside her and understand why they were laughing together. At the same time he wanted to grab her by the hair and smash her face repeatedly into the cold glass of the chilled unit.

A family.

He closed his eyes, gritted his teeth. He took a moment to lean sideways and look out the window. The only new arrival in the lot out front was a dark brown station wagon, evidently theirs.

He put his arm around his plate and put his head down. He ate his eggs and hamburger while he considered what to do.

CHAPTER THIRTY-SEVEN

It was at some point along the road to Las Cruces that Clay Luckman decided to get rid of the gun. He'd been carrying it since Marana, all of two days now, and the weight of the gun itself, the box of shells, felt like trouble and nothing else. He was of the viewpoint that if he kept it, well, it might end up being used, and that would be the cause of nothing but heartache. He was also thinking of Bailey. There was something practical and real about the girl, despite her age, but there was also something wild. He sensed it, perceived it. He believed that she might convince him to keep the thing, believing that they might need it to defend themselves. Against what, she wouldn't be able to say, but he imagined her persuasive, using wiles and flirtatious aspects to get her own way. Girls did that. It was in their nature. It was an instinctual sense of self-preservation that dictated his intention. If you didn't carry a gun you couldn't shoot anyone. Shoot someone, and you were more than likely going to get shot right back.

They had walked a good three miles from the Hatch turnoff. They were still a hell of a way from Las Cruces, and it was Bailey who commented on the marks on the road.

"Look," she said, and pointed to the wide streaks of black that appeared to veer suddenly right and away into the landscape. Beyond thirty yards the landscape dipped and hollowed and they could see the tops of trees. The tracks headed that way but there was nothing visible but more landscape.

"You think there was maybe an accident?"

Clay shook his head. He didn't want to go looking for anything but lunch.

"Maybe there's a car down there," she said. "Maybe someone's in trouble."

It was that sentiment that got him. Would never have thought so, but he was the sort of person who'd come back and help out even if it meant hardship for himself. He was innocent, and yet wound up blamed for things. He shrugged it off like snow, but some of the damp and cold got through. Irritation clouded his features.

"You misery," she said. "What if there's people down there and they're hurt? What if someone's come off the road and they need help and people have been driving back and forth all morning and no one's seen them?"

"Let's go," Clay said, and thought that if nothing else he could dump the gun and the shells en route and she'd never be any the wiser.

From the point the rubber tread marks left the highway they went at a direct thirty- or forty-degree angle. Clay knew nothing of cars, Bailey even less, but from what he could glean with common sense it appeared the car had come away at speed and continued in the same vein.

They walked two hundred, maybe two hundred and fifty yards, and then Clay smelled the gasoline.

He moved more rapidly, his thought for the disposal of the gun falling away from priority. Maybe Bailey was right. Maybe someone had come off the road. Maybe people were hurt.

The ground dipped suddenly, and it was this incline that had hidden the scene from view.

"There it is!" she said even as he saw it. A car, nose down, back end angled up toward them. The car had been stopped by a tree, and there was a static unnaturalness to the scene that seemed so very wrong. Clay expected to see smoke, but there was none. The entire scene was nothing but a photograph.

How long the car had been there he had no way of knowing. By the time Clay caught up with Bailey she was already retching. She leaned against a nearby outcrop of rock and dry-heaved painfully. Clay came up alongside the car. He could see the bowed shoulders and back of one man. The other man he did not see until he was two or three feet from the passenger door, and it wasn't long before he started to get some inkling of what might have occurred.

The driver's head had met the windscreen, and then he had

fallen back against the seat. His face was caked with dark, dry blood. One eye seemed to have burst, the other was closed. Blood had run down from many lacerations in his face and neck. His shirt was soaked, the tops of his pants too, and it was there that Clay appreciated what had taken the driver's attention off of the road. His penis was out, but it seemed to have been severed halfway up. Blood soaked his thighs, his legs, all the way down to his knees. The passenger, another younger man, was sideways on his seat, his shoulder against the dash, his hands and face and arms also drenched in blood. The passenger, leaning sideways, had been doing something that really shouldn't have been entertained while in a car. Maybe they went over a bump, maybe the driver lost concentration and left the road, but it looked like he'd gotten his dick bitten in half. That was the assumption Clay Luckman made, and that was the way he reckoned it had gone. Panicking, hysterical, blood gushing all over the place, the driver just took the car away into the scrubland on the side of the highway and met a tree. In a war between a car and a tree there was only one winner. The driver's head had met the windshield, the passenger's the dash, and that was that. Even had the driver survived the impact, he would have bled out very quickly. This was a loser whichever way it had happened.

Clay surveyed the scene once more and then directed his attention to Bailey. She had staggered away a good ten feet, was down on her haunches, back to the scene, her complexion pale, a thin film of sweat on her face.

"You gonna be okay?" he asked.

"M-maybe n-next week," she stuttered. She retched again. Nothing came up.

"Pretty bad, huh?"

"Yeah, I'd say so. What the hell—" She didn't finish the question. She was going to ask him what he believed had happened, but she was possibly embarrassed. She wasn't dumb. She'd already figured it out. It must have been one hell of a way to die.

Clay walked back to the car. The hood was cold. There was no engine clicking. There was no smoke. Nothing. The vehicle was as dead as the occupants. From the look of the blood—stiff and black and dry—he reckoned they'd been dead a good few hours. Why the scene wasn't haunted by buzzards he didn't know.

Maybe it was the smell of gasoline. He walked around to the other side and took the gun and the shells out of his pants pockets. Leaning down he pushed them as far beneath the car as he could.

Carefully, fingertips only, he reached in and started searching the passenger's jacket. He found a pocketbook and a comb. The comb he dropped in the well, the pocketbook he went through. He found no ID, no driver's license, but there was nine dollars—a five and four ones. He stuffed them in his pocket and dropped the pocketbook in the man's lap.

He did the same with the driver, carefully lifting the lapel of his jacket until he could reach inside. That burst eye stared back at him. It was grotesque, sickening, but necessity alone enabled Clay to do what had to be done. He too had a pocketbook, but he was evidently doing a lot better for himself than his passenger. Thirty-eight dollars, forty-seven all told, and with the few dollars that still remained they now had fifty and change. One man's loss was another man's gain. Things were on the up.

Clay counted the money out. It had a reassuring feel. Felt like full stomachs and maybe a coat for Bailey. Felt like blankets, hamburgers, maybe some hash browns and a chicken-fried steak. He stuffed the dollars in his pocket and went back to tend to Bailey. She was up on her feet, walking back and forth around the rocks against which she'd leaned for support.

"Sick," she mumbled. "Really sick."

"I got us the better part of fifty dollars," Clay told her.

Her eyes widened. "You took their money?"

"Sure I did. They ain't gonna have a helluva lot of use for it."

"But they're dead."

Clay was puzzled. "And this is worse than taking it off of living people?"

"It's different. It's disrespectful. Ain't you superstitious?"

"Superstitious about what?"

"Stealin' money off of dead folks . . . means their ghosts is gonna follow you until you pay it back."

"That's just so much horseshit. Lord Almighty, where did you hear such a thing?"

Bailey turned her back on him and walked toward the road.

"Wait up," he called after her. He let her go twenty feet and then he jogged up behind. "You can have half of it," he said.

"Won't catch me touching dead peoples' money."

"Suit yourself. Won't stop you eatin' the stuff it buys though, will it?"

She stopped suddenly. He near as damn it ran into her. She glowered at him for a while, and then she seemed to lose the will to argue. Her face cleared, she turned back toward the road, and he stayed silent.

They were a good quarter mile down the highway before she spoke again.

"You think we should do something about it?"

"About what?"

"About those two people. About that accident."

"What do you suggest?"

"I think we should tell someone. The police maybe. We should make an anonymous call as soon as we can and tell someone that there's dead folks down there."

"And if we do then you'll shut the hell up about superstitions and dead men's money?"

She hesitated, and then she nodded in the affirmative. "Deal," she said.

"Okay," Clay replied. "Next place we come to we'll find a phone and make your call."

She seemed satisfied. The hunch came out of her shoulders. She looked up ahead as opposed to down to the road. The mood lightened.

Clay walked on beside her, and once again she moved into his shadow and kept up with him step for step.

CHAPTER THIRTY-EIGHT

Circumstance, coincidence, the reason didn't matter. All that mattered was the appearance of Walter Milford's neighbor in the early afternoon of that Wednesday. Walt Milford and Frederick Ross had been neighbors for fifteen years. They had probably spoken about fifteen times. They were old school—both alone, both generally miserable—but never did it occur to them to pool their loneliness and misery and make the most of it. It was like the old story—two Englishmen stranded on an island in the Pacific, and after many years a rescue boat arrives. They both approach the vessel, at which point the oarsmen greets them both, assuming of course that they know each other all too well. "Oh no," one Englishman says. "We've never been properly introduced." That pair of schmucks could have been Walt Milford and Fred Ross—strong, silent types, knew best whatever the situation, never humble enough to be corrected, never wrong enough to be right.

The motivation for Fred Ross's visit that Wednesday was one of extraordinary unusualness, namely a bloodhound called Wagner, a *dumb cooze of a thing* as far as Walt Milford was concerned. Ross had owned Wagner for three years, had inherited him as much as anything else. A family of Californians had moved in down the block, had stayed for little more than six months, and then upped and gone without warning. Wagner had been theirs, and they left the poor dumb thing behind. He howled relentlessly for twenty-four hours, and then Fred Ross went in through one of the windows of the rented house and found him. That was a done deal. Fred was Wagner's savior. Wagner never left his side from that day forward. Fred Ross had never been a dog man. Never been an anything kind of man when it came to domestic pets. But Wagner had a way about him, a kind of understanding nature. He seemed to know when to be quiet, when to be playful, when to leave Fred alone, when to haunt his feet. It was a good arrangement. An arrangement that worked.

Fred Ross might have owned a dog, but he did not own a car. Walt Milford, now unable to drive a car, owned a Ford Galaxie, and it was that Ford Galaxie that Fred Ross possessed the intent to employ in assisting Wagner's journey to a veterinarian. The dog hadn't eaten for twenty-four hours, had barely drunk any water. He was listless and lethargic, and though not an energetic dog at the best of times, such apathy was very much out of character. Had it been six or eight blocks Fred Ross might just have carried Wagner. But it wasn't six or eight blocks, it was a good six or eight miles. There wasn't a way in the world they were going to send an ambulance, so Wagner was going to stay home whilst Fred Ross went to Walt's.

So Ross appeared at the front door, and the first thing he noticed was the absence of the car. The car was gone only on those rare occasions when Milford's son showed up. It would be a bitter coincidence if this was one of those times when he had done so. Just when Ross needed him. That would tell him all he ever needed to know about luck, good and bad. The second thing Ross noticed was the fact that not only the screen, but the inner door was unlocked. Opening the screen he leaned forward and pushed the front door. It swung inward. It made no sense. The car gone, the front door left open? Maybe a moment of forgetfulness, but he somehow doubted it. Seemed from what little he knew of Walt Milford the man was fastidious and organized, much the same as himself. It was an age thing, a culture thing, because these days the younger ones didn't seem to give a damn about much of anything at all. Except maybe girls. Girls and music.

Fred Ross called out. "Walter? Walter? You in here?"

There was nothing. Not a sound.

He called out again. "Walter? It's Fred . . . from next door. You in here, Walter?"

The seemingly inherent and premonitory shift in viewpoint that accompanied aging kicked in. Ten tears, twenty years younger, and there would never have been such a thought. Walt Milford was out. He'd left his door unlocked. These things happen. No big deal. But now? Get past sixty and the first thing you thought of was a fall, an accident, a coronary, a stroke.

Fred Ross let the front door close behind him and he stood in the dim silence of the hallway for quite some time. He could feel the slightly increased pace of his own heart. His nostrils cleared like ammonia. The hairs on the nape of his neck stood to attention.

He took a step forward. He swallowed noisily. He cleared his throat.

"Walter? You okay? Can you hear me?"

Dead, unconscious, even hit with stroke and lying somewhere mumbling and drooling, such questions were irrelevant and unnecessary, but they were instinctual and automatic.

Fred made his way slowly along the front hallway to the doorway at the end. The house was of much the same design as his own. Through this doorway was the sitting room, in the right wall of the sitting room the doorway into the kitchen, on the left the doorway into the dining area.

The door was closed, and before he reached out his hand and pushed it he steeled himself for what he might see. He knew he was being foolish, he knew there was a more than satisfactory explanation for the absent car and the unlocked front door, that Walter had gone with someone to attend to some unexpected matter, had simply forgotten to pull the door firmly closed behind him . . . or perhaps he hadn't meant to lock it. Once again a generational thing. It was only in the last five years, ten at most, that you'd had to consider who might be in the neighborhood, who might be keeping an eye on your house, who might be interested in getting inside while you were gone. Walter might have expected to be away for just a little while, and it hadn't been worth searching out his keys . . .

Fred raised his hand and pushed on the door. It swung inward slowly. The curtains were drawn. Light came in through the windows from the backyard. The room was empty. He took a step forward, immediately alert for Walter's feet protruding from behind a chair, his body hidden from view.

There was nothing.

He breathed his first small sigh of relief.

It was then that he heard it. A scratching sound. Scratching and tapping.

Fred angled his head to the right and frowned. Was that a dog? A cat perhaps? It sound like an animal trapped somewhere.

And then he heard the low moaning, and he started suddenly. He felt a shudder up his back, and the hairs at the nape of his neck rose to attention.

There it was again.

He didn't scare easy, but there was something about the quietly desperate sound that chilled him to the bone.

Scratch. Tap, tap. Uuuggghhh . . .

The door. The basement door.

He closed his eyes. He kept them closed for a good ten seconds. The very same door in his own house went down into the basement. He stepped closer. He ran a strange and inexplicable gamut of emotions, everything underpinned by a sense of chilling dread. He knew. Somehow he *knew* something bad had happened to Walt Milford.

Fred looked around for something, saw Walter's cane lying right there on the floor.

It didn't make sense. Walter, without his cane?

And then two and two began to approach four, and he started to appreciate what had happened here, and all of a sudden his fear vanished and he rushed for the cellar door and started shouting.

He called out Walter's name again, but his voice was weak and it cracked on the second syllable. In his own mind he sounded like a frightened girl.

"Walter? Walter, you down there?"

The moaning sound became louder, and Fred knew where Walter was. He unlocked the door, wrenched it open, and found the old man there, lying right there on the steps, his face dirty, his breathing weak . . .

He helped him up and out of the cellar doorway, shouldered him to the sofa, laid him down, and then he was on the phone, calling for help, the police, ambulance, everybody he could think of.

He looked back at Walter as he stood there with the receiver in his hand, and his heart went out to the old guy.

A half hour later Walter was gone, away in an ambulance to the hospital, and Fred Ross sat in Walt Milford's kitchen and answered questions for a detective called Cassidy.

After Cassidy had left Fred Ross went home. He got two or three shots of whiskey inside of him, and went out for a pack of cigarettes. He'd not smoked a cigarette for thirteen years.

And then a while later the detective named Cassidy came back again. He said he'd been out to see Walter in the hospital, wanted to let him know that Walter would be fine.

"He's a tough old guy," Cassidy said. "Tough as boots."

"He tell you what happened?" Fred Ross asked.

"He did, for sure."

"But he can't tell you who it was, him bein' mostly blind an' all, right?"

"Right," Cassidy replied.

Ross sat and listened as Cassidy started talking. He told him that he believed the attack on Walter Milford was connected to another assault in Tucson, a young girl who lived above a hardware store. He was disappointed that Fred Ross didn't known the license number of Walt Milford's dark gray Ford Galaxie, but he said that it wouldn't take too much work to find out. Already he had called the federal office in Anaheim, California, and had given all the information to the agents there. Apparently there were people working on it, people who might want to talk to Ross directly, and if he was to hear from men by the name of Koenig and Nixon then Cassidy would appreciate it if Fred would answer up as best he could on anything they wanted to know.

Why this Detective Cassidy told him these things he didn't know. Ross certainly didn't want to know any more about the attack on Walt Milford, nor what might have happened to anyone else for that matter. He wanted to try and forget the whole thing. He knew he wouldn't. Not for a long time.

Fred Ross watched Detective John Cassidy leave by the back door and cross the yard. Cassidy accessed Walt Milford's property at the rear and went on up into the house once again. Fred knew that the detective stayed there for another hour or so, because the man's car was parked out front. He wondered what it would be like to have a job like that, to make such things as this your business. He wondered what the hell the world was coming to. He wondered about a lot of things, and not a damned one of them seemed to make a great deal of sense.

CHAPTER THIRTY-NINE

Bailey Redman did the talking while Clay Luckman hung back by the potato chips and pork rinds. They'd come by a gas station with an attached store that sold fan belts, spark plugs, cans of oil, shoelaces, an assortment of handmade bird boxes, packets of seeds, all manner of things that seemed incongruous and unrelated.

"We've walked about an hour," she told the man behind the counter. He had on a red checkered shirt and tatty-looking dungarees. His hands looked like they'd been soaked in crude oil every night for much of his life. A pin badge on his breast pocket read *Clark*.

"Maybe four, five miles back that way," she explained. "A car went off the road. There's two dead men in there."

"And what would you want me to be doin' about it?" Clark said.

"Nothin'," Bailey replied. "Just call someone maybe. The police. Just tell someone so they can go out there and fix it all up. Someone somewhere is gonna wanna know that their kin is dead, wouldn't you say?"

Clark nodded slowly. "Guess so," he said. "Okeydoke, I can do that." He looked at Clay Luckman suspiciously. Maybe this was a scam. Maybe the girl was here distracting his attention with alarmist fabrications while her accomplice was pilfering pork rinds.

"Thank you," the girl said, and she smiled. She didn't smile like a thief's accomplice. Clark relaxed a mite.

The kid came forward then. He had two bags of chips, one of rinds, a packet of Oreos. Didn't look like he was concealing contraband anyplace about his person. He paid with a five-buck bill. Clark made change, gave him a paper bag to put his provisions in.

They went on their way, and as soon as they were out on the highway he made the call to the Luna County Sheriff's Department. Clark Regan was lucky enough to catch the sheriff personally. Hoyt was about to take an early lunch. He knew Hoyt Candell. Had known him for years. Hoyt seemed surprised at first, and then very interested. He said he would drive out himself and check up on it. He wanted to know which way the kids had gone. *Two of them you say? A boy and a girl. How old? You remember what they looked like? If you saw them again could you identify them?*

Clark hung up. Sheriff Hoyt Candell would be by to see him later, to let him know whether or not there were really two dead bodies in a car four or five miles down the road.

Even as Sheriff Candell started out from his office Clay Luckman and Bailey Redman were fortunate enough to get a ride that would take them all the way into Las Cruces. They would be there within the hour, and none the wiser about what was going on just forty or fifty miles behind them.

CHAPTER FORTY

Digger waited until they were done eating.

The more he watched them the more he liked them. The girl had stopped looking like anyone else, and she just looked like herself. The mom and dad seemed like nice folks, chatting with each other, the dad asking the waitress for extra stuff for the kids every once in a while, and when they looked like they were set to leave he took out his wallet and left a good tip on the table.

Nice folks.

Kind of folks who seemed like they'd help someone out who was in a pickle.

Digger got up and started over toward them.

He straightened his jacket as he went. Flattened down his bangs at the front in case they were mussed, and he tried to smile as best he could.

He felt nervous, no doubt about it.

He felt like he was seven, and in trouble for something he didn't do.

The man saw him coming, set down his coffee cup, and frowned slightly.

"Hey there, mister," Digger said. Even his voice sounded like a child.

"Hey, son. What's up?"

Son.

Digger bit his bottom lip.

"Hope you folks is all okay," Digger said. "Hope you all had a good breakfast and whatever."

The girl sniggered.

The boy nudged her silent.

The mom just looked puzzled.

"What's up there, son? How can we help you?"

Son.

Digger closed his eyes for a moment. His palms were pretty much running with sweat. He could feel the drips falling from his fingers. He knew that couldn't be the case, but still he could *feel* it.

"Hey there," he said to the boy, and this prompted yet another snigger from the girl.

Digger felt his cheeks color up.

No, he *could* do this. He *could* deal with this. He *could* get these nice folks to give him a ride out of here. He *could* use this situation to his advantage. A good few miles in the right direction, someplace where he could find another car maybe. People had to be looking for him, of course, but they weren't looking for a family. No, they weren't looking for a family.

This was thinking smart. This is how Earl would have figured things out.

"I was just wonderin' if you folks were heading my way . . ."

"You want a ride, son?" the man asked.

The wife smiled, like she was a little embarrassed, but there was something beneath that, something . . . Jesus, what was the word? Clay would have known the word. Something that made Digger feel like she was looking down on him. The kind of way Shoeshine would look down on him from up on his high horse. *You are not like me. I am superior to you.* This kind of thing.

"Yessir," Digger said, as politely as he could. "I figured you come on up here in that there station wagon, and I wondered whether there was room enough for one more for a while."

"Well, son, I don't know about that kinda thing. I'm just here having some breakfast with my family, and we're lookin' to get goin' as quickly as we can. We have a long drive ahead of us, and very little time to be making detours and diversions, no offense."

No offense. Digger knew what that meant. Earl had told him what that meant. *Folks say "No offense," well what they're really saying is that they're gonna insult you or say something really shitty to you, and they don't want you to get mad. How about that? No offense? How's about you go fuck yourself, huh? How's about that for no offense?*

"No offense?" Digger heard himself say. He meant to think it, but it just came right on out of his mouth.

"Right, son, no offense . . . now if you don't mind, we have to be making tracks."

Digger glanced back at the kids. The girl looked like she was laughing at him. She had on a nervous expression, but underneath he knew she was laughing. Why, Digger didn't know. Did he say something to upset anyone? Did he say something strange? No, he sure as hell didn't. He was polite and respectful, and all he did was ask if they had room in their wagon for one more. Which they did. Sure as hell they did. And they were just disrespecting him . . . just like that guy in the diner, the one with the hat.

Digger clenched his fists. He could feel the sweat creeping out from between his fingers.

There was no reason for him to feel like this.

Earl would not have felt like this. Earl would have just told the guy that he was going to give him a ride, no question, and that would have been the end of it.

Digger didn't move.

"Son . . . if you don't mind . . ." the man said, and he was getting to his feet.

"I didn't mean nothin' by it," Digger said. "I was just askin' if you'd be kind enough to get me a ride, that was all."

The man frowned. He tilted his head as if he was trying to see Digger from some other angle, like there might be something further to this than what he could see if he looked straight ahead. It was a dismissive look, just like that dirty son of a bitch back in the diner. Marlon whoever.

"You asked real polite, son, and I answered real polite . . ."

Son?

What the damn hell was it with this?

Did no one see the man? Did everyone just see some fool kid standing in front of them?

". . . but we have a ways to go, and like I said before, we ain't planning on making any detours or diversions. I hope you get a ride an' all, but we have to get going."

Digger stepped back as they made their way out from the table and started toward the door. He could feel the weight of responsibility crowding against him. He was aware of what needed to be done.

As the boy passed Digger he smiled. It was a dirty little smile. A nasty little smile.

It was meant to make Digger feel like shit. But Digger didn't feel like shit. Something was inside him. It was strong. Earl was there. Earl was with him.

Bide your time there, buddy boy. Bide your time. They make you mad, well, you lost the game already. You set the rules, and hell, you pretty much won it hands down before the get-go.

Digger waited until they'd left, waited until he heard the station wagon start up, and then he went after them.

Digger followed the station wagon for a good three miles. They were headed his way, back west along 180 toward El Paso.

They could have given him a ride.

They could have been nice folks, good citizens, but no, they wanted to be assholes.

Earl would have been *so* pissed. *Hypocrites*, he would have called them. *Shallow, superficial goddamn hypocrites.*

Digger didn't trail them closely. He let them go on ahead by a good quarter mile, and it was only when his anger started to mellow into something a little more edgy and focused that he decided to pull up ahead of them and make them stop. He glanced at the clock in the dash. It was a few minutes after noon.

Why Maurice Eckhart stopped was the question that would later be asked. In reality, it was simply because he had no choice. The young man that had asked him for a ride in the diner, the young man that was now driving alongside them in a dark gray Ford Galaxie had a gun. He pointed that gun out of the window right at Maurice and shouted at him to "Slow down! Slow down, goddammit!" And when Maurice slowed down the young man in the Galaxie nudged him over to the side of the highway and brought him to a standstill.

Maurice was confused and disoriented. The young man got out of the Galaxie and walked toward the station wagon. Linda was asking what was happening. Dennis said he was a psycho, to which Margot replied, "Don't be such a damned fool, Dennis. Stop trying to scare your sister." It was too late. Linda was already scared. The young man was close to the car, and there was something about the arrogance and certainty with which he approached them that frightened the hell out of her. Had there been a chance to ask questions later, then Linda would've been the one who was closest to the truth. *I knew it was trouble from the moment I saw that boy come to our table. I knew something was going to happen. And I knew it was going to be bad.* That's what she would have said had anyone asked her.

Maurice Eckhart, however, was faced with a situation for which there was no context or reference point. A young man with a gun. Was he just some crazy drunk? Was the gun even real?

"Hey there," the gunman said. "My name is Charlie . . ." Then he paused, and he smiled in a crooked kind of way, and he said, "What the hell, eh? I think we're all gonna end up friends by the end of the afternoon. My name ain't Charlie, it's Digger. At least that's what folks call me."

Digger leaned down toward the open driver's side window and grinned at Maurice.

"Maybe you don't remember, but we spoke a little while back. Up there in the diner."

Maurice nodded. "Now look here, son—"

Digger jabbed the barrel of the gun into Maurice's forehead. He repeatedly jabbed him as he spoke, emphasizing each word.

"Don't. Call. Me. *Son.* Get it?"

Maurice didn't say a word.

Digger turned his attention to Linda.

"Need you to get out of the car, sweetheart," he said. "Need you to come right on out of there and come get in my car over there."

Margot reached over the back of her seat and grabbed Linda's arm instinctively.

"Mom? Daddy?" Linda said, her voice wavering.

Maurice turned and looked at her. He shook his head. His eyes were wide with fear. He looked back at Digger. "Mister, I don't know what the problem is here, but my daughter isn't getting out of this car—"

Digger was fast. Whatever Maurice was planning to say was cut short as Digger's left hand closed around his throat. The right hand held the gun, and that gun came through the window and the barrel was pressed against Maurice's forehead—right there between his eyes and above the bridge of his nose.

Margot's complexion visibly paled. She held on to her daughter with one hand, gripped the edge of her seat with the other, and was angled against the door. Her face was rigid with fear. She looked at the young man with the gun, and in her eyes was such an expression, something so basic, something almost wild, as if the sheer force of her maternal instinct possessed sufficient power to stop bullets.

"Hey there!" Dennis said. "I don't know who the hell you think you damned well are, but—"

The gun was suddenly in Dennis's face. His mouth opened to say the next word, and it stayed open.

"Shut the fuck up, little boy," Digger said.

"Okay, okay," Maurice said. "I want to get out. Let me out of the car."

"Only one coming out of the car is the girl," Digger said.

Linda's eyes welled with tears. "Mom," she said, her voice faint. "Daddy . . . no . . ."

Margot reached back farther, almost as if she was trying to hide Linda completely. "My daughter isn't going anywhere with you, mister," she said, her tone direct and unflinching.

Digger was around the back of the car and he'd come up on the rear door before anyone had a chance to appreciate what he was doing. He wrenched the door open, grabbed Linda's arm, and she was out on her knees and being dragged roughly away from the vehicle. Dennis reached out for her, but Digger kicked the door and it came back against Dennis's left wrist. He howled in pain.

Digger hauled the girl to her feet and pushed her around to the front of the car once more.

By this time Maurice was out. He lunged for his daughter, but Digger took one step back and let fly with an almighty kick. That kick caught Maurice in the side of his right knee. He howled in agony and went down like a stone. Despite the pain, despite the fall, he was up again in moments, his body listing heavily to one side.

"Goddamn you!" Digger said. "You just don't know when to say uncle, do you?" He let fly with another kick, and this time he connected with Maurice's shin. Maurice screamed and went down for a second time.

Digger leaned down, his hand still holding Linda tight as anything, and he shoved the gun in Maurice's face.

"Now get back in your fucking car, old man, and follow me. Follow me and you'll get your daughter back. Take off for the police and she's gonna die."

Linda started sobbing, Margot screamed at the top of her voice. Maurice was struggling to get up, managed to reach the outer handle of the door and drag himself to his feet.

Margot started to open the passenger-side door.

"Stay in the fucking car!" Digger shouted. "I'm taking her with me, just like I said. Follow me and everyone's gonna be just fine. Take off and she dies."

Digger didn't wait for a response from anyone within the car. He hurried Linda Eckhart over to the Galaxie, pushed her into the passenger seat, and went around to the driver's side.

With his back to the station wagon for just a moment, Digger didn't see Dennis. Dennis was out of the wagon, and with his left arm hanging limp by his side, he still possessed sufficient presence of mind, sufficient strength in his right, to come at Digger with a coffee flask. Metal, solid, a good pound and a half in weight, Dennis hurled it with every ounce of will he possessed, and it hit Digger in the back of the head and sent him sideways.

Digger, dazed for just a moment, realized that Linda was out of the Galaxie and back in the wagon, as were all the Eckharts, and that the wagon was kicking dirt up from its rear wheels as it skidded away.

"Jesus Goddamned motherfucking cocksuckin' son of a bitch!" he howled, and he got in the Galaxie, jammed it into gear, hurtled away from the side of the road, and went after them.

He was alongside them within two or three minutes, bearing over to their left so he could point his gun out of the window.

"Pull over!" he shouted. "Fucking pull over right fucking now!"

Maurice, his face showing nothing but abject terror, floored the wagon. It nudged ahead of the Galaxie, but the Galaxie was a more powerful car, and it carried only one whereas the wagon carried four. Digger had no difficulty matching his speed.

Digger glanced toward the rear window and saw the boy looking at him.

Motherfucker.

Digger fired once and saw the bullet pass through the rear door just beneath the lower edge of the window.

He knew he'd hit the boy. The boy fell back, his face a stretched mask of anguish and pain.

He believed he could hear the mother and daughter screaming over the roar of both engines.

"Now!" Digger shouted again. "Pull over now!"

Maurice flattened the accelerator, but the engine was grinding. The wagon would go no faster.

Digger fired into the side of the car. He hoped to hit Maurice, but he knew he hadn't.

Steam or smoke or something started to rush from beneath the wheel arch.

Maurice seemed to be losing control of the wheel. The wagon swerved back and forth across the road.

Digger aimed the gun to fire again, but suddenly the wagon angled violently and took off toward the far side of the road. It pitched off the highway altogether, and when the wheels hit the loose stones the car started to roll.

Digger slowed up. He drew to a halt. The car was still rolling.

Suddenly there was a dull *crump*. Digger saw something flare. Before he had a chance to reconcile what he'd heard and what he was seeing the car just seemed to erupt in a ball of bright orange and black. The sound was deafening. *Ba-doooom!*

It rocked to a standstill as the flames just burst from every window. The windshield exploded outward, and—though he knew it could only have been his imagination—Digger was certain he heard those motherfuckers screaming as they roasted.

Digger got out of the car.

He stood there with his hands on his hips.

"Son of a bitch . . ." he said to himself.

Then he turned.

Jesus fuck!

Another car coming down this way. Another damned station wagon.

Digger hurried back to the Galaxie and got his gun. He tucked it into the rear waistband of his jeans and went back to the side of the road.

The car was near, slowing then, getting closer, and then the car came to a staggered halt no more than thirty yards from Digger.

A woman got out, middle-aged, and came hurrying toward him.

"Oh my Lord!" she was saying. "Oh my Lord Almighty . . . what happened?"

Her name was Rita McGovern. She was thirty-nine years old, she was unmarried. Her sister, Mary, worked in an office in Washington, D.C., and had once spoken to Jacqueline Kennedy about a flower arrangement. Mary had told Rita that Jacqueline Kennedy was very nice, not at all airs and graces like she thought she might be. No, she was very pleasant, and she talked to her like her opinion actually mattered. Mary had felt awkward however, because she'd voted for the other one.

Digger didn't know this, wouldn't have cared. She was unattractive to him, and the tone of her voice irritated him.

She stepped closer to Digger, now no more than ten or twelve feet away.

"Did you see what happened?" she asked him. "Did you see what happened to the car?"

"Sure did," Digger replied. "And not only did I see it, I did it."

The woman looked at him. Her eyes were wide. They widened even farther when Digger produced his gun and shot her in the throat.

The sound she made as she hit the ground, the sound of her hands clawing at the huge wound in her neck, the blood that just seemed to bubble up out of that hole like it was never going to stop . . .

Those were the things Digger Danziger heard as he got in the woman's station wagon and drove away. He figured that whoever was looking for him might have found the old guy in the basement, and it was best to leave the Galaxie behind. He also left behind the .38, now empty, that he'd picked up in Wellton.

"Family," he said to himself as he accelerated away from the devastation behind him. "Trouble if you got 'em, trouble if you ain't."

273

CHAPTER FORTY-ONE

"**Y**ou ever get the idea you were meant for greatness?"

Clay frowned. "Greatness?"

"Well, at least meant for somethin'. Somethin' that ain't nothin'. Seems to me most peoples' lives are all chockfull of almosts and maybes. Things that should've been, you know?"

He was silent for a while, and just as he looked about to speak he was silent a while more.

They were on the outskirts of Las Cruces. They'd sat for some time—there at the side of the road where the ride had dropped them—and they'd just talked about nothing of consequence. Smoking cigarettes, eating pork rinds, wondering what the hell was going to happen next. Behind them was a dump. Tread-bare blacks and whitewalls, a rusted bicycle, a doorless refrigerator, hubcaps strewn about like bottle caps behind a late-night bar. There was no color in the landscape, as if drained off and put to better use someplace else. Someplace it would be appreciated.

"No," he said eventually. "I never did get the idea I was meant for much of anything at all."

"I did. I still do," Bailey replied. She flicked the cigarette butt out across the road. It bounced in a small cloud of sparks and came to rest.

It was about one thirty, and back sixty miles or so Hoyt Candell was surveying the scene as reported by Clark Regan from the gas station. Sure as hell there was an overturned car. Sure as hell there were a couple of dead fellers in it. And when he got down on his hands and knees and saw the gun and the box of shells beneath the vehicle the alarm bells went off in his head and he figured this for a good deal more than an accident. Candell, amongst many others, had been in receipt of the federal notice. It was now his responsibility to report this occurrence to the nearest federal office, which—if he was right—was about sixty miles away in Las Cruces. That report went in as soon as he had called up his deputies and had them secure the scene. They marked and taped and barriered, they took preliminary photographs and measurements, and they didn't trample heavy boots all over the place because they knew there would be hell to pay if they messed it up. Hoyt Candell was a backwater burg sheriff, but he wasn't dumb. He'd been in the game long enough to know that there were rules and regulations, there was policy and protocol, and any man who believed he could buck the system and survive was a good deal dumber than he appeared. Nixon and Koenig were right there in Las Cruces when Hoyt Candell's report came in, and they were on the road by three. By the time they passed the dump on the outskirts of Las Cruces Clay Luckman and Bailey Redman had already walked into town, and their paths missed by inches once again. Had they crossed there would have been gunfire. Had they crossed, Clay Luckman would have been dead.

Hungry once again, Clay and Bailey stopped at a diner about a half mile in from the town limits.

"Now you think it was such a bad idea to take that money?" he asked her as he paid up for two hamburgers, a basket of fries, coleslaw, sodas.

She didn't reply. She was being right the only way she knew how.

Seated in a corner booth, stomachs full, they looked at each other awkwardly.

"You really think this is such a good idea?" she asked him.

"What?"

"Going to this Eldorado place."

He shrugged. "Hell, I don't know, Bailey. I don't know what the hell we're doin'. My folks are dead, your folks are dead, and each other is pretty much all we got right now." He paused, and then he smiled a curious smile. "One question I do have is why you go on hangin' with me?"

She smiled. "Polite girl always dances with the boy that brung her."

He smiled back. He turned and looked out of the window—the cinnamon-colored earth, the upside-down ocean of sky.

"Best get going," he said. "Want to see if we can get a ride down to El Paso, stay there the night maybe. Also want to keep ahead of anyone who might be looking for us."

She didn't move.

"Whassup?"

She closed her eyes for a second, and she took a breath deep enough to drown in. "I'm tired," she said.

" 'S why I wanna get to El Paso. Maybe we can find somewhere halfway comfortable to sleep."

"I don't mean like that. I don't mean not-enough-sleep tired. I mean tired in my heart, in my head. Like the spirit of me is tired."

"Hell, Bailey, you ain't seen nothin' yet. You had a bad start, that's all. We've both had a bad start, but things is gonna get better. There's plenty of folks had it rougher than us, and they come out on top. They end up makin' a bunch of money and straightenin' everything out. All of it is about making the future better than what we got now."

"Is that all it's about? You really think that's why we're here?"

Clay turned his mouth down at the corners. "It's lunchtime, Bailey. That kinda conversation is for when it's dark and quiet and there ain't nothing else goin' on."

"My father used to tell me stories, you know?"

"Stories?"

"I was thirteen when I met him for the first time. I took a bus to Scottsdale by myself and I found him."

"Hell, I bet he was surprised enough to have a heart attack."

"No," she said matter-of-factly. "He wasn't surprised at all. I think he expected me to show up."

Clay didn't speak.

"And he was real good. He was a good man in so many ways." She smiled, almost to herself. Clay had the impression he could have been anyone, that she just needed to say some things. Who might be listening was the least of her concerns. "He tried to make up for things, I think. He used to buy me stuff, and he'd make sure that he always had the things I liked to eat in the icebox when I came over, and when I went to bed he'd sit and tell me stories. Made-up things and real things, you know? He just told me stories about whatever he could think of at the time . . ." She hesitated. "This is gonna sound foolish," she said.

"Can't be the judge of that until I hear it," Clay replied.

276

"One time, a ways back, he told me a story about Eldorado. The real one, you know? Not the one in Texas."

Clay was at first disbelieving, then bemused, then just downright amazed. "That is a sign," he said eventually. "That *has* to be a sign."

"I don't know what it is, Clay, but I figured I should tell you. Since you mentioned this place in Texas it's been on my mind a good deal. Maybe it was nothing more than a coincidence or whatever, but I figured I had to say something."

"And what did he tell you about the real Eldorado?"

"Told me that everyone who gets there winds up rich and happy." She hesitated.

"What?" Clay asked her.

"Also told me that a lot of people died trying to find it."

Clay said nothing. She was right. Her father had been right. He understood something about her now. Coincidence, a sign, whatever it was, she was going along *because* of her father, not because of Clay or anyone else. Her father had spoken of it, and thus it mattered. He could have told her Denmark or England or Ding Dong, Alabama, and if he had said any one of those places then that's where they'd be headed. And coincidence? Clay didn't believe in coincidence. What had he heard one time? Coincidence was when God wanted to remain anonymous. *Sure as shit with sugar on top* was his sarcastic response to that homily. It was nonsense. Same as the bullshit church signs they passed every mile and a half.

"You believe that you're going to wind up rich and happy?" he asked her.

"I believe that if you believe anything hard enough then you can get it."

"That's a very positive outlook you have there."

"And you're very sarcastic."

"And you really think you're heading for greatness?" he went on.

She didn't hesitate because she was uncertain. She hesitated because she was thinking how to say what she wanted to say. That was the definite impression Clay got as he watched a faint smile emerge on her lips. "Greatness?" she said. "Hell, Clay, don't you think I'm just the greatest already?"

He didn't say anything. What was there to say? She was contagious, like a disease, but a good disease. A contagious *cure*. Was there such a thing?

"Leave a quarter for the waitress," she said as she got to her feet. "Leave a dollar maybe."

"I'm not leaving a dollar. Hell, we've got little enough money as it is."

"Leave a dollar," she repeated. "That money from those dead men was no more your money than anyone else's. Share a little bit of it. It might do us some good."

"You're serious—"

"Tempt fate if you want, Clay Luckman."

"You're telling me that if I don't leave a dollar then something bad is gonna happen to me?"

"I'm not saying anything of the sort."

He took the bundle of notes out of his pocket and dropped a dollar on the table.

"Jesus Christ," he said quietly.

She led. He followed. The waitress watched them go. Her name was Betty Calthorpe, and she later considered it strange that a couple of kids would leave a dollar as a tip.

Thirty minutes or so later Clay and Bailey picked up a ride into El Paso. The driver was a water-pump engineer called Martin Dove, and he asked their names and Bailey said her name was Frances and this here was her brother, and his name was Paul.

"Like St. Francis and St. Paul," Martin Dove said, and Bailey said a little like that, save that Frances was spelled with an *e*.

"It's *i* for 'im, and *e* for 'er. That's how you remember."

"Clever," Martin Dove said, and then he told them about the water pump he'd just fixed in Caballo, New Mexico, and now he was driving back to the office in El Paso to file his reports.

It was four thirty or thereabouts when they arrived, and the driver waved them goodbye and good luck. He thought they were nice kids, and then he never thought another word about them. Not until later.

CHAPTER FORTY-TWO

Garth Nixon and Ron Koenig were appreciative of Sheriff Hoyt Candell's care and attention to detail.

The gun and shell box had been left right where he'd seen them, and Nixon brought them out carefully, bagged them, asked if Candell would assign one of his deputies to drive them directly to the federal office in El Paso. There they had sufficiently advanced equipment to take prints from the gun. They could also trace the serial number of the weapon, ascertain whether it had ever been legally registered. Candell couldn't have been more helpful. The assigned deputy left the scene at 4:35. The items would be signed into the El Paso Bureau of Investigation Offices a little after six thirty, carrying with it Koenig's written entreaty that the matter be addressed with the utmost urgency. The senior technical officer was called back in from home. He started work immediately. Within an hour he had located the serial number registration of the weapon as that belonging to Harvey Warren, sole proprietor of the Marana Convenience Store & Gas Station in Marana, Arizona. It wouldn't be until the following morning that the fingerprints were formally identified, and this solely because Ronald Koenig happened to have a fingerprint record against which the lifted prints could be compared.

At the scene itself—the overturned car three or four miles from Deming, Luna County—Koenig and Nixon puzzled over the circumstances. At that moment they had no way of determining if the death of the two men had any connection to Clarence Luckman. From all circumstantial evidence it appeared that the two men had been engaged in some sort of sexual activity whilst the vehicle was in motion. The gun and the box of shells might already have been there, the car just happening to stop in the same place. Unlikely, of course, but nothing could be ruled out until certainty ruled it out. The gun may have been placed there later. There was no indication that either man had been shot, and the gun did not appear to have been fired recently. It was a piece of the puzzle that bore no context, or it was unrelated. Nixon suspected the latter, Koenig the former. Had he been asked why, he would not have wanted to cite intuition, but intuition it was. The farther they traveled, the more pieces of this thing appeared, the more he seemed to be able to determine those that belonged and those that did not. At least that's what he believed, and his belief was based on what he felt. The crime scene—the presence of the discarded gun and shells sufficient to classify it as a crime scene in Koenig's mind—*felt* connected. That was all he could say, and he didn't say it out loud. It *felt* connected.

They drove the four miles out to the gas station then, and they showed Clark Regan a photograph of Clarence Luckman, and Clark peered at that picture for a long time before he shook his head.

"I couldn't be sure," he said. "I was more talkin' to the girl. The kid was just hangin' back there by the pork rinds, and then he come on up here to pay for them, but I was still sort of talking to the girl and I didn't really pay him a great deal of mind."

"But it could have been him?" Koenig asked.

"Hell, mister, put it that way it *could* have been anyone."

They returned to the scene with no further certainty than that with which they'd left. Who this girl might have been they had no idea, and if she was in the company of Clarence Luckman and past track record was anything to go by she would more than likely be dead before dusk.

The Luna County coroner was called. Additionally Hoyt Candell sent for a tow truck. Once the coroner had removed the bodies Candell had the tow truck right-side-up the vehicle and then haul it back onto the road.

"What is it with vehicular-related homicides this week?" he asked Koenig.

Koenig shook his head. He didn't comment because he had no comment to make. Three dead men, fifteen miles apart, same county, same route as had been ascribed to the escapee Clarence Luckman. Koenig, irrespective of whatever intuitive shifts he might periodically experience, was also not a believer in coincidence. He thought of the decision that had been made. Luckman was going to die. That was the simple truth of it. There would be no hesitation, no second thoughts. The moment they saw him would be the moment of his death. Sometimes, for the good of all, it just had to be that way.

Satisfied that they had done all they could, Garth Nixon and Ronald Koenig left the scene at quarter past seven and drove the fifty miles back to Las Cruces. There the report from the El Paso office awaited them. The gun had belonged to one of the victims at the Marana Gas Station. Koenig had been right once again. Luckman had followed the I-10, had left the gun and shells at the scene with the two dead men, and then more than likely continued on into El Paso. Why the gun had been left behind, he did not know. Whether Luckman was responsible for the deaths of the two men in the car was also unknown. The one thing he did know was that El Paso would be their next destination. Nixon and Koenig checked out of their hotel and left immediately. They would be in El Paso before nine that evening. Photographs of Luckman had already started going out to the gas stations and convenience stores all the way along the interstate. Every uniformed man had seen that picture enough times to recognize Clarence Luckman from fifty yards. Additional FBI agents were being assigned to the surrounding counties and towns.

Ronald Koenig believed that they were very close to securing Luckman's arrest. The attacks on Gil Webster, Deidre Parselle, and now this Walter Milford. Beyond that the deaths of Laurette Tannahill and Marlon Juncau. Add in the two men in the car outside of Deming—if indeed Luckman had been responsible for that also—and it made four. Four was more than enough for any man. Four was already well over the line. This thing had to stop, and it had to stop right now.

The net would tighten up and close in. It was inevitable.

CHAPTER FORTY-THREE

Clay Luckman felt more than out of place in El Paso. It was a big city, seemed bigger even than Tucson. He wanted to carry on, to get out beyond the suburbs and stay the night in a motel somewhere along the highway. They still had the better part of fifty bucks. They could afford at least one really good meal and a good night's sleep. They deserved it, Clay reckoned, after the distance they'd walked and the things they'd seen. Bailey didn't argue. She seemed just too damned exhausted to bother.

Digger, however, was energized beyond all measure.

The thing with that family had been good. More than good. He'd been back on the road no more than thirty minutes, and he could barely contain his excitement. It had been a shame in a way, because the daughter was good-looking in most every way, and the mother was pretty fresh herself. They would have struggled for sure. But once he'd got inside them and showed them who was boss they'd have quieted down a good deal. Daughter first, then the mother, then the daughter again. After the second or third time he figured that they would have started to like it, started to get into the mood of the thing and all that. At least that's what he thought.

He thought about the boy that had hit him with the flask. He had showed a degree of courage, and courage was a quality Digger could admire very easily. The boy had been courageous, trying to protect his little sister like that. Earl Sheridan was courageous. The only person he could think of in that moment who was not courageous was his damn fool dumbass brother, and he didn't even know why Clay had come to mind. Thinking of Clay made him angry for moment, but then he forgot about him.

He just went about the business of driving, and he drove as

quickly as he could—away from the carnage, the dead bodies, the spent .38 that he'd taken from Wellton's Sheriff, Jim Wheland. He left Rita McGovern on the roadside, his fingerprints on the Galaxie, his shoe prints, the shell casings, and he left behind Walt Milford's dark gray Ford Galaxie that Garth Nixon and Ron Koenig were so desperate to find. He also left behind Margot Eckhart, left her with severe cranial trauma and a broken back. She had been thrown clear of the car as it rolled, and though unconscious and seriously wounded, she was still very much alive. She would come round within an hour of Elliott Danziger's departure. She would crawl from the scene of the burned-out station wagon to the highway and she would be seen by a young couple named Rick Waverley and Samantha Pierce. They were driving from Pine Springs to El Paso in a light blue Chevy that her father had given them for an engagement present. They were going to be married in June of 1965.

The El Paso County Sheriff's Department would be there by seven fifteen, and while Rick comforted the distraught Samantha by the side of the road, the emergency medical services rushed Margot Eckhart to Saint Savior's Hospital. The sheriff himself, a rail-thin sixty-one-year-old widower named Joseph Lakin, permitted no one access to the scene at all. He instructed that a cordon be erected both ways and that all traffic be diverted to another route back down the highway. They had found Rita McGovern's body not fifty yards away, and an abandoned Ford Galaxie, which—Lakin knew—was not Rita's car. Hers was a dark blue Ford station wagon, and it was evident in its absence. Lakin knew Rita McGovern due to the fact that they attended the same church, and now she was dead on the road with a gunshot wound to the throat. In the burned-out wagon there were another three—an older man in the driver's seat and two teenagers in the rear, though he could not tell whether they were male or female as yet.

Standing away from the smoke and the stench he made a call to the county office.

"Alert the feds," he said matter-of-factly. "I don't know what the hell we've got out here, but I reckon they need to come look at it."

CHAPTER FORTY-FOUR

Alice Cassidy stood beside her husband, felt the warmth of his hands on her stomach. Dinner plates were still on the table. He'd eaten like a ravenous thing, said nothing, and then sat for a while in silence while she watched him. He'd come back to her when she mentioned the doctor's visit earlier that day.

"He said it was all good. Everything is normal. Everything is going according to plan."

John did not reply, but she knew from the expression on his face that he was pleased and relieved.

She was waiting for him to tell her about the afternoon's events. There'd been another incident, something connected to the Parselle girl. She knew that much. He hadn't told her, not in words, but she knew him well enough to read the body language, the facial expressions, the silence.

"Same person," he said eventually. "Same one as killed the girl. I'm sure of it."

"And he's still in Tucson?" she asked.

John shook his head. "No, I don't think so. He locked someone in his basement and took his car, and I think he'll be long gone by now."

"And you've given all the information to those federal people that were here?"

"Yes . . ."

"Yes, but?" she prompted.

He looked at Alice, and then he looked away. He smiled at some errant thought, and then he looked back at her and said something that she could have predicted long before he started talking.

"It feels like I should work the case."

There was silence between them for a little while.

"But it's now a federal matter. Isn't that the truth?"

"Sure it is, but the incidents here are still our jurisdiction. I just think that with the murders before he got here, now these attacks . . . well, someone like that isn't going to stop, are they?"

"No," Alice replied. "Not if that's the route they're taking."

"I'm going to call them," John said.

"Now?"

"In a little while."

"But it's after eight already. How will you reach them?"

"I'll just call the federal office here in Tucson and they will know where to find them. They may still be here. They may have gone back to Phoenix, or they might be in El Paso or someplace."

Alice nodded. She started to clear the plates away.

John took her hand as she returned from the sink. He looked up at her.

She smiled, touched the side of his face. "I married you for who you are, not who I thought you might become. You do whatever you have to do. Don't you worry about me, okay? As long as you're safe then I'm fine."

John Cassidy called the Tucson federal office just before nine. He was informed that Agents Koenig and Nixon were in El Paso. If he called the El Paso office they might be able to give him the name of the hotel where they were staying. He called El Paso, he took the name and number of the hotel, and when he called he was informed that the federal people had checked in, received one phone call, and left again immediately. The hairs on the back of Cassidy's neck stood to attention. He thanked the receptionist at the hotel, put a call through to the El Paso County Sheriff's Department, and they informed him that the sheriff was out at a crime scene with the federal agents.

"Somewhere on 180," he was told. "Just a few miles out of the city."

Cassidy thanked them once again, hung up, and dragged out a local map. Interstate 180 ran directly out of El Paso, and then became 62 before heading on up through Pine Springs and into Carlsbad. El Paso was a good three hundred or so miles away. He felt the urgency. He felt the compelling need to go now. Right now. But he did not. He appreciated Alice's understanding, her acceptance of his work, the intensity with which he sometimes approached it, but he needed to reciprocate that understanding. Leaving now for a four- or five-hour drive to El Paso would not be enthusiastically encouraged. It would have to wait until morning, and then he would have to gain Mike Rousseau's permission.

His evident distraction prompted a barrage of questions from Alice. He told her as much as he knew, none of which was certain, all of which was a jigsaw of assumptions based on what little he knew.

"So go now," was her response.

He looked at her, surprise evident in his expression.

"Go now. Get the question answered. At least you'll know. Say you leave it 'til morning, and then you speak to Mike and Mike says no . . . well, what're you going to do then?"

Cassidy didn't have an answer.

"Go," she said. "I'm going to bed anyway. Go and find out what's happening, and then you can either drive back tonight or stay over and call me in the morning and let me know what you're doing. I know how you're going to be until this nightmare is over, and I'd rather have you doing something about it than pacing up and down all night and making me crazy."

John Cassidy didn't say anything. He just held her for a while, and then he kissed her forehead and let her go and he went upstairs to change for a long drive through the night.

CHAPTER FORTY-FIVE

Nine thirty p.m., evening of Wednesday the twenty-fifth of November, just as John Cassidy pulled away from the sidewalk ahead of his house, Elliott Danziger checked into a motel off of the I-10 outside of El Paso. Having driven back into the city after leaving the scene of the Eckhart killings, he took a leisurely dinner at a steak and ribs joint in the suburbs. He ate well. He was surprised by his appetite, but then he hadn't eaten since the diner where he'd first seen that family. And he'd been working, of course. Work like that was sure to fire up a good hunger.

The Sweet Dreams Motel was relatively secluded. It sat back from the highway by a good quarter mile. Nothing more than a crescent of cabins, cabins much as the one occupied by Bailey Redman and Clay Luckman no more than half a mile farther on. They had passed the Sweet Dreams a good while earlier, and though Clay had wanted to stop right there Bailey hadn't liked the look of the place.

"And the name," she said. "Sweet Dreams Motel. It's real corny, and it sounds like the sort of place where people book a room for an hour to have sex."

Caught off guard, a little embarrassed, Clay neither protested nor disagreed. They kept on walking, stopped at the next one they found, the Travelers' Rest, though the neon sign out front read *Th Travel rs R st*. It looked cheap enough to bother without questions, and Clay was right. The man behind the counter merely took their money and gave them a key. Had he been asked for their names Clay would have said anything but Clarence Luckman and Bailey Redman, but the man did not ask, and Clay did not offer. They took the key and made their way out of the building and around the corner to a disheveled cabin with a narrow, low-ceilinged bathroom in back, a TV that took quarters, and a double bed that seemed awful small for a double bed.

They talked about the sleeping arrangements. Clay Luckman, gentleman that he was, offered to sleep on the floor. Bailey said no, they could sleep head-to-toe on the bed. Clay went out to get bottles of Coke from a machine in the forecourt. They spent two dollars in quarters watching *The Patty Duke Show, Shindig!, The Dick Van Dyke Show,* and *The Beverly Hillbillies.* Neither of them wanted to watch the news to see if their respective disappearances were being reported. Perhaps out of fear, perhaps trying their best to believe that the world did not care and would leave them alone. Had they done so, they would have seen Clay's grainy monochrome face staring back at them, and a report that anyone who saw this individual was to report immediately to the authorities, that they should not approach or communicate with this person, that this person was deemed "armed and dangerous." Truth was that Clay Luckman hadn't seen much television at all. He asked Bailey where the pictures came from and how they arrived. Bailey said she didn't know, that it just happened that way. During *The Virginian* she took a bath. Clay turned the volume down and he could hear her singing in there. He didn't know what it was, but she had a pretty voice. She hadn't mentioned her father for a while, nor her mother for that matter, and even though Clay had thought of them both he hadn't said a word. Maybe she'd just closed it all up in the back of her mind. Maybe she was one of those people that bottled everything tight, and then life kept on shaking her and shaking her, and finally she would explode. Maybe she'd last until she was twenty-five and then have some kind of mental disease or something. He'd seen people like that—kids even—at Barstow and Hesperia. Couldn't feed themselves, couldn't talk properly, pushed full of pills that seemed to do nothing but make them a lot quieter or a great deal louder. One of them jumped off a roof and broke his legs. Another of them stabbed a younger kid with a dinner fork. Crazy people.

"You want a bath?" she asked. She stood in the doorway, a towel around her. Her hair was wet and combed back flat against her scalp. "I left the water in there for you in case."

"Sure," Clay said, and he waited for her to come on out so he could get into the narrow room.

Once inside, the door closed behind him, he could smell her. The soap, the warm water, and something beneath that. The scent of Bailey Redman. It made him think of her in all manner of ways that were personal and private, and he felt excited. Then he felt embarrassed because he was seventeen and she was fifteen, and really she was still a kid. But she was smart and she was funny and she was good-looking, and though he'd never had sex he did think about it a great deal, and if he was going to do it the first time then he would want to do it with someone like Bailey Redman. And then he thought that he wouldn't want to do it with someone *like* Bailey Redman, but with Bailey herself.

Clay leaned down and looked through the keyhole in the door. He couldn't see much of anything but the corner of the bed. He cursed himself for being a pervert, and then he got in the bath.

Later, smelling as clean as Bailey, he was aware of how rank his clothes were. Both of their clothes. They needed to get them washed, or they needed new ones. New stuff for both of them, if they were smart, could be as little as ten bucks. That would leave thirty-something.

"I think we should get some new pants and T-shirts," she said moments later.

"I was thinking the same thing."

She looked at the TV. "You ever seen this?"

"What?"

"It's called *The Alfred Hitchcock Hour*."

"Nope, never seen it."

"It's good. It's like spooky stories and whatnot. Come sit and watch it with me."

Clay got up on the bed and sat beside her. They watched it together, clean bodies in grubby clothes, and then they turned the TV off and lay down side-by-side, and neither one of them mentioned the fact that they were meant to be head-to-toe, and it was warm and they fell asleep.

At some point in the early hours Clay awoke. His head hurt and his mouth felt like copper filings, and he could hear a strange fluttering sound. It was a while before he realized it was just moths beating gently at the windows and the screens. They kept on trying, as if within was always infinitely better than without. As if something different was always far greater than something the same.

Bailey was curled against him, and their bodies were like spoons in a drawer. He was busting to pee, but he did not move. He did not want to wake her, because being this close to someone felt good, and it felt right, and it seemed like they belonged.

He smiled faintly, and he closed his eyes, and in a handful of minutes he was asleep once more.

Half a mile away, dreaming nothing, Elliott Danziger slept also. He wouldn't wake until eight thirty, and he would wake with the fiercest hunger and a thirst like the Sahara. He felt other things as well, inside things, things in his mind and his emotions. Among them was a sense of accomplishment, behind that a feeling of so many things undone, and the now-compelling need to hurt someone. It didn't matter who, and why was of even lesser concern. It was simply there, and so strong it was impossible to resist. Not that he would have resisted it. That would have been like saying *No* to ice cream, and who in their right mind would do that?

Again, despite the hour, conversations were taking place in offices and on telephone lines between serious men with serious faces. Agents were being dispatched to towns and cities throughout Arizona and California. Duty rosters were being drawn up, overtime money was being appropriated and apportioned, duty was being called upon, guns were being issued. Scheduling coordinators were being informed that radio bulletins needed to be broadcast more frequently. More pictures were needed. More local newspapers were being asked to run the grainy monochrome image of Clarence Stanley Luckman—escapee, killer, sociopath, teenager. More officers were assigned to locate the murdered body of Elliott Danziger. The pressure and insistence from the upper echelons of the Federal Bureau of Investigation had become relentless. No quarter would be given. No reason for failure would be acceptable. Luckman took pride of place as the most wanted man in the entirety of the continental United States.

And yet Clay Luckman, Bailey Redman, even Elliott Danziger remained oblivious to it all.

DAY SEVEN

CHAPTER FORTY-SIX

The surprise that Garth Nixon and Ron Koenig experienced when Detective John Cassidy presented himself at their hotel at a little after eight on the morning of Thursday, November 26, was matched only by Cassidy's seeming intensity. He was unshaven, looked somewhat disheveled, and they soon learned that he had driven from Tucson very late the night before, had found their hotel, but not wishing to wake them at two o'clock that morning had slept as best he could in his car. Inquiring after them a little before seven, Cassidy learned that they had already left. Apparently they were at a hospital somewhere. Beyond that their movements were unknown. Cassidy had then waited impatiently until their return more than an hour later. They had come back with the good news that Margot Eckhart was still alive, the not-so-good news that she was unable to answer questions and would remain that way for some considerable time. The nursing supervisor had their contact details, would inform them of any change in her condition. However, she had described the likelihood of Margot's recovery and subsequent ability to give them any information about her attacker with the phrase *as slim as it gets*.

The initial identification of the Eckharts and Rita McGovern at the crime scene had been straightforward enough. Employing all the resources they could muster from Deming, Lordsburg, and Las Cruces, ably supervised by Sheriff Hoyt Candell and Doña Ana county sheriff Michael Montgomery, Nixon and Koenig sent black-and-whites every which way. They backtracked every possible route the Eckharts could have taken, and they found the diner on 180. The agents had spent two hours there the evening before, had again spent two hours there that morning, and were now all set to cross-reference and confirm the numerous reports

295

they had taken from the employees. Koenig was certain beyond any question that Clarence Luckman had been at the diner on Highway 180 outside of El Paso. The diner owner, Ralph Jackson, had seen the dark gray Ford Galaxie outside, had noticed the fact that the young man who drove it was obviously an ex-con. "Either that or ex-military," he said. When asked how he knew this he said, "It's obvious. It's only ex-cons and ex-GIs that eat like that. Hunched down low, one hand holding the fork, the other hand around the plate like they're guarding it." Jackson also remembered the Eckharts. "Station wagon, I think," he said, "though I couldn't be sure. Nice people. Kids were very polite. Please and thank you and whatnot without having to be reminded by their folks. Seeing that less and less these days." Jackson could not confirm whether the Eckharts or the young man had left first. He saw neither the station wagon nor the Galaxie pull away. He was in back for a while sorting out a troublesome deep-fat fryer, and when he came back both the young man and the family were gone. He did not remember what the young man was wearing, and when Ron Koenig showed him a picture of Clarence Luckman he merely said, "I don't know, sir, I really don't. Teenage kids, young 'uns . . . hell, they all look the damn same to me."

Ralph Jackson's report placed the Eckharts in the diner around eleven or eleven thirty the previous morning, Wednesday the twenty-fifth. That's where Clarence Luckman saw them. He must then have followed the Eckharts out along 180 toward El Paso. From appearances Luckman had shot at the station wagon while in motion, and the driver had been wounded or sufficiently agitated to lose control of the vehicle. The woman had been thrown clear, but the car went on to ignite and kill the three occupants, now confirmed as the father and both the teenage children.

Rita McGovern, presumably arriving at the scene with an intent to help, had been shot in the throat by Luckman, and then Luckman had taken off in her station wagon, leaving behind the Ford Galaxie.

What was left was nothing but forensic evidence.

Unfortunately, the prints on the Galaxie and discarded .38 revolver were too smudged to be readable. The arrival of the print report from the weapon beneath the car gave them as much evidence as they needed to place Clarence Luckman in the locality of this latest atrocity. That gun had belonged to Harvey Warren in Marana, and these were undeniably Clarence Luckman's prints. Clarence Luckman was close, and with the utter brutality and violence inflicted on the Eckharts and Rita McGovern he was sure to be carrying all manner of evidence on his person. It was now simply a matter of finding him. And once they found him, it was going to be just as simple to shoot him right where he stood.

John Cassidy's appearance at the El Paso hotel was a curveball out of left field. There was no reason for him to be there. He had the attacks on Deidre Parselle and Walter Milford to investigate back in Tucson. This was a viewpoint not shared by John Cassidy.

"Luckman has moved on, right?" was his opening gambit. Koenig and Nixon had walked up to their room with him. Stacks of papers were piled around the carpet. The room looked more like an office than a hotel suite. "And if he's moved on then the case has moved on with him. I don't have any forensic skills above and beyond what your federal people have already employed in Tucson. I can't get any more out of those crime scenes. I've been to both of them, twice in fact, and I can't see anything else that is going to help you. You know who you're looking for, you have a damned good idea where he is, or at least the direction he's headed in, and I want to help."

Koenig looked at Nixon. Nixon looked at Koenig and then back at Cassidy.

"Your sheriff know you came out here?" Koenig asked.

Cassidy shook his head.

"Well, I don't know what to tell you, Detective. This is a federal matter. Your jurisdiction and authority stops right there at the Tucson city limits. We got your report about the attack on Walter Milford, and the fact that you identified his vehicle as a dark gray Ford Galaxie has been very helpful in this most recent case, but—"

Cassidy raised his hand. "I know all this, sir, but I have a feeling about this thing, and it's growing stronger by every minute . . ."

"And what feeling would that be?"

"That there's a little bit more to this than we might think.

There's something about this thing that just keeps nagging and nagging at me, and I can't let it go."

"And that would be?"

"Well, that would be the fact that it doesn't make sense. All we have are the reports from Barstow and Hesperia about this boy, but the idea that he could be capable of changing from someone who's never had any real trouble before to someone who is capable of doing all of this—"

"Oh, believe me," Nixon interjected. "People are certainly capable of doing this, and often it's the people you'd least suspect."

"I know it's nothing but intuition at this stage, but my intuition is good. I could be wrong, and I'm more than happy to admit I'm wrong, but I just cannot get the idea out of my head that there's more to this Clarence Luckman than we think."

"Detective, we have plenty of circumstantial evidence that Clarence Luckman has been everywhere where these killings have happened."

"So what happened after he took Walter Milford's car and left Tucson?"

"What d'you mean, what happened?"

"Where did he go? Who saw him next?"

Koenig smiled. "Look, Detective, I really appreciate your persistence on this, and I appreciate your willingness to help, but this is a very serious multiple homicide case, and you have things to deal with back in Tucson, and you really shouldn't be out here talking to us about this . . ."

"I'd just like to know what happened after he left Tucson, that's all," Cassidy replied. "If you can tell me that much I'll be happy. Tell me that and I'll turn right round and drive back to Tucson."

Koenig was hesitant, and then he said, "Well, there isn't any reason *not* to tell you, Detective. You are involved in this case, albeit within the Tucson city limits, but I don't see what good it's going to do you, and you have to understand that we are now dealing with another series of murders, two of which are uncertain as to cause at this time, and a further victim in a hospital here in El Paso with cranial trauma and a broken back who may or may not make it."

"Uncertain? What do you mean, uncertain?"

"Well, we have to now assume that the other two men who were found dead were not the work of Clarence Luckman."

"What other two men?"

"Okay," Koenig said. "I'll tell you what has happened since Luckman left Tucson, and then you go back and work on the Parselle and Milford cases, okay?"

Cassidy hesitated.

"You have no authority here, Detective," Koenig said. "The fact that you drove out here three hundred miles in the middle of the night tells me that you are a hard-working and dedicated detective, but you are not a federal officer, and this really is a federal case—"

"Tell me what has happened since Tucson and I'll go home," Cassidy said.

"Right. Okay." Koenig leaned back in his chair. He took a moment to light a cigarette, and then he told Cassidy about the murder of Marlon Juneau east of Deming, the two dead bodies in the car, the discovery of Harvey Warren's gun beneath, the identification of Clarence Luckman's prints on that gun, the fact that a report went in to the police from a gas station owner in Deming called Clark Regan about the two bodies, and the subsequent sighting of Clarence Luckman at the diner where the Eckharts had stopped. Koenig went on to detail the discovery of the four dead bodies—Rita McGovern on the highway, Maurice Eckhart, Linda, and Dennis in a burned-out car, and the fact that Margot Eckhart was now in Saint Savior's Hospital and unlikely to recover sufficiently to confirm or identify anything or anyone.

Cassidy asked for the timeframe they were working with, and it was as Koenig was explaining this that Cassidy stopped him.

"There's something right there that doesn't make sense," he said.

"You mean the fact that Clarence Luckman was supposedly reporting the discovery of the two dead bodies in the car at a gas station at about the same time that he was seen in a diner outside El Paso . . . and that these two locations are approximately a hundred miles apart?"

"Yes," Cassidy said. "That couldn't have happened."

"And the answer to that question is that it could not have been Clarence Luckman who reported this to the gas station owner. The gas station owner, name of Clark Regan, remembers that there were two people, a teenage girl and a teenage boy. He spoke only to the girl, and could not identify Clarence Luckman from the photo we showed him."

"But the guy in the diner did identify Clarence Luckman from his picture?"

"No, he didn't identify him either. But he remembered the Ford Galaxie, and he remembered the Eckharts. We also now have a revolver at the McGovern murder scene that has been identified as having belonged to Sheriff James Wheland from Wellton. That's where Clarence Luckman and Earl Sheridan carried out the bank robbery."

"So if the young man who reported the overturned car at the gas station was not Clarence Luckman, then who was he? And who was the girl with him?"

Koenig shook his head. "We don't know."

"And if it wasn't Luckman at the gas station, and yet Luckman was the one who had Harvey Warren's gun, then how did that gun end up beneath that car such a short way from the gas station?"

"Again, we don't know yet."

"Seems to me that Luckman doesn't have that much of a problem with being identified by the weapons he's using. If he did have then he wouldn't have left Sheriff Wheland's gun at the McGovern scene."

Koenig leaned forward. He smiled genuinely, and shook his head. "Detective Cassidy, you have a discerning and rapid sense of logic. I only wish that there were more federal people as smart as you. You are asking precisely the questions we are asking, and we don't have answers to all of them. All we have to date are seven known victims, and the two further attacks from Tucson. Additionally we have Margot Eckhart in the hospital, and— inexplicably—we have two dead men in a car east of Deming with a handgun under the vehicle, said handgun having come from the convenience store in Marana. That's what we have. What we *think* is that Clarence Luckman is either here in El Paso, or has now left El Paso in Rita McGovern's station wagon, and he's continuing southeast along the I-10 toward Fort Hancock and Van Horn. After Van Horn the highway joins the I-20, which goes on to Odessa, then on to Fort Worth and Dallas, whereas the I-10 carries on to San Antonio and Houston. The farther he goes the less likely we are to find him. The bigger the city he reaches, again the less likely we are to find him. If he decides to go south and gets into Mexico there is a strong likelihood that we will *never* find him. Those are the facts and the suppositions. Those are the scenarios we have, and also the scenarios we are trying to avoid. We have the sheriffs of pretty much every county within a three-hundred-mile radius working with us, we have continuous bulletins on the televisions and the radio, we have photographs of Luckman being distributed to every gas station and convenience store along the interstate and connecting highways. We have hundreds of men at our disposal, and we are using every single one of them in the most effective and efficient way we can to locate this individual before he kills anyone else, so—"

"So I should be on my way home?"

"With respect, Detective, yes, you should be on your way home."

"I know, and I'm grateful for your time. It seems that you have every base covered."

"We hope so, Detective. You appreciate what we're dealing with as well as anyone, and you know how these things can sometimes succeed or fail based on the smallest detail."

Cassidy rose from the chair. "I appreciate your time, gentlemen," he said, "and I wish you all success." He shook hands with both Garth Nixon and Ron Koenig, and Nixon showed him out.

"Not the last we've heard of him," Koenig said as Nixon shut the door. "Good man. Would be good to have him come work with us."

"Ask him," Nixon suggested.

"Next time I see him I might just do that."

CHAPTER FORTY-SEVEN

Clay and Bailey rose early, there was little to eat, and with empty stomachs they departed the Travelers' Rest and headed out toward the highway. Bailey said nothing as they walked. Clay's thoughts were all questions and no answers, and yet later—had he tried to recall those questions—he would not have been able to.

Within an hour they caught a ride heading away from El Paso on the I-10.

The driver's name was Emanuel Smith. He wore a shirt that was already dirty back when Coolidge was president, over it a black vest that was all shiny with grease around the pockets. "Smithy," he said. "Just call me Smithy. No one but my ma called me Emanuel and she's been dead these fifteen years, and hell she was crazy anyway." He laughed from the base of his gut and his whole body seemed to shudder with the effect. "Hell kind of name is Emanuel? Like callin' a kid Abednego or Ham or something. Crazy shit if you ask me. Darn crazy shit."

The pickup was wide, and they sat up front together.

"Can take you as far as Sierra Blanca," Smithy said. "Eighty some miles. Shouldn't take much more 'an about a coupla hours if we don't get no trouble." He reached forward and caressed the dashboard. "She's a good ol' girl, but a little temperamental, you know? Like all women."

Clay glanced at Bailey. Bailey smiled.

"Either o' you pair drive?"

"No, sir," Clay replied.

"Then we won't be sharing the workload, will we?"

"No, sir."

"Either o' you pair had breakfast?"

"No, not yet," Clay replied. "We were going to keep on walking until we found somewhere."

"And then I came along and spoiled the plan," Smithy said with a smile. "I don't know about you, but I'm gonna be arrivin' at hungry real soon. I think it'd be a good thing to stop and take something. Then we can do a flat straight run to Sierra Blanca." He tugged a pocket watch from his vest. "It's just after eight. Say we stop for half an hour someplace, we're back on the road by quarter to nine . . . hell, we could be there by eleven or eleven thirty. How does that suit you for an arrangement?"

"Suits us just fine," Clay said, and settled back.

Not five minutes passed before Smithy went from friendly banter to curious inquisition.

"You don't fool me for a minute," he said when Bailey hesitated over their names. "You ain't brother and sister. I seen the likes of you too many times to know you for anything other than what you is. Runaways, right? You got troublesome folks or drunkards or some such, and you figured that whatever was out here was better than back there."

Neither Clay nor Bailey replied.

Smithy nodded sagely, and then he smiled. "Hell, you don't need to worry about me. I been runnin' away from somethin' or other my whole darn life." He laughed coarsely. "If it weren't a mother or father then it was a wife or a mistress or a pissed husband with a loaded gun." He paused and shook his head. "Got a boy up there in Blanca. Twenty-five years old, talks like he ain't through kindergarten, crazy as a shithouse rat. Don't know what the hell to do with him but struggle on. Shee-it. But you keep on going, you know? Sometimes you work hard at something solely to prove you can do it. Only person who needs to know is yourself. But it is hard, I'll say that much . . ."

Smithy's voice trailed away. Clay looked at Bailey. Her expression said everything. They hadn't been picked up out of pity or sympathy or decent human kindness. They'd been picked up because Emanuel Smith was the loneliest man in the world.

"Sometimes wonder if I haven't had my fill of regular folks." Smithy looked at Clay. He half-closed his eyes as if to more closely discern his thoughts. "Know what I mean, son? Kind of folks who figure that life is all about going to church and feeling guilty, that there ain't no derivation of pleasure until you're dead and gone to heaven. Always reminding people how sinful they are. Doing what they need to make everyone else as miserable and anxious as themselves. Can't abide such attitudes. All high and mighty."

Smithy reached forward and took a pack of cigarettes from beneath the dash. He lit one awkwardly, releasing the steering wheel with both hands for just a moment.

He went on talking, his words issuing from amidst a cloud of smoke. "No one ever did anything worth anything in this world by coloring inside the lines. That's a fact. It's always harder to be good. Honesty is a tougher road. Wears you out sometimes. Sometimes people take a tough road because they're too mule-dumb to quit. Others take a tough road 'cause they know it's right and they got a good heart. All they ever had, all they ever will have is a good heart. Maybe people like us are destined to want but never get. Some peoples' lives are like that, I guess. Empty, you know? Like a balloon."

"I know what you mean," Bailey interjected. "I know exactly what you mean, Mr. Smith."

Smithy looked sideways at her, the expression on his face like he was about to tell her that she knew nothing. Hell, how could she? There wasn't nothing to her. She was just a slip of a girl and could never have experienced anything even close to what he had. But he didn't. He looked at her, and then he nodded his head and said, "Yes, my dear, I think you do."

"It's not been easy," she said. "We want to get to Eldorado in Texas, and then we're going to make some decisions about what to do."

"Sounds as good a place as any," Smithy said. "Shame I ain't goin' there myself, otherwise we'd be travelin' companions all the way."

"Sierra Blanca will be just fine," she said.

"And whatever trouble you've had back home," he said. "You just look at the things you like and squint your eyes so the rest goes blurry. See what you want to see. Don't see nothin' else. Sometimes it feels like life is there to teach you as many things about hurting as it can. That may be true. You can experience all the trouble you want, but that don't mean you have to spend all your time thinking about it. Bad memories have long shadows.

Spend the rest of your life inside of them and you never get warm."

He smoked his cigarette to the butt and then he flicked it out the window. He smiled kind of knowingly. "I hear it says in the Bible that Jesus will follow you to the end of the road, to the ends of the earth. Tell you something now. Been some places, seen some things that no one—not even the Lamb of God—would have followed me. Far as I'm concerned life is mostly a great number of somethings for pretty much nothing in return. Think that's how it's designed so you don't take what you got for granted. Truth is that when all is said and done, the only thing we end up fearing is time."

And so he went on. Everything he said seemed to be a judgment, an ultimatum, a handful of words from a sermon about fortitude, resilience, persistence, and unwillingness to quit. His slant was dark, pessimistic, but there was a sober level to it that Bailey found reassuring and practical. Emanuel Smith was a dreamer. He'd watched his dreams die, but that hadn't changed his belief in the dreams. Like her father. He was dead, but that didn't mean he'd never lived.

"Tell you now, it's a hundred percent tough ninety percent of the time, or ninety-five percent tough a hundred percent of the time. They sound the same but they're not. They're very different. A man carries his burden in silence. Makes a complaint, well, then he ain't a man."

"Mr. Smith?" Bailey asked.

" 'S up, sweetheart?"

"What happened to your wife?"

"My wife? Which wife would that be then?"

"The one who had your boy?"

"That one? Well, she's dead, sweetheart. Dead as they get."

"You miss her?"

"Miss her?" he echoed. He was quiet for a moment. "Try not to, I s'pose, but yes, I miss her."

"I lost my dad."

"That's why you're running away?"

"That. Some other things."

Clay listened to her voice. There was something there he hadn't heard since she'd cried at the side of the road.

"Hell of a young one to be losin' your father," Smithy said. "And your ma? Where's she at?"

"Lost her too."

Smithy frowned. "You ain't doin' so good there, girl. Seems to me you should start takin' better care of the people around you, save you lose 'em all."

"You remember what your wife looks like, Mr. Smith?"

"Sure I do. Hard to forget that."

Bailey was quiet for a moment, and when she spoke again there was a hitch of suppressed emotion in her voice. "I try and remember what he looks like," she said. "My dad. I try and remember what he looks like, but when his face comes . . . well, it looks like him but then it kinda doesn't look like him. Like there's always something slightly wrong. The shape of his eyes, you know? The shadow around his jaw."

Smithy smiled. "Well, hell, of course he's gonna look different now, sweetheart. He's dead . . . well, I mean he's dead in our terms, but every other way you look at it he's just someplace else. He's wherever folks go when they die, and they have different air there, or there's a different light, and that makes 'em look different."

"You're sure?"

"Sure I'm sure."

"How come you're so sure, Mr. Smith?"

"Well, hell, girl, it's easy. Every time I think of my wife now she looks pleased to see me, and that didn't never happen when she was alive."

He was deadpan for a moment, and then he cracked his face with a smile, and then he started laughing, and Bailey looked at Clay and Clay looked right back at her, and then the pair of them broke up rowdily, and the cab of the pickup was such a ruckus of noise the engine was drowned out.

"You only got two kinds of time in this life," Smithy said a while later. "Too much or too little. That's the truth, bare-faced as it gets. Trouble is that most folks is always looking for what's ahead, what's in front of them. Gotta pay attention to what's going on around and about as well. That old thing they say has some truth in it, you know. Never so much joy in the destination as there is in the journey. Something of that nature."

"You can't help it though sometimes, can you, Mr. Smith?" Bailey said. "Sometimes you just can't help thinking that you were born under a bad star and you were just fixed for bad luck the whole of your life."

Clay heard nothing after *bad star*. He was looking up ahead at the road, but all he could see was the night sky out through the window as he lay on the floor with his mother. All he could remember were the prayers he made and the fact that they were never heard.

"Well, those thoughts are just the variety you should never think. You just put up a sign someplace in your head and you never let them in, okay?" He said it with certainty, and he said it with some degree of conviction in his voice, but all three of them knew that it was not always how you wanted it to be. Sometimes those things just found a way right on in, and once they were in you were done.

"Clay? Clay?"

Clay turned, and in the same moment he realized Bailey was talking to him he also realized that she had used his real name.

Smithy said nothing, but it didn't pass by him unnoticed.

Clay looked at her for a moment and then shook his head.

"You okay?" she said.

He nodded. He mumbled something, and then he added, "Just hungry . . . I think I'm just hungry . . ." to which Smithy replied, "Good enough for me. Next place we see we stop."

He didn't speak for a moment, and then he said, "Hey, hey, what do we have here?"

Bailey looked up.

She saw a line of three or four cars up ahead a couple of hundred yards. By the side of the highway there was a police vehicle—unmistakable—and Smithy was quick to ask her if the police might be looking for them.

"No," she said. "Why would they be looking for us? We haven't done anything wrong."

"Give me your word now, girl . . . tell me straight you ain't done nothin' I should be concerned about."

She looked at him dead-square. She was as honest and open as the day was long. She gave her word.

"Good enough for me," Smithy said. "Well, they's sure as hell lookin' for someone, and if they find you in here—"

"Then they'll separate us and send us to juvie and we'll get beaten to hell and back again and we might even die," Bailey interjected.

Smithy smiled ruefully. "Well, sweetheart, I don't know about that, but I seen them places and I sure as hell wouldn't wish for you to be in one of them. Get down on the floor. Get yourselves as far back under the seat as you can."

Smithy reached into the back and tugged up a dirty, damp-smelling blanket. He managed to shuffle it over them as best he could, and then he was slowing up, coming to a stop, waiting at the end of the short line of cars for his turn to be questioned.

Bailey didn't dare breathe. Clay could hear his heart thumping like a drum in his chest.

Smithy wound down the window, smiled at the young officer at the side of the road, and asked what was up.

"We're looking for an escaped convict," he said.

Smithy laughed. "Well, it ain't me, Officer, and that's for sure."

"Yes, that's fine, sir. I want you to take a look at this picture and see if you recognize this young man."

Even as the officer brought the picture up, Smithy saw the men back at the side of the road. Armed they were, bearing both rifles and shotguns. Whoever they were looking for must have been one dangerous son of a bitch. This drama sure wasn't happening because of a couple of runaways.

Clay felt Bailey's hand around his, and she was squeezing it tight enough to hurt, and though he could see almost nothing beneath the blanket he was aware that her breathing had quickened. He could feel sweat along his hairline. He felt nauseous. He knew they were looking for him. He knew they had found him. He knew they were both done for and he would be on his way back to Hesperia before the day was out.

And Smithy—eyesight like a bat—squinted at the vague blur of something or other that was held in front of his face, and he said, "No, Officer, can't say I have . . .", and that picture could have been Jimmy Cagney or Mickey Mouse, it wouldn't have mattered, because no way in the world was Emanuel Smith going to tell the officer that he'd left his reading glasses back at home and couldn't see shit from Shinola.

"Very good, sir," the officer said. "Well, you watch how you go now, and if you do see this young man then you need to call the nearest sheriff's department or federal office. For your own safety we have to advise you that this man is armed and dangerous, and that you should not approach him or communicate with him under any circumstances."

"Well, that's as clear as it gets," Smithy said. "I'll be on my way, then."

"Thank you for your cooperation, sir, and drive safely now."

Smithy gunned the engine into life, shifted gear, and started to pull away.

"Sir?" the officer said.

Smithy frowned, depressed the brake and slowed to a halt.

The policeman was still there, had walked the two or three yards that the car had traveled, and was once again at the window.

"Sir, we need you to hold up just a moment longer."

Smithy glanced to his left. There was something going on. A couple of the officers were talking, a third joined them. Perhaps some word on the radio?

Beneath the damp and filthy blanket Clay was beginning to feel sick. Bailey's shoulder pressed against his side. Was she shaking? What was going on? Why had they been stopped again? Beneath his line of sight there was a small hole in the floor of the truck. Through it Clay could see daylight, the surface of the road, and then there was the sound of an engine revving.

"Sir?" Smithy hollered as the young officer started back toward his colleagues.

The officer raised his hand. "You just wait there a moment," he replied.

"What the hell is this?" Smithy said under his breath.

Clay felt for the edge of the blanket.

"Stay still for God's sake!" Smithy hissed. "Jesus Christ, boy, stay still!"

The car that was revving fell silent.

Bailey's hand was still holding Clay's. She was gripping it so tight that Clay's fingers started to throb with the pressure.

Footsteps. Heading back toward the vehicle.

"So am I outta here," Smithy asked, "or is there some problem?"

"I need to see your license and registration, sir," the officer said.

"You what?"

"As I said, sir, your license and registration."

"Jesus, what the hell is this all about?"

The officer didn't reply.

Smithy reached out to the glove compartment. He flipped the catch and it opened. He tugged out a fistful of papers—envelopes, unpaid bills, receipts from the garage, all manner of things. He started through them, couldn't see a damned thing clearly. He had his license. Got that. That was easy. Now his registration documents. Jesus, it could be any of them. He started to feel anxious. He went through the papers faster. Where was it, where was it? He dropped a couple of pieces, and then he had his hand down around his ankles trying to retrieve them.

Bailey saw what he was looking for. She snatched it, held it up with just the tips of her fingers.

The officer took a step closer to the window.

"You okay there, sir?" he asked.

Smithy snatched the paper from Bailey's fingertips and thrust it out of the window at the officer.

"Here we are," Smithy said.

Clay's heart was ready to burst. Now, whatever happened, whoever they were actually looking for, if he and Bailey were found hiding in the foot well . . .

And then it hit him.

Digger? Earl? Was that who they were looking for? Was that the reason for the roadblock? Were they covering every direction possible?

No. It couldn't be.

The officer had his notebook out. He was writing something down. A line, a couple of lines, and then he closed it again.

He stepped back to the side of the vehicle. He returned Smithy's documents.

"That seems all fine, sir," the officer said. "You have a good journey now."

"Thank you," Smithy said. He stuffed the papers back in the glove compartment, turned the key, and restarted the engine. He let the car roll ten feet or so, and then he floored it and took off.

Clay came out from under the blanket feeling the most intense sense of relief.

"Jesus in a jelly jar," Smithy said. "That was something, wouldn't you say? Damned near scared the wits out of me."

Bailey appeared from under the blanket, her face red, sweat sticking her bangs to her forehead.

"Good you got that paper for me there, girl," Smithy said. "Couldn't tell one damned thing from the other. He'd have got me for that, you know? He'd have figured that out, and then he'd have realized I couldn't have seen that picture he was showing me."

"You don't know who they were looking for?" Clay asked.

"Ain't a clue," Smithy said. "Sure as hell wouldn't be looking for you pair though, right?"

"Right," Clay said, and he wanted to believe that, wanted to be sure of that, but if they weren't looking for him and Bailey, who were they looking for? Earl Sheridan and Elliott maybe? Surely not. Surely they'd appreciate that even Earl and Digger weren't dumb enough to just keep heading the same way.

Clay and Bailey stayed on the floor for a good two or three minutes before they struggled out from under the blanket.

"It's all fine," Smithy told them. "They're looking for some crazy with a gun, not a couple of runaway kids." He smiled, went for another cigarette. Clay couldn't help hear the nerves in the man's voice. Not only had he been shaken up by the incident, he also sounded like he was trying to convince himself that he'd done nothing wrong.

"Now," Smithy said, "let's get some chow."

CHAPTER FORTY-EIGHT

It nagged at Cassidy's thoughts as he drove. He even had to pull over and write down as much as he could remember from what he'd been told in the hotel room. Marlon Juneau. Clark Regan in Deming. Rita McGovern. The Eckhart family. And then there was the gun beneath the car. A gun that came from the store in Marana. That scenario versus the one that found Clarence Luckman in a diner over a hundred miles away as the Eckharts came to eat. It gnawed at John Cassidy and it wouldn't leave him alone. Someone could not be in two places at once. Didn't matter who they were, they could not be in two places at once. Back along the I-10 to El Paso, three hundred miles or thereabouts, and though he had agreed with Agents Koenig and Nixon that he would lay down and go to sleep, he had no intention of doing any such thing. Behind him he left the Sweet Dreams and the Travelers' Rest, behind him he left the Eckharts' crime scene, but most of all he left behind Elliott Danziger, a young man who'd woken in a motel room not five miles from where he himself had shared words with Koenig and Nixon. But that could not have been, because Elliott Danziger was dead and the person they really needed to find was Clarence Stanley Luckman.

The I-10 ran a line out of the Rio Grande and followed it some fifty miles before dog-legging back toward Sierra Blanca. As if it couldn't keep pace with nature and wanted to cut out and rest. The Rio Grande separated Texas from Chihuahua, ran a further nine hundred miles along the borders of Coahuila and Tamaulipas to the Gulf of Mexico just south of Port Isabel and South Padre Island. Smartest thing Elliott Danziger could have done was to get in Rita McGovern's station wagon and follow that river as far as the land would let him. But no, Elliott had never been one for the best thing, and thus he rose in the Sweet

312

Dreams Motel, stretched and yawned and washed his face, and wondered what excitements this new day would bring him. Whatever sense of responsibility and conscience he might have possessed had slipped its moorings and drifted unobserved toward the horizon of his mind. Soon—again unobserved—it would fall off the edge of the world and be gone forever. Such was the way of things.

Elliott ate well—bacon and scrapple and eggs and coffee, and then he went back to his room to collect his few things together. He needed new clothes and he needed another gun. Now all he had was Marlon Juneau's .45 and three bullets. A party with three bullets would be no kind of party at all. It was nine thirty by the time he left—following the same route as Clay Luckman and Bailey Redman, passing the highway-side diner where they shared breakfast with Emanuel Smith. Elliott went in the opposite direction to John Cassidy, Cassidy driving as fast as he could, imagining the questions Mike Rousseau would fire at him regarding where he'd been, why he'd been gone at all. Events transpired, but they did not conspire. For a brief while all concerned parties had been within a handful of miles of one another, the police, the FBI, the runaways, and yet fate—or dark stars or luck or simply chance—colluded to prevent coincidence. This—it seemed—was also to be the way of things.

Elliott made good time, passing through Fort Hancock just after ten, Sierra Blanca a little more than twenty minutes later, and it was on the road to Van Horn that he eventually saw the signposts indicating a fork in the highway. If he continued on 10 he would be aiming for San Antonio, thence to Houston. If he took 20, well, that would take him through Odessa and Big Spring to Fort Worth and Dallas. He pulled over for a while—just to think, just to figure the odds, and it was then that he saw a small house in the far distance and became curious. It was a house out of nowhere. Such a sight lit a slow and inextinguishable fuse in his mind, and he sat there for a while longer appreciating the simple and uncomplicated isolation of the building. From the highway you would see nothing. From such a house the highway might as well have been a million miles away—a different country, a different continent—and whatever happened out there would be unknown to the world. He hesitated a moment longer—not from indecision or uncertainty, but simply to savor the sense of anticipation—and then he pulled left and took the dirt road away from the highway toward the isolated house. Had he known that he was right in the heart of the Diablo Plateau he would have smiled.

Elliott drove the three or four hundred yards to the front of the property, and then circled around the back so the station wagon was invisible from the highway. The owner of the house, a tall man in his late forties, was already at the back porch when Elliott got out of the car and started walking toward him.

"Help you?" the man said.

Elliott produced the gun from behind his back. He held it out at shoulder-height, unerring, unwavering, aimed directly for the man's head, and the man lowered his eyes for a moment.

"Seems to be the problem, son?" he said when he again looked up.

"No problem here," Elliott said.

"You in some trouble?"

"No trouble here."

"You wantin' for somethin'?"

"Ain't we all," Elliott replied.

They were now no more than twelve feet apart. The man had a towel in his hands. He'd been drying dishes perhaps, maybe fixing something and had cleaned his hands afterward.

"You alone here, mister?" Elliott asked.

"Sure am . . . 'sides from the dog, but he's out someplace runnin' around after his own damned tail or somethin'."

"You got some guns in there?"

"Sure have."

"What you got?"

"Got a shot, couple of handguns, a Remington."

"You got shells?"

"More shells than you'd know what to do with."

Elliott smiled wryly. "Oh, I don't know about that, sir, I really don't."

"Whatever you say, son."

"You a farmer?"

"No," the man said. "I do some work around here and

elsewhere. Fences, handle the stock in season, run a tractor for those who ain't keeping one theirselves."

"What's your name?"

"Randall. Morton Randall."

"You believe in God, Morton?"

"Sure do."

"I don't."

Morton nodded. "Figured that'd be the case."

"You think if I kill you I'm gonna go to hell?"

"The look of you . . . well, I figure you're pretty much there already . . ."

"No one's good," Elliott said. "All bad. Most folks is all bad. I figure hell is overcrowded already."

"Believe me, son, however crowded hell gets I believe they're gonna be savin' a special hot place for you."

"Soon as I get to hell I'm gonna tell 'em you made me do it."

Morton smiled. "You gotta get straight with the Lord. 'S the only way you're gonna get yourself out of this mess."

"Get myself out of it?" Elliott said. "Hell, man, I've spent too long gettin' into it to wanna get out of it."

Morton Randall—perhaps aware that his death was now due—paused for a moment. He glanced down at his shoes, and then he half-smiled. He tucked the towel in his back pocket and looked at Elliott Danziger with no expression at all.

Elliott glanced away toward the horizon, and then he turned back. "I think it's time we did this thing, Morton . . . I really do."

CHAPTER FORTY-NINE

The place was half-beat to death, not so much a house as a ramshackle collection of walls with a roof above. The roof slanted drunkenly. Behind it was a barn of sorts, one side angled awkwardly against gravity, the other walls coping with the pressure with a nonchalant degree of concern.

"Hell of a mess," Smithy said as he pulled up ahead of it. "If I hadn't lost my wife . . . hell, if I didn't have the boy to deal with I would have taken more care of the place. But what the hell, eh? I'll stay here until it falls on me, and then I'll probably be dead so I won't need to fix it."

Clay and Bailey had agreed to come—just for a little while, just for an hour or so—and then they were going to be on their way. Clay had a mind to try and make it to Fort Stockton by the end of the day. At least Fort Stockton. Find the right ride and they could get to Eldorado itself by nightfall. Hell, it was only three hundred or so miles from Sierra Blanca. For some reason Eldorado now seemed analogous to something—something better, a change for the good, a little piece of hope. Maybe nothing would be different. Maybe Eldorado would be just one more kind of disappointment, but it was a purpose and it was a goal and it was a destination. It was a reason to keep moving.

The boy of whom Emanuel Smith spoke was waiting for them in the yard. He had to be six three if he was nothing. Smithy had said he was twenty-five, but he had the complexion and coloring of a ten-year-old kid. He had the slack-jawed, vacant-eyed, hang-dog-jowled expression of an idiot. His arms hung like plumb lines from his shoulders, dead straight like stair posts, and his hands—each the size of a ham hock—were clenched into fists.

He smiled when he saw the pickup pull up ahead of the house. The smile vanished when he saw that his father was not alone.

"Jonas," Smithy called as he exited the vehicle.

Jonas was backing up around the corner of the building readying his escape.

"Jonas . . . you mind your manners now. We got guests here and you better be civil or I'm gonna get mad."

Jonas hesitated. He looked down at the ground. He started rubbing his palms together like he was planning on setting a fire, and a low rumbling sound came from somewhere in his vicinity. At first Bailey could not believe that the sound came from Jonas, but it did. It didn't sound human. It was an animal sound, dark and troubled, and it scared her.

She glanced nervously at Clay, but Smithy saw her expression and smiled.

"Don't be concerned. He's a helluva lot scareder of you than you are of him. He's harmless, sweetheart. No more trouble than a puppy dog. He gets over his nerves and he'll hang around you both like you're long-lost. Once he decides you're his friends . . . well, you won't find anyone more loyal than Jonas." Smithy looked up at his son. "Right, Jonas? You're the best friend anyone could ever wish for, isn't that so?"

Jonas fell silent. He stopped rubbing his hands together, but the palms stayed flat against each other as if he was fixing to pray sometime soon.

"Come on in the house," Smithy said to Clay and Bailey. "I'll fix us some coffee, make you some sandwiches or something for your travels, and then you can be on your way. I'd take you on down to Eldorado, but I got a mountain of things to do and I really don't want to leave the boy alone any longer than I have to—"

"It's okay, Mr. Smith," Bailey interjected. "We're really grateful that you've brought us this far."

Smithy walked to the steps and paused. He turned to look back at Clay and Bailey.

"Your name I know," he said to Clay. "I know it because she said it." He looked at Bailey. "But you? I only know the name you gave me and it ain't your real name. That much I'm sure of. Now, I don't know what trouble you got yourselves into, and I ain't gonna ask, but whatever the hell it is I can tell you one thing for free. There's never a trouble in this life that's solved by runnin' away from it—"

Bailey opened her mouth to speak.

"Let me finish, girl. Do me that much as a courtesy. Most often I'm out here with the boy and I don't get a great deal of time to talk anything but simple stuff he'll understand. You pair are as sharp as pins, I can see that without looking too hard, but I can see the trouble you got around you as well. Hangs like a second shadow. Don't see that there's gonna be anything good coming out of this 'cept if you try and fix it."

"There's nothin' to fix," Bailey said. "We're not running away from anyone. We don't have anyone to run away from. We're going to Eldorado simply because it's somewhere different. We ain't done nothin' wrong and we sure as hell ain't runnin' away from anyone—"

Smithy raised his hand. "If that's the truth then I've heard enough. If it ain't then I don't wanna hear any more. We're done with this conversation. Come on in and I'll make you something to take on your way, and then we'll say our farewells and be done with it."

Clay and Bailey followed Smithy into the house. Jonas was now nowhere to be seen.

In the kitchen Smithy went straight for the whiskey. The room was not so much dirty as unkempt, uncared for. Spiderwebs decorated the corners, traipsed across the spaces between things. Around the white sink was a clean space where food would be prepared. It was from a cupboard beneath this that Smithy took the bottle.

He turned and looked at Clay, held up the bottle with the five or six inches of amber swilling in the bottom.

"You want a drink?"

Clay shook his head. "Can't say I do. Don't have a taste for it."

"Me either," Smithy said. "I keep expecting to take a liking for it. Thirty years ain't done it yet."

"Why don't you quit?"

"Ain't one for quitting. Besides, you deal with something like that—" He jerked his head toward the front of the house. There was no doubt that he was referring to Jonas. "Deal with something like that every day and you find a depth of sorrow that you didn't think you could find. You wait until darkness and then drink enough to forget. Drink enough to sleep. Before long it gets to a point where you don't wait until darkness."

He uncorked the bottle, poured an inch into a glass, downed it in one and poured another. He drank half, set it aside on the counter, and then reached for bread and such things to make sandwiches for the runaways.

Later—half an hour or so—the sandwiches made and wrapped in paper, the three of them stood on the porch and looked at the road that would take Clay and Bailey away from there.

"Been a mighty pleasure havin' your company for a while," Smithy said.

"Been a pleasure meeting you, Smithy," Bailey said, "and we're real grateful for your help in bringing us this far."

"Well, you take care now. You look after each other good, 'cause it seems to me that no one else is gonna be doin' that."

Clay shook Smithy's hand. Bailey leaned up and kissed the old man's cheek.

They started walking, and it was only when they reached the end of the long path that Bailey looked back.

Jonas stood there at the corner of the building, and when he saw her he waved. Just once. A left-right motion of the hand. She raised her hand to wave back, but even as she did so he was gone.

CHAPTER FIFTY

The house was neat and clean. No denying the fact that Mr. Morton Randall kept a tidy place. Mr. Randall himself was behind the kitchen. There was an extra room in there. Not so much a room as another space separated by a doorway with no door. Washing machine, a drier of sorts, a rope to hang stuff up. Anyway, Mr. Randall was in there with a bullet hole in his face. Digger had planned to shoot him a couple of times, maybe use all three .45 slugs, but Randall went down and stayed down with the first one. Digger had shot him just above his mouth and beneath his nose, so either the bullet ricocheted up and went through his brain or it went out back and severed his spinal cord. There was no exit wound, so whichever and wherever and how, that baby was still inside there and wasn't coming out anytime soon.

Digger figured that later he might cut Randall's head off and see if he couldn't find it. It wasn't important, not at all, but it was something to do for want of something better.

After Digger had cleaned himself up he went out back and sat on the porch. He kicked off his boots and pulled his socks away from his aching feet. He massaged the balls and the arches, even the spaces between his toes. It felt good. He was hungry and he wanted to fuck someone. He thought about fucking Randall in the ass but it didn't really interest him. He wanted a girl. He wanted quite a young girl. Or maybe he wanted two. He would have to see what was available.

He understood things better now. The girl from the bank, the one in the apartment, even the old man who'd owned the Galaxie. In some way they had been tests. He had failed the tests, but that was part of learning. It was better now. He had a good sense of control. His emotions were in check, his needs were being fulfilled, and he was aware of the simple fact that those who achieved something in life were simply the ones who took what they wanted when it was there. It was not complicated. It was a sentiment and a philosophy that he knew Earl would appreciate.

Back in the kitchen he found some pork and beans in a dish in the refrigerator. He lit the stove, dumped half of the mess into a pan, and warmed it. He ate it tepid with a spoon straight from the pot. He looked for liquor, found a half bottle of rye on a shelf above Randall's bled-out head, and he took a couple of sips. It was raw-edged, but it would do.

Randall's guns were in a shed at the back of the property. As he'd said, there was a twelve-gauge shot, a good Remington rifle, a couple of Colt revolvers that had seen better days. There was also a mountain of ammo. Amongst everything Elliott found two and a half boxes of .45 caliber. He left the revolvers behind, but took the shotgun and the rifle. With the .45 shells he could just stick with Juneau's weapon as his sidearm.

He carried his arsenal back to the house and laid out the guns on the floor of the sitting room. He covered them over with a blanket, but before he did that he took a good handful of the .45 shells and filled his pockets. He was out for hunting, and the .45 was gonna serve him best.

He left Rita McGovern's station wagon behind the building and looked for the keys to Randall's pickup. It was a good pickup, a Ford, maybe three or four years on it. Had a bed in back, and a wide cab—enough room for four. Anyone he was bringing home he'd want up front and close. He wouldn't want anyone in the backseat. Wouldn't want anyone behind him, even if it were some slip of a girl, all bones and no meat.

He checked around the place. He locked the back door, closed the windows, shut up the back kitchen door and the door to the stairwell. Where the hell the front door key was he didn't know, but he didn't think anyone'd be coming down here in the next hour or so. He figured the closest Morton Randall ever got to company was the sound of people on the highway leaving him behind.

Elliott Danziger got into the pickup and revved the engine into life. He took one more look at the house—*his* house—and then he headed back for the I-10. He planned on driving to the nearest town and seeing if there was any entertainment. If not, well, he'd keep on driving until he found something.

The nearest town was Van Horn, and it was all of ten or twelve miles away. Quarter of an hour and Elliott was idling at a junction waiting for a light to change. There was a diner, a post office, a bank, a mercantile, a clothiers, a saloon called The Buffalo Bar, another couple of places. Elliott drove on over and took a right at the corner. He was on Merchant Street, and down on the left was a garage with a girl sitting out front. From what he could see she looked pretty enough, maybe twenty or so, and Elliott pulled into the forecourt, checked the .45 in the back of his pants, and got out.

"Heya," she said. She smiled. Her teeth were really white. She had shoulder-length ash-blond hair, much of it tied in a ponytail. She wore jeans, a checkered shirt, cowboy boots. She looked like she was on her way to the rodeo to see her dumb boyfriend get kicked to death by a steer.

"What can we do for y'all?" she drawled, and immediately the nasal Texan twang irritated him.

Elliott smiled. "Don't tell me that you're doin' all the fixin' and mendin' here, little girl."

She smiled again. Such white teeth. "Well no, that'd be my daddy you'll be wantin', but he's on out tendin' to somethin' that ain't movin', you know?"

"Sure do," Elliott said. "So he just leave you all here on your lonesome?"

"Case folks come by and need somethin', sure. Can take a message, can tell me what's wrong and I'll tell him when he gets back . . ."

Elliott smiled. He wished his teeth were as white as hers. "What's your name, sweetheart?"

"Name's Candace," she said.

Elliott couldn't help himself laughing.

"What's so funny?"

"Candace?"

"Sure, you ain't never heard that name before?"

"Hell, sure I have, just never figured it for what it was. Stick the letter *y* in there somewhere and you'd be candy-ass."

Candace frowned. She took a step backward. "Now, that's just rude, mister. There ain't no call for sayin' things like that."

Elliott nodded. "Well, I'm real sorry, miss." He could hear himself imitating her nasal drawl. "I didn't mean nothin' by it."

"So you have something wrong with your truck or what? You have somethin' my daddy needs to fix?"

Elliott looked down at his feet. He used the toe of his boot to kick a little indent in the dirt. He reached behind his jacket and took out the .45. He held it down by his side and it was a moment before she realized what it was.

"Oh no, sweetheart," he said. "I ain't got nothin' your daddy needs to fix."

She didn't struggle a great deal, but then most people don't when faced with a .45 and a smile like the one Elliott Danziger wore.

He indicated she should go on into the garage itself. There was a high overhanging roof, and once beneath its shadow the workshop proper was visible. Hydraulic jacks, a couple of inspection pits, shelving on all three internal walls loaded with a fabulous array of black machines and tools. Everything smelled of oil and diesel and gasoline and sweat. Across the concrete floor were the memories of a thousand oil leaks and brake fluid spillages.

"Now, look here, mister, I didn't do nothin' to upset you—"

Elliott pressed his finger to his lips. "Sssshhh," he whispered, and he did the smile again and there was something so indescribably chilling about it that Candace just fell silent.

There was a bench down in the corner and he told her to sit. She did so. He told her to take the band out of her hair. She complied.

He stood in front of her for a moment, and then he put the gun in his left hand and held out his right.

"Give me your hand," he said.

"Mister . . . please . . . please, no . . ." She looked scared then. Really scared. Too scared to cry.

He hefted the gun in his hand, raised it, and touched the muzzle to her right temple.

"Give me your hand," he repeated.

Candace held out her hand and closed her eyes.

Elliott took the girl's hand and pressed it against his crotch. He was already nearly there, and when he felt her fingers through the fabric of his pants he was erect within moments. He unhitched his belt, maneuvered his hard-on out of there, and held it in front of her face.

"Open," he said, and jabbed her in the side of the head with the gun.

Candace looked up at him. Her eyes were now filled with tears.

"Mister . . ." she whimpered.

"No talking," Elliott said.

She opened her mouth to speak again, and Elliott grabbed her face. His fingers reached the back of her head and his thumb was in her mouth. He twisted her head sideways and leaned down. His nose was no more than three or four inches from hers.

"You're gonna do just exactly what I tell you to do. If you don't, I'm gonna shoot you. I ain't gonna kill you. I'll shoot you in the gut or something. That'll hurt a great deal and it'll take you a good couple of hours to die. While you're dying, I will fuck you in the ass. When I'm done with fucking you in the ass we'll sit here together and wait till your daddy gets back, and then you'll see me shoot him in the head fair and square. That's what'll happen, you understand?"

She closed her eyes tight, as tight as they would go, and Elliott felt her nod her head despite the pressure he maintained on her neck.

"Well, good enough," he said.

He released his grip. She kept her eyes closed.

"Open your eyes and your mouth," he said. He jabbed her once more with the .45.

Candace opened her eyes, and then her mouth, tentatively at first, and then wider.

"Okay. Good. Now we're in business."

Elliott took her hand once more and closed it around his erection. He made her massage back and forth a few times until he was hard again, and then he held the back of her head and put it in her mouth. She sat there without expression. Her eyes open but looking right through him.

"You gotta suck it now, sweetheart," he said, and he smiled like he was explaining something to a child.

It was then that he saw it. The flash of hatred in her eyes. He saw what she was going to do. He saw the intention in her face as clear as daylight. The way the muscles tensed along her jaw line. The way the color rose in her cheeks suddenly.

She was going to bite his damned dick off!

Elliott grabbed her throat. She opened her mouth involuntarily. He jerked back and his erection was clear of her teeth.

The relief he felt was enormous. Well, hell, he nearly damned well came with the relief.

"Fucking bitch," he said, and his voice was barely audible.

She looked at him. The same sad hangdog look she'd given him when he first sat her down. Pathetic. *Don't hurt me. Please don't fucking hurt me.*

"Fucking bitch," he said, and he raised his hand.

She flinched and withdrew. A tiny gasp escaped her lips. She raised her hands to protect herself, and ever so slowly Elliott lowered his hand and watched her expression change. The fact that he hadn't shouted, the fact that he hadn't hit her was more unnerving than anything.

Elliott took one step back. He put his erection back in his pants.

"Okay," he said quietly. "You wanna play funny fucking games, sweetheart, then we'll play funny fucking games."

With one strike of the gun's handle she was unconscious. He picked her up as if she were no heavier than a sack of laundry, and he walked on out to the truck.

No one saw Elliott Danziger. No one saw Candace Munro. One person did see Morton Randall's pickup pull away from Sam Munro's garage at approximately ten past noon on Thursday the twenty-sixth of November, but thought nothing of it.

Candace had intended to stay at the garage for a couple of hours at most. She'd told her dad that she might go on up and see a friend in Monahans, up near Odessa. He'd offered to drive her, but she said she liked to take the bus. She was twenty-one, she was a good girl, trustworthy and good to her word. She had never been a problem, not a day of real difficulty since her mother had died fourteen years before. The arrangement to visit her friend was informal. They'd spoken of it on the telephone but made no firm plans. Thus, later, when Sam Munro returned to the garage at quarter to three, he figured she'd taken the bus. There was no note, but then there would only have been a note had someone come in with a message for Sam or some work that needed doing. Evidently there had been none, and there was nothing strange in that. And the friend in Monahans? Well, she'd never really expected Candace to show up. Candace had said she would come a couple of times before, and then her dad had needed her and she'd had to stay back. She would arrive when she arrived. It was that kind of arrangement because it was that kind of friendship.

Thus Elliott took Candace Munro back to Morton Randall's house for lunch. No one was any the wiser, and no alarm bells were ringing. Unknown to Elliott, he had almost committed the perfect abduction. Not that that would have pleased or impressed him either which way. In that moment he had far more pressing issues on his mind.

CHAPTER FIFTY-ONE

An hour later—Clay and Bailey still on the road from Sierra Blanca to Van Horn—John Cassidy pulled up to the curb in front of his house and killed the engine. He needed to get to the office, but he wanted to speak to Alice first.

He needn't have worried. First thing she said to him as he opened the door was, "I called Mike. Told him you weren't good. Said I thought you had some fever or something and it'd be best if you stayed away for a day or so in case it was contagious."

He hugged her. He started to speak before he'd even let her go.

"No," she said. "You're going to have something to eat and a cup of coffee first. From the look of you—and the smell, I might add—you've slept the night in your car and you've driven here without any breakfast."

Cassidy sat down. He watched her silently as she made an omelet, packing whatever she could into it in the way of protein and nutrition. She made coffee, poured two cups, though hers was merely an inch or so in the bottom.

Cassidy ate. It was hard work. He wanted to talk to her. He wanted to express in words all the thoughts he'd been having on the drive from El Paso. She made him clear the plate, and then she sat across the table from him and told him to speak slowly.

When he was done she looked at him and said, "When there's two people."

A vague frown crossed his brow.

She smiled. "The answer to the only question that really needs an answer. How could someone leave a gun beneath a car in one place, and yet be in a diner a hundred or so miles away about to kidnap and kill a family? When there's two people . . . exactly as you have already convinced yourself."

"I *have* convinced myself of this," Cassidy replied. "I really have. It makes sense, Alice. It is the *only* thing that make sense. The only report they have of the death of the other boy who was taken hostage by Earl Sheridan is from Sheridan himself. This Danziger boy. Sheridan told the police in Wellton that he and Clarence Luckman had killed Elliott Danziger. There's no body that's been found, not as yet anyway. Where did they kill him? And why? These two boys spent their lives together, sent from one juvenile facility to the next, but always together. You don't have brothers like that going off and killing each other. It does not make sense. Second, there's this report from the owner of the gas station . . . something about whoever reported the crashed car on the highway being a girl, and there was a boy with her. Two teenagers, not one. The crashed car was where they found the gun that came from the convenience store in Marana. That's the thing that bothers me now. There's some significance to that gun. Some significance to where it came from. This convenience store in Marana."

"Marana is thirty miles away," Alice said. "It's no distance at all."

Cassidy nodded. "I know."

"And you think there's something there that can help?"

"Who knows? But I can't just let it rest. The federal authorities are not going to wait to ask questions. If they see this Clarence Luckman they're going to kill him."

Alice reached out and held his hand. "So go. Go on, take a drive up there. Take a look at where it happened. Speak to the police. They'll talk to you."

"Yes," he said. "That's what I wanted to do, but I'd planned to go tomorrow or the next day."

"Well, I got you the day off so you may as well get on up there now."

He squeezed her hand. "Thank you, Alice."

"No thanks needed. Go on. Get out of here. Call me if you're not going to make it back for supper, okay?"

"I will," Cassidy replied, and he leaned forward to kiss her.

"Not good," she said once he'd pulled back.

"What?"

She crinkled her nose. "You smell like a hobo. Go on and take a wash before you leave. I wouldn't want anyone thinking I let you out of the house looking and smelling the way you do."

Cassidy rose from his chair. He touched her face gently. "Too good for me," he said.

"Don't I know it," she replied.

An hour later he was on the road again, driving the thirty miles or so to Marana. He found the convenience store without difficulty. Marana was not a big place, and it was the only store appended to a gas station. It was closed. It had been the scene of a brutal double homicide only three days earlier. Cassidy looked about the place, but there wasn't a great deal to see. He asked for the sheriff's office and was directed to the small office manned by Officer Nolan Sharpe, representative of the Pima County Sheriff's Department.

Sharpe was young, no more than twenty-three or -four, but he was personable, and he had about him an organized manner that demonstrated a desire to be there and to undertake the job properly. He seemed pleased to have Cassidy consult him, as if the attention from a Tucson City detective elevated his position and gave it greater stature and credence.

"Harvey Warren we all knew," he told Cassidy. "Harvey was an institution here in Marana. His family has owned a store here for decades, but Harvey was the one who built the gas station alongside it. Good man. Terrible tragedy. Unbelievable."

"And the other victim?" Cassidy asked.

"Frank Jacobs. Franklin to give him his full name. Shoe salesman out of Scottsdale. Passin' through, as far as we know."

"And there was no one else in the store at the time of the shooting? Just Earl Sheridan, Clarence Luckman, Harvey Warren, and Frank Jacobs?"

"As far as we know. There was no one else dead, and there was no one hangin' around either. We went in there, found the two dead men, and Jacobs's Oldsmobile was gone. They also emptied his wallet and took whatever was in the till."

"And this Frank Jacobs was down from Scottsdale, you say."

"Yes, Scottsdale. He was a traveler. Sold shoes. Wingtips, work boots, whatever."

"You have an address for him?"

"Sure do." Sharpe found the file, wrote down the address, handed the slip of paper to Cassidy.

"You gonna go on up there and take a look in his house?"

Cassidy shrugged. "I don't know," he said. He wished to appear nonchalant. He didn't want Sharpe reporting to Koenig and Nixon that he'd been snooping. "We'll see which way the wind blows my thoughts when I get out of here."

"Well, anything I can do you know where I am."

"That's appreciated."

"And if they're looking for any trainee detectives in Tucson . . ."

Cassidy smiled. "Then I'll put your name down."

"Obliged, Detective Cassidy."

Cassidy and Sharpe parted company. Cassidy looked at his watch. It was a little past four. Scottsdale was at least ninety miles and he wanted to be there before it got dark. He planned to call Alice from the nearest phone. No, he wouldn't be home for supper, but he wouldn't be so late that she couldn't keep it warm for him.

With the address of this Franklin Jacobs in his pocket he took the I-10 toward Phoenix. There was something he couldn't shake loose—the idea that there was someone else. Just as Alice had said earlier. How could someone be in two places at once? Well, it was easy, of course. When they were two people.

CHAPTER FIFTY-TWO

They walked and walked, and when Bailey figured they were done walking Clay just wanted to walk some more. By four o'clock they had covered the better part of ten miles. They had spoken little. At first Bailey looked like she didn't want to speak. Clay tried a few times. Started a few things up but they fell flat and the silence returned. After a while he let his imagination run. He began to think of himself as a cowboy, a ranch hand, a herder separated from his crew and his charges in some terrible storm, and now responsible for the daughter of some murdered land-owner. Murdered by redskins. Danger all around them. It kept him amused for half an hour and then he figured it was just dumb. Not one car passed them. They did see one man along the way. Must have been eighty or a hundred years old. Clay asked him the name of the next town on the road.

"Van Horn," the man said. He spat the words out like they were something bitter-tasting. Like he couldn't get them out fast enough. Clay's attention was drawn to a five-inch scar down the side of his neck. Maybe he'd talked too much one time. Maybe someone figured he'd shut the hell up if his throat was cut, but got talked out of it when he was only halfway done. Now the old man was being careful. Half a dozen syllables at a time, no more, no less. "Thirty miles or so," the man added.

Clay thanked him and they went, left the old man behind with his scar and his limited conversation.

They stopped at a store and bought a few things. Bread, cheese, peanuts, soda. It was a grim store, selling things for a dime that weren't worth a nickel. Seemed to stock more dust than it did anything else.

Eldorado was somewhere close to the other end of the world.

Silence again but for their footfalls. The landscape around them was every different kind of big. In a way he felt both lost and a little overwhelmed. He ate the bread, the cheese. He broke off pieces and gave them to Bailey. She took them, said nothing, but a few minutes later her hand came out for more.

Finally they stopped. It was growing cooler.

"We have to make a decision," Clay said. "Whether we're gonna keep walking toward Van Horn and hope we pick up a ride, or we try and find somewhere to sleep the night."

Bailey turned and looked at him. "You think I'm pretty, Clay Luckman?"

Clay frowned. That was a low curveball out of somewhere with the sun in your eyes. "Pretty? How d'you mean?"

"Well, shoot, Clay, if I have to explain what I mean by that question then it seems I got my answer already."

"Hell, Bailey, I know what you mean. Jesus, girl, you're fifteen years old—"

"And that matters? I knew a girl one time, she was pregnant when she was thirteen."

"Just because someone else does it doesn't make it right. No girl should be pregnant at that kinda age . . ."

"Well, that and everything else aside, you still have to answer my question."

Clay felt himself blush. He remembered being in the hotel, the way he'd crouched to look through the bathroom keyhole in the hope that he'd see her naked.

"Well, sure, Bailey, of course I find you pretty. Pretty as a picture, I'd say."

"And do you love me, Clay Luckman?"

"Now, what the hell kinda question is that?" Clay stopped dead. He was getting annoyed now. This really was crazy talk.

"If I was a little older, would you love me then?"

Clay looked down at the ground. He shook his head. "Bailey, I'll tell you something right here and now. You are pretty. Of course you are. Anyone who doesn't think you're pretty . . . well, they ain't gonna be right in their mind—"

"Well, how come you ain't never tried to . . . you know, tried to get me out of my clothes?"

Clay's eyes widened. He knew what was going on. She was clutching at things—*anything*—that would make her feel less lonely. "Now you're just being . . . Christ, Bailey, I don't even know what to say to that. If this is something that's come about because of what's happened, like you're feeling all lonely and whatever—"

Bailey Redman stepped forward suddenly. She grabbed Clay Luckman's face with both her hands, her palms flat to his cheeks until he felt his eyes were going to meet, and then she kissed him dead center on the lips. He was too shocked to move, too shocked to say anything at all when she released him and stepped back.

She looked at him unerringly. She had a fool grin on her face. "Say after me, 'I love you, Bailey Redman.'" She paused for a moment. "It ain't hard, Clay Luckman. Just say it so's I can hear it. I. Love. You. Bailey. Redman."

Clay started breathing again. He wasn't aware he'd stopped. "I . . . er, I lo-love y-you, B-Bailey Redman."

"Good. Now again, but like you mean it."

Clay blinked hard. "Er, okay . . . I love you, Bailey Redman."

"Well, all right, then," she said. "Now that's done we're all set. I love you, you love me, we're on the way to Eldorado, and everything's gonna be fine an' dandy."

Clay started walking again. She came up alongside him, put her hand around his arm, and squeezed it reassuringly.

"And when I'm a little older . . . you know, however old you think I have to be, well then we can do the sex thing as well, okay?"

Clay didn't say a word. He was still speechless from the *I love you, Bailey Redman* thing.

They walked for thirty minutes more. They'd held hands pretty much the entire way. Clay was convincing himself that this uncharacteristic overture from Bailey was little more than a coping mechanism related to the loss of her father. The man had been dead three days. She'd cried two times, two times only, sobbing and hyperventilating and the whole thing, and then nothing. There was the odd moment she'd disappear completely, her mind elsewhere, her gaze fixed on some indistinct middle ground between one thing and another, but the emotional release at the side of the road had been her only real expression of grief and anguish. Now she was adopting Clay as her mentor, her big brother perhaps, and she wanted his assurance that he loved her. What did it mean? It meant that he promised to look after her, to protect and defend her, to care for her as her father would have done had he still been alive.

Clay knew how she felt. He'd had a big brother one time. He knew what it was like.

Clay reckoned he could do those things, and do them to the best of his ability. That—in all honesty—was the very least he could do.

"Ain't been no cars, Clay," she said eventually. "Doesn't look like we're gonna get a ride, and I'm tired."

"We'll have to find somewhere to sleep for tonight," he said.

"We should have asked Smithy for a blanket."

"For sure."

A half mile on they saw a barn to the right of the highway. Three or four hundred yards away, a sound roof, the sight of bales in there, and Clay made a straight line for it as if it were an oasis in the desert.

Adjoining a tract of pastures and fallow ground, the barn provided storage room for the feed and hay for whoever's herd grazed there in summer.

Once inside they sat cross-legged. They ate the rest of the bread, some more cheese, some peanuts, and then they drank soda. Dry chaff floated in the last weak sun bars. Bailey moved her hand and motes rushed away and back. After a while Clay lit a cigarette just to see whorls and curlicues of smoke in the sunlight. He felt good, inexplicably so, and he wondered if some small part of the shadow that had been following them had now been left behind.

CHAPTER FIFTY-THREE

Candace Munro was not a virgin. Two years before she'd had sex with a young man called Dan Forrest whose father owned a hardware store in Grandfalls. Candace had met Danny when old Mr. Forrest's truck broke down outside of Van Horn. Sam Munro was called out. Candace went with him for the ride, and there she met Danny. Danny was a sweet boy. They talked on the telephone. He drove over a couple of times and they had root beer floats and talked about nothing specific or consequential. They held hands. One time they kissed. Next time he came over and he told her that he was joining the army and they were sending him to Fort Benning in Georgia and this was possibly the last time he would see her for a while. She knew it would be the last time she *ever* saw him. She perceived it. They made love. He'd brought a rubber. He'd never done it before and nor had she, but they managed to figure it out. That was the late summer of 1962. August he went to Fort Benning. December he fell twenty feet from a tree bough and broke his neck. They were doing maneuvers, the red team and the blue team. They weren't shooting real bullets or nothing. It was just training. The team leader sent him up the tree to see where the blue team had laid low. He got up there, and just as he was about to report the enemy position he slipped and fell and he was dead. Candace's perception had been right. Since that time a couple of other things had happened. Katie Garrett's boy had a puppy and the puppy ran away. They looked and looked but couldn't find it. Candace got the thought into her head that the puppy was in a drain or something, and she told Katie Garrett this. Katie looked surprised, and then she rushed down to the end of the yard and heaved open a metal cover that was once a hatch over the flood outlet for the town's auxiliary generator. The puppy was in there—wet, cold, starving, but alive. How he'd gotten through the pipe work and down into the outlet no one knew, but it didn't matter. Dog and boy were reunited and everyone was relieved. Another time Candace knew that someone planned to not pay her father for the work on his truck. He was just passing through, had a flat, asked for a tire change. Sam was almost done with the tire and Candace told him. She said, "Make him pay now," and Sam said that it wasn't done that way. You did the work, *then* you got paid. She insisted, even threatened to ask the man herself. Sam did as his daughter asked. The man looked awkward and sheepish, and then he made like he was going through his pockets, and then he expressed surprise and alarm that he didn't have his pocketbook or any cash with him. He said he would to call someone, and call someone he did—right from the garage phone—and he told whoever to come down and meet him and bring some money. "How did you know that?" Sam asked his daughter after the one had paid and then both of them had driven away. "I don't know. Sometimes I just get a really strong feeling about something and I know I'm right." Sam kissed the top of his daughter's head. He hugged her and told her he loved her despite the fact that she really should be burned as a witch.

So Candace trusted her perceptions, and as she lay face forward across the kitchen table in Morton Randall's house, her ankles and wrists bound and tied to the four legs, naked as the day she was born . . . as she heard Digger Danziger muttering and mumbling to himself as he walked around behind her, as she felt him come up behind her and start massaging her inner thighs again, readying himself to stick it in her yet another time . . . as she tried to ignore the pain that she felt down there, the sure sensation that she was bleeding, she also understood that none of it really mattered anymore. The perception she had, and perhaps stronger than any before, was that this was the very last day of her life. She had been there for three hours, though after the first hour she'd lost any real awareness of time passing. She tried to think of something good. Anything at all. She tried to see Dan Forrest's face, his smile, the way his eyes lit up when she smiled back. She could see only blackness. Perhaps that was best.

After he'd raped her, she knew he was going to kill her. Perhaps because he never looked directly at her, perhaps because he never said her name, perhaps because he never touched her with anything but force and violence, or perhaps simply because of her perceptions. She knew she was going to die. It was just a matter of when. And how.

She knew it was time when he appeared with two knives. They were the kind of knives you used to cut meat, the blades a good six inches long. He had one in each hand and he held them like they were extensions to his own arms.

She closed her eyes and gritted her teeth. Once he was inside her, she heard the knife leave the table and she knew this was it. At the same moment that he thrust between her legs as hard as he could he plunged the knives into her sides. It was as if someone had switched a light on inside her head. Brilliant, brilliant whiteness. It wasn't even pain. It was a sensation, yes, but not like any sensation she'd ever experienced before. She thought she made a sound, but she wasn't sure. Everything started to blur, and then whiteness became yellow became green, and then it was a fierce turquoise, so fierce she didn't know whether her eyes were open or closed. He tugged one of the knives out then started stabbing down into the small of her back, her shoulders, her neck, the side of her face, and he was screaming then, and the last thing she heard before she died was his voice. Mad, enraged, like something possessed, and he was shouting "Bitch! Bitch! Fucking dirty fucking bitch!" but she couldn't be sure what he was saying because consciousness was deserting her, and the last thing she thought of before she died was the way that Danny Forrest used to call her Candy.

After he was done Digger stood there for a while. He tugged the knives out and threw them into the sink.

There was quite a lot of blood. More blood than he'd expected.

He looked down at himself. Her blood was on his thighs. He felt sick. He grabbed a towel from the edge of the sink, turned on the faucet, and got it wet. He wiped the blood away, retching as he did so.

He glanced back at the girl. Her eyes were open. Was she looking *at* him? Was she *smiling*?

Digger reached out tentatively. He used the tip of his right index finger to close one eye, and then the other.

He pulled up his pants. He walked back around her and looked at her from the side of the room.

He closed his eyes.

The nausea passed as quickly as it had come.

This was a terrible thing. This was a powerfully terrible thing. He knew that. She was dead. He had fucked her and killed her at the same time.

He had done this thing.

He had done this thing. This powerfully terrible, mighty, wonderful thing.

Not anyone else.

Not *Earl*.

Digger felt the rush in his chest. It was like finding God. He had found God. God was inside him. It was like being baptized. Maybe that's what it was. A *religious* experience.

Earl was there. Earl had always been there. Earl had guided him, shown him, talked to him, encouraged him, but now he was on his own.

Digger was alone.

Earl was here, here *inside* him, but it was *not* Earl, just the memory of Earl.

Digger was hyperventilating. His whole body was varnished with a cold sweat.

Oh, how alive he felt! How utterly and truly *alive!*

He'd never felt such a thing in all his life, and there was only more to come. Good God, could it ever feel better than this?

This is exactly what Earl had meant. The *realest* thing you could ever feel. A human being takes the life of another human being, and they own that life. It becomes theirs. They walk away with the life that they've stolen, and it is now their own. They have the power of two lives. And the more you take, well, the stronger you become.

Digger stepped back and put his shoulders against the wall.

He looked at Candace.

She made him angry. He didn't know why. She just did.

Bitch.

She was a bitch, a fucking bitch, a fucking asshole mother-fucking bitch!

God, how she made him mad!

"Fuck you!" he screamed at her. "Fuck you, Candy-Ass!"

Then he started laughing.

Digger stepped back until he felt the sink behind him. He reached to his right and took a skillet from the stove top.

"This is for you, Earl," he whispered. "For all you did for me. Loved you, man, but I'm on my own now. All on my own fucking lonesome."

Digger took a step forward. He raised the skillet, hesitated for just a moment, and then he beat Candace Munro in the head again and again and again until she was unrecognizable.

He stood there with the bloody skillet in his hand, and he was sad for a moment because she was *really* dead now and she was just too much of a mess to fool around with anymore. He washed up, set the knives aside, cleaned his hands, and sluiced cold water on his face. He ate a couple more spoonfuls of cold pork and beans from the pan, and then he untied the girl and dragged her behind the kitchen. He leaned her against the wall right next to Morton Randall. Morton was on his side, and there was a good deal of dried blood and Digger skidded some, but he gained purchase and got the old boy sitting up again like he was waiting for lunch. They could have been father and daughter. Elliott went upstairs and fetched a bedsheet from the first room he came to. He draped it over the pair of them, careful to position the sheet so that it did not come into contact with any of the girl's blood. From the kitchen you could just see the doorway, the shadows within, and nothing else. There was room in there for a good half dozen or so.

The exertion had done him good. He felt alive. It had been a rush, and a good one at that, and he figured he would do it again. Maybe tomorrow.

CHAPTER FIFTY-FOUR

Entrance to Frank Jacobs's house was easy, as was often the case with homicide victims, especially those who possessed no immediate family. The back screen was open, the interior door unlocked, and Cassidy just walked on in there like he was coming home for the evening. It was a little after half-past five. Already it was darkening, and Cassidy had hoped he would be able to search the place without employing the electric lights. He'd brought a flashlight from the car, but the damn batteries were pretty much dead, and the light it issued was a weak distraction as opposed to a bright illumination.

The first and most striking perception was the sheer lack of home comforts. The sitting room was nothing more than a couple of chairs, a low table centering the room, a lamp standard, a TV, and against the back wall—literally floor to ceiling—were stacked shoe boxes, three deep and fifteen high. Men's, women's, children's, both leather and synthetic. Pumps, sandals, wingtips, loafers, brogues, oxfords, an endless variety. Cassidy could smell the leather inside the cardboard. It was a good smell. Seemed that Frank Jacobs's life had been shoes. He wondered how long he'd been doing it, how long he expected to go on doing it. He wondered if selling shoes had been a stepping stone to something else, but the stepping stone had become the safe harbor in the river. Or maybe Frank Jacobs had always wanted to sell shoes. Maybe he was a born shoe salesman, never wanting for anything, aspiring toward no other goal than the recommendation and purveyance of footwear to America's working folk. Whatever the case, it was now Frank Jacobs's history. A handful of minutes in the sitting room and Cassidy figured there was nothing to see. There was a small bookcase beneath the window—a half dozen dime novels, a few periodicals, a stack of shoe brochures from a company in Flagstaff. There was a wireless, the TV, a pair of battered slippers parked beneath the low table, a heavy amber-colored glass ashtray, the rug on the floor. This was where Frank Jacobs came to relax after a long day of driving and selling.

Aside from the kitchen the only other downstairs room was the dining room, and perhaps would have been the dining room had Frank Jacobs possessed any reason to decorate it as such. Again more shoes, this time a good hundred or a hundred and fifty boxes. Cassidy didn't need to count them. There was no significance to their presence. Upstairs in the bathroom was the medicine cabinet above the sink. Toothpaste, soap, a shaving brush, a razor, a stick of shaving soap, a styptic pencil, aspirin, mouthwash, toothpicks, some kind of compound tonic for *When Your Get Up and Go Has Got Up and Gone!* Nothing out of the ordinary, nothing unusual.

It was in the bedroom that Cassidy believed he'd hit pay dirt. Pictures of a girl. Five of them. One in a small frame on the nightstand, another framed on the windowsill, three more in an envelope on the shelf of Frank's wardrobe. The last one was of the girl and Frank together, and there was no mistaking the similarity. His daughter? And the envelope bore a name, printed carefully in pencil. *Bailey.* Her first name, or her second? More than likely her first. Bailey Jacobs? Was that who this girl was?

Cassidy felt a rush of something in his chest. Had she been with him at Marana? Had she been in the store but somehow survived the attack? And if so, where was she now? Had this Clarence Luckman—or whoever the hell he might be—kidnapped her, taken her hostage, and was even now traveling the country with her? Or had he killed her and dumped her body somewhere, as yet undiscovered? Cassidy remembered what Nixon and Koenig had told him in the hotel room in El Paso. That the discovery of the crashed car had been reported by two people, one of them a girl. That's where Harvey Warren's gun had been found, and that gun had come from Marana. He tugged out his notebook, leafed through the few scribbled notes he'd made when he left the hotel room after his discussion with Nixon and Koenig. *Clark Regan in Deming.* That was who he needed to find. That was who he needed to show one of these pictures to. *Was this the girl that came that day, Mr. Regan? Was this the girl who told you about the overturned car with the two dead men inside?*

Cassidy went through the pictures, chose one from the envelope on the wardrobe shelf. It was perhaps not the most flattering, despite the fact that she was a pretty girl, but it showed her looking directly at the camera, a slight smile on her lips, her hair tucked back behind her ears. A clear and unobstructed view of her face. This is what *Bailey* looked like. From this he hoped that she could be identified by someone.

He looked at his watch. It was six o'clock. Deming was— what?—a good two hundred miles on the other side of Tucson? That wouldn't work—not tonight. And showing up there at nine or ten o'clock, finding the gas station closed, trying to track down this Clark Regan by knocking on random doors? Cassidy didn't think so. No, he would drive home tonight, have Alice call him in sick again tomorrow, and he would drive out to Deming first thing and find this Regan character. He held the picture of the girl in his hand, and in the dim light of a dead man's bedroom he looked at the face of a teenager that could be alive, could be dead, could be nothing at all to do with this. But he felt something. He really felt *something*. In his own mind he couldn't resolve the mystery surrounding Clarence Luckman. How could a boy— never in trouble, never anything other than an orphan, an unfortunate social outcast—suddenly become a homicidal maniac? And again, clearer than ever, Alice's words were there. *When they are two people.*

CHAPTER FIFTY-FIVE

Why there were fireworks they did not know, but there were fireworks.

Clay lay silently, could hear nothing but the sound of Bailey's breathing beside him, and then it was there in the distance—*crack! crack! fffssstttt!*—and he started upright, and sat there for a moment wondering if he hadn't been dreaming.

"What is it?" Bailey slurred, roused from her sleep.

"Ssshhh," he whispered. "Listen . . ."

There is was again—*crack! crack! fffssstttt! CRACK!*

"Fireworks?" she asked.

"I think so, yes."

"Let's go see."

They gathered their shoes up and put them on. They went like scared children to the doorway of the barn, and peered out into the darkness.

"There's a lake," Bailey said.

Clay could see it in the distance—perhaps half a mile or so. Beyond it the arc and flare of fireworks reflected in the surface of the water.

"Come on!" she urged. "Let's go watch!"

Clay—thinking now that he was only one sly smile shy of true love, the kind of love that means suicide if you don't get it—went with her, dragged along by her enthusiasm, his hand in hers, the feeling of her fingers around his own, and watching as the ground rushed beneath his feet, leaping stones and rocks, skirting outcrops of tough Texan scrub, and all the while the ever-approaching promise of magic as another firework exploded and lit the sky.

They reached the edge of the lake, and the surface of the water and the base of the sky had no seam between them, and for a moment they were one, and it appeared as if the ground beneath their feet was somehow suspended in infinite space, and there was no beginning and no end to anything.

And then the sound again—the sudden rush as a streak of color lit the sky, and then it was if the heavens themselves exploded. Pinwheeling, pirouetting, fishtailing. A sudden flower of light, the smell of sulfur, glycerin, cordite, hot metal. A thousand instant flares in the sky like pepper sprinkled over a flame. Sparks like an ax blade against a grindstone.

Bailey gasped with each one, a breath captured for a second in her chest. She tugged his arm excitedly, and it was all he could do not to grab her and kiss her. He stood behind her, his chin on her shoulder, and as he held her he could feel her heart beating frantically just inches from his own. The skin and muscle and bone that separated them was as nothing.

There were tears in his eyes, but they were not tears of sadness or loss. They were tears for something else that he did not understand.

Soon it was over. Bailey was flushed with excitement. She sat down on the ground and couldn't speak for a while.

Eventually she said, "Wow!" and then she started laughing.

Clay helped her up. They walked back to the barn hand in hand.

Lights had come on in nearby houses. Houses they had not seen before. Distant windows stared back at them with their bright square eyes.

Lying down once more, beyond the barn door the murmuring darkness more alive than any night, Clay knew he would not now sleep, whereas Bailey—before he had even registered how closely she lay beside him—was gone.

The night grew bitterly cold. The air was dry and the heavens were cloudless, and somewhere beyond the flat horizon the flicker of lightning identified the presence of a storm he could not hear. And then he was really afraid for the first time. Afraid of the present, the uncertain future, more afraid of the past, for the past he could not change and everything from this point forward could have been predetermined by circumstances beyond his control. Perhaps fate, destiny, astrology. Perhaps Bailey Redman was destined never to see her next birthday, and by mere association he was also doomed. The star beneath which he had been born was dark, but hers was darker still. Perhaps their shadows were doubled, now feeding off one another and doubling again.

As unavoidable as weather, or time, or rust, or death.

He was scared to be feeling what he was feeling. He was scared to love this girl. What had she said? *If love is so great, how come it breaks so many hearts?*

And what of Elliott? What of the love that they'd had for each other, the years they had spent together with no one but each other to protect them against the vagaries of a cruel and desperate world? Where had *that* love gone?

Clay closed his eyes. He willed himself to sleep but he could not.

Not tonight.

Perhaps not ever.

DAY EIGHT

CHAPTER FIFTY-SIX

The press had blood on their teeth. And they would not rest until their bellies were full. Unsubstantiated reports found their way into the newspapers. The local journals and rags picked up on it, and would be followed by squibs in the nationals within a day or so. The FBI and the sheriffs' departments had known it would merely be a matter of time. Once they started disseminating pictures, once the radio broadcasts reached the wider world, well, the world would start to look in their direction. There had been a bloodbath someplace in Texas. El Paso, according to initial word. A family had been killed. It was just like that case in Holcomb, Kansas, a few years back. Cassidy caught word of it on the radio when he woke on Friday morning. As if fate conspired to keep them ignorant, neither Clay Luckman, Bailey Redman, nor—most importantly—Elliott Danziger, had been exposed to radio or TV broadcasts; not in cars, nor in diners, stores, or motels, and thus they were oblivious to the world's awareness of what was happening. The press now knew some names—Clarence Luckman, Garth Nixon, and Ronald Koenig—and reporters were dispatched from numerous offices to track the latter two in their hotel in El Paso. By the time the enclave of journalists arrived both Nixon and Koenig had departed, first to the Eckhart–McGovern crime scene to seal it completely, to put a barricade of sawhorses and uniforms around it and close it off from the rest of the world, secondly to Las Cruces, the nearest town that could provide them with an adequate telephone service, an acceptable hotel, and a handful of county officers who could be assigned the more mundane tasks associated with such a case. Time was now against them. Once a case reached the national headlines it would then run against the clock. The federal authorities and the respective representatives of each of the involved county sheriffs' departments would be clamoring to get it out of print and off the television. The appearance of reporters, the fact that the locals were aware of national media interest, made it all the more difficult to keep the investigation discreet. Some folks, understandably, became very wary of speaking to the federal or county officials. They did not want to see their names in the press. To be considered instrumental in the progress of a homicidal maniac's arrest . . . well, enough said. A homicidal maniac was not going to take too kindly to that kind of interference in his business.

Cassidy went out to Deming regardless. He trusted that news of what was happening around El Paso had not traveled the hundred or so miles northwest to the gas station and Clark Regan.

Digger Danziger, however, woke with a hellacious thirst, the same kind of thirst that had prompted his desire for a bottle of Shoeshine's root beer all those many years earlier. Clay Luckman was not there to do his work for him, and in thinking of that incident—an incident that seemed part of someone else's history—he realized how little he had thought of his brother during recent events. They were not the same, had never been the same, and in that moment Digger was proud of the differences. He thought of the love he had once possessed for Clay, but there seemed to be nothing there. Where he had once respected his brother, there seemed to be a vacuum. Such a consideration did not trouble him. In that moment, had he been asked whom he wished to be reunited with—Clay or Earl—it would have been Earl. No question. Every time it would have been Earl.

Digger went downstairs to look in the refrigerator. There was nothing of use. Half a bottle of soured milk. A carton of orange juice. He tasted it, found it too bitter. He threw the carton in the sink, tipped the milk in after it, and then searched out some clothes and money.

Out of the corner of his eyes he noticed the sheet-covered bodies in the room beyond the kitchen. He walked on through, lifted a corner of it, and looked at Candace. Her eyes were in that mess somewhere, but he couldn't see them. Her head was over to one side like she was bored. *Bored to death*, he thought, and smiled to himself.

Digger drove into Van Horn in Morton Randall's pickup. It was early, a little before nine, and the place was dead. He drove around some, found a mercantile, went inside and bought milk, some cream, some cheese and ham and bread and eggs. Whether there were such things in Randall's house didn't matter. There was a woman behind the counter and he wanted to get her talking. She had on a pin badge. *Sue-Anne* it read.

"Hey, Sue-Anne," Digger ventured. The woman looked at him. She was about thirty-five or forty. She was slim but she was hefty up top. She wasn't exactly pretty, but she had a pleasant face.

"Hey there back," she said. She smiled. It wasn't genuine. She smiled like it was eight o'clock in the morning and she didn't want to be there.

"Kinda get the idea you don't wanna be here," he said.

"I'd say you was pretty much right there, son," she replied.

Digger's nostrils cleared. *Son?* What the hell was that supposed to mean?

He saw the face of that man in the diner. The one with the hat. He had a chair for his fucking hat!

Digger closed his eyes for just a second.

"You okay there, son?" the woman asked.

She said it again. *Son?* What the hell was it with this bullshit?

Digger gritted his teeth. He could keep it together. She was talking down to him? Treating him like a kid? Just like that bastard back in the diner. But he *could* keep it together. Earl would have kept it together. Earl would have just smiled and taken it all in his stride. Earl could handle trouble, but he wasn't one to go making trouble for himself.

Digger thought about the .45, the fact that it was back in Randall's pickup.

He took a deep breath. He could feel the rage somewhere in his chest. And he could hear Earl's voice in his head.

Earl was no *kid*, and neither was he. This woman—this *bitch*—needed to understand who she was dealing with.

Sue-Anne rang up his provisions. "That'll be two dollars ten," she said.

"I think you should give me this stuff for free," Digger said.

She looked at him. Her expression had that same bored-to-death thing as Candace.

"I think you should get your wallet out and pay me," she said.

"I think you should shut the fuck up," Digger replied.

"What?" she said. "What the hell kind of thing is that to say to me? Jesus Christ, what on earth gives you the right to come in here . . ."

Digger leaned across the counter and slapped her across the face as hard as he could.

Sue-Anne staggered back a step, and before Digger knew what was happening she had a gun in her hand. It had come from beneath the counter. There was nothing, and then there was a gun.

"Whoa," he said, genuinely surprised.

"Get the hell outta my store," she said. Her eyes were on fire, her teeth gritted. Digger could see the muscles jumping along her jaw line.

The gun was steady, but it was a .32, maybe even a .25. Even if she fired it, and even if it hit him, well, a popgun like that wasn't gonna give him much more than a scratch, was it?

"And if I don't?" he asked. He felt playful, mischievous. Sue-Anne was no more going to pull that trigger than Digger was going to let her live.

"Then . . . well, son, I'm gonna shoot you right where you stand."

"Son?" he said. "What the fuck is this 'son' bullshit?"

"What I say," Sue-Anne replied. She was edging along behind the counter. She was planning on coming out into the store and walking him to the door at gunpoint. Like that was going to happen!

"Just exactly what I say," Sue-Anne went on. "You ain't nothin' more 'an a teenager. You come on in here badmouthing me, and then slap me for Christ Almighty's sake . . . Jesus Lord Almighty, who the hell do you think you are?"

"I'm your worst fucking nightmare," Digger said.

Now he was angry. Now he was riled. Now she had spoken to him disrespectfully. Said he was nothing more than a teenager. Well, a teenager he might be, but he could still take that .32 off of her and stick it where the sun didn't shine before he pulled the goddamned trigger.

352

"So get the hell outta my store, boy," she said. "Get the hell outta here and don't come back . . ."

She didn't finish the statement. Digger had reached out and grabbed her arm. He twisted that arm with all his strength, but Sue-Anne was no Laurette Tannahill, no Dee Parselle. Sue-Anne was used to hauling fifty-pound bags of seed and feed, gallon drums of molasses and whatnot from the back of her truck and into the store. Once Digger got ahold of her arm she just wrenched back the other way and relinquished his grasp.

Digger, surprised at first, then mad, advanced at her again.

She fired.

The sound was deafening in the enclosed space.

Digger thought he felt the air move as the bullet whizzed by his face and hit the wall behind him.

"Jesus—"

She raised the gun again, all ready to shoot him down. Just like Earl. Just like they did to Earl, the bastards!

Digger let fly with a wild swing and caught her on the shoulder.

Sue-Anne staggered back and lost her balance.

Digger just ran.

He was out of the store and into the pickup before Sue-Anne had a chance to gain her feet once more.

"Fucking bitch!" he shouted as he hurtled away. He saw her in the rearview, standing there in front of the store with the gun in her hand.

"Fucking bitch, fucking bitch . . . God Almighty, what the hell!" he shouted, and slammed his hands on the steering wheel.

Back on the frontage Sue-Anne watched him hightail it out of there. She was terrified, hyperventilating, more scared than she'd ever been.

Elliott Danziger was there, and then he was gone, like an errant, ill-omened wind.

He drove away feeling a sense of tension and hatred right through his mind and his body. He had been challenged, and— once again—he had been found wanting.

What would Earl have said?

Earl would have said nothing. Earl would have turned right around and headed on back to that store, and he would have taken that bitch and beat her head in, no question.

Digger looked back one more time in the rearview. He could still see her, standing right there in front of the store with that gun in her hand.

Now he needed to hurt someone more than ever.

And hurt them bad.

CHAPTER FIFTY-SEVEN

Clark Regan looked sick. He was maybe sixty or sixty-five. Not an old man, but he really did look sick. He had the sort of face that belonged to this part of the country, these kinds of people. People who'd spent their lives looking at nothing but distance and dust storms. Kind of people who could predict weather from the shape of shadows around the moon. And were always right.

It was just after ten. The drive from Tucson had consumed the better part of three hours, and Cassidy hadn't dallied or delayed. He'd wanted to get to Deming as early as possible. He'd wanted time to go on from there to wherever else he needed to in order to pursue this thing. That, and minimize the possibility of news from El Paso reaching Clark Regan. Cassidy needn't have worried. The last thing in the world that concerned Clark Regan was the possibility that he might be hunted down and killed by a homicidal teenager.

There was no hesitation in the man's voice or his body language when Cassidy showed him the picture of the girl.

"Yep," he said. "That's the one."

"And she told you about the dead people in the car?"

"Couple of dead fellers she said, back a ways. Asked me to phone the sheriff's department." Regan nodded his head. "So you're in with the other two fellers that came here? The federal people?"

"I am, yes. We're working the same case. They're federal, I'm police from Tucson."

"So you're a good ways from home, then?"

"I am."

"Well, now you know the same as me, no more, no less."

"The boy that was with her . . ."

"Yeah, he was here too."

"And you didn't see him so well?"

"Nope. He was back there some." Regan nodded toward a rack of potato chips. "I reckoned he was gonna steal something while she distracted my attention. I thought it was just a story. Come in here and raise an alarm about something or other, get me all flustered, get me making telephone calls to the sheriff for no reason, and meanwhile the accomplice robs me blind. But it wasn't that way. He didn't steal nothin', and what she said was the truth. There were indeed a coupla dead fellers under a car back a while on the highway. Seems from what I heard that they was a coupla hummersexuals doing stuff they shouldn'a been doin' in a car on the highway . . . shouldn'a been doin' anyplace, I reckon."

"Okay, I really appreciate that, Mr. Regan. And there is no doubt in your mind, no doubt whatsoever, that this girl here is the one that reported that to you and asked you to make the call?"

"On my life," he said. "Not that there's a great deal of it left, but yes, I'm sure, on my life, that that was she and she come in here and told me what she did."

"Okay, okay . . ." Cassidy paused. He could feel his heart in his chest. That same rush of something. Not because he had something that no one else had, but because he had *something*. He felt like he should buy something.

"Gimme a carton of Luckies," he told Regan.

"You don't smoke," Regan replied.

Cassidy frowned.

"You ain't got the smoker's teeth, nor the fingers nor the skin. I should know. Been smokin' them damn things all my life, and now they got me." He touched his midriff. "Say there's cancer in my gut, in my kidneys, ever-where, you know? I'll be here a few months more, and then it's all done and dusted."

"I'm really sorry to hear that," Cassidy said.

" 'Preciated, son, but it don't matter. We ain't kin and we ain't never gonna be, so don't lose your head over it. You wanna buy something, well, I ain't gonna stop you, but buy something you need. We don't make more 'an a dime on them smokes anyhows."

Cassidy loaded up the counter with cookies and potato chips.

He got candy bars and cans of soup and a wrench and a pair of leather gloves.

Regan totaled them up and took his money. He packed everything in a brown paper bag and pushed the bag across the counter.

"You enjoy them candies, now, you hear?" he said.

Cassidy smiled. "Thank you, Mr. Regan. I really appreciate your help."

"Well, you're welcome, son, and I hope you do just fine, and I hope you catch whoever it is that you folks seem so busy lookin' for."

"Thank you."

Cassidy managed the door with one hand, and he was back in the car before he really understood the import of what had happened.

The girl—this *Bailey*—had been alive on Wednesday, just two days before. She had walked into Clark Regan's gas station and reported the car, and beneath that car had been Harvey Warren's gun. Had she put it there? Had she taken it from the gas station in Marana after the death of Frank Jacobs—her father?—and had she then put it beneath the overturned car? If so, why? And *was* she Jacobs's daughter? If not, then who was she? And who was the boy with her?

He drove away with more questions than those with which he'd arrived. But the most important question had been answered, at least with a degree of certainty. Whoever had appeared with the girl at the gas station, and whoever had followed the Eckharts from the diner were different people. And now he was looking for three, not one. Of this Cassidy felt sure.

CHAPTER FIFTY-EIGHT

Southwest a hundred and fifty miles or so, no more than seventeen or eighteen miles from where Digger Danziger had recently driven away from Sue-Anne McCarthy's mercantile in Morton Randall's pickup, Clay Luckman and Bailey Redman sat on the floor of the barn where they had slept. The fireworks of the night before could have been a dream. The day was bright and fresh and cool, and though they knew the lake was somewhere down the hill they could not see it.

"Eldorado . . . I'd say it's only about two hundred and fifty miles now," she said. "If we could get a good ride, someone that would take us to where the highway divides, then we'd be within striking distance."

"And when we get there?" Clay asked her. He turned sideways and looked at her profile. The more he looked at her the prettier she got. Was it that way with all girls, or just with Bailey Redman?

"I don't know, Clay, and it's no use askin' me. You know we ain't got no reason to go there more than any other place. We're just going, that's all."

" 'Cause of your daddy."

She hesitated, and then she nodded sagely. " 'Cause of my daddy maybe, but more because of your dumb magazine advertisement."

"What was he like?" Clay asked. "I only ask because I never really had one."

"I'm the wrong person to ask," Bailey replied.

"Look . . . if you don't want to talk about it—"

"I do want to talk about it," Bailey interjected. "It's just that . . . well, it ain't the easiest thing in the world to talk about so you gotta let me do it in my own time."

Clay bit his lip. He stayed silent. He wanted her to know that she could take all the time she wanted. "He sold shoes, right?" Clay prompted.

"Yeah, shoes. Nothing wrong with selling shoes. You gotta do something for a living and he sold shoes."

"Nothing wrong with selling shoes at all."

Bailey looked away toward where the lake had been the night before, toward the memory of reflected fireworks. "He sold a lot of shoes, I think. He had a house full of shoes. His whole house smelled of leather." She paused. "It was a good smell. I used to go visit, and I would wait until he opened the door, and then when he did I would just stand there for a second and I could smell the leather. That's a smell that will always remind me of him."

"Leather is a good smell."

"And he was good too," Bailey said. "He didn't smoke much, and he hardly ever took a drink, at least from what I saw. He wasn't a religious person. He didn't go to church or nothin' like that, and I never saw him reading the Bible or anything, but he was a good man. The sort of man who says he's gonna do something, and then he does it. Sort of man who treats people kindly no matter who they are. I mean, he used to go on down and sell shoes to the black folks, and he would charge them less than the white folks 'cause he knew they had less money. And he wouldn't tell 'em he was givin' them an extra discount because he didn't want to hurt their pride. He treated everyone the same as everyone else, didn't matter who you were—man, woman, white, black, Chinese, or whatever you were; as far as my dad was concerned everyone was the same."

"My dad got shot in a store . . . just like yours did."

Bailey turned and looked at Clay. A frown creased her brow.

" 'Cept my dad was tryin' to rob it, and there was a cop in there and he shot my dad. Earlier that day my dad killed my mom. He hit her in the head with a baseball bat and broke her neck."

"Christ Almighty, Clay . . ."

Clay raised his hand. "I didn't mean to interrupt you talking about your dad. I just thought it was strange that both our dads were killed in a store, that was all. Sure, my dad was a crazy man and your dad wasn't. I just never mentioned the coincidence before."

"You want to talk about him?" Bailey asked.

"There ain't nothing to say. Reckon he was the kind of man who would be in jail if he wasn't dead, or if he wasn't in jail he'd be on his way."

Bailey looked back toward the horizon. "Life is weird," she said.

"No disagreement there."

"You have something, and then it's gone. In an instant. Like clicking your fingers. Everything's one way, and then bang, it's all gone lopsided or back-to-front."

"The nature of things, I guess."

Clay was silent for a moment, and then he turned back to her and said, "And what about your mom?"

"What about her?"

"What was she like?"

"You mean, her being a prostitute an' everything?"

Clay hesitated. "No, I don't mean that. That was what she did, not *who* she was, right?"

"Ain't a lot of people who saw it that way."

Clay smiled. "My brother was a nice guy, and then he went crazy. Ain't no shortage of dumb people, Bailey, you know that."

"She was good. I knew she loved me, right from the get-go. She didn't have no shame about what she did, and when she got sick she didn't think it was a punishment from God. She wasn't like that. She was a great mom, and I loved her back just as much."

"Shame people've gotta die too early. But, like I said, that's just the nature of things."

"Well, to hell with the nature of things, Clay Luckman. We're just gonna have to change the nature of things, aren't we? We're gonna go to Eldorado and we're gonna find out what nature has waitin' for us there, and if we don't like it then we're gonna damned well change it or go lookin' for it someplace else."

Bailey got up. She brushed down her pants and stamped her feet until her cuffs dropped.

"We'll get something to eat on the way," Clay said. "That's if you're hungry."

She smiled. "Slap on enough ketchup and I'd eat a raccoon sandwich."

CHAPTER FIFTY-NINE

One time Elliott Danziger heard a story. Where he heard it, the place it was about, well, he couldn't remember these things, and they were unimportant details anyway. It was true and that was all that mattered.

The story went that there was a valley someplace, and on the side of the valley was a town. It wasn't a big town—maybe two or three hundred houses, a thousand or so folks living there, and these men came along to talk to the people about buying up their land and their houses so they could turn the valley into a reservoir. "We're going to build a dam," they said. "Each end of the valley we're going to build a dam, and then we're going to fill up the valley with water and we're going to make a reservoir that will service the whole county. Crops will get irrigated, wells can be drilled, there'll be plenty of water for everyone and prosperity will abound." The townsfolk got together and they had a meeting. They discussed the issue back and forth, and finally a representative from the town went to see the reservoir men and told them to fuck themselves. "Go fuck yourselves," they said. "We don't want your dam and we don't want your reservoir. We have enough water for our needs and that's the way it's going to stay. We built these houses with our own bare hands and we ain't movin' for no one."

Well, the reservoir men had this paper from the government, see. And the paper said that the people in the town had no choice but to let the reservoir men build their reservoir. The town representative said, "Go ahead, build the dam. See what happens."

So the reservoir men came, and they started building. They built all day, and then they came back the next morning and found that everything they'd built had been taken down and had disappeared. Bricks, stones, concrete, banks of earth—everything was gone. Tires were punctured on digger machines, tools had vanished, and aside from the machinery it was as if no one had been there. So they started again. They built and built all day, and then they left someone there overnight to guard the site. Came back the following morning and the guard was hogtied and gagged, all the building work was undone, and the guard didn't have the faintest idea what had happened. So it went on for two more days. Everything they built was taken down. Machines went missing. Tools vanished. A man came from County Water & Power. He met with the town representative. The town representative sat patiently, and without a word he listened to everything the man from the County Water & Power had to say. When he was done the man from the county said, "So, what do you have to say to that?" and the town representative leaned forward and said, ever so quietly, "I think you should go fuck yourself."

Now they were mad. County Water & Power got an eviction order from the governor's office, and because the governor was in the pocket of the company, financially speaking, and because he was going to earn a handful or two from the whole deal, he signed the eviction order without one bat of an eyelid or a shake of his tail feathers.

County Water & Power came down to the town all excited. They had an official eviction order. If the townsfolk didn't move on out now . . . well, they could call in the sheriff's department. And they would do that if the need arose.

This time the town representative didn't even look at the paper. The man from the county handed it to him, and the town representative took it and tore it in half, and then half again, and then a few times more until it was confetti. He threw it up in the air and it came down like a shower, and then he turned to the county man and he said, "I told you last time, but you didn't seem to hear me. Go fuck yourself."

The county man called the sheriff's department. The sheriff was the town representative's brother-in-law. When the sheriff answered the call he asked if this was the man from County Water & Power. "Yes," the man said, "it is I." The sheriff said, "I believe you've been talking to my brother-in-law," and the county man said yes, he had. "I wasn't aware he was your brother-in-law, but yes I have been speaking to him and he still is unwilling to comply

with the eviction order." "Well, okay," the sheriff said. "I understand we have a standoff here . . . and it seems to me, sir, that had
you complied originally with the order given to you by my
brother-in-law, well, we wouldn't be in this situation right now."

The county man was puzzled. "What order was that?" he asked.
"What order did your brother-in-law give me?"

"If I seem to remember rightly," the sheriff said, "he told you to
go fuck yourself."

Now it was scaled up to a full-blown battle of wills.

The town versus County Water & Power. County came in. They
erected barricades and fences, and behind the barricades and
fences they went on building their dam. They went on building
as if everything were in order. There was no way around the
fences and barricades and the townsfolk couldn't stop the building, so they gathered up their provisions, and they sent out for
more, and they hunkered down for the duration, determined not
to move, determined never to give an inch to the County Water
& Power people. Which would have been fine. Which would have
worked out just fine if it had just stayed a war of territory and will.
Maybe they would have battled it out forever. Maybe County
would have opted for another valley. Maybe the townsfolk would
have run out of food and finally conceded defeat. But it didn't
work out that way. Now there was a valley with a dam at both
ends and a town on the western incline. It was not a deep valley,
and when the storms came it got awful full awful fast, and the
mud turned into swampland, and the foundations of the houses
became waterlogged and they started to slide. Folks came out
to buttress the foundations and they got swept into the water
and were drowned. County heard what was happening and they
didn't do a damned thing. There were no emergency calls, and
later they said that the storm must have taken down the telephone lines because no word of distress was heard from the
people. That may well have been true, but it was more likely that
the County people just flat-out lied. A town with a thousand dead
folks was a town they could now turn into a reservoir. And that's
what they got. Everyone drowned. Every damned one of them.

Come morning the bodies floated out there like fall leaves on a
lake. You could barely see the water for dead people. They called
it a national disaster. There was an officially recognized day of

mourning. The governor wore a black armband for a week and he said some things in church. He attended the memorial service, and then he went to the meeting with County Water & Power and they gave him a bucket load of money for being such a good guy, and the governor signed the order that granted permission to go on and build the reservoir.

And they did. You can now take a boat out across that reservoir. In the summer the water is clear. Crystal clear. You can look down and there are all the houses. They never moved one of them. Not a damned thing. The houses, the little church, the fences, the trees—everything is still there, just as it was before the storm. How long it will last—who knows? Who cares? It's there, and you can look down at the little doors and the little windows, and because the water is so damned clear it looks like there's no water at all. Like you wouldn't be surprised to see one of those little doors open fifty feet below you and for someone to come out and look up at you and wave.

That was the story of the town that drowned.

Elliott heard that story some years before. He'd listened intently, heard every word, and he'd never forgotten it. It told him that there wasn't no such thing dumber than people. It told him that people who fight a losing battle are the dumbest of all. It told him that you got to get yourself on the side with the most power and the most authority, and that's where you got to stay. No one gave a damn about the townsfolk. No one cared about the fact that these were their homes, this was where they carried on their lives, and intended to carry them on indefinitely. No, no one gave a damn about that. All they gave a damn about was money and power and control. Those were the important things, the things you had to get. Money and power and control. As much of it as possible.

He had money. What he did made him feel powerful, but he wasn't in control. That dumbass bitch in the store had shown him that. That was the missing element, he felt. He had himself a house. Morton Randall's property was now his. He also had Randall's pickup, and he had plenty of guns and ammunition, and he could pretty much stay there as long as he wanted. But still, despite all of this, he wasn't in control. His immediate circumstances, yes, perhaps. But his fate? His destiny? No, he was not in control of these, and this was what he needed to resolve. He could stay right there, go out hunting and fetch someone back every once in a while for his entertainment, but that could go on for only so long. Someone somewhere would get wise, and then they'd come a knocking, and he didn't reckon he had enough bullets to shoot the whole damned county sheriff's department.

The woman in the store would call the cops, he knew, and even as he turned back the way he'd come—intending to leave Van Horn and drive the ten or so miles to the house—he saw a sheriff's department car coming up behind him. The car passed. The driver didn't take one blind bit of notice of him. Soon he understood why. He passed the mercantile and the car was parked right outside, doors open, cops evidently inside, and he knew that the woman had already talked. What was it? Fifteen, twenty minutes? He was tempted to pull up, to go on inside that store and just shoot every motherfucking one of them, the woman, the cops, everyone. Whoever else would come down later and they wouldn't have a clue who'd done it.

But he didn't stop. He wasn't that dumb. He put his foot down and he cruised right on by, reached Randall's house in less than a quarter hour, and when he sat in the kitchen he realized his heart was beating rapidly. Why, he didn't know. Was it because the police were already at the mercantile? Was it because it had taken only twenty minutes for the woman to get the cops there? And if so, how many minutes had elapsed between his leaving and their arrival? By how many minutes had he evaded being seen? Was he scared that they would find him? Was he scared that someone would say they saw Morton Randall's pickup outside the store, and the police would come on over to check out the accuracy of that report?

Elliott got up and walked to the kitchen window. It looked out toward the highway. There was nothing out there. No one was driving toward the house. But if they came, they would come later. It was still too soon for them to think that Randall might know something.

And if someone—if the police—came to the house, what would he do? Hide? Would they come inside if no one answered the door? Would they just walk on in? Was it one of those little places where everyone knew everyone else by their first names, and the sheriff would just make himself at home, coming right on in here to see what had happened to Morton Randall? And he would come in here—the kitchen—and he would check in back and find Randall and the girl. And then all hell would break loose.

No, it couldn't work this way. Elliott needed more time. He had more things to do. He couldn't have the police coming in here and finding two dead bodies.

The bodies had to go. He had to get them out of the house.

Elliott left by the back door. Ten yards down to the left was the outhouse. There was more than enough room for Randall and the girl. Enough for ten or twelve of them.

He took the girl down first. Wrapped her in the sheet and hauled her up onto his shoulder. She didn't weigh a great deal, and soon he had her down in the corner of the outhouse behind a couple of feed sacks. Randall was a different prospect altogether. Randall was a big guy, bigger than Elliott, and it took every ounce of Elliott's strength and determination to even drag him as far as the back door. Elliott went back into the front of the house and took a rug from the sitting room. He laid it out on the steps that went down from the back door, and then he managed to maneuver Randall onto the rug. He grabbed the rug and hauled Randall across the ten yards to the outhouse, managed to sort of roll him over the threshold, and then got him in the corner beside the girl. He threw the rug over the pair of them. He stood there for a minute, and then he saw a pitchfork hanging on the wall. He took it down, smiled, and then thrust it like a spear into the carpet. It made him laugh. The feeling of the pitchfork stabbing into Randall. He had to use the sole of his foot against the rug as leverage to get the thing out. He ran his finger along the tine of the pitchfork but there was no blood. He hung it up again and closed the outhouse door behind him.

Back in the kitchen he felt better. The exertion, the fact that the bodies were out of the house, simply the feeling that he'd done something as opposed to nothing. There was a little blood, more than likely from the girl, on the floor at the back. He used a towel to clean it up, and then put the towel in the trash bucket beneath the sink. All done. No one would ever know that two dead folk had been sitting there, and unless the police went into the outhouse they wouldn't be found. That hadn't been so hard. He'd gotten overanxious for no reason. Maybe he was just hungry. Maybe he was a little tired. He would eat something, he would take a nap maybe, and then he would have a good think about where to find some more entertainment.

CHAPTER SIXTY

Culberson County sheriff was an Everhardt. The Everhardts had always been in law enforcement, all the way back to frontier days when Lyle Everhardt shot a man named Gilbert Hardy in June of 1877. He shot him in the face while Hardy was trying to rape a sixteen-year-old Methodist girl named Greta Jansen. The Jansen girl's father was town mayor. He ran the campaign start to finish in seventy-two hours and gave the sheriff's job to Lyle. Lyle took the job because he figured it would help him keep sober. It didn't. Regardless, from that day forward, one son out of every litter had wound up in the law, and Kelt Everhardt was the choice for his generation. His younger brothers—Clint and Radley—were farmers. Clint perpetually wore an anxious expression, as if always fearful of what might happen next. Farming was an un-predictable business, a business for fools as far as Kelt was con-cerned. "I would never be a farmer," he'd once told his brothers. "Have all your successes and failures governed by things that you can't even talk to. That and the weather. Spend your whole life smelling of shit. If I wanted to be that lonely it'd be out of choice." They agreed to disagree.

The law, however, was predictable.

So it was that on Friday morning, November 27, 1964, that Kelt Everhardt—representative of the law—was called down to Sue-Anne McCarthy's mercantile, and he heard what she had to tell him.

The officer who had responded to the emergency call from Sue-Anne, a young pup called Freeman Summers, was still there on the scene. He stood by the bullet hole in the wall as if it would take off if he didn't mind it some.

"Just came on in here, asked for his stuff. I put it right out there and asked for the money. First of all he said I should give it to him for free, and when I told him to pay up he bad mouthed me and then he slapped me."

"Close up the store," Everhardt told Summers. "Call the office, tell them to send two of anyone they can find. You are responsible for the crime scene, young man. Not a footprint, not a fingerprint, not a hair, not a breath is to make a mark on this scene. I'm calling in the federal people. I have an idea that this young man is the one the federal people have been looking for, and they're the only ones who have the wherewithal to examine something like this and find prints and whatnot to confirm it."

Summers took the order without complaint. He merely nodded, touched the peak of his cap.

Everhardt drove back to the office. En route he called his dispatcher and told her to find him a nearby federal office.

"Federal what?" she asked. Her name was Doreen. She had worked dispatch for nine years. She was known for her business-like manner, the edge of truculence and irritation she forever seemed to possess, and she was as insubordinate with the sheriff as she was with her long-suffering husband.

"The Federal Reserve Bank of America," Everhardt said dryly. "I want to know if they will print me enough money to pay for your funeral, Doreen."

"You're a very funny man, Sheriff," she replied sarcastically.

"Yes, Doreen, I am. From a family of circus people, you see."

"And what would you want to be telling these federal people?"

"I'll be telling them just exactly what I want to tell them when you find me a number and a person to tell it to. I'll be at the office in ten minutes, maybe less." He hung up the car radio before she had a chance to respond.

Doreen had found someone called Agent Grant Grierson at the office in Las Cruces.

"And how does this relate to us?" was Grierson's question once Everhardt had explained the matter at hand.

"The memo that came from your people," Everhardt said. "Came only a few days ago, if I remember rightly. Which I usually do. It was quite specific in its tone. Anything beyond ordinary or routine in the way of homicides or attempted homicides and suchlike was to be reported to the nearest federal office. I considered, in my professional opinion, that a young man challenging a woman in a mercantile and near as damn it getting his head blown off for his trouble is somewhat out of the ordinary for a town that's not seen any drama since Harriet Yarnham stabbed her husband with a breadknife nearly seven years ago this Christmas."

"Yes, of course, Sheriff," Grierson said, aware then that his own lack of attention had shown him up. "I'll have to contact the agents responsible for overseeing that case."

"Well, you go on and do that, son, and we'll wait here till you come back to us. The lady in question ain't goin' no place, and if she ain't then we ain't neither."

Koenig and Nixon were still in Las Cruces themselves, and had they delayed their departure from the office by a mere half an hour, they would have been there when Everhardt's call came in. As it was they were taking an early lunch at a diner in the suburbs, and it was another quarter hour before Grierson managed to find them. Once briefed, they called Everhardt themselves, took what little information he could give them, and decided immediately that Van Horn was their next destination. From the description that Everhardt had passed on from this woman in the store down there, well, this sounded an awful lot like Clay Luckman. They drove the hundred and fifty miles considerably beyond the speed limit, and arrived a handful of minutes before two, no more than twenty minutes before John Cassidy pulled up in front of his own house in Tucson. Cassidy was eager to tell Alice of the news, that the picture he held in his hand was not only the potential daughter of the murder victim from Marana, but that this girl had more than likely been with Clarence Luckman in Deming only days before. And if not Clarence Luckman, then maybe she had accompanied Elliott Danziger, the boy supposedly murdered by Earl Sheridan.

Nixon and Koenig, however, were somewhat more sober and reserved as they entered the mercantile in Van Horn.

The woman was remarkably level-headed about the whole incident.

"Sue-Anne McCarthy," she told them.

"M, small c, C-A-R-T-H-Y?" Nixon asked.

Sue-Anne nodded in the affirmative.

The four of them stood in a square—Everhardt, Nixon, Koenig, and Sue-Anne. She told them precisely what had happened. She told them what the young man had touched, where he had stood, and when Nixon showed her the grainy monochrome of Clarence Luckman she said, "Yes, a coupla years older than that, but the eyes are the same. I really think it was him."

Koenig looked at Everhardt. "No other reports? No witness statements? Nothing out of the ordinary?"

Everhardt shook his head. "Nothing. My officer was here by ten, and the place has been closed up since."

"I want to commend you on maintaining the integrity of the scene," Koenig said. "Most often people walk all over it like it's . . . well, I don't know what they're thinking, to be honest."

"Sue-Anne missed getting herself killed by a whisker, right?" Everhardt asked. "Otherwise that memo wouldn't have found its way out here, and I wouldn't have had any business calling you."

"That's right," Nixon replied.

"How many?"

"That we know of . . . somewhere in the region of seven, maybe more."

"Seven?" Sue-Anne asked. "That young man has killed seven people?"

"Yes, ma'am," Nixon replied.

"He's been busy, then, your boy," Everhardt said.

"Has indeed."

"Seems it'd be a good idea to get me as many of them pictures as you can and I'll put 'em out all over the place," Everhardt said. "Times like this it seems best to unofficially deputize everyone."

"Perhaps," Koenig said. "He's close, evidently. I wish we'd been here sooner, but that's no one's fault. He has about four or five hours on us now, so he could be anywhere within—what?—a two-, three-hundred-mile radius."

"Or he could be right down the street a couple of blocks having a soda in the drugstore," Everhardt said.

"He could. The only downside of putting his picture everywhere is that he might see it before someone sees him. Then he'll vanish like a ghost."

"I see your point," Everhardt said. He tipped his hat back again and put his hands on his hips. "So what do we do now?"

"We'll have someone come and take pictures, prints, whatever physical evidence they need."

"You gonna tell me his name?"

"Luckman. Clarence Luckman."

"Luckman. There's an irony there if ever I heard one. Seems to me it's about time his luck ended."

"I'd say you were right on the nail there, Sheriff Everhardt, and as soon as we get sight of him he's going to be looking back at the world through a hole in his head."

CHAPTER SIXTY-ONE

The entirety of John Cassidy's journey home had been spent considering the import of what he'd learned. The picture of the girl burned a hole in his pocket; the image of her face burned a hole in his mind.

"As I said," Alice commented matter-of-factly, "two people. Seems to me that your bank robber told the police in Wellton whatever he wanted them to hear. He said the other boy was dead and I think that perhaps he wasn't."

"Answers my question about how someone could change so dramatically overnight. A kid that's never been in trouble suddenly becomes a homicidal maniac. Well, I see now that he didn't. I think this other one—this Elliott Danziger, the one that Sheridan said they'd killed—I think he's our boy. He had a history of violence at this Hesperia place. I think he's the one that's doing these killings. Explains why his body has never been found."

"And his half brother, this Clarence Luckman, is on the run?"

"I believe he is. He must have been there at Marana, and he wound up with the gun. He then put the gun under that car. For what reason, I do not know . . ."

"And he's got the girl with him."

"I would say so."

Alice nodded. She sat down and held the picture of Bailey in her hands. "And you're guessing that this girl is the daughter of the man who was killed along with the convenience store owner?"

"I am. She sure as hell looks like him, and if she is it would make more sense than anything else."

"His name?"

Cassidy hesitated. He was never supposed to name names. "Frank Jacobs," he said.

"So this is Bailey Jacobs."

"Seems that way."

"She must have been there and seen her father killed."

"Looks that way."

"Kind of thing is that going to do to a youngster like that?"

"Whatever it does, it isn't going to be good."

"So the question now is why are they running, and where are they running to? And why on earth did they put that gun beneath that crashed car outside of Deming?"

Cassidy shrugged. "Same question I've been asking myself all the way home."

Alice was quiet for a time. She couldn't take her eyes off of Bailey Jacobs's face. "And the federal people think that Clarence Luckman is their killer, and they're circulating his name and his picture, and if they see him they're going to shoot him down like a dog in the street."

"Yes, they most definitely are. They are not going to wait around to talk things over. They want this thing to end, and they're not going to want the cost of a trans-state investigation and a lengthy trial."

"So you have to make sure they don't, John. You got to go find those two fellers that came here and tell them what you know. You have to tell them about the girl, and that this other one—this Danziger boy—is more than likely still alive and he's the one they should be looking for . . ."

"I know, Alice, I know."

"So what are you waiting for?"

"Was hoping we'd have some lunch or something."

She shook her head. "You don't have time for lunch. Wherever it is you're heading you can get a sandwich on the way."

"You could always make one for me while I call up the federal office in El Paso and see if they're still there."

Alice got up. "That I can do," she said. She hesitated at the door and turned back toward her husband. "You have to fix this, John," she said.

He opened his mouth to reply, and she raised her hand to silence him.

"This is one of those things that you don't even think about. You don't even question it. From the way it looks, there's a couple of teenagers out there on their own, and right now the world takes one of them for a killer when he isn't. The other one saw her dad murdered in cold blood, and maybe she can identify who did it. The federal people are going to want it out of the papers and off the radio. I'm not saying they're going to rush in blind, but right now they don't know what you know, and they need to know it fast." She looked at the picture of the girl on the table. "You find that girl and you bring her here if she's got no place else to go. No one deserves a start like that in life . . . no one."

Alice left the room. Cassidy watched her go and then he made his way across the room to the hallway. He picked up the receiver and dialed the operator.

"Federal Bureau of Investigation in El Paso," he said quietly, and then, "Yes, I'll hold."

CHAPTER SIXTY-TWO

Clay and Bailey had eaten, and then they'd walked for a good two hours, and by two o'clock they'd covered another six or seven miles, and they were maybe ten miles from the outskirts of Van Horn and no one had stopped to give them a ride. Three cars had passed them, one of them a station wagon jammed with kids, all of them peering through the windows—wide eyed and vacant of expression, as if a sense of disbelief accompanied seeing anyone in such a place. The I-10 was flat and featureless and gave onto a distance that the eye couldn't determine and the mind couldn't fathom. It seemed like this was a road that would go on forever, and then some. Walking it was like being in a rocking chair. You're moving plenty, but you ain't going nowhere. It was perhaps the loneliest road in the whole wide world.

She said that at one point. Bailey. They hadn't spoken for a good while and she just said, "I think this must be one of the loneliest places ever, ever."

"Lonely is a state of mind, not a place," Clay replied.

"That's very deep."

"What do you mean? That's very deep? Or that's very deep for me?"

She smiled. "I don't mean nothin' but what I said."

"Well, I'm sure there's some folks up in New York City or someplace where there's millions of people every which way you look, and they feel that they're in the loneliest place ever. That would be worse, I reckon. Have a hundred thousand neighbors and not know one of them."

"That would be sad."

"Reckon you'd have to work hard at being that lonely. Seems to me everyone can find someone to love them, no matter who they are. Hell, even that Hitler guy in the war got a girlfriend."

She laughed. "You're crazy."

"And you're real smart yourself," Clay replied sarcastically.

"You're saying I'm dumb?"

"I'm sayin' you wouldn't recognize a smart thing if it ran you down in the street."

She swung her hand sideways and thumped his arm.

He pushed her back.

Bailey made a serious face and came at him with fists.

Clay ran, pulling faces as he went.

No matter how many names she called after him, none were his.

She caught up with him eventually, the pair of them still laughing.

"I reckon you now have to be the one person in the world I know best," he told her.

"You don't know me at all," she replied.

"I knows you is dumb," he said in a fool voice.

"Enough already," she said, and then her expression was serious. "There is something we need to talk about, Clay." She paused. She came to a stop. He was no more than six feet from her and the expression she wore was grave.

"It's something I've been meaning to say for a while. It's just that . . . well, it hasn't felt the right time or whatever, and I can't put up with it anymore."

Clay frowned.

"It's just . . . er, well, you know how we're . . . well, how we've kinda gotten close an' everything?"

Clay nodded. He felt the color rising in his cheeks.

"Well, the thing is this. I think that maybe . . . I mean, I don't know an' all, but maybe, maybe . . . if we . . . if we stay friends an' everything, and I mean like proper friends and whatever. Well, you know what I'm saying, right?"

Clay wanted to tell her what she was thinking, but he didn't dare.

"You know what I'm going to say, don't you, Clay?" she asked.

He nodded.

"Well, if we were like *together*, you know? If we became like a couple and everything . . . if we were in love and we decided to get married or something—"

Clay's heart was running overtime. He felt short of breath. He wanted to grab her and kiss her, but he couldn't move an inch.

"Well, I have to tell you now, Clay, and I want you to know that I really mean this . . . I really do. It's taken a lot of time to work this out and to come to this decision, but if we were in love and we got married and everything . . ."

Bailey took a minute step backward. She inhaled deeply, as if finding the courage to say what she needed to say.

"You see the thing is, Clay . . . well, it just wouldn't be possible for me to have children with someone as pig-ugly as you . . ."

She held her deadpan expression for no more than a heartbeat, and then her face broke with a smile as wide as the Mississippi, and then she was laughing as whatever was going on in Clay's heart reconciled itself with his ears and eyes, and he realized he'd been had.

"Useless . . . goddammit . . . oh my God, I don't believe you said that . . ." he was saying, but none of it came to anything because she was off down the highway and out of earshot before he realized how far he'd fallen into her trap. Hook, line, and sinker. For a minute or two he just sat down on the road and took some deep breaths. He'd never felt anything like it in the world, and it was at that moment—that moment more than any other before, more than any that would come in the future—that he knew, he *knew* beyond all question, that he loved Bailey Redman with everything he possessed.

She slowed and stopped at some point and waited for him to catch up.

"You're a son of . . . a daughter of a bitch, that's what you are, Bailey Redman, a goddamned daughter of a bitch. I don't believe you said that to me."

"Too late, I said it," she replied. "You should have seen your face."

"You wanna see your face when I stomp all over it? Damn you . . . that was a mean trick to play on me . . ."

She stepped close. She reached up and touched the side of his face. She looked him right in the eye and she smiled like a California sunset, and then she leaned forward and brushed her lips against his.

His arms hung limply at his sides. He wished he could hold her close just for a second, just so she'd know how much she meant to him. But there was something, something right there inside him that rendered him unable to respond.

"You're always going to be the one for me," she said, and for a second she held his gaze, and then she turned and started walking, and Clay hesitated before following on behind her, and then next thing she said—something about how she was getting hungry again—was said in such a way as the moment that had happened might never have happened at all. But it had, and he knew it, and he knew that she knew it, and it was perhaps the most important thing that had ever happened to him in his life. No, he thought then, it *was* the most important thing that had ever happened. No question about it.

They needed a ride. They needed some Samaritan driver to come barreling along the highway and give them a ride to the next town. Van Horn, that's what it was called. They needed a ride to Van Horn so they could get something to eat and something to drink and just take a moment to figure out if they were now going to just keep on walking to Eldorado. All of two hundred and fifty miles. Clay thought about it. Two hundred and fifty miles. Seemed like a hell of way, but it wasn't. They could do it in—what?—two or three weeks. Ten, fifteen, twenty miles a day. How fast were they walking? Hell, yes, they could do it, and with Bailey Redman beside him he reckoned it would be a breeze. The way he felt in that moment, damn it if just about everything didn't seem like the easiest thing in the whole wide world. Maybe he'd been wrong. Maybe one dark star had the power to cancel out another. Maybe it really was going to be good from this point. Maybe this really was the point at which everything just got better and better.

CHAPTER SIXTY-THREE

The federal people came and they did whatever they had to do in Sue-Anne McCarthy's store. They were in the place for a good two hours, and Everhardt had Summers stand on guard outside the mercantile to keep away the sensation-seekers and the press. Word was out already. Reporters were likes flies on shit. However many you shooed away there were always more who got the whiff of it. They were small-time, and it didn't take much more than a few stern words from Officer Freeman Summers, and they slunk away with their noses out of joint. But newspapers being what they were, the platens were being inked up regardless of the lack of substantiated facts. There was a killer on the loose in Texas. He was a homicidal maniac. He'd killed a family outside of El Paso, and now there was rumor of some other attempted atrocity in some wide part in the road called Van Horn. There had been a confirmed eyewitness identification of this boy, and he was close. By the time they got wind of Margot Eckhart, still breathing through a tube in Saint Savior's Hospital, there was a flurry of activity going on that would soon wind up in a hurricane.

Everhardt knew this, and he knew that he'd get some of the fallout, some of the aftershock. A town like Van Horn was not equipped to deal with a case such as this, and he was more than happy when the federal people left. He'd been given a stack of photographs of this Clarence Luckman, some of which he was going to give to his officers, others he would deliver in person to the storeowners, the manager of the bank, the people at the train station, the Greyhound ticket office. People who needed to keep a weather eye open for this character. Had Everhardt realized the nature of the thunderstorm that was on its way . . . well, had he known, there wouldn't have been a great deal he could have done about it. Forewarned was not necessarily forearmed, certainly when it came to the likes of Elliott Danziger.

As Clay Luckman and Bailey Redman prayed for a ride to take them into Van Horn, as John Cassidy urged his car forward to Las Cruces, where he hoped he would find Ronald Koenig and Garth Nixon, Elliott Danziger rose from his nap, stretched, yawned, felt the tension of muscles in his neck and back, and wondered what time it was. It was actually a handful of minutes after five. The evening was coming in. The air had cooled. He was hungry, he was thirsty, and his mouth tasted like buzzard had crapped there while he slept. He also had a raging erection.

In the kitchen he moped around for a while. He was irritated by the lack of proper food in the place. He called Morton Randall a "cheap no-good son of a bitch skinflint." He wanted ham and eggs and scrapple and ketchup and some slabs of homemade bread. He wanted coffee with cream and five sugars and maybe some soda as well. He figured he would clean up some, and then go on into town. There would be someplace he could eat. He could also see if there were any more police hanging around the mercantile, or if they'd all gotten confused and overwhelmed and given up already. Evidently no one had seen Morton Randall's pickup, and the woman in the store had no more known his name than he hers, so it looked like he was in the clear. Still, he would have to find some way to get back there and kill her just for being a bitch. I mean, this wasn't some big city. Wasn't even a big town. Some podunk, East Jesus nothing of a place where people stayed because they didn't have the good sense to leave. Wouldn't catch him dead in a place like this, Digger thought as he made his way back up to the bathroom. He figured on a bath. There was a bad smell around the place. Could have been the memory of Morton and Candace moldering some in the kitchen, but just in case it was his own stink he reckoned he should wash up some. Didn't want to be drawing attention to himself, after all. Hadn't Earl said that very same thing on the drive from Marana to Wellton? *People like us ain't given shit, so we gotta take it. You have to keep your own self-respect. That's the important thing. You can't let yourself slide. You gotta stay sharp, on the money, right? Only time you're in trouble is when you can no longer smell your own stink.* Sure he did, and even as Digger remembered it he could hear Earl's voice, the pride and self-respect in it, the sense of self-worth and value that the man possessed. He really was a star. But he was dead. Fucking tragedy. Fucking shame. A man like that, a man of that caliber, shot down dead in the street like a dog. And all the while that faggot son of a bitch Clarence Luckman was walking around the streets some-place with a shit-eating grin on his face. *Oh me, oh my*, Digger thought, *what I wouldn't give to cross paths with that motherfucker just one more time.*

Half an hour later Digger lay in the bath thinking about the girl from the bank, and then the other one, the one who'd tried to call the cops. Then he thought about Candace. And then he thought about tonight. Tonight was Friday night. Friday night was party night. Tonight he wanted something real special to take his mind off the fact that he missed Earl Sheridan and that he was really beginning to hate his no-good, piece-of-shit brother, Clarence Luckman.

He remembered back a while—Hesperia, maybe before that. They'd been working someplace and had come across a hornet's nest. The others wanted to steer clear, to get far away from the thing. Not Digger. He took a half pint of gasoline and soaked the nest but good. Then he set the son of a bitch afire. Those motherfuckers came out mad and hot, most of them losing their wings as they escaped. As he watched it he laughed like a drunk hyena. He remembered that feeling. The feeling that there was nothing they could do but die. He knew that Clay could never understand a feeling like that. He was just too dog-dumb. Digger smiled. He got out of the bath and dried himself down. Maybe somewhere Morton Randall had some cologne or something. Maybe a clean shirt and a pair of pants that would fit him. He wanted to go out looking the part. Make an effort. You had to make an effort, otherwise where was your self-respect?

He needed to go out and find someone. He needed to go out and find some girl and he needed to fuck her until her heart burst.

That's what he needed to do. And then when he had done that he needed to chop her into little pieces and throw her all over the house, and then burn everything down to the fucking ground and leave it all behind in a smoking pile of blood-soaked ashes.

That would make him feel better.

That would help him get over the idea that he needed to have friends.

CHAPTER SIXTY-FOUR

A couple of minutes after seven a dark gray pickup slowed at the edge of the I-10 and waited while the two kids ran to catch it up.

Leaning for the handle to open the door on the passenger side, the driver—a man by the name of Dennis Hagen—smiled when he saw Bailey Redman. A cute kid, and what the hell she and her friend were doing out here at such a time was beyond him.

"Where y'all headed?" he asked.

"Van Horn, or farther . . . wherever you're going," Bailey said.

"Van Horn is where I'm going. It's only a handful of miles, but I can take you there if that's your fancy."

"That'd be great," Bailey said, and she tugged open the door and came on up to sit beside him. Clay followed her, saying, "Thanks, mister. Really grateful that you stopped."

"No problem to me," Hagen said, and yet before he pulled away he hesitated, looked at the pair of them for a second longer and said, "Well, I guess it ain't a problem . . . but that depends on what problem you kids are carrying with you that puts you out here on your own."

Bailey smiled her sweetest smile. "No problem," she said. "My mom is up in Odessa waiting for us."

Hagen nodded. "She is, is she?"

"Yes, sir, she is."

"And what would any halfway decent mother be doing letting her kids out on the highway at nighttime more than a hundred and fifty miles from home?"

"It's a long story," Bailey replied.

"And I bet it's got a beginning, a middle, and an end that are all as fanciful as one another. Anyways, whatever your business, I can't see you out here on the highway at night. I'll take you into Van Horn and you can do your explaining to Sheriff Ever-hardt."

As if to make the point Dennis Hagen leaned across both of them and locked the passenger door, and then he kicked the pickup into life and sped off.

Clay looked at Bailey, his eyes wide. Bailey gave an almost imperceptible shake of her head. *Don't say a word*, that gesture said. *I got it all under control*. Somehow Clay doubted that, but he didn't know what else to do in that moment.

They headed into Van Horn, no more than ten miles, and were there in a quarter of an hour. Dennis Hagen pulled up in front of the sheriff's office, the lights ablaze, the appearance of greater activity than was usual, it seemed. Hagen got out on the driver's side, and it was then—as he was walking around to unlock the passenger side and deliver his passengers to the police—that Bailey scooted along the seat, dragging Clay with her, and out they went through the driver's side door.

"Run!" she said, even as Hagen realized what was happening and started around the front of the vehicle again.

"Son of a bitch!" he exclaimed, and watched as the pair of them hightailed it away and down the street faster than he could ever have hoped to catch them.

He stood there for a moment feeling dumber than a donkey, and then he shook his head. "Hell in a handbasket," he muttered, and then wondered what business it was of his anyway. He'd gotten them off the highway, brought them into town. At least they'd be safer here than out there. And he sure as hell wasn't going to go report it. Didn't want to tell Kelt Everhardt he'd been outsmarted by a couple of wiseass kids.

CHAPTER SIXTY-FIVE

"It's that question," Cassidy repeated. "It all comes down to that question, Agent Koenig. How could Clarence Luckman put the gun beneath the car outside of Deming, and yet be in a diner with the Eckharts . . . both at the same time? That's what bothered me more than anything, so I went on up to Scottsdale, and that's where I found her." Cassidy indicated the photograph of Bailey Jacobs that Koenig held in his hand. "The likeness between her and the homicide victim from Marana is undeniable, and when I took it out to Clark Regan, the owner of the gas station, he had no doubt that this was the girl who reported the overturned car to him."

Koenig was nodding. He glanced up at Nixon. The three of them were seated in a small office in back of the Las Cruces Sheriff's Department building. This was where Cassidy had found them—the first place he'd looked.

"I said to Agent Nixon here back in El Paso yesterday that you were a smart man, Detective Cassidy, and I have to say I am impressed by your progress in twenty-four hours. Your sheriff know you're out here with us again?"

Cassidy shook his head. "I'm off sick."

"You don't look so sick to me."

Cassidy didn't reply.

"So what do you want to do?" Koenig asked.

"I think we should put Elliott Danziger's face everywhere we can. I think he's still alive. I think he's the one that's doing these killings, not Clarence Luckman. I think Clarence Luckman was with Sheridan and Danziger at Marana, as was Frank Jacobs with his daughter. I think Luckman and the girl got away, and they've been running ever since. I think Danziger is on his own one-man killing spree, and we've been looking for the wrong boy ever since this started."

"And if you're wrong? If Sheridan and Luckman did kill Danziger, just like Sheridan said? If it is Clarence Luckman out there doing these things, and whoever the hell turned up at the gas station to report that car is unrelated to this in every way? Then what?"

"Well, we keep looking for Luckman as well. The only thing now is that we're looking for three people, not one. We're looking for Elliott Danziger—"

"Who is dead," Nixon interjected.

"Who *may* be dead, we don't know for sure," Cassidy said. "The only word we have on that is from Earl Sheridan. He's been shot, he knows he's not going to make it, he thinks that the last thing anyone's going to expect is that he'll lie about something like this. But it means he can go on causing trouble after he's gone. I believe he was *that* crazy. I believe that throwing the police off the scent completely was a wonderful idea for him. I think it made him as happy as he could be even as he died. Like he's still able to screw everyone up even when he's no longer around."

Koenig looked down at the picture of the girl once more. He stared at it like it could have been the winning hand with a thousand-dollar pot. He looked at Cassidy, he looked at Nixon, he looked back at the girl.

"I think you're wrong, for what it's worth," he said quietly. "The fact of the matter is that the entirety of the FBI, most of the county sheriffs' departments in southern California and Arizona, even a few in Texas, have a clear description of Clarence Luckman, and a clear understanding of what needs to happen when he is sighted."

"They will kill him," Cassidy said.

"They sure will."

"That cannot be allowed to happen—"

Koenig raised his hand. "It may already have happened, Detective Cassidy, and we have yet to receive the report. There are hundreds of men looking for this boy, and we are not in a position to suddenly switch tack and alert them all at once of some potential identification error."

There was silence between them for a moment.

"However," Koenig went on. "I also think that one of the worst human characteristics is lack of humility. Your theory . . . well, you may be right, and I have to commend you for your forthright attitude and your determination. I really am *very* impressed. What we can do now, at this time in the evening, I do not know. I also know that an officially sanctioned collaboration between the Tucson Sheriff's Department and the Bureau is not on the cards, and more than likely won't ever be. However, I do understand what we're dealing here . . . potentially. We will obtain photographs of Elliott Danziger and circulate them to all offices in this and surrounding states. We will get a wire out, we will get people informed. We will get reproductions of this picture of the girl made up and get them circulated too. That's what we will do. And as for you? Well, tonight you can either stay here in Las Cruces, or—if you can face it—I would turn around and go home. I would go into work tomorrow morning and get on with your other cases."

Suddenly Koenig's demeanor seemed to cool, almost as if Cassidy's interference and insistence had exhausted his patience. "I will keep you informed," he added, "and I will ensure that any and all credit that may be due to you at the point this case resolves is afforded in writing to your department, and to the relevant officials at the Bureau." He paused, and then he nodded his head as if resolving something for himself. "And if this turns out to be the case . . . that Elliott Danziger *was* alive all along, and that he has been responsible for this killing spree, then I'm sure a commendation of the very highest order will find its way into your personnel file. However, we still have a very definite view that this is the work of Clarence Luckman, and if he is seen . . . I have to tell you that if he is seen and he attempts to escape, well, he *will* be shot."

Cassidy didn't speak for a good while. He didn't know what to say. The idea of driving back to Tucson . . . well, he just didn't want to leave until it was finished. He remembered Alice's words, once again her voice playing inside his head like a recording.

You have to fix this, John. This is one of those things that you don't even think about. You don't even question it.

"Have there been any more?" Cassidy eventually asked.

Koenig was slow to respond, but in his eyes he betrayed the answer before he even opened his mouth.

"We believe so," he said. "In a town called Van Horn about a hundred and fifty miles southwest of here."

"Still on the I-10?"

"Yes," Koenig replied. "Still on the I-10."

"What happened?"

"Woman in a mercantile was challenged by a young man. From what little information we have obtained, it could well be Luckman. It was only a physical assault, but the direction he was headed, the description . . ."

Cassidy leaned forward. He rested his elbows on his knees and looked down at the floor between his feet. "Okay," he said. "I'm staying here tonight. I'll deal with my own sheriff and my own job. You don't need to concern yourself with that." He looked up at Koenig. "I need to be here to see it through."

Koenig opened his mouth to speak.

Cassidy raised his hand. "You have to give me that much rope," he said, "and if I end up hanging myself with it, then so be it."

Koenig didn't reply.

Cassidy got up. "I'll find a hotel nearby."

"There's one across the street and down a block," Nixon interjected. "Stay there. That's where we are. Then if we need you we can find you."

"Okay . . . and I'll come see you in the morning." Cassidy paused halfway to the door, and then he turned back and looked at the picture of Bailey Jacobs in Koenig's hand. "For her sake, if no one else's . . . I have to see this through to the end."

CHAPTER SIXTY-SIX

They hid in the shadows between streetlights, and then they were running, crouched low to the ground, laughing as quietly as they could as they skirted the back of the sheriff's building and came out on some other street. Clay caught a glimpse of someone emerging from a doorway, and they hunkered down behind a wall until the person had passed. Like the drive-in movie theater, Clay felt excited, a little scared, very much alive.

They found a diner on Crown Street near the center of Van Horn. The guy in there was just closing up, but he said he'd make them some grilled cheese sandwiches and they could have a root beer or a Coke or something.

Bailey did her flashing eyes and coy smile thing, and she got the guy talking, and he made them two grilled cheese sandwiches each and he was as friendly as could be. Clay ate one and a half, Bailey finished her own and then finished his, and she drank two glasses of root beer and then she had some ice cream, which the guy brought from out back.

"My sister makes it," he told Bailey. "She has a hand crank and she makes it herself. People around here love it."

Bailey loved it too, and by the time she was done even the guy was surprised at how much a little girl could eat.

"So what are you doing out this evening?" he asked her.

Bailey smiled. "We're on a date," she said.

"A date, is it?" the guy said. "Well, I'll be . . . you've come to my place on a date."

"Our first date," she added.

"Well, that," he said, "is a cause for celebration, and as it's your first date then dinner is on the house."

Bailey smiled, but she shook her head. "No, we couldn't do that. We have money to pay—"

"Won't hear a word of it. You go on now, enjoy yourselves, and come back some other time, okay?"

"Hey, thanks, mister," she said. "That's really kind of you."

He waved them out of the diner and closed up. He watched the pair of them head off down Crown Street and he wondered what it would be like to be young and in love and have the whole world out there before you.

Bailey wasn't thinking about the whole world at all. She was thinking about how much money they had and whether or not they could afford to sleep in a motel again.

"Sure we could," Clay said. "I mean, what the hell, we're damned well nearly in Eldorado. We can make it."

They walked to the end of Crown Street, turned left, headed away from the diner and the sheriff's building, and it was toward the end of the third or fourth block that Clay saw a motel on the other side that looked like the kind of place they were after. A main office, a semicircular arrangement of small cabins out behind it, a neon sign that announced *Comfortable Beds Hot Water Reasonable Rates*.

"I'll go over alone," Clay said. "I can get away with being old enough. You wait here, and once I've got the cabin I'll come back out and get you."

"Hurry," Bailey said. "It's getting cold."

Clay jogged cross the street and entered the main office. For a moment she saw him standing there behind the desk, and then he moved left and disappeared.

Bailey rubbed her hands together and stamped her feet. She could see her own breath.

It was dark now, and there was a bitter breeze down the street that made her shudder.

She saw Clay leave the office and head along the cabins with the attendant.

Wouldn't be long and she'd be inside—warm, comfortable, able to sleep on a real bed with real blankets. There'd be a TV. They could watch TV again like they had last time, sat up there on the bed amidst pillows and blankets. Alfred Hitchcock and whatever.

She heard a door close somewhere, and she shifted back a little as a pickup came down the street and the headlights illuminated her against the wall where she was standing.

She dug her hands in her pockets and put her head down.

The pickup slowed ever so gradually, and came to rest not six feet from where she stood. She looked up, and through the open passenger window she saw the driver looking at her. He was young, and he was smiling.

"Everything okay here?" he asked.

She nodded. "Sure, mister . . . just waiting for someone."

It was then that the gun appeared.

"Waiting for me," he said slowly. "Now get in the fucking car before I blow your head clean off your fucking shoulders."

CHAPTER SIXTY-SEVEN

"Las Cruces," Cassidy said. "I'm going to stay overnight. I'll call you early tomorrow and let you know what I've decided."

"How were they . . . the federal people?"

"I reckon they've got me for a crazy one. But they listened to what I had to say, and they're going to get some pictures made up, at least. I mean . . . well, the truth is that we don't know. We really don't know if it is Clarence Luckman doing these things, or if the Danziger boy is still alive—"

"It's a terrible thing, John," Alice said. "He *is* a boy, isn't he? I mean, he's not even out of his teens, and he's somehow capable of doing these hideous and dreadful things."

"If he's the one who's doing them."

"He is, I feel sure of it. The more I think about it the more it makes sense."

Cassidy smiled. "Sometimes I wonder whether you're the one who shouldn't have been the detective."

"As if there'll ever come a day when they'll let women do this kind of thing," Alice replied.

"They should get started on it now . . . female intuition, you know? Could save us a fortune in lengthy investigations."

"So did you have dinner?"

"I did, yes."

"What did you have?"

"I had a sandwich—"

"Go get some proper dinner, John. You can't live on candy bars and Coca-Cola. Go somewhere and get a steak or something."

"Alice, really—"

"John."

"Okay, okay, okay. I'll go get a steak."

"And try and sleep. I know you don't sleep well when you're

away, but try your best. Have a glass of whiskey or something. That always does the trick for me."

"You get some rest yourself, Alice."

"I'm all right, John. I'm not the one running around Texas like a maniac."

"Okay, sweetheart. Miss you. I'll call you tomorrow."

"And I'll call Mike and tell him you're doing better but I still don't want you out of the house."

"Appreciated. Love you."

"Love you back."

She hung up and Cassidy listened to the dial tone for a moment before replacing the receiver in its cradle.

He glanced at his watch. Twenty to nine. Dinner. He had to get some dinner. He'd said he would, so that's what he would do.

CHAPTER SIXTY-EIGHT

Clay hesitated at the side of the road.

Bailey was talking to someone. Someone in a pickup truck.

Hell, he thought, this is the last damned thing we need. Interference from some do-gooder.

Clay backed up and walked across the street and around the back of the truck. The guy in the truck was saying something.

"Bailey?" Clay said quietly.

Bailey didn't look back at him.

"Bailey?" he repeated, a little louder.

It was then that he saw her hand. Down by her side, just her one hand, and she was making a motion with it. *Get back*, that motion said. *Get away from here.*

There was silence then. The rustle of the wind through the leaves on the ground. The purr of the engine. Aside from that nothing.

Clay shivered. He stood still for a moment, and then he took another step forward.

He caught sight of something moving in the corner of his eye.

The driver had seen him.

He felt something then, something dark and terrible, and he waited, barely able to breathe, as the driver moved along the seat and opened the passenger-side door.

As he stepped down, that sense of dark terror gripped Clay Luckman with such ferocity he could not think. He could not think even as the driver stepped down and stood in the road ahead of him, as he leveled the gun at Clay's chest, as he started to smile in recognition. Whatever sense of relief he may have felt in learning that his brother was alive was overwhelmed by his utter disbelief and horror in seeing what he had become.

"Well, fuck me sideways with a baseball bat," Digger said. "If it isn't my own fucking useless son of a bitch dumbass cocksucker of a brother Clarence motherfucking Luckman. Jesus Christ Almighty, what a coincidence we have here."

"Digger—" Clay started.

Bailey looked at Clay, back to the driver. It was there in her eyes. *Digger? Your brother?*

"Shut your fucking mouth, Clay," Digger said. "You cocksucking son of a bitch motherfucker piece-of-shit coward fucker asshole . . . Jesus, I should shoot you right in the head and leave you dead in the fucking street, you cunt! You left me to die back there. You left me and Earl to die back there at the store. You fucker. You asshole. You utter piece of shit . . ."

"Digger, seriously . . . I didn't mean—"

Digger stepped forward. He grabbed Bailey's hair and pushed the gun into the side of her neck. "So this is how you've been entertainin' yourself, is it?" he said. He wrenched the fistful of hair and Bailey screamed. "This is the company you've been keepin', eh? Not good enough for you, were we? Me an' Earl not good enough for the likes of Clarence motherfuckin' Luckman, is that it?"

"Digger, you got to let her go. She's done nothing. You want someone, you take me. I'll go with you. I'll go with you, Digger . . . just leave her alone—"

"Shut your fucking mouth!" Digger shouted. He tugged Bailey's hair again, and she screamed, louder this time, and he hit her in the side of the head with the gun. For a moment she lost her balance, her knees giving way beneath her, and Digger wrenched her to her feet once more.

He walked forward, gun out ahead of him. "I'm taking her," he said, his voice barely more than whisper. "I'm gonna shoot you in the head right now, and then I'm gonna take her and tie her up and fuck her until she can't remember her own fucking name, and then when I'm bored of her I'm gonna cut her head off and piss all over her and then I'm gonna set her on fire. That's what I'm gonna do to her, you piece-of-shit coward lying motherfucking son of a bitch!"

Clay stepped back, and then with one sudden movement he lunged forward toward Digger. He went with everything he had— every ounce of strength and courage, every ounce of love he felt for Bailey, every morsel of willpower and determinism. He just rushed Digger and he didn't care then whether he died. He had to keep Digger from hurting Bailey.

The gun went off. Clay felt himself thrown to the side of the road. His head caught the edge of a tree trunk, and for a moment he lay there dazed.

He heard scuffling. Bailey screamed again. Another shot. A third. The sound of the bullet thudding into the wood merely inches from his head. He rolled sideways, flattened himself to the ground, and was up on his knees even as the pickup pulled away.

It was then that he felt the pain in his right upper arm. He grimaced, held his left hand against the torn material of his T-shirt, felt the shallow flesh wound beneath, the warmth and moisture of the blood.

Clay was disorientated, confused, thought to return to the motel and call the police, decided against it. He started running, falling over his own feet as he went, the breath burning cold in his chest, his throat, his eyes filled with tears, the sense of abject terror as he thought of Bailey, of Digger, of what he was going to do to her . . .

A sense of utter panic invaded his senses. Clay shuddered as he ran. He felt nauseous, light-headed, out of control. He reached the junction, turned right, right again, and then cut across toward the sheriff's office once more. He didn't know Van Horn, but he knew where the sheriff's office was in relation to the motel.

He didn't stop to think of how Digger had found him. He didn't stop to wonder if Digger had followed him all the way from Marana. He didn't wonder at how his brother had become someone he barely recognized. He could think of nothing but what Digger had promised to do to Bailey.

Even as he neared the sheriff's office he was aware of something else. He wondered how he would explain himself, explain what had happened. This was it now. This was it for both of them, even if Bailey survived. Was he now a kidnapper? Had he kidnapped a young girl against her will and crossed state lines? Would he be in jail for the rest of his life?

Clay clutched his bleeding arm and hurried on.

Distracted, upset, anxious, he failed to notice Officer Freeman

Summers getting out of the patrol car ahead of the building to his right.

Clay walked past him, no more than ten or fifteen feet between them.

"Hey there," Summers said.

Clay stopped dead in his tracks. He should have turned around immediately. He should not have hesitated. Hesitating made him suspicious. Instantly suspicious.

"You," Summers said. "Aren't you Rachel Montague's boy?"

Again Clay hesitated, but he did not turn. "Yeah," he muttered. And then louder, "Yes, I am . . . ."

"Turn around, son . . . you look at me now while I'm speaking with you."

Clay turned—slowly, cautiously. He felt the rush of anxiety in his lower gut, the tension, the sense of dread.

"No, you're not," Summers said. "You ain't no more Rachel Montague's boy than I am. What the hell—"

Clay thought to run then. He thought to just hightail it in any direction he could. The likelihood that the police officer would shoot him? Slim, probably wouldn't even think of it. And then whatever doubt Clay Luckman might have had about Freeman Summers's inability to handle this as a potentially threatening situation evaporated as Summers drew his gun and aimed it directly at Clay's chest. Clay felt his knees turn to Jell-O. He wanted to piss himself. He felt light-headed and nauseous and for a moment he felt so disoriented he couldn't even remember his own name.

"Hands out to your sides where I can see them, son," Summers said. His voice was direct and commanding.

Clay was aware of the blood running down inside his sleeve. He didn't want to move his hand. He had to move his hand.

"Hands out to your sides!" Summers repeated. "I'll not tell you again!"

Clay dropped his hands to his sides. The quantity of blood on his jacket, his sleeve, right there on his hand was clearly visible in the light from the office windows.

"What the hell?"

Clay opened his mouth to speak.

"Don't wanna hear nothin' but your name, son," Summers

interjected. "And don't give me the wrong name, now. I'll soon find out the truth, and if you BS me then you're gonna be up to your neck in trouble."

Clay looked back at the young officer and he knew it was all over. He thought of the days he had spent traveling with Bailey. He thought of her dead father in the convenience store in Marana, of the money they took from the drive-in, of the night they spent in Tucson and their plan to reach Eldorado, of the gun he hid beneath the overturned car outside of Deming, of the motel—the first one—and how he'd crouched to spy through the keyhole in case he could see her naked, of Emanuel Smith and his crazy son, of how the I-10 represented their lives together for the past five days . . . He thought of how long it had seemed and yet how short it was. Five days. Monday, Tuesday, Wednesday, Thursday, and now Friday . . . and here he was, in Van Horn, looking back at the muzzle of a police forearm, and this officer, the one with really short hair, and how he couldn't have been much older than Clay himself, and how he was now asking him his name and there was no way in the world he could tell him anything but the truth . . .

And then he thought of Bailey and his own brother, and what he was doing to her in that precise moment . . .

And so he said it. Said it loud and clear so Officer Freeman Summers would have no doubt.

"My name is Clarence," he said. "Clarence Luckman."

And he watched as Officer Freeman Summers's eyes seemed to perceptibly widen, and then Clay noticed how he frowned, and how the gun he was holding seemed to waver for a second, and then the officer was shouting something at the top of his voice, shouting for the sheriff . . .

"Sheriff! Sheriff! Goddammit, someone get the freakin' sheriff!"

And Clay didn't understand what was happening. All he knew was that whatever journey he and Bailey Redman had made together was over. That, and the fact that he loved her.

And so he took a step forward, and he raised his hands without thinking, and the gun steadied, and the finger tightened against the trigger, and the sound of the bullet as it left the muzzle was like a firework reflected off the surface of a lake a million years before . . .

Once again, for some strange reason, there was no pain. He spun sideways. He was aware of that. He spun to the left, and the lights of the sheriff's office went by at a thousand miles an hour, and then he was looking at Freeman Summers's shoes as he hurried toward him.

And then there was shouting again, and then there was darkness and silence, and he wondered how long he would hear his own heart as it slowed down to nothing.

CHAPTER SIXTY-NINE

She was the best-looking of all of them. There was no question in Digger's mind that she was the best-looking of all of them. Young for sure, maybe fifteen or sixteen, but that meant that no one had spoiled her for him . . . And then he thought of Clay, and he wondered whether Clay had screwed her.

Once again he felt just plain bitter and resentful toward his brother. How come someone like Clay could get a girl like this? The whole balance of things was skewed beyond belief. Well, right here and now, he was going to set that balance right.

In the car the girl didn't say a word. Not the whole way back. He tucked the gun between his legs and he kept to a good speed and he kept his eyes on the road, and she was sitting right over the far side of the passenger seat, right against the door, like she was trying to stay away from him as best she could, and there was a look in her eyes like she was scared, but something else . . . like a cornered animal, ready to fight back given half a chance.

But there wasn't nothing to her, and if she made any kind of move on him then he would just whack her in the head and that would be that. Not to kill her. She wouldn't be so much fun dead. Just hit her hard enough to put her down so he could get her in the house easy.

So all the way back—ten miles or twelve miles or however far it was—she never said a damned word to him, and the more he looked at her—just a glance over to his right every once in a while—the more appealing she seemed to him. She really was a catch. This was what he needed. A girl like this. This one he could fuck until her heart burst, and then he could fuck her some more.

But the more he thought about it, and he did think about it, the more he realized that the reason this felt so damned good was that she was Clay's girl. That was just the best shit ever.

Well, how about that for coincidence and fate and destiny and all the rest of that shit, eh? Clay winds up out here in the same place at the same time, and Digger gets to take his girl. Un-fucking-believable! Just un-motherfucking-believable! Maybe the balance had been set straight already. Yes, maybe that was closer to the truth of things. Now he was set to get what he deserved as opposed to being endlessly overlooked.

It didn't matter whether Luckman was dead. In fact, it was probably better if he wasn't. Where would he be now? Running around like some fool chicken with its head cut off. He didn't have a damned clue where the girl was. All he'd know was that she was dying in the most horrible way, and that he—Digger—was doing it to her. Ha! Who said there wasn't such a thing as divine intervention and universal justice?

He didn't pass one car on the way, and no one overtook him. He went unseen, and it felt so good to just be in control of everything, and to have some time to fool around with the girl, and to not have to worry that someone was going to come knocking on Morton Randall's door. Places like this people stayed home after dark.

He could barely contain his excitement and anticipation.

He had a hard-on like a fence post.

Digger drove the pickup around back and parked. He didn't want it seen from the highway.

He walked around the front of the truck, the gun in his right hand, and he opened up the passenger door.

"Get out," he said.

She hesitated.

He stuck the gun in her face, just inches away, and he told her again. "Get the fuck out of the fucking car, you fucking bitch." He said it slow and precise, like he had all the time in the world, which—as it happened—he did.

Bailey Redman—more terrified than she believed possible—inched along the seat and came out slowly. One foot on the ground, then the other. She had never seen Elliott Danziger directly. Only Earl Sheridan. She would never forget the face of the man that had killed her father, but his accomplice . . . This young man's face was new, unrecognized, but she believed it would perhaps be the last face she ever saw.

She knew with certainty that tonight she would die. It horrified her. It left her speechless, dry-mouthed, unable to think or feel much of anything but the nightmare that awaited her, but it did possess some small saving grace.

Whatever happened tonight, whatever he might do to her before he killed her, however long it took and however she might hurt, at the end of it she would find her father. Of that she was sure.

Digger walked her into the house through the back way. Up the steps, through the screen, opened up the door into the kitchen, and then they were inside.

He told her to sit at the kitchen table.

"What's your name?" he asked.

"I-I'm n-not telling you," Bailey replied.

Digger smiled. Her eyes flashed at him. She was challenging him.

He put the gun in his left hand and he grabbed her hair. As he hauled her to her feet she summoned every ounce of self-possession she owned to keep herself from screaming in pain. Digger dragged her across the kitchen to the back door once again. He marched her down the steps and across the yard to the outhouse. He tucked the .45 into the waistband of his jeans and opened the door. He tugged the light cord and the place was suddenly illuminated in stark shadow-less brilliance.

Still holding her hair, Digger pushed her face right up against the dead girl's.

"This is Candace," he said. "Or, as I liked to call her before I stabbed her to death, Candy Ass. Now say hello to pretty Candace, little girl . . ."

And with that he twisted his grip on Bailey's hair.

Bailey shrieked in agony. She felt like her hair would come loose and her eyes would just burst out of the front of her face.

"Say hello to pretty Candace, little girl," Digger repeated, and with her face no more than two or three inches from the gray, cold features of the dead girl before her, Bailey opened her mouth and said, "Hello, C-Candace . . ."

"Good. Now say goodbye, Candace."

"G-Goodbye, Candace."

He hauled Bailey up by her hair again. He tugged the cord, the outhouse was dark once more, and then he walked her to the steps and through into the kitchen. He sat her down again, took the gun from his waistband, and put the muzzle against her nose.

"Tell me your name," he said.

"B-Bailey," she replied.

"Bailey what?"

"Bailey R-Redman."

"My name is Elliott, but people call me Digger. You can call me your worst fucking nightmare."

Bailey looked up at him, and through tear-filled eyes she watched as he took his jacket off.

He had the gun in his left hand then, and she knew he was right-handed. Remembered that he was right-handed. His left would be weaker.

He threw the jacket on the other chair and then he leaned close and pressed the muzzle of the gun between her legs.

"I'm not going to tell you what's going to happen tonight because I don't want to spoil the surprise," he said. "But you're here for a party. A special kind of party. Just you and me are invited, but you're the guest of honor, Bailey Redman. This is a party for you, Bailey Redman, an early Christmas party, a birth-day party, a party for no other reason than to have a party. We would have had cake and liquor and all that shit, but you know something . . . I really couldn't be fucking bothered. We have the entertainment, you see, and as far as I'm concerned it's the quality of the entertainment that makes the party. Wouldn't you agree with that, Bailey Redman?"

Bailey tried to keep herself from crying. She had felt nothing but shock since he pointed the gun at her through the passenger window of the pickup, that and the intense pain as he dragged her by the hair, and then there was the utter horror of being faced with a dead girl in the outhouse . . . But now there was some-thing else. There was the memory of Clay. Of where he was, what he was doing, and worse than all of that . . . if he was dead. This, above and beneath all else, served to bring her to the present, to bring her into focus about what had happened, what was *going* to happen . . .

"I said wouldn't you agree with that, Bailey Redman?"

Bailey choked back her fear. "Fuck you, you sick son of a bitch."

Digger laughed coarsely. "Fuck me? *Fuck me?* Somehow I don't think so." He leaned down until his face was mere inches from hers. When he spoke she could smell his breath. It smelled like something had crawled down his throat and died right there inside of him.

"You listen to me now, Bailey Redman. There's two ways this is going to go. The hard way, or the really hard way. You want it the hard way, believe me. You do not—not in a million years— want it the very hard way. Whether or not you die tonight . . . whether or not you die right here tonight in this kitchen—is your decision, and the more fun I get the better your chances. You understand me?"

Bailey didn't move, didn't move a muscle.

He slapped her suddenly, a vicious backhand, and before the pain reached her she found herself on the floor.

He dragged her up again, the gun in his left hand, his right around her throat, and he sat her down once more.

"You understand me?" he hissed.

He held her by the neck and he nodded her head up and down for her.

"Good," he said. "I'm so thrilled that we now understand each other."

He let her go. She gasped for breath. She held on to the edges of the seat to keep herself from falling to the ground once more.

"Okay, so first things first, sweetheart . . . take your clothes off."

CHAPTER SEVENTY

The call to the hotel in Las Cruces came in a handful of minutes after ten. By quarter past Ronald Koenig and Garth Nixon were in the car. Koenig had asked at the desk for Cassidy's room number. They had called him from the foyer but there was no response. Nixon had even gone up there to hammer on the door in case Cassidy was already sleeping. Again no response. They left word at the desk that they had gone to Van Horn, a town some hundred and fifty miles along I-10.

Clarence Luckman had been shot. They knew this much. They left word of that as well. Just so Cassidy would appreciate the speed with which he should depart Las Cruces. Cassidy had wanted to be there at the end, and it appeared the end was in Van Horn.

Cassidy, having enjoyed a steak in a restaurant on the outskirts of Las Cruces, returned to the hotel at 10:51. He received the note from the night manager at 10:54. By 11:10 he was in the car and had reached the end of the street. He was doing ninety miles an hour by the time he hit the I-10, but he was still a good thirty minutes behind Koenig and Nixon. He wanted to be in Van Horn within an hour and a half. All that mattered now was Clarence Luckman, and—according to the sheriff of Van Horn—he was there. The fact that he had already been shot told Cassidy everything he needed to know.

At the same time Sam Munro, concerned now that he'd had no word from his daughter or the friend in Monahans, drove back down to the garage and put the lights on throughout the place. He had searched the house for any indication that Candace had left. Nightclothes missing, her cosmetics, other such stuff that she always took with her. All of it was present, at least as best as he could tell. He didn't have a number to call the friend in

Monahans. He knew her first name. Charlene. That was all he had. Charlene what? He didn't have the faintest clue. He went down to the garage to see if there was anything he might have missed. A few scribbled words on a scrap of paper. A note on one of the pages of the receipt pad. He looked, but he found nothing. He found nothing because there *was* nothing. Of that he was now sure. This feeling, this sense of *unknowing*, began to worry him. He decided he would knock on some doors in the vicinity. Okay, it was late, too late really to be bothering folks, but this was Candace. Everyone knew Candace around there. They saw her pretty much every day. But if anyone had seen anything happen to her then they would have called him immediately. He knew nothing had happened to her. It couldn't have. It was fine. There was an explanation. She was up in Monahans with Charlene and she'd just got too involved with whatever they did to call her dad. Boys, no doubt. Always boy trouble. At the bottom of this there would be a boy, and more than likely a no-good one. That's what it would be.

Aware that he was doing nothing but trying to convince himself that everything was okay, Sam Munro still went and knocked on some doors, and it wasn't until the fourth or fifth door, already getting on for 10:45 that he even spoke to anyone who'd seen her the day before. That person was Dan Caldwell, a retired schoolteacher who owned a Chevy station wagon that was too big for his purposes and forever failing to start.

"Seen her before Morton came over," Caldwell told Sam Munro. "Morton Randall, sure. He was over sometime yesterday. Saw Candace before that, and then didn't see her afterward. Saw the doors closed, that was all. Bay doors were never opened as far as I recall, so I don't know what she was doing all afternoon."

"But you're sure Morton Randall was here?"

"Well, I seen his pickup, or one that was exactly the same. I remember seeing it and thinking that he must've been over there. He wasn't there long, and then he was gone. Candace had been sitting out front reading a magazine or something, but after Morton left I never saw her again."

The thing about the doors made sense, Munro thought. Candace struggled to open the bay doors by herself, and if she could get away with it she just left them closed. They only needed to be opened when a car was in over the inspection pit. Otherwise all the fixing and whatever was done on the forecourt.

Munro thanked Caldwell and went on his way. He sat in his car for a while trying to explain things to himself, and then he started the engine and headed out to the highway. Randall's place was—what?—maybe ten or twelve miles, and though he felt sure the man wouldn't be able to help him any, it was still something he couldn't let go of.

So Sam Munro took off down the same highway as Koenig, Nixon, and Cassidy, believing that his journey out to Morton Randall's place would be nothing other than a vain attempt to find out where his daughter had gotten to. He drove within the speed limit, unlike the police, and he was out there in a quarter of an hour. The lights were on downstairs, and he sat on the high- way for another ten minutes or so until he convinced himself that he couldn't rest until he'd spoken to Randall. It was late—a handful of minutes shy of eleven thirty—but the lights were on down there, and if Randall was anything like him then he was going to be up for a good while yet.

Munro started the car again, turned left, and made his way down the long drive toward the house with an odd feeling in the base of his gut.

CHAPTER SEVENTY-ONE

"**I** have to tell you that the federal people are on their way," Everhardt said, "and whatever difficulty you think you're in right now . . . well, son, I gotta tell you that this really is the end of the line for you."

Clay Luckman looked back at Everhardt with some indefinable expression. He felt everything and nothing. He believed he had arrived in hell. He lay on the floor of the jail cell, blood leaking from his upper arm, a hole right through his waist, the pain ebbing and flowing in dark, scarlet waves that made it difficult to think of anything but the last time he'd seen Bailey Redman's face. The terror in her eyes. The utter, indefinable terror.

"The things you've done . . . well, I can't even get my hat on. I can't even begin to comprehend the kind of person you must be to do the things you've done—"

Clay opened his mouth to speak for the fourth or fifth time, and once again Everhardt raised his hand and silenced him.

"I told you before, and I'll tell you again. Ain't no use you tellin' me a goddamned thing. First and foremost you should not say a word until they bring some sort of public defender down here from the El Paso district attorney's office, and second because I really don't want to hear a single word out of your mouth. You are whoever you are, and that is something I will never understand . . . something I *hope* I will never understand, and as far as I'm concerned you did the very best thing you could do by showing up here, 'cause I got you now and you ain't goin' no place at all and when the federal people get here, which should be about"—Everhardt paused and glanced at his watch—"which should be about an hour or so from now, then they're going to take you out to wherever they take people like you and put you in a box that you ain't never gonna see the outside of until they execute you."

Everhardt leaned forward, his expression grave.

"You understand that that's what's gonna happen here, son. I gather you must, unless you is just downright crazy or dumber than a dog's ass. You are gonna fry for this, or they're gonna hang you or whatever the hell they're doing these days . . ."

"But—"

Everhardt reached down and put his hand over Clay's mouth. One hand behind his neck, one over his mouth, and then he leaned forward until their eyes were no more than six inches apart. "Not a word. Not a fucking single goddamned word out of you. You are one almighty sick son of a bitch, and if I had my way we'd go back to the old days, you know? We'd just drag you out the back here and horsewhip you unconscious, and then we'd hang you from the nearest tree and be done with it. We'd take our time doin' it, you know we would. And we'd bring some beers and we'd get a little gathering together, and we'd kill you the long way round. But the law is the law, and the law stands here. You're going on up to the big house with the federal people, and from the point you leave here you ain't my concern anymore."

Everhardt released him. He stood up and stepped back. He paused before he opened up the cell door.

"The girl . . . Bai—" Clay struggled to get up.

Everhardt let fly with a backhander. The knuckles of his right hand connected with Clay's cheekbone and Clay went back down like a stone.

"Son, you keep your fucking mouth shut, you hear me! Only girl you is ever likely to see is your own mother when she comes to identify your body."

Clay possessed insufficient awareness to even register what Everhardt was saying. He lay on his side on the floor, his knees up against his chest, his hands protecting his head, and he knew that whatever had happened here, whatever was happening here, was all the more evidence that the bad star had followed him from Hesperia, from Barstow, perhaps from the dingy apartment where his mother had died and he hadn't even known it.

The door opened. The door slammed shut.

"Now, I'm gonna make a call and get some people down here

to sort out this matter once and for all. I ain't in a hurry, mind, as you've probably already guessed. It sure as hell doesn't pain me none to see you lying there and hurting so bad. Only thing I care about is that you don't up and die on us before we have a chance to see some kind of justice done here. That's all that's going on here, son, just so's you don't get the wrong impression and think I give a damn about you."

Clay's awareness of what he was hearing drifted then, and he laid his head down on the cold stone floor, and he heard nothing at all then but the sound of Sheriff Everhardt's boots as he walked away.

DAY NINE

CHAPTER SEVENTY-TWO

Several minutes before midnight, in that brief window of time before Friday the 27th became Saturday the 28th, John Cassidy arrived in the small Texan town of Van Horn. He was a good half an hour behind Koenig and Nixon, and as he pulled up outside the sheriff's office he was directed to the other side of the building by a young uniformed officer.

Getting out of the car he was asked for some form of ID, and when he told the officer his name, that he was here with Koenig and Nixon, the young officer shook his head and looked away down the road.

"They took him already," he said.

"Took Luckman?"

"Sure as hell did. Bundled him out of here and into the car and drove off down that way." He indicated with a tilt of his head.

"I heard he was shot," Cassidy said.

"Twice, as far as I could tell."

"By you?"

"Nope. I shot him only the once."

"So who else shot him?"

"Who the hell knows? By the time he rocked up here he was already bleeding."

"And they took him . . . the two men from the FBI? They took him in their car?"

"Sure as hell did. Them and Sheriff Everhardt, off down that way."

Cassidy got back in the car and gunned the engine. He knew what was going to happen. He knew he was too late. His heart was racing, his hands were sweating. He could see Alice's face as he tried to explain to her that he'd been too late. That he went out for dinner and he got back half an hour later than he should

415

have, and he drove out here as fast as he could, but he was too damned late. He hoped then that he'd been wrong. That they'd both been wrong. He hoped that Clarence Luckman was the one who'd done these things—a young man who had been kidnapped from the Hesperia Juvenile Correction Facility and yet had become a worse nightmare than even his kidnapper; a young man responsible for the killings of Laurette Tannahill, of Marlon Juneau, the entire Eckhart family, of Rita McGovern and Lord only knows who else. He could face the prospect of being wrong in his assumptions with far greater ease than he would ever accept the death of an innocent young man.

Cassidy hit the accelerator and took off in a skid of gravel.

He left Officer Freeman Summers standing there ahead of the sheriff's office with a smile on his face and a sense of pride in his heart. After all, hadn't he—Freeman Summers—been the one to shoot Clarence Luckman, the worst murderer anyone had ever heard of? Sure as hell he was.

He found them no more than two miles away. The beams of his brights illuminated the scenario in stark brilliance, and he knew then exactly what was happening.

There were four of them—Sheriff Everhardt, Koenig, Nixon, and out ahead of them, leaning to one side, seemingly barely able to stand, was Clarence Luckman. His arm, his pants' leg, the lower half of his jacket were all soaked with blood. He moved awkwardly to one side, and then as Cassidy's car approached he tried to raise his hand against the brightness of the headlights.

Koenig was there as Cassidy skidded to a halt.

Koenig wrenched the door open. The man's face was varnished with sweat. His cheeks were reddened, his eyes bright and fierce and accusative.

"Get the hell out of here!" he shouted. "This isn't your business now. Get the hell away from here, Cassidy!"

"No," Cassidy said. "You're not going to do this. You *can't* do this! Is this what you've been ordered to do? To just kill this boy in cold blood in the fucking street?"

Cassidy pushed past Koenig and walked toward Nixon.

Nixon stood there, a cigarette in his hand. It was the sheriff who held a gun, and it was aimed unerringly at Luckman.

"Do as he says!" Nixon shouted. "Get the hell out of here! This isn't anything to do with you anymore."

Cassidy felt the rage burning in his chest. "What the hell are you talking about? Isn't anything to do with me? You're going to let this man murder him? You're just going to let this happen?"

Nixon looked at Koenig. Koenig looked at Luckman.

Luckman looked back at the four of them, his eyes wide, rolling white every moment or two, unsteady on his feet, his hand clutching his side, his mouth open. He took one staggered step forward and fell to his knees.

Cassidy rushed forward. He stood in front of Luckman.

"Get out the fucking way!" Nixon said. "For Christ's sake, get out of the fucking way!"

"It ends now," Koenig added. "This is it, Cassidy! This is where it ends! He's gonna die right here and now for what he did. He's not going to jail. He's not going to plead insanity and get three years in some fucking nuthouse. He's gonna die right here and now. Think of the people he killed! Just think of what he did to those people!"

Cassidy backed up. He knelt beside Luckman and put his arm around his shoulder to hold him up.

Luckman looked back at him, blood on his lips, his eyes unfocused, his hair plastered to his face.

Uuugghhh, he gasped, and then he dry-retched and grimaced in pain. He clutched his side even harder and moaned once more.

Nixon was there then, Koenig too, and they stood over Cassidy and Luckman, and there was such desperate rage and hatred in their expressions.

Luckman opened his mouth, an attempt to speak perhaps, but Cassidy cut him short.

"Not a word, son. Not a single word until you answer one question."

Clay Luckman—his face smeared with blood, the disbelief and shock and horror so evident in his eyes—waited for whatever that question could be.

"You tell me the truth now, son," Cassidy said. "You tell me the truth, and don't you even think about lying or misleading us. You have no idea how much trouble you are in. You have absolutely no idea what will happen to you if you lie to us or mislead us. You understand me?"

Clay—slowly, deliberately—nodded his head.

"You tell me—"

"My bro-bro-brother . . ." Clarence gasped.

"Your brother?" Cassidy asked, and then he looked up at Nixon and Koenig. "What did you say?"

"Bro-brother . . . he took . . . took Bail . . ."

"Bailey?" Cassidy said. "Elliott Danziger took Bailey?"

Clarence Luckman moved his head. He nodded once, and then his eyes rolled back once more and he went limp in Cassidy's arms.

Cassidy, feeling a rush of adrenaline and fear the like of which he had never experienced, did his best to get to his feet with the deadweight of Clarence Luckman in his arms.

Nixon was then beside him. "Is that the girl?" he asked. "Is that the girl you were talking about?"

"Bailey Jacobs," Cassidy said. "He said that his brother has taken Bailey Jacobs."

There was silence for a moment, and then Nixon stepped forward to help Cassidy.

"Into the back of the sheriff's car," Nixon said, and then he looked back at Cassidy, and in the stark illumination of the car headlights Cassidy could see the bloodless fear in the man's face.

"Not a word," Nixon said. "Not a word, okay?"

CHAPTER SEVENTY-THREE

Digger saw the lights through the window before Sam Munro had made it halfway from the highway.

"Fuck! Shit! Fuck!" he said. The girl hadn't even gotten all her clothes off and now some interfering motherfucker asshole was coming toward the house.

"Jesus Christ Almighty," he said.

He grabbed Bailey by the arm and hurried from the kitchen and up the stairs.

Once in Morton Randall's bedroom he shoved Bailey onto the mattress and grabbed a pillow. She lay there for a second, motionless, wide-eyed, and then she realized what he was going to do.

"No!" she screamed, and tried to get off the bed. Digger snatched at her foot and held her. He used the butt of the gun to sideswipe her. He caught her a glancing blow across the face, and for a moment she was stunned.

That moment was all he needed. He held a pillow in his left, pressed the muzzle of the gun into it, and then pulled the trigger.

The sound was quieter than he'd imagined. He had steeled himself for an explosion, but it sounded like nothing more than a bottle hitting the ground.

She was motionless. Utterly motionless.

"See," he said. "Try and run away now, you little bitch."

He dropped the pillow, left the room, and hurried downstairs to deal with whoever had come from the highway to bother him.

When he opened the door and saw Sam Munro there was a moment's recognition. Something in the man's face seemed familiar. Had he seen Sam Munro standing beside his daughter he would have understood precisely why he felt a sense of déjà vu, but in that second it was unimportant.

"Oh, er, hullo there . . . er, I was . . . I was looking for Mr. Randall. Is Mr. Randall in?"

Digger smiled his best smile. "Sure he is. He's right inside. Who are you?"

"Oh yes, my name is Sam Munro, and I wondered whether Mr. Randall might have seen my daughter yesterday."

Digger frowned. "Your daughter?"

"Yes, my daughter. Candace Munro."

"Right, right, right . . . Candace," he said, and two and two made four and he knew that he would have to kill this son of a bitch as fast as possible.

"Come on in, Mr. Munro. I'll get Mr. Randall for you . . . He's just in back. I'm Elliott by the way," he added. "I'm Mr. Randall's nephew."

"Oh, okay. I didn't know he had a nephew."

"Oh yes, Mr. Munro, there are a good few of us. We just don't make a visit that often."

"Well, it's a pleasure to meet you, Elliott," Munro said, and he held out his hand.

Digger shook it, and then he stepped back to allow Sam Munro entry into the house.

Digger directed him to the kitchen, and it was there—seated in the same chair where Bailey had sat only minutes before—that Munro waited for Elliott to bring Morton Randall down to speak with him.

And it was there—with his back to the door—that his view of Elliott Danziger was obscured. He didn't think anything at all until a strange sensation overcame him, and then there was a feeling of intense pain in his shoulder. He reached up, and there he discovered the handle of a kitchen knife protruding from his upper arm. The profound and indescribable disbelief then evident on his face stopped Elliott in his tracks. He had planned to drag the knife out and just stab the guy in the neck, but he couldn't stop laughing.

It was a surreal scene. Sam Munro, here on a mission to try and find his daughter, seated in the kitchen of Morton Randall's house, and Randall's nephew, this Elliott, had just dug a kitchen knife into his arm and was now howling like a hyena.

Munro tried to get up. He felt faint. He lost his balance. He sat down again—hard.

Digger went on laughing.

Munro tried to get up again, and this time he managed it.

Digger took one step forward and pushed him.

Munro went sideways and collided with the stove. He reached up to the stovetop to gain his footing, and there his fingers met with the edge of a glass dish. He grabbed it.

When Digger came for him again he just lashed out with that dish. He hit Digger fair and square in the side of the head. Cold pork and beans scattered across the floor. Digger went down like a stone. *Boom.*

His arm howling in pain, Munro went for the back door, wrenched it open and stumbled awkwardly down the steps into the yard. He knew enough to understand that pulling the knife out was not a good idea. The knife had maybe severed whatever veins and arteries, and there was little blood, but to pull it out would be to dramatically increase the risk of enormous bleeding, and already he was starting to lose the feeling in his fingers and his hand. He had to drive. He had to get in the car and drive back to Van Horn.

It did not occur to him in that moment that there was any connection between what had just happened and the apparent disappearance of his daughter. There was no reason for him to consider such a thing.

All he knew was that he had to get to Kelt Everhardt. He had to find him and tell him that there was a kitchen knife in his shoulder and a crazy boy in Morton Randall's house.

CHAPTER SEVENTY-FOUR

"**H**e is out there somewhere, I tell you," Cassidy said again, and he seemed to be saying it for the hundredth time.

"I appreciate your opinion, Detective Cassidy," Koenig said. "I really do appreciate your opinion on this, but right now we have what we have. Clarence Luckman is the suspect. Sheriff Everhardt is going to see him to the hospital, and as soon as they have addressed his immediate wounds he will be arrested. If he makes it, and as soon as he's out of danger, he is going to be charged. We charge him, then we interrogate him. That is the way it goes, and we have no reason to do anything different right now—"

"And no real reason *to* charge him aside from circumstantial evidence . . . hell, no evidence at all, if I'm looking at this the way you are. However, if you have evidence that I don't know about that puts Clarence Luckman anywhere near any of these killings, then I suggest that you tell me now and I'll go ahead and fill out the goddamned paperwork myself."

"Look," Koenig said. "I . . . *we* really appreciate your help on this, Cassidy, but you have to appreciate what we're dealing with in return. This is a capital case. This is a killing spree the like of which the federal authorities have not seen in . . . Christ, I can't think of a case that even comes close to it. Handled incorrectly, one mess-up, one failure to do this by the book, and we lose him. We have to get a confession, and it has to be an unbiased confession, and someone from the public defender's office needs to be gotten here right now, and we start this thing without delay—"

"But—"

"But nothing, Detective. It *has* to be done this way, and if as a result of the interrogation we learn that this Elliott Danziger is still alive, and that he has been responsible for these killings, then obviously Clarence Luckman will be released."

"If he doesn't die from the gunshot wounds . . ."

"A police officer acted bravely," Koenig said. "He did his duty. He was authorized to employ deadly force as needed to apprehend the criminal."

"But we don't know that he's even a criminal! Jesus, can't you see what's there right in front of you? He even said it himself. The brother is here, for Christ's sake. He said it! He said that the brother had taken Bailey Jacobs—"

"*He* said that. *He*. Clarence Luckman said that. Right now Clarence Luckman is our suspect, Detective Cassidy, and I'd appreciate it if you would step aside now and let us do our job. The fact that his brother might or might not have taken this girl doesn't change the fact that Luckman is a killer . . ."

"You're going to blow it," Cassidy said. "Danziger is out there. I am certain of it. If we waste time now when we could be looking for him, then we will lose him. A couple of hours and he could be in Mexico, and then we are screwed."

"And the evidence that you have that says Danziger is out there, that Danziger is the one that did these things, is no less circumstantial than the evidence that implicates Luckman."

"Just look at him! Look at the boy! You saw him. You're telling me that he was capable of doing the things we've seen, like Deidre Parselle? You really think that that boy was capable of stabbing a girl that many times? Of doing what was done to that girl?"

"And your boy Danziger is no less a teenager, Detective Cassidy," Koenig retorted. "All we have now is Clarence Luckman. He's been on the run for a week. We have him now, thanks to Sheriff Everhardt. Now we get someone here from the El Paso DA's office. This boy needs legal representation before we even get a word out of him, and then, and *only* then, will we find out what has really happened here."

"Un-fucking-believable—"

"Detective Cassidy, seriously . . ." Koenig started, but he was interrupted by the appearance of Freeman Summers outside Everhardt's office door.

"Mr. Koenig?" Summers asked.

"Not now, Summers. I'm busy."

"But, sir . . . ?"

Koenig turned. "Seriously, Officer Summers, I am dealing with something very important right now, as you can well see—"

"Sir, I'm sorry, but I got Sam Munro out here and he desperately needs to see someone, and Sheriff Everhardt isn't here . . ."

"Hell, Summers, you can deal with it!"

"No, sir, I think you're gonna wanna talk to him. He has a kitchen knife sticking out of his shoulder and he says there's a crazy boy with a gun out in Morton Randall's place . . ."

Koenig's eyes widened.

"Oh, and another thing . . . he says that his daughter has gone missing."

CHAPTER SEVENTY-FIVE

Digger was pissed. There was so much blood all over the girl upstairs that he couldn't fuck her. I mean, even for him, it was just too much. That aside, he just could not work out how the dead girl in the outhouse . . . I mean, *how the fuck* did her father know to come out here, all the way down the highway to Randall's place? He wrestled with that question for just a minute, and then he got it. It could only mean that someone had seen Randall's pickup outside the garage where he'd gotten the girl from. Fuck. *Fuck!*

Now what was he going to do? Hide in the house? He didn't think so. Go on the road in Randall's pickup? Not a good option. They knew what he would be driving, and they would find him in no time. What would Earl have done? Earl would have taken a hostage. That's what Earl did in Hesperia, and that's what he would do now. Oh, how he wished Earl were here! If Earl were here he wouldn't be in this situation. Motherfuckers had to shoot the poor man down. God, it made him mad!

Digger got the .45 and the rest of the ammo. He thought about taking other guns with him, but he didn't want to be weighed down, especially if he was getting out of there on foot. That, now, was really the only option. Just make it however far he could until he got another car. Hell, a half mile down the highway he could flag down a ride, shoot the driver, and take the car. That would be fine. Then he'd be on his way, right out of here, perhaps down into Mexico where these sons of bitches couldn't even touch him if they came knocking at his door. Sure as shit stinks, that's what he would do.

Digger spent a few minutes gathering up some items of clothing. He and Randall were close to the same size, maybe a couple inches in height, a couple on the waist, but it would be fine. A pair of pants, a shirt, a couple of T-shirts, an extra pair of shoes. He stuffed everything in a bag and dropped it in the front hallway. He then went out to the pickup and checked if there was anything in there he needed.

Back in the house he gathered up his money, his jacket, a couple more knives from the kitchen, which he dropped in the bag in the hallway, and he was all set to go.

That's when the lights came on again. Out front. Right out there in the front yard. And it was like daylight through the windows, and he didn't understand what the goddamned hell was going on . . . It was like a fucking spaceship had landed outside of Morton Randall's house, and then he heard a voice, and it was loud, and it cut through everything inside his head, and he knew the rules of the game had just been changed.

"You! You inside! We have you surrounded back and front. There is nowhere for you to go! Come on out here, son . . . drop whatever weapons you have and get on out here with your hands on your head!"

"Fuck!" Digger said. "Fuck! Fuck! Fuck!"

It was the girl. He would have to use the girl as a hostage, somehow hold her upright, make them believe she was still alive. Now there was no other way. Earl had made it work, and now he could too. The bitch upstairs was his ticket out of the shit.

CHAPTER SEVENTY-SIX

The drive over to Randall's place had been at breakneck speed. A convoy of three cars, which rapidly became five, six, then seven, as Nixon and Koenig, Cassidy, Summers, another sheriff's department vehicle, and two more civic volunteers were called in to make the ten-mile run out there.

Cassidy knew that Bailey Jacobs was dead. He knew it in his heart. He tried to convince himself that this was not the case, that the irony that would place Bailey Jacobs within the grasp of Elliott Danziger could not have happened. No God could be that cruel. But he also knew that this was what had happened, as if Clarence Luckman and Bailey Jacobs had somehow attracted Danziger back to them. As if some strange dark star had overshadowed them all the way from Hesperia, and now it had finally caught them.

He wanted to speak to Alice. He wanted to tell her that he had done everything he could. He wanted to hold her, to shed his tears, to hear her tell him that she understood . . . but he knew that there would always be that edge in her tone, that wonder, that unspoken question . . .

Did you, John? Did you do everything *you could to save her?*

"Yes, I did," he said out loud. "Yes, I did. I did everything I could," and he pressed his foot down on the accelerator and urged the car forward to Morton Randall's house down along the highway.

Nixon and Koenig were up front, Cassidy behind them, Summers behind him, and the other vehicles in the convoy following close on their tail.

And then Koenig's car was slowing, he was indicating left, and they were turning, and in the distance Cassidy could see the lights of Randall's house, seemingly the only house for miles . . .

and he knew that it was here, here in the middle of nowhere, that the nightmare was going to end. There was relief, and there was fear, and there was grief, and there was a slow-burn sense of disillusionment as he appreciated all that had happened, all that could have been done but was not. Just one more hour, one more day, one more slim clue, and Bailey Jacobs might have made it.

They came to a stop, each of them lining up in a semicircle around the front of the house, Koenig out of his car now, directing the unit car and the two volunteers around to cover the back of the building. Their collective headlights illuminated the scene like daylight, but it was a stark and cold illumination, almost monochrome, and Cassidy knew that this image—Morton Randall's lonely house off of the I-10—would now be burned in his mind forever. The nights he could not sleep—when the nightmares came, as he knew they *would* come—this was the scene that would play over in his mind again and again and again.

The lonely house in the middle of nowhere. The dead girl. The sense of guilt

Nixon had a bullhorn then, and he was speaking into it, his voice commanding and direct.

But Cassidy just wanted to push them all aside and get in there. He wanted to see her. He wanted to see what Elliott Danziger had done to her. He wanted to see the dead body of Bailey Jacobs and start dealing with his pain.

CHAPTER SEVENTY-SEVEN

Digger was at the top of the stairs. He was mad. Mad enough to burst.

"Where the fuck are you?" he screamed. "Hey! You ain't gonna get away from me, you bitch!"

He went back to the bedroom. There was the bed, there was the mattress, there was the extraordinary amount of blood on the sheets . . . and there was *no girl*!

He did a double-take. He had even rubbed his eyes like he was in a cartoon and could not believe what he was seeing. Where the fuck was she? How the fuck had she moved? She was dead! She was fucking dead! He saw the blood. He heard the gun. He had pulled the trigger himself! Goddamn motherfucker piece of shit son of a bitch cocksucking bitch fuck shit fuck! What the damn hell was happening?

It wasn't another room. He hadn't moved her. There was the blood. There was the bed where he'd put her before he picked up the pillow. There was the damned pillow, right there on the floor with a bullet hole burned right through it.

Fuck! Fuck! Fuck!

Digger gripped the .45 even harder.

The bathroom! She was hiding in the bathroom!

He backed up a step, turned silently, and on the balls of his feet he tiptoed carefully to the door. It was ajar no more than six inches, and with his fingertips he edged it open, hoping it would make no sound. The bath. The shower curtain. She was in the fucking bath hiding behind the fucking shower curtain!

Digger smiled. He tightened his hold on the gun. He could edge up against the faucet end of the bath, and with his left hand he could whip the curtain back and there she would be. Bitch! The fucking bitch was gonna die this fucking time, no fucking doubt about it! But first she would get him out of here. This was better; maybe luck was on his side. Alive, she was a far better hostage.

He heard the bullhorn outside again. He ignored it. He needed the girl. He needed to take her out of there alive or otherwise—preferably bleeding and kicking and screaming at the top of her lungs, and they would give him a car, and they would let him drive the fuck on out of here, and this would be the last time Texas or anyone in this shithole would see him. He was gone, man. Gone like the wind!

He was beside the bath then, and he reached out slowly, carefully, tentatively, and he gripped the shower curtain.

One swift tug and it would disappear, and there she would be—in all her glory—and he would have his one-way fare all paid up and ready to go.

One-two-three, and he yanked it back, and he was looking at the vaguely yellow-stained porcelain of Morton Randall's bathtub . . . and no girl!

"Fuck!" he said out loud.

The bullhorn voice started up again.

"Motherfuckers!" he said. That was it. Enough was enough! He was going to go out there to the front of the house, and he was going to shoot those sons of bitches in the yard. Shoot them down like dogs, just the way they had Earl Sheridan. An eye for an eye, a tooth for a tooth.

He turned, the gun in his hand, and he looked up.

And she was there.

Right there in front of him.

He opened his mouth. He smiled.

She had been right behind the door all along.

And Elliott Danziger kept on smiling—imagining the fast ride to Mexico, the slow cruise across the border, the *cerveza*, the pretty girls, the . . .

And he kept on smiling until Bailey Redman showed him the scissors clenched in her fist, and then took those scissors and plunged them right into his eye.

"Fuck you!" she said defiantly.

He stared back at her with his one good eye, and he was still smiling when his finger jerked involuntarily, and it kept on jerking until that .45 was all emptied out . . .

And it was the sound of those gunshots that prompted Koenig to drop the bullhorn. He went at a run, far faster than a man of his size could be expected to run, and he went up the steps and through the front door of Morton Randall's lonely house like an unbroken horse.

The door came off its hinges, and Nixon, Cassidy, all of them went after him as fast as their legs could carry them.

CHAPTER SEVENTY-EIGHT

It took the surgeons at the El Paso General Hospital an hour and a quarter to get the .45-caliber bullet out of Bailey Redman's thigh. As Digger had fired, as he'd leaned toward Bailey, the pillow in his left hand, the .45 in his right . . . as he'd aimed for her chest and pulled that trigger, she had instinctively raised her left leg to kick him. The bullet had stopped dead in her bone.

While she underwent the operation, Detective John Cassidy sat beside a bed in a room three doors down. In that bed was an unconscious Clarence Luckman, himself having undergone an operation to repair the flesh wound in his right upper arm, the through-and-through that punctured the side of his stomach. Even as he slept, and despite being given sufficient sedatives to floor a horse, he was nevertheless handcuffed to the bed frame.

Nixon and Koenig had found Morton Randall. They had found Candace Munro. Sam Munro was being attended to. They had taken the knife out of his shoulder, stitched him up, and then they'd had to tell him his daughter was dead. They'd sedated him too, and now he slept—perhaps believing, as Cassidy would have—that it was all a nightmare. The sense of relief when he woke would last only so long as the unawareness of his location. Then there would be a moment of recognition, of orientation, and it would all come flooding back. The nightmare, at least for Sam Munro, was real. As real as it had been for all of them—the Eckharts, for Laurette Tannahill, for Marlon Juneau, his head blown apart at the side of the highway for no other reason than he was there . . . The very same reason for all of them.

And those gunshots. The ones they had heard in the house. They had gone through the floor—one after the other after the other—as Elliott Danziger spasmodically reacted to the collapse of his nervous system. Those scissors that Bailey held, a good six-inch blade on them, had gone directly through his eye and into the frontal lobe of his brain. Elliott Danziger was dead before he hit the ground, though perhaps not so quickly as to miss the grim smile on Bailey's face as he fell to his knees. That's what Cassidy wanted to believe. That's what he told himself had happened. And that's what he would tell Alice.

Later, when Clarence Luckman came round, Cassidy told him where the girl was, and of all that had taken place. He would remain handcuffed, just for the meantime, just while they got everything straight. Clarence would be there for a while, and no, he would not be able to see the girl. Not yet. She was going to be fine, as he was, but there was a procedure and a protocol to follow, and follow it they would.

"Bailey Redman," was his reply. He had looked at Cassidy with those wide and terrified eyes, and said, "Her name isn't Jacobs. Her name is Bailey Redman."

CHAPTER SEVENTY-NINE

She walks with a limp. There is a strong possibility she always will. It does not tire her, nor does it seem to bother her, and the scarring has healed well and it is like the memory of another life.

She is sixteen years old, and she lives in Tucson City. She lives with John and Alice Cassidy and she looks after their baby. The baby's name is Evan, and he is a handsome boy, and he has dark hair like his father and hazel eyes like his mother, and Bailey believes that he will grow up and break as many hearts as there are to break. This is what she believes, and her belief is strong.

She also believes that there is a dark star for her, and one for Clay Luckman, and though the dark stars have not left them behind, nor have they moved forward, they have somehow counteracted one another. If that was not the case, then how come they both survived? This she believes too, and her belief is equally strong.

Some time after the nightmares began to diminish Cassidy told her about Earl Sheridan and Elliott Danziger, of all the things they did, the people that they were, and that her father—the shoe salesman from Scottsdale—was not the only one to die. Bailey understood then that there was a circle, and that the circle was present in all things, and that it was strange kind of justice that had delivered her into the hands of Elliott Danziger. She had been there to exact retribution for her father. Bailey wondered about the others who had lost their loved ones, and where they would find their justice. Perhaps she had delivered it for them. Perhaps she had channeled all of it. Perhaps she had been chosen to bring it all to an end.

She spoke about this with Clay, and Clay listened and he did not try to explain. He just listened, and he heard her, and that was enough.

They do not talk about it now, though sometimes when he holds her, when there is nothing but inches of muscles and skin and bone and blood separating their hearts, she feels that the bad sign still worries him and she knows better than to speak of it. To grant it voice is to grant it strength, and this she will not do. For now, perhaps forever, it will remain unvoiced, and in this way it will grow weaker and weaker with time, and soon it will disappear altogether and worry him no more.

And he—Clay Luckman—living no more than four or five blocks away, walks over to collect her, and they go out, and they spend time together, and they speak of the future that they will have. That they too will have a child like Evan Cassidy, and he will break as many hearts as there are to break. And one day—perhaps—they will go out to Eldorado, Texas, to see if there is anything there for them. Whatever it might be, it will wait until they are ready.

It took weeks, but people came forward. Clark Regan. Betty Calthorpe, the waitress in Las Cruces who found it strange that a couple of kids would leave her a dollar as a tip. Martin Dove, the water pump engineer who picked them up on the I-10 and set them down in El Paso. Emanuel Smith from Sierra Blanca. Dennis Hagen, the last ride they took, the ride that took them into Van Horn that night. They even found George Buchanan, the short-order cook from the drive-in. Ronald Koenig and Garth Nixon found them all, and they took their statements, and those statements put Clarence Luckman in different places and at different times, and thus they understood how he could not have been responsible for the killings that had taken place. And they tried to understand why Clarence Luckman, Bailey Redman, and Elliott Danziger had all made their way along the same highway, and why they all arrived in Van Horn that night. But there was no explanation, at least none they could rationalize.

"Maybe my brother had the darkest star of all," Clay told Bailey one night. "Or maybe we were always gonna be drawn back together. I don't know. Perhaps I don't *want* to know. He died in Van Horn, and we were there when it happened, that's all."

And then he never spoke of it again.

"Doesn't matter where you are in the world, you're always looking at the same sky," she tells him.

And he says, "The same stars too."

"And the sky and the stars can see you right back."

"They can for sure."

"Love you, Clay Luckman."

"Love you right back, Bailey Redman."

And then he holds her, and she holds him, and the circle is evident, and it closes tight around them, and somewhere in the world it is always nighttime, and the stars never sleep.